the

OPERA SISTERS

the OPERA SISTERS

BASED ON A TRUE STORY

MARIANNE MONSON

SHADOW
MOUNTAIN
PUBLISHING

A portion of the author's royalties are donated
to Holocaust memorial efforts.

© 2022 Marianne Monson

Visit us at shadowmountain.com

This is a work of fiction. Characters and events in this book are products of the author's imagina-tion or are represented fictitiously.

Library of Congress Cataloging-in-Publication Data

CIP on file

ISBN: 978-1-63993-046-3

Printed in the United States of America
Alexander's Print Advantage

10   9   8   7   6   5   4   3   2   1

FOR ALICE AND AFTON,
TWO INSEPARABLE SISTERS WHO
LIVED THROUGH THE GREAT WARS

CHARACTER CHART

HISTORICAL FIGURES

Louise and Ida Cook

Mary and James Cook
  (their parents)

Bill and Jim Cook
  (their brothers)

Sir Walford Davies

Rosa Ponselle

Amelita Galli-Curci

Peter Bailey

Ezio Pinza,
  his daughter Claudia,
  and wife Augusta Cassinelli

Florence Taft

Noel and Freda

Friedl Orlando

Rettie Douglas

Saanvi Patel
  (real name unknown)

Thelma *(real name unknown)*

Mitia Mayer-Lismann, her
  husband Paul, daughter Else,
  and brother Carl

Elfriede and Herr Basch

Maria Bauer, her mother Irma,
  her father Ezra *(real name
  unknown)*, and her fiancé
  Leopold Winter

Mr. and Mrs. Beer,
  neighbors to the Cooks

Lulu Cossmann and
  her brother Paul

Perla Galaznik
  (real name unknown)

Jakob Taube
  (real name unknown)

Sir Benjamin Drage

Adolf Eichmann

Annelies Ribbentrop

Frajda Bekerman
  (real name unknown)

Alice Gerstel *(real last name unknown)* and her husband Oskar *(real name unknown)*

Afton Foskett
  (first name changed)

Isadore Greenbaum

Robert Smallbones and his daughter Irene Smallbones

Berta Grynszpan and her brother Herschel

Jacques Heliczer

Frau Jack *(location changed)*

Walter Stiefel

Dr. Hirsch
  (real name unknown)

Dr. Israel Taglicht

Clemens Krauss and his wife Viorica Ursuleac

Theo Markus Vineberg
  (real name unknown) and his mother Gelle

Vera Lynn

Gerda, Georg, and Krysia Maliniak

Helmut Rosental
  (real name unknown)

Mirjam Sonneberg
  (real name unknown)

Julek Zunz (real name unknown) and his wife Herta

Irmgard *(real name unknown)* and her son

Silvio and Corine Ahrens
  (real names unknown)

PART 1

"Louise and Ida Cook have derived more from living than anyone I know."

–ROSA PONSELLE

ONE TRILLION MARKS

MUNICH, 1923

A long horn blared through the factory courtyard sounding the morning break. Expectant workers streamed out into the courtyard, wiping sweat from their faces.

Through the gates, rumbled a lorry filled with stacks of bound rectangles, fluttering in the morning breeze. When the lorry halted with a grunt, the chief cashier and his two assistants climbed up onto its bed.

"Schulz," the cashier called, and a man stepped out of line, cap pulled low. The assistant gathered a bundle of notes, heavy as a brick, and tossed it down to the waiting man who grabbed it, shoved it into his knapsack, and turned on his heel, sprinting toward the factory gates.

"Koch," the cashier called next, tossing down a bundle so large the man below could scarcely carry it.

"Neumann."

The ritual repeated itself. Each man sprinted to the street and barreled into shops, begging to exchange his stack of money for a bit of potatoes. A lump of coal. A small bottle of paraffin.

Prices rose by the hour.

Restaurants didn't bother printing menus. By the time the bill arrived, the price had changed.

American visitors couldn't spend their money because no German had marks enough to exchange them. People carted money through the streets in wheelbarrows. The cost of one loaf of bread rose to 4.6 million marks.

In the long, cold winter of 1923, people who once had savings and still had jobs, broke up their furniture and shoved the pieces into the stove to keep from freezing. They used banknotes as wallpaper to cover over the cracks. Women sewed paper money into dresses. Children taped the bills together to make kites or toys. They shoved handfuls of the stuff into the stove where at least it bought them a few minutes of warmth.

Desperate men pried copper off drainpipes to trade for food to feed their families. Gas was siphoned out of any automobile left on the streets. Petty thieves stole knapsacks and suitcases but left the worthless paper money inside behind. In dark alleyways, counterrevolutionaries clashed with communists and with bands of state police.

On a double-decker bus, a pale and sickly woman rocked herself back and forth. "Six hundred billion!" she muttered repeatedly.

Seated around her, red, worn, and angry faces looked shrewdly at each other, wondering what orchestrated magic could be at play. Their savings, incredibly, had disappeared, absorbed mysteriously into the ether after a lifetime of patient work.

What wizardry, they wondered, could explain this strange upending? And in every mind, as they watched their neighbor from the corner of their eyes: *Who*? *Who was to blame?*[1]

HIGH TREASON

MUNICH, 1924

In the People's Court of Bavaria, a failed artist, former soldier, and unknown political upstart stood trial for his failed attempt to overthrow the Bavarian government.

He had burst into a beer hall, fired a single shot at the ceiling, and declared a "national revolution had begun." It was over quite quickly. When the police began to fire, he tried to sneak away, fell, and dislocated his shoulder. When he was arrested two days later and charged with treason, everyone assumed this was the end of the Nazi party.

The defendant refused a state lawyer, though, and represented himself, giving long-winded and passionate speeches that the press carried in headlines and snippets around the country and beyond. Indignant and unashamed, he used the next twenty-four days to put the government of the Weimar Republic on trial instead.

When the judge sentenced him to five and half years in prison, the defendant spoke to a courtroom hanging on his every word:

"I ask you: Is what we wanted high treason?

"You, my Lords, will not speak the final judgment in this case; that judgment will be up to 'History,' the goddess of the highest court, which will speak over our graves and over yours. And when we appear before that court, I know its verdict in advance. That Court will judge us as Germans who wanted the best for their people and their fatherland, who wished to fight and to die.

"You may speak your verdict of 'guilt' a thousand times over, but 'History,' the goddess of a higher truth and a higher court, will one day laughingly tear up the verdict of this court, for she declares us to be innocent!"[2]

By the time he was released from prison early, only ten months later, Adolf Hitler had never been more popular.

CLOUD SEEDS

APRIL 1933

Storm clouds gather, dark and rolling, mounding into a plume near the horizon.

From Berlin and from Hamburg, from Dresden and Cologne, they come. First one and then another, leaving with one backward glance at all they have ever known. Some wonder if they should have waited longer. Tried more.

Why should they have left a six-room apartment? A legal practice? Their students?

Why leave to become a stranger? To start life over again in the United States or Palestine, in Switzerland or Argentina?

The broken windows. The smeared graffiti. Hostile glances in the streets.

Those who stay find reasons to believe it will be okay. It will be better for the craftsmen, they say. For the factory worker. For those who fought in 1918.

"I cannot leave my parents."

"We've been German for centuries, and where would we go?"

But a few glance at the sky and turn away. They pack the crystal. They sell their grandmother's chair. "I feel in my bones that worse is coming."

The rain begins to fall so lightly at first, no one is even sure what is happening. One drop condenses, lifts on a downdraft, and plumets toward earth. And then another.

The drops become a small but growing rivulet, making its way down crevices of crooked cobblestone streets. Moving outward and beyond.[3]

SENSIBLE

LONDON, SUMMER 1934

Ida's lace-up Oxfords echoed on the long tile hallway as she fell into step behind others leaving the Foreign Office at workday's close. She concentrated on a woman's reasonable black pumps progressing in an orderly fashion ahead of her and forced herself to slow down. *Steady,* Ida chastised, as her fingers gripped her purse tighter in frustration. *Be sensible.* She drew a deep, calming breath, fighting against the urge to leap all the way down the hall.

You're nearly thirty years old now and should be able to contain yourself, the mature part of her brain lectured, but the secret beating its way through her brain wanted nothing of restraint. Forcing her steps to slow once more, she told herself to be calmer. More practical—more like her sister.

Ida made her way outside, down the steps, and around the corner, to the meeting spot where her sister waited. With a rounder face, smooth hair and wider eyes, her older sister had always been considered the prettier one, and Ida thought Louise looked a picture as she leaned slightly against the limestone base of the Lord Robert Clive statue wearing a tweed polo overcoat and pintucked gray gloves.

In the last twenty meters, Ida could hold back no more and practically skittered across the walkway.

Louise looked up in surprise. "You all right?"

Ida clutched her arm. "Louise," she said. "Take a deep breath. Prepare yourself. You may be unable to control yourself at this news."

Louise laughed. "Rather doubtful, that. I believe you're the one who has a difficult time containing yourself. Whatever is it?"

Ida inhaled with the pleasure of anticipation. "Over lunch, I walked by Albert Hall. They had just posted the concerts for the new season."

Louise raised her eyebrows, piqued. "And?"

"On her London debut, Amelita Galli-Curci is coming to sing in concert." Ida paused to let the news sink in. "Galli-Curci is coming *here*!"[4]

A smile broke over Louise's face, her stiff posture melting momentarily in the face of her sister's enthusiasm. "That's rubbish!"

"Three performances. Oh, Louise! I'm chuffed to bits! It's still months off, but do you think if we scrimp on lunches—do you think we can buy tickets—to them *all*?"

"We must!" Louise pronounced, and Ida thrilled at her sister's decisive response, because she knew that if Louise said a thing, it was as good as done.

Ida threaded her arm through her sister's, and they turned to walk up King Charles Street, toward Whitehall, as Big Ben clanged out the time in the distance. How often had they listened to Galli-Curci's record in the past year? Over and over again they'd played it, until their mother, father, and younger brothers insisted on anything other than that. The mere thought of hearing Galli-Curci's voice in person, of seeing before them the singer whose image they'd admired upon the record label, sent Ida into a paroxysm of anticipation.

"Oh!" Ida stopped mid-stride on the pavement. "Whatever will we wear?"

Louise laughed. "We've heaps of time to figure it out, Ides."

◆ ·· — ··· — ·· ◆

Six months previous, Louise had blown through the back door, rain and wind gusting in with her, removed her hat, and announced to the kitchen at large: "I simply *must* have a gramophone."

She'd wandered into a lecture by Sir Walford Davies over lunch, she explained. With his gramophone beside him, he'd discoursed on the beauty of music and the modern possibility of enjoying a range of styles in one's very own parlor.

"They're no longer only for the wealthy," Louise said, quoting from the lecture.

Ida laughed, "I doubt very much Sir Walford was speaking of civil servants earning three pounds fifty a week."

"Nevertheless," Louise replied. "I must have a gramophone. I've just received a cost-of-living alteration I can use for the deposit."

Ida had never known the likes of Louise for obstinacy, but she didn't see how even she might manage it. Still, she wasn't going to miss seeing the marvel, so she went with her sister to a showroom full of H. M. V. gramophones.

When the shop assistant dropped the needle down upon a record, expertly played violins and cellos filled the shop with sound. "Oh!" Ida exclaimed, touching the polished walnut case and hand crank. "Suppose I chip in my cost-of-living increase too? We can share it and some records to boot."

"Ten records are on offer right now," the assistant said, pleased by their reaction.

"We ought to have some Beethoven and Mozart, I'd think," said Louise. "And Bartok and Stravinsky, according to Sir Walford."

"I would suggest vocal records as well," said the assistant. "Rosa Ponselle's *La Forza del Destino* is one I think you might enjoy. And there's a new Amelita Galli-Curci record out."

They exchanged blank looks.

He held up the Galli-Curci record, and they both studied the proud woman on the cover, swathed in embroidered fabrics.

"Ida," Louise asked coyly as the attendant moved away. "What does her outfit remind you of?"

Ida blushed. "I know what you're thinking of, but I doubt she's wearing draperies nicked from her secondary school."

"Are you certain?"

Ida rolled her eyes. "Do you remember that Christina Rosetti poem that says, 'There is no friend like a sister'?"

"Of course."

"I doubt very much she ever had one."

Louise laughed. "We'll take the records," she told the assistant when he returned.

They left the shop that day clutching ten records, with the gramophone promised to follow in a few days' time.

When the lovely creation was unpacked in the front parlor beside the Chesterfield, Mum, Dad, and their brother Bill gathered round for the occasion and waited as Louise drew a record from its packaging, laid it carefully upon the spin table, and dropped the needle upon the lined surface of the disk.

Louise chose the Ponselle record at random, and the flat filled with the soaring tones of an incomparably beautiful voice. In response, Ida sank down upon the hard floor in stunned silence. "Oh, Louise!" she managed. "You've cut open a hole to heaven and let it drain directly into our parlor!"

"Imagine that," their father said, stroking his chin and fiddling with the handle on the gramophone, pretending to understand how it worked. "Imagine that. It's a concert hall in our front room."

◈ · · — · · · — · · ◈

"Shall we walk and save the bus fare for concert tickets, then?" Louise asked, bringing Ida back to the present and the streets of Westminster.

Ida nodded. "We can bring bits from home to eat for dinner and save on that as well."

Since the day the gramophone had arrived, it had been much easier for Ida to ignore the lack of interest she felt as she set off for the good-and-solid-job-with-a-pension she knew she ought to feel grateful for, especially in the middle of an economic depression.

The twenty-three pounds had been paid off now; and somehow, the music also made it easier to forget that many of their grade school friends had found love and had babies of their own now, though plenty remained single given the shortage of men their age alive after the Great War. Like so many others, Louise had fallen in love in her teenage years with a boy who had fallen on the battlefield. And though Ida loved dreaming of all the ways she might find romance, she had not met anyone whose reality could contend with the fantasies her mind could conjure or the plots of the romance novels she hid under her bed.

Both their brothers, Jim and Bill, would soon be married to women Ida and Louise deemed nearly worthy of them, and more and more they were gone from home. Day after day, Ida returned to her copy typist desk, taking dictation and typing careful notes, though her eyes often strayed to the window where the rays of a westering sun turned the clouds pink along the edges.

Perhaps, she sometimes thought, perhaps reality would be easier to accept if only her mind didn't insist on inventing so many stories of all the other impossible ways it could go.

CURTAIN RISE

Three months later, beneath the massive glass and wrought-iron dome of Royal Albert Hall, Ida clutched Louise's hand and held back a cry of anticipation as the lights began to dim. "It's happening!" she whispered fiercely.

Louise didn't reply, but she appeared only slightly more composed.

Onto the stage stepped a woman they would have recognized in any setting. With a clear olive complexion, dark shadowed eyes, and a pronounced Grecian nose, Amelita Galli-Curci looked like a goddess dressed in an elegant white gown with a black velvet ribbon circling her throat. Her dark hair hung in ringlets adorned with a simple white rose pinned above one ear. Larger than life, she seemed, glowing without any need of the stage lights.

Galli-Curci opened her mouth, engulfing the auditorium with sound. For one moment, Ida wondered if a nightingale had shapeshifted into the white, ruffled creature before her. Verdi's *Sempre Libera* sounded like play in Galli-Curci's mouth, and her tongue ran up the impossible birdlike trills as if she were dancing up a flight of stairs. She laughed in the middle of the song before extending the ridiculously high note at the end, while it hung in the hall. Shimmering, endless.

When she finished, the audience erupted in applause. She sang other songs too, a collection of arias from a multitude of operas. When the lights came up for intermission, Ida fought her way back to reality, wondering how to possibly translate the experience into words. She followed Louise toward the foyer, encountering other patrons exiting from the box seats, finely dressed and obviously at home in a concert hall. One older woman in a splendid evening gown leaned toward her friend and said something that sounded like: "Cabaletta, shift about with tempi and ornamentation," to which her companion replied: "Extended cadenza before hitting an endless high E flat."

Ida and Louise exchanged perplexed glances but hesitated, listening.

"One of the most incredible Lucia di Lammermoors in the world," the woman continued. "How truly she captured the feeling of a person gone mad."

Their words were obscured by the shuffle of others passing, but they managed to hear, " . . . the vibrancy and wildness of the cadenza . . ." as they moved away.

"That woman from her first song went mad," Ida remarked to her sister when the women had moved on. "You know, I *felt* that. I suppose when you know all the operas, these songs become stories. Oh, Louise, do you think she was driven mad because her lover was seduced by a siren? Or drowned at sea? Or perhaps her only child had been wrongly imprisoned?"

"We obviously have a great deal more to learn if we'd like to speak about the music with any sense," Louise replied, looking after them.

"I know it's silly, but her costume and this theater remind me of our old plays at Alnwick Castle," Ida said.

Louise raised an eyebrow.

"Yes, I know you tease me about it, but listen." Through Ida's mind rolled a Northumberland meadow dotted with contented sheep and droning bees beside the sluggish river Aln. Beneath the spreading branches of sessile oaks and the parapets of Alnwick Castle, she had reenacted her favorite stories with secondary school friends. Her best friends Rettie and Saanvi had played Pharoah and

Moses, while she'd been Miriam, pulling an indignant baby doll from the reedy edges of the river. On another occasion they'd been creepy goblins prancing from Christina Rossetti's market, crying: "Come, buy! Come, buy!"

"Don't roll your eyes," Ida insisted. "We were only silly children, but when we play acted, it pulled me straight out of everyday life and lifted me to another world completely. A more beautiful and fascinating world. This concert *feels* like that. Like one of my romance novels come to life before my eyes." She thought of the cupboard next to her bed that held bits of stories. "Ida's scribbles," her family called them. "You know I tease you, but I do understand," Louise admitted. "It's magical, truly. Every bit as beautiful as I hoped it would be. Do you know '*Sempre Libera*' means 'Forever Free?' I think I must learn Italian if we're going to do this more often."

"As we must! Given your marks in Latin, I've no doubt you will figure it out."

The second act was just as incredible. Ida felt herself soaring through the sky above Alnwick Castle grounds on the sound of a voice that turned from breaking lament to idiosyncratic ornamentation, depending on the emotionality of the phrase. Once again Ida wanted to understand the stories that could inspire such passion and pleading.

When the curtain dropped for the final time, applause filled the hall in waves. People wiped tears from their eyes and demanded an encore as the applause stretched on and Galli-Curci bowed again and again. Little did she know she'd won over two particularly avid fans in the gallery, their hero worship cemented.

A few days later, the sisters shared their dinner break on a hall bench to save on the expense of a café. Louise carried a book of

Italian verbs while Ida read the libretto of *Lucia di Lammermoor*. In between bites of roll, Ida asked, "Did you realize most opera librettos aren't written by musical composers but by some of the best writers in the world? I had no idea. And the plots are just as dramatic as the ones I like to make up."

"Or nearly as dramatic," Louise prodded.

Ida ignored her. "Our Lucia falls in love with her family's sworn enemy and sees the ghost of a girl killed on the same spot by one of her ancestors. Then she goes mad and kills the bridegroom she's being forced to marry."

"That does sound like something you'd make up," Louise said, appreciatively. "And then make all your friends act out. But listen to this review. It nearly does her justice: 'A splendidly rounded artist, the possessor of a voice of ample power, of an extraordinarily thrilling quality, and one absolutely uniform. Command of legato, delicacy of phrasing, color her tones, project a vibrant pianissimo, propelled by her full power. The sense of pitch is exquisite, the flexibility of utterance, and delicacy of her coloratura is beyond all praise.'"

"They've captured it," Ida said. "Only they've forgotten to say that she has a voice of oxidized silver, reminiscent of a nightingale's call."

"You really ought to write that rubbish yourself."

"Mm-hmm," Ida answered absently. "I want to hear her sing a full and proper opera!"

"But she only does that in America."

"Then we should go to America."

Louise laughed. "We haven't even been to a full and proper opera at Covent Garden. We could begin there before hauling off to America."

Ida pulled out a perfumed sheet of paper from a folder.

"What are you doing?"

"Writing a letter to Amelita Galli-Curci."

Louise scoffed. "And what will you tell her?"

"That we've attended all of her performances here thus far and should like very much to come to America someday to hear her sing, but it will take us a few years to pull it together."

"So long as we both manage to hold onto our jobs," Louise qualified. "I fancy she has other things to do besides answer notes from copy typists."

"Perhaps," said Ida, but she wrote steadily on.

When they'd been children growing up in a brick row house in Cumberland, Ida had often been confined to their small square garden, identical to all the other gardens straight down the road. She'd entertained herself hunting for diamonds or making up stories. In the air, the scent of Cumberland's factories had mixed with the smell of oil from prosaic breakfast stoves. But sometimes, from beyond the orderly row of houses, had come a whiff of salt air, carrying with it the promise of oceanscapes and islands beyond.

Ida remembered placing one small hand upon the black iron gate, sniffing after that hint of saltwater promise, dreaming of the seashore as she swung the gate on its hinges, open and closed, longing for an adventure.

As she wrote to Galli-Curci, the thought of that old, black iron gate rose up in her mind, though she hardly knew why. She could nearly hear the rust rattle squeak of it and feel the movement beneath her hand as the metal hinge turned and began to swing open.

◇·· —— ··— ··◇

Two days later, a response envelope with elegant handwriting arrived by post. Ida ripped it open.

How very dear of you to attend all my performances. If you do ever make it to America, you shall have tickets to everything I'm singing. If you would like, you're very welcome to come round to my dressing room at the Albert Hall on Sunday evening to say goodbye.
—Amelita Galli-Curci

"Louise!" Ida shrieked, waving the paper like a banner.

"Well. I'm gobsmacked," Louise said when she read the letter in Ida's shaking hand. "I'll go to the foot of the stairs. Sometimes, I suppose, a person just has to be cheeky enough to ask."

◆ ⋯ ⋯ ◆

Amelita's dressing room was as elegant as they'd imagined, with red velvet curtains, glassy mirrors, a silver toiletry set, and lights that reflected in the diva's glossy black curls.

"The Cook sisters?" Galli-Curci asked, throwing open the door and holding out her hands. "How sweet of you to write to me. And to come to every performance! We opera singers don't always have such loyal fans as the big band musicians do."

Dazed and starry eyed at seeing the prima donna at close range, Louise curtseyed, shook her head, and couldn't think of a single thing to say.

Ida reached round her sister to take the star's outstretched hands. "Oh, Miss Galli-Curci, it is an honor to meet you. Your concert was received a treat, not just by us but by all of London. I hope you read the paper that said, 'Magic is spelled 'Galli-Curci'? That was our favorite."

Her silvery fluted laughter sounded just like her singing voice.

"Please, you must call me Amelita—or Lita, dears. Come in, come in, and sit down, and tell me *all* about you."

And so, they did. Or Ida did, at least. And Lita told them of her passion for music and the challenges of traveling about from city to city performing most nights. When they rose to leave a quarter of an hour later, Ida felt they would be friends for life. "I've never met anyone who lives the way you do," Ida confided.

"As a slave to my art?"

"Not that so much," Ida said, thoughtfully. "Do you mind very much if we take a snap of you?" She held up the Brownie box camera she'd purchased for the occasion and then debated ad nauseum whether it was proper to even ask.

"Of course not," said Lita, posing in front of her dressing table as Ida snapped the shutter.

They said goodbyes and departed through the side door of the theater. Ida sighed, trying to hold onto the glow of that moment, of the heightened sense of vitality. "Louise?" Ida demanded once the door had closed firmly behind them. "Did you say anything at all that entire time?"

"Yes," said Louise, scrambling after the scraps of her dignity. "As you may recall, I managed to stammer out both 'hello,' and also, sometime later, I said, 'goodbye.' Fortunately, you prattle on enough for the both of us."

BERLIN, THE REICHSTAG

MAY 21, 1935

"War," Chancellor Adolf Hitler intoned to a smattering of polite applause, "is senseless. It is useless as well as a horror. Germany has not the slightest thought of conquering other peoples. Germany needs peace and desires peace. We shall adhere to the nonaggression pact with Poland unconditionally. We recognize Poland as the home of a great and nationally conscious people."

He touched one hand to his clipped moustache. "As for Austria, Germany neither intends nor wishes to interfere in the internal affairs of Austria to annex or conclude an Anschluss."

He droned on, his mood tolerant, conciliatory even, as he explained the need for lifting restrictions imposed by the Versailles treaty. "For Germany, this demand is final and abiding," he promised, utterly sincere. "Germany needs peace and desires peace. Whoever lights the torch of war in Europe can wish for nothing but chaos."[5]

American and British journalists looked on, nodding approvingly; tomorrow they would reassure each other through their confident lines of type. Around breakfast tables Londoners would read analysis in the *Times*: "The speech turns out to be reasonable, straightforward and comprehensive. . . . No one who reads it with an impartial mind can doubt that points of policy laid down by Herr Hitler may fairly constitute the basis of a complete settlement with Germany. . . .

"It is to be hoped that the speech will be taken everywhere as a sincere and well-considered utterance meaning precisely what it says."

MITIA MAYER-LISMANN

FRANKFURT AM MAIN

Mitia Lismann's feet could not hold still.

On pointed toes, the young girl would gawk up at the quaint gabled houses clustered at odd angles around Frankfurt am Main's

Römerberg square. Her Russian papa and German mami would lead her dancing feet over cobbled stones to the Fountain of Justice, where she'd look up, wide-eyed, at the goddess Justitia in her billowing gown, holding aloft the tilting scales. In her lowered hand, the goddess clutched a sword.

Frankfurt am Main. A city of medieval towers and bridges.

In winter, Mitia and her brother Carl would join neighbors in the square for the five-hundred-year-old Advent market. "Guten Tag," she'd say to her parents' friends, wiping marzipan cookie crumbs from her mouth. The flickering lights of menorahs in windows blended with the candlelight on the Christmas trees, all reflecting in her sharp, almond eyes.

By summer, blossoms spilled from garden boxes mounted to half-timbered houses, and Mitia would recite the odd house names as she scampered beneath them: Golden Griffin. Great Angel. Black Star. The ornamented and jeweled balconies were like a fairytale rendered in stone and plaster, as delicate as a hand-decorated egg.

◇·······——··—··—·······◇

As she grew older, Mitia devoured opera and music performances like they were finely crafted strudel. By the age of twenty-three, she began lecturing, illuminating the profundities of Beethoven's *Fidelio* at the Frankfurt opera house. Her eyes were usually subdued, but when she spoke of opera, her passionate gestures could fill a room with lightning.

Beneath a canopy, she married Paul Mayer, a professor at Frankfurt University who reminded her of Papa. A few years later, she gave birth to a daughter who she named Else, Hebrew for "God has promised." With all the passion of a new mother, she swore to fill the girl's waking moments with exquisite sound. In their lovely home in Frankfurt, Mitia never imagined needing any world beyond this one, beyond the charming town that turned flowers to snow and back again.

But there in Römerberg square, the scales on Justitia's fulcrum hung precariously, tilting at an odd angle, cutting up toward the sky. And no one remembered that in her lowered hand, the goddess held a sword.

◇ ·· ··· —— ·· ◇

When the National Socialist German Workers Party won 43 percent of the vote but managed to bring Adolf Hitler to power anyway, Mitia turned to Paul, faint worry etching a line between her brows. "Do you think...?"

"Do not worry, *Engelchen*," Paul replied. "Frankfurt University is the most liberal of all the universities in Germany. The faculty pride themselves on democracy and independent scholarship. And you, Mitia? What is your news?"

A smile grew over her thin lips, like the opening of the window shutters. "I have been invited to be the official lecturer for the Salzburg Music Festival."

"You, see?" he said, waltzing her one turn around the piano. To Else, seated at the keys, playing a simple gavotte, he said, "Your mother is so brilliant. Everything will be just fine." The words came out with such confidence, such absolute surety, that Mitia knew they must be true.

But in March, Paul returned from a meeting, pale and gaunt.

"*Was ist passiert?*" Mitia asked, feeling a chill bloom through the room with the door he had opened. *What is it?*

"The new commissar announced Jews are no longer permitted on university premises." He held up his hands in shock. "Faculty dismissed without salary. Research money reserved for 'racially pure science.'"

Mitia reached for the back of a chair—a carved and gracious chair that had belonged to Mami. "And your colleagues? What did they say?"

"Martin Heidegger said that Germany's soul needs to 'breathe fresh air,' and National Socialism will provide it. That freedom of inquiry and expression are selfish ideas and we should dedicate ourselves and our work to something larger than ourselves—the Nazi state."

Mitia closed her eyes. "And those who will not?"

"Sent to Dachau. A work camp."

"Mein Gott," said Mitia, drawing her husband's arms around her. "Paul, what will we do?"

The following spring, young German boys in uniform papered Papa's shop with a sign in calligraphic script:

Germans, Defend Yourselves

Do not buy from Jews

The boycott lasted only one day, but afterwards the sign remained, rain-drizzled and splattered with mud. Papa didn't dare remove it.

Then, in May 1933, came a flurry of activity in the streets. Else and Mitia watched, wide eyed, as trucks, carts, and wheelbarrows transported books through the streets to Römerberg square. They hauled volumes of Helen Keller's *How I became a Socialist* to stack onto a pyre alongside Ernest Hemingway, Jack London, and Karl Marx. Franz Kafka. F. Scott Fitzgerald. Upton Sinclair. Sigmond

Freud, Albert Einstein, Proust, and Joseph Conrad beside James Joyce, Oscar Wilde, Leo Tolstoy, and Dostoyevsky.

This literary purging, the soldiers said in hard, decisive words, would purify the German language from communists and socialists. From pacifists and those who had criticized Germany. From homosexuals, and from Jews.

They lit the stacks, then, chanting as they burned.

Nazi officials addressed the crowd, goading students to throw more volumes into the flames.

A torch-lit parade and fire oaths continued late into the night.

A few blocks away, charred pages and fragments of lit ash descended on the streets of Frankfurt like the exhale of a great forge. Standing by their darkened window, Paul wrapped a shawl around his wife's shoulders and softly whispered a phrase from the German lyric poet Heinrich Heine: *"Dort wo man Bücher verbrennt, verbrennt man am Ende auch Menschen."*

Where they burn books, they will, in the end, also burn people.

◆ ·· — ··· — ·· ◆

The following year, Else, now thirteen, tugged on her mother's sleeve as they walked across Römerberg square, pointing upward to the sleek lines of a massive airship. "Look, Mami," Else said, as the zeppelin maneuvered across the blanched spring sky. "Why does it turn again and again?"

Mitia followed the angled corners, noting the radial symmetry of the arcs overhead. "It's tracing the shape of a swastika," she said, flatly.

A portent of the future hovered over Frankfurt's medieval buildings like an omen. From somewhere inside, a hatch opened and a flurry of white leaflets descended, scattering through the air, turning

23

spirals as they fell. Else laughed and ran to snatch one from the sky, carrying it back to her mother like a small white bounty.

Mitia took the prize, glancing down at the printed words: "The führer gave us freedom and honor! Our thanks is our voice." Then there, in the corner, smaller: "We know how you vote."

As Mitia crumpled the flyer with her hand, she watched her sweet daughter with her friends, pirouetting through the square, dancing after leaflets descending like confetti from the sky.

QUEUEING

LONDON, 1936

"Neville Chamberlain is quite right," father insisted, looking round the table over the top of his spectacles as if someone might want to contradict him. James Cook had been an officer in Customs and Excise, and though a streak of compassion lay beneath his every interaction, at times his mannerisms placed his children under review and demanded they perform accordingly. "Germany has every right to re-arm and occupy the Rhineland after that ridiculous Paris agreement. Hitler is chancellor and may set the country back on the path toward economic stability. We all see the efficiency of the upcoming Berlin Olympics. He's built an autobahn and wants every family to have a Volkswagen. Well, I say a stable Germany is far better for Europe."[6]

"Quite right," mother murmured absentmindedly as she poured herself another cup of tea. Even as she aged, she'd retained elegant, arching brows and a face that reminded Ida of a Madonna. Mary Louise looked more like her namesake, while James had bequeathed his longer face and prominent nose to his fanciful younger daughter.

"Winston Churchill seems to think Hitler won't be content until he's started a war," Louise observed.

"Hogwash. Stoking fears, as usual. Churchill can't even decide which political party he belongs to," said father, as though that decided his credibility forever. "We must allow Germany to rebuild. A few years ago it took a million reichsmarks to buy a loaf of bread. No wonder Germans want a powerful central figure at the helm. I say a stable and prosperous Germany is the best way to keep peace in Europe. No one wants another Great War."

His look implied that Louise, particularly, did not want another Great War.

"Peace," Ida interrupted. "We all agree that is the goal." She glanced protectively on her big sister, who had become preoccupied with her biscuit. "Come on then, Louise. We'd better go. Good bye, Mum, Dad." Ida leaned in to kiss them. "We'll be home late, don't wait up."

"Another opera night?" Mum asked. "And where are you getting all the bees and honey?" Mary had been born within the sound of Bow Bells, and when alone with her family she sprinkled Cockney phrases thick as currants in her dough.

"Same way we plan to get ourselves to America to see Lita someday: by eating scraps from home for dinner and walking our shoes thin," Ida said.

With a thankful glance, Louise rose. "Rosa Ponselle is on, and if we want any chance at landing tickets, we must be standing in queue by 7 am."

"Well, it's your sleep at stake," said father, "but I don't know how you do it, scrimping and saving, eating hardly any dinner to save every shilling."

"I'll leave tea in the ice box," said Mum.

Ignoring her father, Ida said lightly, "We're as keen as mustard about it, and if you came with us, you'd understand why." How could she explain to her parents that she felt like she spent each prosaic day trapped in an office before a typewriter and a few evenings a month in seventh heaven? How could she describe to her parents what it had meant to meet someone who lived with such passion? How could she explain how dreaming of watching her perform in New York City someday helped her get out of bed?

The collapse of world markets had left them grateful to have jobs and a stable home with their parents, though it meant delaying plans. It was easy to feel guilty for even thinking about opera as they walked past long queues for unemployment. Ida felt a longing both to help those suffering and a conflicting desire to enjoy every scrap of music that lit her soul on fire. So they gave as they could and saved every spare penny for the next show.

Ida and Louise arrived at Covent Garden under a gloriously blue sky and greeted other gallery regulars who had become familiar over the past years of ardent attendance at every possible opera. They set up their camp stools to hold their place in the queue, then hurried off to work.

Work hours always passed even more sluggishly on concert days, but eventually it was time to tidy up her desk and rush to meet Louise, returning to their stools an hour before the box office opened. Ida brought her Brownie box camera just in case they saw opera stars as they entered for rehearsal, a novel, and an issue of *Mabs Fashions* magazine to help pass the time. "Listen to this, Louise," Ida read aloud. "'A Million Women Too Many: Husband Hunt.' Thanks to the Great War, Miss Fanny Evans explains, only one in ten women our age have married."

"That's old news! You can learn that much from years of social dances where five girls crowd around every breathing male," Louise replied. "You don't need an article."

"She offers advice for how it still might be managed," Ida replied.

"Even at our age? Go on, then. What does she recommend?"

"She's quite practical. She advises: set up your paint easel outside an engineering school. Get lost at rugby games and tell an eligible man you need some advice."

Louise laughed. "Do you have to pretend to be empty-headed to find a husband, then?"

A few feet ahead of them, they recognized regulars Noel and Freda, who had started chatting with them in the queue more than a year ago. Louise gestured toward the couple, now staring rapturously into each other's eyes. "Betting Freda beats the odds."

"It's so romantic," Ida said. "An opera queue romance. It's straight out of a romance novel."

Gesturing over her shoulder, she whispered, "And who's that behind us? I haven't seen him before."

Louise turned. The man seemed to have been waiting for an entry. "Excuse me, Miss, but is that a Brownie box camera?"

"It is," Ida replied, grinning up at the stranger.

"What is your favorite subject to snap?"

"Opera stars, when I can have them."

Just then, a young girl walked by, holding firmly to her father's hand. She was, perhaps, four years in age, and wore a flowered hat atop her black curls and an embroidered dress with a starched white collar. Ida waved, and the girl waved primly back, letting go of her father's hand for a moment when she saw Ida's camera.

"Don't you want to take my photo?" she asked, speaking with

an accent that might have been Italian and twirling a little to show her dress.

Ida laughed as the girl's father sought to redirect her. "Claudia, don't bother the nice lady."

Definitely Italian.

"Oh, she couldn't possibly be a bother," interjected Ida, intimidated by the distractingly handsome man in a meticulous suit. He had to be someone important. "I bring the camera to take snaps of opera stars, but I'm very happy to have a photo of such a charming fan."

The father nodded, and the little girl smoothed her dress and smiled as Ida snapped the photo. "Would you like one of us both?" the father asked. "To be in this queue, you must be a true opera lover."

"That's one you'll want," prompted the gentleman behind them, who seemed to have taken great interest in her conversation with the father and his little girl.

"Thank you ever so much," Ida said, snapping them both. "I'll print them and bring them to the queue next week if you'd like to see them."

"We'll be here," said the father as he led the girl toward the theater.

"Did you not recognize that fellow?"

"I'm afraid not," Ida admitted. "Should we have done?"

"Ezio Pinza, quite a star for your collection," he said. "And I am Peter Bailey. Not the least bit famous, I'm afraid, but charmed to meet you."

"Ezio Pinza? The famous bassist?" Louise asked, looking after the retreating figures as Peter nodded.

"Oh, we're hopeless," Ida said, laughing.

"I wouldn't say so," said Peter, looking down at her with respect. "I'd say if you're after snaps of opera stars, you've done quite well of a morning."

"Mr. Bailey, by any chance did you see that new soprano sing *Rigoletto* last week?" He nodded.

"And what did you think of her?"

Peter looked uncomfortable.

"Yes, do give us your view of it," chimed in Louise.

"I'd say she had an enormous voice . . ." he began, wincing apologetically. "though I'm afraid a good deal of it came from her nose."

"Quite so," Louise agreed.

Ida bolted surprised laughter, and her estimation for the man grew even higher.

Some hours later, in a moment romantic enough even for Ida, Rosa Ponselle swept onto the stage as the druid priestess Norma, her dark hair tumbling free past her waist.[7] With moonbeams resting on her gown, she took her place beneath a sacred oak, and a kneeling crowd encircled her. Beseeching the heavens, she sang:

> *Chaste goddess, who dost bathe in silver light*
> *These ancient, hallowed trees,*
> *Turn thy fair face upon us. . . .*
> *Enfold the earth in that sweet peace*
> *Which, through Thee, reigns in heaven.*

Though they had heard some remarkable singers, Ida and Louise both agreed they'd never heard another with such unbelievable vocal control. Her voice had a shimmering tone—warm, smooth as velvet, dark and luxurious. Ida felt slightly disloyal to Galli-Curci for the thought, but the tall, striking Rosa with piercing black eyes commanded the stage like no one else they'd ever seen.

When it was over, the audience remained on their feet for six straight minutes of applause, and the sisters clapped madly from the gallery. As the crowds thinned, they moved to the front of the theater, though the stage was now empty. Ezio Pinza spied them and saluted. "Well, was it worth it?" he asked.

"Worth what?" Louise replied.

"The twenty-four hours queueing you must have done to be here." He smiled jauntily.

"Certainly! Every second of it!" Ida chimed in.

Peter Bailey waved from across the auditorium and made his way toward them.

"Hullo again," Ida said, with a touch of color rising to her cheeks.

"And what did you think?" he asked them both.

"I agree with the reviewers," said Louise. "She must be the greatest lirico-spinto that has ever lived."

Ida nodded. "No matter how many more operas we see in our lives, I can't imagine any will touch this night. Such artistry! She began in pure serenity, then rose to a lyric tornado of revenge."

"A lyric tornado of revenge?" Mr. Pinza repeated with admiration.

"She says such things often," Louise said, smiling.

"An apt expression of her greatness," said Mr. Pinza. "I believe you do understand the art form."

"Oh, we're still novices, though we've been at it a few years," Ida corrected. "But Ponselle handles Bellini's merciless ornamentation just as magnificently as I imagined from our gramophone parties."

"Gramophone parties?" asked Peter; Mr. Pinza also looked intrigued.

Louise nudged her sister. "They're heaps of fun. Perhaps you would like to join us for the next one?"

"I'd be charmed," said Mr. Bailey.

"And what does a gramophone party involve?" asked Mr. Pinza.

Ida started, flattered that a star himself would take any notice of their prattle. "Not much, really. Just our family's flat in South London, a light supper, a small collection of records, and lively conversation about various performers and performances."

"How lovely," said Mr. Pinza. "I think I should like that very much."

Thinking of how simple their home would be compared with Ezio Pinza's, Ida stopped to clarify, "I'm afraid our parties are not the least bit grand, only gatherings with ordinary, though passionate, opera enthusiasts."

"That sounds utterly delightful," said Mr. Pinza.

"Your wife and daughter are welcome too, of course," Louise added. "And yours, Mr. Bailey?"

Ida was not disappointed when he shook his head and clarified he would come solo.

24 MORELLA ROAD

"Louise!" Ida shrieked. "Have you pressed the napkins?"

"Yes, they're here," Louise replied coolly. "Have you finished the tea?" She entered the kitchen and found her sister struggling to force a rolled pastry into a tin. "You've got flour in your hair."

"Really, you are *not* helpful."

"Hold still, then." Louise brushed powder from Ida's coarse curls, while Ida managed to turn the crust into the tin and began piecing the broken bits back together.

The shrill ring of a telephone sounded across the flat. "Ida, call for you," Mother called.

Ida scurried across the kitchen, wiping her floured hands on her apron. "Hullo?"

"Hello, darling, it's Ezio Pinza with a question for you. Would it be all right with you if I bring another guest to our little gathering tonight?"

"Quite all right. Who is it?"

"It's Rosa Ponselle. She's with me and the family at the hotel and says she'd be charmed to come."

Ida sat down hard on the nearest stool.

"You all right, love?"

Ida forced her voice to stay steady. "Mr. Pinza, you are *quite* sure she realizes she's coming to a completely *ordinary* home?"

"She assures me that's just the type she loves best."

Ida struggled to calmly hang up the phone before screaming: "Louise!"

◇ · · — · · · — · · ◇

On Morella Road, men in bowler hats walked sedately home from the tram to plates of boiled root vegetables and sides of meat. They glanced up in surprise at the three-storey flat with its wood-work painted in sober raisin tones, which glowed with lights and liquid sound like an impromptu dance hall.

Inside, guests used well-pressed cocktail napkins to manage sausage rolls and Ida's lemon drizzle cake; they washed it all down with Mother's sangria. Ezio Pinza played a new recording of *Tristan und Isolde*, which led to a debate over Lauritz Melchior and if he had successfully trumped Hermann Winkelmann's interpretation of Tristan, with the party being divided over the matter.

Noel and Freda tossed flirtatious lines at each other, and Ida and Louise both tried desperately to pretend that they had attended parties with such acclaimed attendees before.

Just as magnetic off stage as on, Rosa Ponselle moved among the party smiling and chatting so comfortably, Ida grew convinced she really *was* charmed by their simple home and their sincere passion for her art.

With a little coaxing from Mr. Pinza, Rosa agreed to sing. Standing beside the family's white marble fireplace, she clasped her hands, and her large, shadowed eyes assumed a look of tragedy. When she opened her mouth and began to sing, Ida felt like she'd eaten stardust.

Rosa's voice poured out in tones like warmed and radiant honey that must have reached to the furthest corners of the building.

"*Casta diva . . .*" she sang, and all fell silent before the spell of her soaring upper register that managed to seem even more magnificent outside of a concert hall.

"*Tu fai, fai, tu fai nel ciel . . .*" she sang. *Spread peace on the ground as you do in heaven.*

The group applauded enthusiastically when she had finished.

"I feel so lucky to live in London," sighed Ida. "Miss Ponselle, you cannot possibly understand what this evening has meant to us."

"Call me Rosa, please," she urged.

Mr. Pinza, less dazed than the sisters, said, "Other than London and Miss Ponselle in New York City, of course, much of the best opera is actually happening in Vienna, Milan, and Munich." With his olive complexion, dancing eyes, shock of thick, curling hair that fell about his temples, and cleft chin, Ezio Pinza was distractingly good looking, but as he spoke, Ida found herself looking up at Peter Bailey and wondering what it would be like to travel to see operas by his side. She blushed and dropped her gaze.

"If you and your sister wish to see some marvelous opera," Mr. Pinza turned to Ida, "you should come with us to the Salzburg Festival this summer. Clemens Krauss and Bruno Walter will be conducting under the peaks of the Alps. It will be exquisite."

"Oh, that sounds fabulous," said Peter Bailey. "I could be talked into coming." He didn't look like he would need too much persuasion.

"Now, Pinza, don't forget they've already promised to come see me in New York," Rosa interjected. "And they'll have back-stage access at the Met."

Ida sighed. In a parlor lit up by candlelight and sparkles, filled with the majesty of Rosa's voice, it was so easy to think of flitting across the continent, traipsing after opera performances as if they didn't have to scrimp for gallery seats at Covent Garden.

Reading her face, Pinza added, "The festival tickets are quite reasonable. Max Reinhardt said he wanted the festival to be 'luxury food for the rich and saturated, but also food for the needy.'"

"'Food for the needy'" repeated Ida, idly. "Music *is* that, isn't it?"

Refilling sangria cups, Louise and Mother watched Mr. Bailey's eyes follow Ida—their own awkward, all-angles Ida—each time she crossed the room. Far too soon, Rosa rose. "The silver, small moon climbs all night upon Time's curving stalk," she paraphrased.

Ida and Louise moved to gather her things and hug her good-night. When Rosa walked down their front stairs, it seemed to Ida that she had taken all the silver moonlight out the door with her.

◇··—··—··◇

Daylight streamed through their window the next morning by the time Ida sat up in bed, wondering if the glorious evening had been a wonderful dream. But there lay her party dress, now in need of a good pressing, still draped over the seat of her dressing table.

How could she possibly manage to return to her office and the prosaic duties of a copying typist after such a night such as *that*?

The Salzburg Festival.

She had to be there. And not just for the chance to see Peter Bailey again either. But she couldn't possibly do it on three pounds a week, no matter how many dry, white rolls they ate for lunch. She simply needed more money.

Mabs Fashions magazine sat open on the floor of her bedroom, where she'd left it the night before. Romance novels were stacked beside it, along with pages of Ida's story scribbles. Yawning, Ida rose, stretched, and then began flipping leisurely through the magazine's pages.

Louise was already splashing water on her face at the dressing table. "Better dress fast if you don't want to be late."

"How much do you suppose writers get paid for these bits in here?" Ida asked.

"Not enough, I'd imagine. Oh, do hurry, Ides. I can't be late."

Ida pulled a dress over her shoulders and turned to the end of the magazine. *To submit a story idea, write to* Mabs Fashions, *Amalgamated Press, Farringdon Street, London.*

Ida chewed her bottom lip. She thought of all the bits of stories she had tucked away. They were fluffy nonsense she didn't want to show anyone, but what if she tried to write a proper article? *Sometimes you just have to be cheeky enough to ask*, she thought of Louise saying as she joined her sister in front of the looking glass, patting down her hair. "Louise, do you think *Mabs* might want a bit about the opera dresses I made from their patterns?"

"Maybe," Louise said noncommittally. "I'm off now—"

On her dinner break, between bites of a hard, white roll, Ida wrote up a query: "Dear Sir or Madam, would you by chance be interested in reading an article about opera dresses I made from your magazine's patterns? . . . "

Several days later, she carried the return post to her room: "Dear Miss Cook, we would indeed be interested in reviewing your proposed article."

"Well then!" she announced to her bed.

She hauled the family typewriter up a narrow second flight of stairs to the attic, where motes of dust circled through the air like creatures from another world. Their orange tabby cat they'd named Prince Igor followed her on stealthy paws.

With its tiny, white, scrollwork fireplace and a grate just large enough for a bit of coal, the attic had a steeply slanted roofline that ended in a dormer. Everyone else in the family found the attic too dark and out of the way, but Ida loved it. Tucked away, she could look over the tile rooftops of London and imagine sailing over them all. It was the only really private spot in the house. She settled in and started putting ideas onto paper. For hours she worked on the article, revising and polishing, shaping and re-shaping the draft.

A few weeks later, while the family had gathered for tea with their visiting brother Bill, the evening post arrived. Ida darted up from the tea table to snatch it off the entry floor and tore open an envelope.

Returning to the table, triumphantly she waved a cheque for five pounds like a little flag of wonder.

"Where'd you get that, then?" Louise asked, astonished.

"A bit of hanky-panky, no doubt," Bill suggested.

Ida laughed. "Hardly. I—in fact—have sold an article. To *Mabs* magazine. I'm rather shocked myself, to tell the truth of it."

"You didn't!" Bill bent to look closer at the cheque. "Well," he shrugged. "It appears that she did."

"Is this another one of those 'How to Catch a Man' pieces they're always printing?" countered Louise.

"No," Ida laughed. "I'm afraid I'm not qualified to write about that. I wrote about the dresses I've made for the opera. And I might try writing another." She looked at the check as if it might disappear.

"Why would their readers want to read about something crumby like that?" Bill asked. "Just kidding, Ida. Nicely done."

"Nicely done, indeed," said father, tapping the table. "You're in print and paid for it."

"And how will you use your earnings?" asked Mum.

"To attend the Salzburg opera festival," Ida announced.

"You're *not*," said Louise.

"I am," Ida said with a still astonished smile. "And, of course, you must come, too."

"PERHAPS NOT FOR LONG"

Salzburg was like something out of a dream. Church spires and palaces reflected on the smooth channel of the Salzach River. The white walls of Hohensalzburg Fortress looked down from a rocky outcropping over the city. Behind all the castles and palaces, loomed the grandeur of the Alps.

And the music! Ida and Louise soon found that to walk the streets of Salzburg in the morning was to encounter music as commonplace as wind. Through an open window came an aria from a singer warming up, the fluttering notes of a piano sonata, or a choir rehearsing in any of the baroque churches. Musical pilgrims flocked to concerts in Mirabell Palace, haunted the chambers where Mozart had first played the harpsichord, and marveled after Elisabeth Rethberg and Bruno Walter the way Americans trailed after actresses in Hollywood: star struck, adazzle, mouths slightly agape.

They wore the new evening gowns Ida had sewn and written about in her article: a scarlet, satin crepe for Louise, and a pink and silver taffeta for herself, with crushed velvet capes trimmed in rabbit fur to complete the ensembles. They sat beside the handsome Peter Bailey at a Mozart serenade at the Residenz and *Le Nozze di Figaro*, conducted by Clemens Krauss, at the Festspielhaus. Ida couldn't help but wonder if her own romance story might finally be beginning.

Ezio Pinza had brought his family to the festival, and they met in passing in the central square, where he generously insisted they join him for dinner after the performance of *Don Giovanni*.

Mr. Pinza's smooth, sonorous voice and startling good looks made him a perfect Don Giovanni. It took little imagination to believe him a consummate heartbreaker as he praised wine and women as the "support and glory of mankind."

On stage, in that great, final moment of catastrophe, a statue of the dead commendatore appeared at the top of a double, curving flight of stairs. "Don Giovanni!" the marble appeared to shriek. "You invited me to dine with you!"

Giovanni pressed his back against a massive pillar as though, confronted by this horror, he needed something solid behind him. In a desperate attempt to escape, he threw himself down the steps, but flames sprang up, blocking his way. The pillar collapsed, the solidity of the world giving way, and Giovanni was consumed, dragged down to hell for all his sins. "Such is the end of the evildoer," the ensemble sang reassuringly. "The death of a sinner always reflects his life."

When the lights came up, Ida was rather shocked to see Peter Bailey looking more than a little spellbound by a blond Austrian woman across the auditorium.

Louise followed Ida's eyes. "Oh dear," she said a touch too loudly. Then, "Come away, love. There's no reason to watch."

Ida let Louise lead her out of the concert hall, a little numb, trying to hold on to the magic of the performance that had truly been one of the best they'd ever seen.

"Never mind him," Louise told Ida sternly. "He clearly doesn't deserve you under any circumstances if he doesn't see all that you have to offer."

"Oh," Ida said, trying to control her lower lip that did insist on shaking. "I thought . . . I'd hoped . . ."

"I know, my love," Louise said, taking her arm and squeezing it in an uncharacteristically affectionate way. "I hoped too, but really, what could I possibly do without you? You may not have a handsome man beside you, but you do have a sister who loves you desperately."

Ida's eyes spilled over. "Oh, Louise! I love you too. Sometimes I think I've addled my brain with too many romance novels."

"No," her sister insisted. "You have good, solid brains and you have me, Ides. You will have me forever."

Ida dashed her tears away and squeezed Louise's arm as they entered the elegant hotel restaurant Ezio had reserved. It was easy enough in that space to recapture their glow from the magnificent performance. "What artistry!" Ida gushed to their host.

"What drama, Mr. Pinza!" Louise murmured in agreement.

"Oh please," said Ezio, leaning toward them, not looking a bit like he wanted them to stop.

Suddenly the door was flung open, and Clemens Krauss called into the room: "Don Giovanni! You invited me to dine with you!"

"So, I did," Ezio laughed. He rose to introduce his daughter, his wife, Augusta, and Ida and Louise.

In turn, Clemens Krauss presented his wife, Romanian opera singer Viorica Ursuleac, who had played the Countess in *Le Nozze di Figaro*. With dramatic sideburns and a dark shaft of hair swept back to the right, Clemens Krauss had piercing eyes that looked down the length of his not insubstantial nose as if he could ferret out shoddy musicality and vanquish it with a flourish of his baton. Viorica Ursuleac's golden curls were pinned neatly into place; a curtain of pearls she might have worn on stage dripped round her commanding neck.

Clemens settled beside Ezio, and the two began debating whether Mozart had intended Don Giovanni to be read as a hero or a villain, while Viorica and Augusta seated themselves beside Ida and Louise. Neither woman spoke English well, though Viorica was more comfortable than Augusta.

"Your portrayal of the Countess was flawless," Ida said, a bit awed. She wondered for the dozenth time how she and Louise had become lucky enough to now count such glittering illuminati as acquaintances and friends. Just like she'd first felt upon meeting Lita, it was invigorating to be around people pursuing their life's passions so unapologetically.

"Thank you, dear," Viorica said graciously.

"So much power," agreed Louise. "Particularly in your upper registers. I believe it must become one of your signature roles."

"Are you ever terrified to get up on stage in front of everyone?" Ida asked.

Viorica smiled. "I was, at first. But I've realized, this was my own work to do in this world. You understand? So, I put up my hair, go out onto the stage, and do it."

Ida nodded, her admiration for the woman growing even greater.

"We should ask the Cooks," Ezio said a short time later, pausing his conversation. "They're astute students of the art form, and I value their opinions." The sisters looked in his direction.

"Ladies, all of you, please, what is your reading of the character of Don Giovanni?"

"Any man who enjoys violent conquests of women is a consummate villain through and through," Viorica said, and there were nods of agreement.

"Yet we still feel empathy for the man," Louise offered. "We're still drawn by his passion and charisma, which drive the work as a whole. Otherwise, we would not mourn his destruction. It is the mastery of Mozart that allows this ambiguity, don't you think?"

Bored by the adult conversation, young Claudia sidled close to Ida and pointed to her wrist. "I like your little time," she whispered.

Louise laughed at the darling phrase. "My watch?" Ida asked.

The girl nodded shyly. "Next week is my birthday. I hope to have one for a gift."

"I hope she isn't bothering you," Augusta said.

"Oh no, she couldn't," said Ida.

"Ten minutes more, Claudia," Augusta said, "then ze bed for you."

Mr. Pinza perked up at her words. "Oh, let her stay, Augusta;

41

she isn't harming anyone," he called down the table, his voice flush with a few cups of wine.

His wife's brows lowered, and her words came out with more anger in them than Ida and Louise had expected: "Ezio, I tell you, you'll spoil ze girl. You let her do however she pleases."

The sisters exchanged awkward glances, neither of them wanting to be present for a domestic argument. But before Ezio could spit back a response, Viorica leaned toward Claudia, her eyes bright and shining for the child's sake: "Who's afraid of the big bad wolf?" she sang, her sumptuous voice no less exquisite than when she was on stage.

The song was a popular one, and Claudia's face lit up at the familiar tune. Mr. Pinza joined in, and suddenly the pair was singing a striking duet, notes twining around each other.

Tension eased from the air, and Claudia joined in at "tra la la la la . . .

Music fixes everything, Ida thought, awed. *Perhaps, then, it could even fix a broken heart.*

◇ ···· —— ···· ◇

The next morning, they dashed off postcards to their parents who were likely worried at home over the state of things in Austria: "Oh Rapture!" Ida wrote, scrawling a few lines describing the concerts, shows, and spires of Salzburg. "Mum, you can breathe easy. The only soldiers we've seen were strolling along in the sun grinning and not keeping very good time. Yours, in a state of *fizzle!*"

For the final performance of the trip, Ida and Louise pinned each other's hair in place, donned opera dresses and cloaks, and headed for the Festspielhaus. Hoping to savor each final moment, they arrived early—so early, they were surprised to see a white-haired woman on the stage gesturing dramatically and banging away on the piano between each point.

Ida paused at the door, whispering. "Was there a pre-concert lecture scheduled for *Fidelio*?"

"Yes," Louise whispered back. "You said you didn't want to see it because the woman presenting it had a double-barreled name and you said they're never very good. Remember?"

Ida smothered a giggle. "*That* wasn't very nice of me. Let's just pop inside, and we'll find our proper seats after she finishes."

"The musical precision," the lecturer was saying, waving her arm about, "the Mozartian banter. It holds until the moment in the first act when Beethoven breaks with tradition and enters new territory with the counterpoint of his fugue and the slashing chords of the villain's aria.

"With its hymn-like music and repeated motifs of light and dark, it is ironic that this opera about an unjustly imprisoned political prisoner premiered in Vienna shortly after Napoleon's army occupied it. But *fidelity*—in the form of love—enters that prison, offers our hero nourishment and ultimately redemption. There he sits, unable to recognize his love, as he cries out in pain: 'God, how dark it is in here!'"

"This is actually quite interesting," whispered Louise. "We would have learned something if we'd come sooner."

Ida agreed. Shadows hooded the speaker's eyes and fervor electrified her body. "Above all," she continued, "Beethoven's *Fidelio* elicits nostalgia for lost liberty by appealing to the best in ourselves and reminding us of the sacred religion of humanity." The speaker appeared deeply moved and nearly shaken by her own words for some reason. The few dozen people who had come early for the lecture applauded as she bowed.

"Well, we can toss my previous theory," Ida said, looking after the woman as she left the stage. "I should very much have liked to have heard the rest of her lecture."

"There's nothing like having a German explain Beethoven, is there?" asked Louise.

Hours later, as they sat in the darkened theater and listened to Beethoven's soaring melody, Ida remembered the lecturer's words as Florestan's voice rose up from the pit: "God! How dark it is in here!"

◇ · · — · · · — · ◇

By the end of the festival, they had successfully avoided awkward meetings with Peter Bailey and considered Clemens Krauss and Viorica Ursuleac true friends. Still, they were a bit surprised when the couple offered to see the sisters off at the Salzburg train station. The station was a bustle of commotion, filled with passengers traveling home with parcels and packages from the Festival. Across the crowded platform, Louise spotted Viorica, golden hair pinned in place, with Krauss beside her. She motioned to Ida, and they moved across the space eagerly, then stopped, surprised to see the *Fidelio* lecturer with the double-barreled name by their side.

Ida, still feeling extra sensitive due to the lapsed affection of a certain handsome young man, felt a pinch of annoyance. "What's she doing here? I thought we were to have a moment alone with Viorica and Clemens."

Louise murmured agreement, but they both did their best to shrug off the ungracious thoughts as they approached.

"May we introduce you to our friend?" Kraus, asked intently.

"Of course," said Louise, extending her hand.

Ida, further away, glanced toward the train, wondering if the woman would leave and give them time alone with their friends before they'd have to board.

Viorica smoothly laced her arm through Ida's and turned her aside from the gathering. She moved her lips close to Ida's ear, the sound lost among the busy station noises. "My dear, might I ask a favor?" she said quite earnestly.

"Of course," said Ida. "What is it?"

"You understand, I hope, that this is a great personal friend of ours. She's going to England for the first time to deliver a lecture." She squeezed Ida's arm with surprising insistence. "Could we count on you? Can you please promise us that you and your sister will look after her?"

Ida glanced at the woman, wondering why she needed taking care of. True, she was a lone woman traveling, but her pearls and elegant, tailored wool suit showed class and confidence, with perhaps a touch of wear. Still, the request seemed odd, and Ida stumbled after a response.

Viorica paused for an answer.

"Certainly," Ida murmured, still confused, "of course we will."

Viorica gave a sigh of relief and steered her back to the others. Releasing Ida's arm, she took the woman by the shoulders, reassuringly. "There," she said. "Now you'll be all right."

Louise raised her eyebrows, and Ida felt just as baffled.

"Miss Ida," said Clemens Krauss, "may I introduce you to the official lecturer for the Salzburg Festival? This is Frau Mitia Mayer-Lismann."

◇··—···—··◇

On the train, Frau Mayer-Lismann said few words, and Ida and Louise soon gave up trying to make conversation. The woman

45

seemed haunted, though by what neither could say. To pass the empty moments, Ida started making up stories about the woman. Perhaps she was a jewel thief, wanted for a series of heists, who offered opera lectures as a cover. Had she been betrayed by her husband? Was she a wealthy widow who left her home only for opera festivals?

Baffled, Ida pushed the strange woman from her thoughts, wanting only to relive every moment of the festival and plan for next year (without Mr. Bailey), which couldn't come quickly enough.

"Krauss said if the Nazis gain control of Austria, the programme next year will likely be different." Ida sighed. "I guess we'll just have to wait and hope they don't."

Frau Mayer-Lismann continued staring out the window as if the words "next year" meant nothing at all. She did seem to relax a bit by the time they reached Amsterdam. Perhaps she's coming to trust us, Ida thought, but she was still such a bore, responding to their polite questions with only the slightest responses. So different than she'd been during the lecture.

◆…—…—…◆

"Well, here you are," said Ida, as they deposited Frau Mayer-Lismann her in front of her hotel." The woman paused as if she didn't want them to leave.

Unable to stand the awkward silence, Louise half-heartedly offered, "If you'd like, we could show you the sites tomorrow?"

To their utter amazement, she agreed.

"Why did you ask her that?" Ida asked when they were out of earshot.

"Because I never dreamed, she'd say 'yes,'" Louise admitted.

◆…—…—…◆

Beneath the soaring gothic arches of Westminster Abbey, the three women considered the colored domes and scrolling woodwork. Gazing up at the stained glass, Frau Mayer-Lismann politely inquired: "Is this a Protestant or Catholic church?"

"It's a Protestant abbey," Ida said, smothering a smile. For such a brilliant woman concerning all things Beethoven, she knew precious little about London. "Though we do have Catholic ones if you prefer them. Which are you?"

"Me?" Frau Mayer-Lismann asked in surprise.

Ida nodded.

She lowered her voice. "Why, I'm Jewish—didn't you know?"

"No." Ida replied truthfully. "I thought nothing about it. We're not violently anything, but we call ourselves Christian and try to do our best."

Frau Mayer-Lismann's face relaxed at the response, as if she had decided something. After seeing Big Ben and the Tower of London, they walked her back toward her hotel. On a quiet corner of the sidewalk, she glanced around. "I must confess something."

"Yes?" said Ida and Louise, baffled once more. Ida remembered her jewel thief hypothesis, but brushed the whimsical thought away.

Frau Mayer-Lismann lowered her voice. "I'm afraid I've not only come to deliver a lecture. I've come to begin making arrangements because my family must leave Germany."

"Leave?" Ida said.

"Germany is quickly becoming an impossible place for us to live."

"Because of the Nazi party?" Ida asked.

Frau Mayer-Lismann nodded.

"I don't mean to be rude," said Louise, "But do you think it might be only bluster? Our father certainly thinks so."

For the first time since they left Salzburg, Frau Mayer-Lismann showed a touch of the same vitality she'd exuded on the lecture stage. "I'm afraid not," she said fervently. "They've boycotted my father's business. There are rumors they will seize it entirely. My husband has lost his job."

"But surely he can find another one?"

"Very unlikely."

Struggling awkwardly to reassure her, Ida said, "This is the twentieth century. And there are, of course, thousands of Jews in Germany."

There was a sharp silence before Frau Mayer-Lismann replied, "Perhaps not for long."

Ida and Louise walked home in bewilderment, reassuring themselves that somewhere there had to have been a misunderstanding. They'd promised to keep in touch, but Ida couldn't help but wonder what correspondence with the gloomy woman would bring. "What if she's being tricked into coming here?" Ida asked, her thoughts rambling. "Held for ransom? She acts so nervous. Maybe she's committed a crime and they're tracking her down."

"You're being ridiculous," laughed Louise. "She isn't a character in one of your stories."

That night, as Ida lay in bed, listening to Louise's long, slow, steady exhales, Frau Mayer-Lismann's shadowed eyes hovered at the edges of her mind—the swift despairing expression she adopted when she thought no one observed her—the palpable alarm that seemed to propel her down London's darkened streets as if something sinister tracked her every movement. Was the woman paranoid? Was there a sensible reason for the way she acted? The question seemed like a long and tangled knot that would not unravel, no matter which way Ida turned it. Germany couldn't possibly expect all the Jews to leave.

But the words *Perhaps not for long* echoed again through the shadowed corridors of her mind.

REHEARSAL

MÁLAGA, SPAIN, FEBRUARY 1937

The moon rose, thin and slender, over the Moorish stone walls of the Alcazaba Fortress. Wan lunar light touched the stone, culled from Roman ruins, raised into silver terraces built along lines of glacial outwash.

Winter remnants of persimmons and custard apples decayed back into loam. Lychee. Star fruits and coriander. Pomegranates, the fruit of the dead.

The moonlight touched them all but could not enter the dungeons where Christian slave girls had once been locked after each day's work was finished.

At the edges of stone gardens and limpid pools, shadows moved, bent over by the weight of bundles, slipping beyond the reach of the moon. *Refugiados.*

They felt the tremor of the earth, the movement of great armies bearing down. The creak and turn of Mussolini's tanks. The streaks of light from Nationalist ships and the shimmer of air preceding the Luftwaffe's whirring blades of the Luftwaffe.

Their breaths came in small gasps that might have been the burble of a fountain. Or a thin inhale of terror.

The pale moonlight made it impossible to tell.[8]

SERIAL ROMANCE

LONDON, 1937

"Post for you, Ida!" Louise said, plunking a letter down in front of her sister.

Miss Taft, Fleetway House, 25 Farringdon Street, London, read the envelope.

Ida tore it open.

"Well. What is it?"

"Miss Taft wants to meet me," Ida said, surprised. "The editor who bought my little articles for *Mabs*."

"Perhaps she doesn't believe you wrote them, then?"

"Oh, hush."

The next day, Ida left work early and hurried across town.

At the door to Fleetway House, she stood, straightening her hat and adjusting the pins in her curls. Finally, she pushed open the door and gave her name to the secretary. The woman went off with the message, as Ida glanced at the people hovering over their typewriters and arguing over copy, magically coercing books into existence.

The secretary led her to a glass-doored office, where Miss Florence Taft waited, smartly dressed in a tailored skirt, finished with a simple strand of pearls. Two telephones lined her desk, along with stacks of papers. Dozens of notes were pinned to a board behind her. She dropped the receiver of one phone back in its cradle as Ida entered. "Hello, Ida. Thank you for coming."

"My pleasure," Ida replied, perching herself on a chair facing the editor's desk.

After nearly a year of submitting articles to the seasoned editor, Ida knew that Miss Taft was not someone who wasted time. Miss

Taft tucked a stray bit of hair behind her ear and came straight to the point. "I've enjoyed your articles for *Mabs*. They're entertaining, well-written, with just a bit of cheek to them if you know what I mean."

Ida smothered a grin, pleased at the description. "Thank you."

"I'll tell you what I'm after at the moment, though, is someone who could write a serial for us. Have you ever thought of writing fiction?"

Ida thought of all the stories she'd tucked away. Silly things, really. As childish as dressing up in draperies in secondary school and parading across the lawn of Alnwick Castle. Ida pushed the thought away and struggled after being an adult. "Oh, I've scribbled things here and there," she confessed. "Nothing very substantial."

"Do you know the serial stories I'm talking about?" Miss Taft asked.

"Installment stories?"

Miss Taft passed over a copy of *Weldon's Ladies' Journal* opened for Ida. "Exactly right. Stories told out by bits. The public goes mad for them. You get one chapter this week, with a hook to keep you reading on the following week. They're mostly romances; but there are other types—the main thing is they keep the readers reading."

"Right," said Ida, running her finger down the page of the fiction serial in the magazine. *The Girl in the Flat,* it was called, by E. M. Winch. It looked to be about a naïve country girl who went to the big city and got herself into a jam. The piece ended with the words *To be continued . . .*

Romance. The word was so fanciful, like turning cartwheels down the street. Ida had always imagined the stories in the cupboard next to her bed were fanciful and ridiculous. A waste of time. Could real people actually publish such stuff? Obviously, someone wrote all the novels she read, but it seemed like real authors must be much smarter, wealthier, and luckier than a simple copy typist.

"Would you like to give it a try?"

"I can't promise anything," said Ida. "But may I take this with me?"

Miss Taft waved her hand. "Of course, of course. Here's another issue too."

Ida thought of Viorica Ursuleac, stepping onto the stage. "This is my own work to do in this world. You understand?" Viorica had told Ida in Salzburg all those many months ago.

Hesitantly, Ida asked: "—And if I come up with something? When would you like to see it?"

"Yesterday?" said Miss Taft, throwing her arms up and gesturing round the office. "You can see we've plenty to do here, so take the time you need, but yesterday is ideally when I could use a new serial." She straightened one of the stacks of papers on her desk and bid Ida good day.[9]

◇··——···—··◇

Back at home, Ida climbed the stairs to the attic, settled on a cushion, and spread a stack of her scribbles and some magazines on the floor around her. Her cat, Prince Igor, followed her and settled down right in the middle of one. Ida laughed. "You're a secret romance reader too, aren't you, Iggie?" She pulled *Up the Garden Path* by Anonymous from under the cat and skimmed through the light romance between a gardener and a woman who loved flowers. *With Folds of Darkness* told the story of a young woman who cleverly solved the mystery of a wealthy old man who'd been poisoned by his servants. She compared these to the stack of "scribbles" spread out on the floor. Not that different, to be honest. In one, she'd written about a girl who loved to sing and met a wealthy man who promised to make her a star. In another, two sisters with a sick father to care for tricked a wealthy man into marrying one of them.

She picked that one up. That idea might do with a bit of tinkering. It was about two sisters named Vicki and Margery. She doodled an opening with two sisters in their bedroom, a setting she knew intimately:

> *Vicki glanced abstractedly at her sister, where she curled up on the end of the bed.*
>
> *"How marvellous if you could meet a really rich man at Conways and marry him."*
>
> *"Yes, marvellous, but horribly unlikely. Do get off the bed, Margery."*

Ida scrawled new dialogue across the page for a practical, hard-working older sister and a younger, dreamy sister who spent her days caring for their ill father and dreaming up impractical solutions to their problems.

> *The doctor said, "If you can't get your father out of England before the winter he—"*
>
> *"What?" Vicki's voice was sharp with sudden fear.*
>
> *"You might as well ask how long it would take to go to the moon and fetch it back."*
>
> *"It's so awful to think that it's just money that's needed to keep him alive."*
>
> *"It is always money." Margery's voice was hard.*

Pages later, Ida wrote:

> *Vicki never forgot her first sight of Christopher Kentone: his head thrown back, his dark eyes alight with amusement, as he stood in the*

light from the room behind him, framed by the dark paneling of the hall.

Never mind that Christopher looked a bit like Ezio Pinza. Or maybe Peter Bailey. Ida frowned. No one would ever make the connection, except possibly Louise. It was nearly impossible to hide oneself from Louise.

"Were you waiting for someone?" Christopher asked Vicki.

A servant appeared and leaving her to his care, Christopher said, "Now you will be all right."

Ida stopped, her pencil hovering over Viorica's words on the page, words she'd put in Christopher's mouth. But they felt right there, so she let them stay.

Hours later, when Ida descended from the attic, she clutched a dozen manuscript pages to her chest, her mind still floating with Vicki, Margery, their father, and the handsome Christopher, whose love might hold the key to setting all things right.

It needed work; she knew that. There were plot holes, fluffy words that needed scrubbing, details that needed nailing down—but the drama was there, the romance—so much of it, in fact, it was difficult to think about anything as prosaic as dinner biscuits and a manual she needed to read before work tomorrow. She was shocked to realize how many hours had passed, as her mind still floated through that *other* space, like a dust mote, aloft, turning, turning, lit by moonlight.

⟡ ·· — ··· — ⟡

"I'll buy it," said Miss Taft one week later.

"You will?" said Ida, trying to smother her shock.

"Yes, I will." Miss Taft dropped the manuscript to her desk. "It's not the best thing I've ever read, but it's far from the worst either. It will keep reader's reading. And if you enjoyed writing it, there can be more—many more—after you finish this one should you want there to be. I'll have an editor go over it and send you her notes so you can see how to improve the next installment."

"I have *ever* so many more ideas," Ida said, unable to hold back a grin.

"Jolly good. I'll put a check in the mail, then. Fifteen pounds. And you'll bring the next installment?"

"*Fifteen* pounds?" Ida said, staggered.

"Oh yes. Serials pay much better than little magazine pieces."

"I had no idea."

◇ ·· — ··· — ◇

As Ida walked home, the autumn leaves that shone like jewels fell, drifting toward the sidewalk like petals on a stage at the end of a performance. Puddles from a recent rain lined the corners of the streets, and maple leaves submerged beneath the surface like glittering stars receding beyond a layer of smooth glass. The world, Ida thought, had never looked this beautiful.

Her every footfall echoed the words in her head: "fifteen pounds." *Fifteen pounds!* And the promise of the same again next week! And the week after that! She'd never had so much money in her entire life. Whatever would she do with it? New shoes? Marks and Spencer ready-made dresses? Travel! And of course—so many opera tickets.

She found Louise straight away. "How shall we spend it?"

"*You* spend it, you mean?" Louise looked slightly awed.

"It's *our* money. I wouldn't want to spend it without you. Where would be the fun in that?"

"What a dear sister you are," Louise took her arm. "Oh, Ides. All those times I told you to stop imagining. And now I shall become the reliable spinster with a proper job, and you can be the eccentric millionaire authoress."

Ida laughed. "Now who's being ridiculous?"

"Did I mention I had a letter from Viorica yesterday? Krauss is conducting at the National Theater in Munich. Do you think, perhaps, we should go?"

"Yes!" Ida insisted. "Of *course*, we should go. Remember the photographs of Munich decorated when Berlin hosted the Olympics? It looked grand! What are they playing?"

"*Rienzi*, I think. Apparently Hitler and his lot are mad about Wagner."

"Can he truly be terrible if he likes opera?"

Louise laughed. "That's your measure of a person, is it? Should we stop in Frankfurt-am-Main on the way and see poor Frau Mayer-Lismann? She's written and asked us to."

Ida sighed. "Oh, I suppose we should. That woman is so gloomy. But yes, you're right, of course, Louise. Shall we get new dresses?"

"Will there be enough?"

"With *fifteen* pounds this week and next for as long as I keep writing serials? There will be enough. I have a whole cupboard full of ideas! I intend to begin saving for our trip to America right away! I am determined to finally hear Rosa sing at the Met, and you must come too! Oh, Louise! I'm all *a-fizzle*!"

"You well and truly did it! Looks like your fantasies might make heaps more money than my practical brains and Latin verbs can muster. How's that for irony?"

Ida stopped mid twirl. "Oh, Louise, it's such a glorious dream. It's the stories, the work, that thrill me most, not the money. It feels nearly wrong somehow to believe I can do something that makes me so happy! Only, I'm dizzy with fright that I'll wake up tomorrow and Miss Taft will have changed her mind."

BOMBERS

SPAIN, APRIL 26, 1937

They arrive from the south on a Monday afternoon.

It is market day in Guernica. Wooden carts filled with artichokes and asparagus rattle into town, to the city center where Basque women with their hair tied back with *zapis* sell broad beans and garlic ristras. Chanterelle mushrooms. Furniture makers set up their cider barrels and cabinets, and a man sells *makila* sticks fashioned from wild medlar wood.

The Plentzia River flows smoothly through town on its way to meet the turquoise waters of the Bay of Biscay. Here, under the branches of ancient oak trees, the councils met in the Middle Ages to work out defense policies. Sovereigns pledged to leave the people in peace beside the river.

Outside of town, to the east, is a bridge. A bridge that spans its divide so cleverly, it is wanted now.

The Italians come first, from Soria in SM.79s, dropping light explosive bombs as they travel south, toppling the church of San Juan. Imploding the bridge first, and then the roads.

Junkers and Heinkel bombers come next, sending aluminum incendiaries to drift down upon the town center as civilians scatter. Some take refuge in the fields, so the pilots turn their planes about, plunging low to strafe the roads and then the crop lands.

Half-timbered houses three hundred years old burn on, well into the next day.

Learning of the massacre, Pablo Picasso finds himself a piece of unbleached muslin and sets up a ladder. He begins sketching. A gored horse. A woman screaming over her dead baby. A disemboweled soldier. All of them burning.

From the remnants of a shattered sword, a flower grows, spreading across the fabric in hues of black and white. And endless gray.

JUSTITIA

As the train pulled into the *bahnhof* at Frankfurt, Ida and Louise scanned the crowd for Mitia's daughter, Else. "I'll be wearing a pink hat," she had written.

And there she was, sitting on a bench in the station, with a pink velvet hat perched on top of her silky brown curls.

They loved her immediately. Her brown eyes shone as she talked about her studies at the Frankfurt conservatoire and led them across Römerberg square. The plaza of angled medieval buildings was decorated with Nazi banners. In the center of the square stood an elegant fountain with a statue of the goddess Justitia, scales hanging askew.

"You're nearly as knowledgeable about opera and music as your mother," Louise said, admiringly.

With none of her gloominess, Ida thought but did not say.

They passed a store window plastered with notices. They could not read the German but could guess one word—*Jude*—clearly enough. Ida averted her eyes, embarrassed, and followed Else's pink hat over the cobblestones.

A block off the main square, Else led them up to a luxurious flat. "My family has been here for four generations," she explained as she led them inside.

"What a music room!" Ida exclaimed, admiring the elegant grand piano and carved bookcases filled with books on musical theory.

"Hello again, and welcome," said Mitia, embracing them. She turned to the tall man beside her. "This is my husband, Paul."

"Thank you," Louise replied. "You have such a lovely home."

"You can't possibly still plan to leave this place?" asked Ida, gesturing about. From all she'd seen of Frankfurt so far, it was nothing but a beautiful, thriving city.

Mitia laid a finger to her mouth. "We'll talk of it later."

⋄ ·· —— ·· ⋄

The next day, Paul motored the Mayer-Lismanns—including Mitia's older brother Carl—and the Cook sisters through verdant stretches of green meandering along the Main River to Offenbach, a hamlet ten kilometers from Frankfurt. The Mercedes turned up a wide, circular drive in front of an impressive villa and stopped beneath a stone porte cochere. Ida and Louise climbed from the car, mouths agape.

It was clear from the greeting with Frau Elfriede Basch that the families were dear friends. Frau Basch ushered their guests into a large oak-paneled library where the furnishings were grand, though a tad worn about the edges.

"What a splendid estate!" Ida exclaimed, but Elfriede waved off her compliments.

"You should have joined us in happier years when we used to hold musical soirees here with ever so many glittering guests. Isn't that right, Mitia?"

Mitia nodded. "Shall we show them the music room? They will appreciate it."

59

Elfriede led them into the hallway, past a massive Venetian mirror Louise paused to admire. The upper landing, where an elegant divided stairway met, was adorned with matching glass cabinets. The cases held a decorative glass collection that included delicate hand-painted vases, a Roman-era rainbow patina cruet, and delicate glass filigree decanters from Murano, Italy.

The walls of the music room were ornamented with heavy framed Dutch paintings; a grand piano inlaid with palisander, lemon, and boxwood details took up one corner of the room.

Ida and Louise looked about in awe, and Ida wondered if she should have worn something other than her six-and-eleven-penny satin jumper.

"Let's have tea, such as we have, and music," said Elfriede, looking over toward Else. "Did you know our darling Else will be the last Jewish student to graduate from the Frankfurt Conservatoire?" Else took the cue and sat down before the pianoforte. They clapped for her melodies, which were genuinely superb.

"The fact remains," Else was insisting to Louise a short time later, "all the characters in *The Magic Flute* must face the prospect of their own death."

Ida talked with Mitia and Carl, who was such a sweet man that he had both her and Louise calling him Uncle Carl in no time. Mitia looked more relaxed than they'd ever seen her, and the old fire they'd once glimpsed on the stage flashed at the corner of her eyes.

But after the empty teacups had been stacked upon the sideboard, Elfriede said, "There. It's best we truly talk. Else's English is better than mine, so she will explain things."

Ida and Louise looked up in surprise.

"Miss Cooks," Else began, "I'm afraid we must leave Germany . . ."

"All of you?" Ida asked, looking round the circle at each of the refined faces, so clearly rooted in this world. "Are you certain?"

"Very certain," came Else's answer, and heads shook in unison.

"And—you'll leave all this behind?" Louise asked. It seemed too incredible. This house represented centuries of accumulated wealth beyond anything the sisters had ever imagined. Just a few moments before, they'd been singing parts from their favorite operas as if they'd no greater cares.

Frau Basch flew off in rapid German, and Else nodded. *"Da, da.* Her husband has been taken," Else explained.

"Taken where?" Louise asked.

"To Dachau, a work camp," Paul interjected. "Accused of being a communist."

"Gracious," said Louise. "Do you think things will get worse than they already are?"

Ida chimed in. "Wouldn't you want to try to wait? My father says—"

Uncle Carl, his skin creased like parchment, spoke up in English with a heavy German accent. "It is becoming difficult for us now to buy even food. Things could get much worse, *liebling.* Much worse."

Ida realized with a strange awakening that it didn't matter much what her father said, for her father had never been here, had never spoken with these people. The newspapers at home, written by a correspondent from a comfortable armchair behind a British desk weighing strategy and politics could not possibly understand the reality these families lived with. For the first time, she felt a branching of reality and sensed that beneath the grandeur of this mansion, beneath the tea and music and elegant furnishings, simmered a rising wave of dread she could not comprehend. To consider leaving this behind—they must be facing impossible circumstances. "If you aren't allowed to buy food, what do you eat?" Louise asked practically.

"Fortunately for us, our neighbors are farmers. For this time, they allow us to barter. We trade them a rare book, a piece of family silver in return for sacks of potatoes and a chicken."

The way Mitia and Paul were nodding at each word Else spoke told Ida things were even more difficult for the Mayer-Lismann family. She felt a wash of shame for judging Mitia for being *gloomy* of all things. The crude and harrowing signs from the streets of Frankfurt rose to her mind: *Jude.* An awkward silence followed, and she cleared her throat. "Frau Basch, can we help somehow?"

The woman's face, as regal as a queen's, warmed to kindness at Ida's words. "Else believes there may be a way."

"Going to England may be the best choice for us," Else explained. "My mother and Elfriede can apply to receive visas as 'domestics.'" Ida and Louise exchanged a glance. The very idea of women such as these pretending to be domestic servants. Wholly unbelievable.

Else continued, "I can apply for a student visa. It's my father and Uncle Carl who are most at risk, I'm afraid."

"Don't fuss about me! I'm old!" lectured Uncle Carl. They'd clearly had the conversation before.

Else continued, "They're liable to be rounded up and taken at any time, especially if they are not employed, which they can't be thanks to newly passed laws. Guarantees are what we need. British citizens must sign documents agreeing to be financially responsible for us as long as we remain in Britain—or until we receive permission to go to the States."

Ida and Louise exchanged nervous looks again. A hefty promise. Their family certainly didn't have the resources, and yet, as Ida

watched the fire flash in Mitia's eyes, she knew they must do everything in their power to help these two families. Finally, she understood the full weight of Viorica's words: "There, now you will be all
right." Viorica had, perhaps, trusted them to help beyond a train
journey.

"I'm afraid we know nothing about the immigration process,"
Ida confessed, feeling guilty that she'd thought of little besides romance stories much of late. "I feel foolish that we haven't paid more
attention to the situation. The newspapers in London have covered
the political situation, of course, but not the impact on . . . real
people like yourself."

"On Jews," Mitia said directly.

Ida nodded helplessly.

"We will look into it," Louise promised. "We will help if there's
any way we can. Our family is quite ordinary, I'm afraid. I'm not
sure we'd qualify to give a guarantee."

Else explained it all back into German, and there were more
nods around the circle. "We have one more request of you." Else's
pretty face flushed. "It may be quite dangerous, and we understand
if you choose not to."

"What is it?" Ida asked, a sinking feeling in her stomach.

"Have you heard that Jewish houses and all their belongings
must be registered with the Nazi government?"

Ida shook her head; they hadn't known. There was so much they
hadn't known.

"Everything above five thousand reichsmarks must be registered.
We believe they intend to confiscate it all. Without money, no foreign government will allow any of us entry, and we will be unable to
leave Germany."

"Would they do that?"

Elfreide moved to the buffet, where a velvet box sat upon the polished surface. She brought it back to the circle and withdrew something. Ida noticed for the first time how prominent the older woman's veins were, tracing up both sides of her hands like vines lacing up the sides of a tree.

"You asked to help," she said. "If you can help us get these to England, they will make the difference." She uncurled her hands to reveal a gorgeous ruby brooch surrounded by glittering diamonds. Nestled beside it was an ornately carved emerald ring.

"Oh!" Ida started. "They're like something from the Queen's jewels!"

"Ida," said Louise, nudging her.

The two exchanged a long, tortured glance. There was a name for this. *Smuggling.* Smuggling jewels legally required to be registered with Nazi officials. They'd had no idea of the real situation in Germany. What else didn't they know? And if they were caught . . . ? A flash of fear struck Ida's heart—fear of never being able to get home, of being trapped in a twisted carnival mirror with a deep sea rising.

Dachau. Elfriede's husband had been sent there. A fierce homesickness swept over her.

Ida picked up the ring—a dazzling rectangle as large as the knuckle on her ring finger. Light from the windows passed through the gem, reflecting shimmering emerald shafts deep within the faceted stone. What if it had once belonged to a Bavarian princess? What if it contained secret powers? If any ring did, it would look just like this one.

"It's exquisite," Ida said. "I've never seen anything like it—outside of a museum."

"Perhaps," Louise suggested. "Perhaps. If we wear them openly?"

Ida was amazed that her sedate and practical sister who had never done anything even slightly dishonest was considering it.

Louise held the ruby brooch against her sister's satin jumper. "If we wore them with our simple clothing, they *might* be taken for Woolworth's paste."

"Do you think so?" Ida stammered.

The Baschs, Uncle Carl, Mitia, Else, and Paul watched them try on jewels, debating, as if the jewelry were costumes one could simply slip in and out of, rather than a family's inheritance, the last remnant of an entire estate, a faint and final hope.

"*Da, da,*" Elfriede said.

"Can we possibly?" Ida whispered to her sister, the emerald ring luminous in the palm of her hand.

"How can we not try?" Louise replied with tortured eyes, and Ida marveled at the strength and goodness of her older sister.

So they nodded their agreement to Elfriede, and it was done. Gratitude. Relief. Laughter. Else returned to the pianoforte to play. What a solace the music was; clearly one of the few things of light and beauty still there for them exactly as it had been in times before.

MUNICH

Munich. The scale was impossible to believe. In a nod to Bavaria's illustrious past, buildings had been built on a massive scale and were now being renewed under Nazi order. Sumptuous Corinthian columns supported the Palace of Justice. The Residenz. The Marienplatz. Each surface was resplendent with a Grecian frieze or some other ornamentation.

After a debate about whether it would be safer to leave Frau Basch's jewels unattended in the hotel room or risk wearing them out in public, Louise and Ida decided it would be safer to wear the finery out in plain sight, so Ida pinned the ruby brooch to her opera gown, and Louise wore the enormous emerald.

As they made their way from hotel to opera house, they passed several advertisements for an art exhibition in the Hofgarten: *Entartete Kunst*. Degenerate Art. The advertisement portrayed a man in a stark black kaftan, gold coins in one hand, a whip in the other, with sharp red letters below. *"Der ewige Jude,"* Louise, who had been picking up some German, sounded out.

"Do you know what it means?" Ida asked.

"I think . . . the Eternal Jew," Louise guessed, as Ida drew her cloak tighter against the chill night air.

The grand colonnade of the Bavarian State Opera was adorned with crisped swastika banners riveted into the stone. Pretending they didn't usually buy the least expensive gallery seats in London, they joined Viorica in her box, their jewels blending into the sea of finery around them. Viorica greeted them with enthusiastic kisses on both cheeks, eying their jewelry but saying nothing about it. Five golden tiers of seats rose from the floor, illuminated by a chandelier hanging from a festooned rotunda. Crimson fabric upholstered the walls and seats, and Ida and Louise tried not to gawk at Munich's bourgeoisie out for an opera with the great Clemens Krauss conducting.

The crowd stirred, and the audience rose in unison. A man with severely swept back hair, a pinched face, and thin lips entered the royal box seats, a woman dripping gemstones by his side. All eyes turned toward the pair, as he stretched out his straight arm in attention over the crowd. En masse, the crowd returned the greeting.

"Herr Joseph Goebbels," Viorica explained. "This is one of Hitler's favorite operas—he was here himself last week." When the

Goebbelses took their seats, the audience followed suit. "And how are our friends in Frankfurt?"

"They're . . . fine," said Ida.

"Anxious to see about a visit to London," Louise added.

Viorica nodded. "Of course."

Ida bent close to Viorica. Surely no one could hear their voices over the rustling of programmes and people settling? "They believe they may be in some danger," she whispered in a low voice.

Under the dazzling lights, it was easy to believe that Viorica might laugh and dismiss the idea with a wave of her elegant hand. This was Germany after all—a land of order and elegance, of opera and science. And this was the twentieth century, for heaven's sake.

Viorica's gracious smile never wavered, and she continued to nod to those around them as if she had not heard. The slightest incline of her head brought Idea close enough to hear her whisper: "They are, indeed, my dear, in gravest danger."

Shocked, Ida tried to settle back into her seat as the lights in the theater dimmed and the crowd fell to silence. Clemens, resplendent in a tuxedo with his shock of hair swept back, took his place on the stand, bowed to the appreciative audience, then raised his baton as he drew the wind section into sound.

The curtain rose.

Fully armored, the Roman tribune Rienzi took the stage, quelling a riot while promising peace and magnanimously courting the favor of his countrymen.

In gratitude, the countrymen fell down before him, singing lines the sisters had reviewed on the train into Munich: *"Rienzi, mach uns großartig und frei!"* Rienzi, make us great and free!

Later, the gorgeous chorus rose up, soaring, a hundred singers on the stage joining their voices in praise:

Rienzi, hail!
Rienzi, hail!
Rienzi comes! Our shame is past!
Deliverer! Savior! Glorious knight!

Ida recalled Viorica saying that this opera was Hitler's favorite. No doubt he imagined himself as the anointed Savior of the German people.

Only Adriano, whose father led an influential group of Romans, seemed to be concerned. On stage, he warned:

To the goal of thy proud dreamings,
thou canst but come through paths of blood.

. . .

Desist from battle!
Oh desist!

But Rienzi insisted on the path to war:

Ere thou shalt move my heart,
let all the world in ruins fall!

"So be it!" Adriano replied:

Fate shall even take its course.

Ida felt a sick sensation rise in her stomach in spite of the beauty of Wagner's triumphant melodies.

The final scene opened with Rienzi, Adriano, and Irene—Rienzi's sister and Adriano's beloved—trapped in a tower. Flames licked the base as people sang:

Let death his arrogance arrest.

From the burning, ruined tower Rienzi called out with dying breath:

Is this your thanks for all I've done?
Degenerate folk!
The last of the great Romans curses you!

And then the curtain fell down upon the scene of misery, as the glittering audience rose, and applause broke over the sumptuous theater.

It should have been a stunning artistic achievement. The performance had been a triumph—the technique perfection, the setting divine. But Ida found herself intuitively pulling her wrap around her shoulders tighter, as if to ward off the glittering applause and somehow guard them all from an inevitable future.

◇·····—·◇

As they neared the Dutch border, Ida and Louise tried to push down their nervousness, to wear the jewels casually, as if they'd always been their own. As the train rocked, a memory she'd not thought of in ages came into Ida's mind.

"Louise, do you remember that game I used to play when we were little? When I would hunt round the garden digging in the dirt and peering under things, looking for lost diamonds?"

Louise laughed. "We had a row about it a few times, remember?"

"Because you said if I found one, I must give it back to its rightful owner and it would be wrong to expect a reward simply for doing what's right." Ida smiled at the memory and looked down at the exquisite ruby brooch circled with diamonds. "This is just as gorgeous and sparkly as the jewels I imagined as a child."

"Am I to suppose you've matured since then, and that you're planning to give it back?"

Ida laughed. "You had an unusually sensitive conscience for

69

a child, Louie. And yes, I shall give this treasure back when the Baschs come to claim it." The train slowed as they reached the border, and the smiles dropped from their faces.

"And what was the purpose of your trip?" a German official inquired.

"Opera," said Louise, adjusting the white gloves that covered Frau Basch's emerald ring, as Ida flourished a *Rienzi* playbill.

His eyes momentarily rested on Ida's brooch, but as he took in the rest of her outfit, he appeared to dismiss it. Nothing about them looked like gentry.

"Next," said the official, and he waved them through.

A few hours later, they boarded the ferry that plied the route between Rotterdam and Harwich, and, as the hammered water receded, the sisters relaxed at last, melting into the ship's railing as each minute increased their distance from Germany.

By that evening, they were back in the parlor at 24 Morella Road, which looked just like they had left it; they embraced their parents for a long time. How different everything felt. No longer could they wave off news about Germany. Suddenly the political climate had become interesting in a way no newspaper could manage. Ida thought of how she'd planned to use her new writing earnings to buy clothes and opera tickets. The memory made her a little sick. Back in their shared bedroom, Ida gingerly placed the emerald ring beside the brooch, wondering what to do with the lot. "I suppose we need a safe deposit box for them," said Ida.

They settled into their beds and turned off the lights, a silence stretching between them.

"We must get those dear people out," Louise said at last. "All of them."

Ida nodded into the darkness, surrounded and lifted by the safety and protection of her home. "Tomorrow, we begin."

DOLPHIN SQUARE

The morning after their return from Munich, Louise began organizing tasks with the cool aplomb of a general. "Now then," she said briskly. "There are several things we must do: find English sponsors for them. We've smuggled out their belongings, but we need to convince the British Government they're not paupers. It's simple, really, but Ida, we must organise and coordinate. One mistake and . . ."

"And they're trapped," Ida finished, overwhelmed by the enormity of it all. "I'll work on it. It will be easier for me since my job is less strenuous than yours."

By midmorning, Ida had realized Else was correct about the visas: she could get a student visa easily enough, and Mitia and Frau Basch might be passed off as domestics, but the men presented a much more challenging task, while also living with the greatest risk of being captured. Finding a guarantee would be the easiest way to get around the problem, but the guarantor had to assume full financial responsibility for as long as the refugees remained in England, possibly for the rest of their lives.

Ida sighed and scrutinized the paperwork over her dinner break. So much bureaucracy, so many rules spelled out in exhausting legalese—with none of it matching the fervor and importance of those families trapped in a villa in Germany, bartering off their family's possessions in exchange for potatoes.

By the following afternoon, she was able to telegraph Else's student visa to Frankfurt. The family would have to travel separately and reunite in London, she wrote to Mitia. There was no other way.

Putting the rest aside, she climbed the narrow stairs to the attic and began working feverishly on the latest installment of *Wife of Christopher*, grateful to escape to a story she could control. As she typed her way through the dramatic scenes, they carried a new weight, the lightness of the romantic serial belied by the people now potentially relying on its success.

◆ ·· — ··· — ·· ◆

A few weeks later, she was summoned back to Miss Taft's office.

"Ida, I'm pleased to tell you a publisher we often work with has expressed interest in your serial when it is finished."

Ida couldn't hide the smile that spread across her face. "They wish to publish it as a book?"

"A romance novel, yes. They've forwarded a publishing contract for you to review."

Ida reached for a pen.

"Oh no, my dear, you mustn't sign any contract right away. Take it home, look it over with your family, and let me know."

"Is it fairly standard?"

"Yes," Miss Taft said. "The advance is smaller than it will be once you're established with a record, but Mills & Boon is an excellent publishing company. If you're sure you can finish the serial on a strong note, I suggest you accept their terms. They've indicated that they're interested in seeing more from you if it does well."

Ida glanced down at the contract: "To be received: one completed manuscript." A shiver went down her spine. "Oh yes, I will finish it, Miss Taft. I must."

Miss Taft glanced up at the odd response but didn't question her. "Review it and let me know then. Do you want to publish it under your own name or use a pseudonym?"

"A writing name? I'll give it some thought."

As Ida left the office behind, she leafed through the pages of the contract to find the advance amount. One hundred twenty-five pounds! More money than she'd had in her entire life. While she would have spent it gladly a few weeks before on opera tickets and festivals, the thought only briefly crossed her mind. Would it guarantee one of their friends? Maybe more? She thought of sweet Uncle Carl, and the idea of having him safe in London made her step light as she hurried home.

⋄ ⋯ — ⋯ ⋄

"Mitia's received her visa," Louise said weeks later, glancing up from the letter she dropped onto a book of German verbs. "She'll arrive a week after Else. Wherever shall we put them?"

"I've been thinking about that," Ida said. "We might lease a flat in Dolphin Square."

"A *flat*? Are you crackers?"

"If the Mayer-Lismanns and the Baschs arrive in London like we hope they will, don't you think we'll need a place to put them?"

"What will you do with the flat when they're finished with it?"

"We can terminate the lease, or I can use it as a writing studio and a place to hold gramophone parties."

Louise laughed. "Are you sure you're not spending sterling faster than you can make it?"

"I'm trying not to," Ida confessed, "but we can't possibly squeeze them all into the attic here."

"Let's look at flats," said Louise.

⋄ ⋯ — ⋯ ⋄

They found a three-bedroom apartment in the newly built Dolphin Square, near Westminster, with a wide expanse of lawns, bricked shops, and formal gardens for strolling. The flat received south-facing sunlight, leaving it far brighter than most of London. Ida paid the deposit with a thrill of independence. While she had no real desire to leave her parents' home, knowing she had the ability to do so still filled her with quiet pride.

Else arrived that Saturday, her dark hair covered with a silk scarf, her eyes shaded by the heavy brim of her hat. Ida and Louise met her at the station. She stepped onto the platform cautiously, scrutinizing onlookers, then startled at the sight of them, rushing to hug them close. "I can't tell you how wonderful it is to see you," she said, her voice emotional.

"Come," said Ida, linking arms with her and whisking her off to Dolphin Square. You would have thought the flat was the Baschs' villa in Offenbach by Else's reaction.

"What a view of London! Oh, you dears! We never imagined. How can we possibly ever repay you?"

"You'll think of no such thing," said Ida firmly. "You're our guest, as we were yours in Germany. We hope to get your father, Uncle Carl, and the Baschs here soon."

Else nodded joyfully, but her eyes slowly filled with tears. "I'm sorry," she said, brushing them away. "I can't help it. There are *so* many dear people—friends, neighbors, relatives—in desperate circumstances, you've no idea. I wish this flat could fit them all."

Ida and Louise looked at each other, crestfallen. They'd scarcely thought beyond the Baschs and the Mayer-Lismanns, but, of course, there were others. So many, pressing behind them, seeking a way out. There were half a million Jews in Germany.

Though, just as Mitia had said on their first introduction, *perhaps not for long.*

Mitia arrived a week later, wearing the haunted, anxious look they remembered well but no longer judged gloomy. She clung to her daughter, chest heaving, holding her close. Turning at last to Ida and Louise, she hugged them too. "We will never forget what you've done for us. Never."

Embarrassed, Ida and Louise tried to shrug it off. "I'm sorry we haven't discovered a way to get your husband here yet," added Louise. "Or the Baschs."

"We're going to keep trying," Ida promised. To her sister, she said: "We will likely need to go back."

MARIA BAUER

VIENNA

By the time Ilse Maria Bauer had turned seven, she could sing all the verses of a popular song:

> *Wien, Wien nur Du allein*
> *Wirst stets die Stadt meiner Träume sein!*

> *Vienna, Vienna, only you*
> *will always be the city of my dreams.*

And the city *was* a dream. Hushed stands of beeches, oaks, and hornbeams sloped down to the sluggish blue of the Danube Canal in the charming Viennese neighborhood of Döbling. Being a child in Vienna had meant hiking after Papa through lush vineyards dotted with wild garlic flowers; it had meant visiting the palace with its splendid gardens arranged in curls of color around graceful fountains; it had meant marveling at the animal house at the Schönbrunn Zoo and shrieking with delight on the enormous Ferris wheel turning through space at the Prater amusement park, and swimming on the Alte Donau.

Being a child in Vienna had meant lighting shabbat candles, learning to braid the challah and brush it with egg until the rising curves glistened in the light. It had meant being Jewish, but not the way the Zionists were Jewish, or the way those who spoke Yiddish on Matzo Island in Leopoldstadt were Jewish. From their apartment in Döbling, Maria had gone to school with Czechs and Yugolavs. Croats, Poles, and Serbians. Her papa wore no beard and explained that though their family had come from Ukraine, they were Viennese now, and there was room for everyone in this vibrant, brimming city.

At barely sixteen, Maria attended her first Vienna Opera Ball in a long gown that swept the floor and white gloves to the elbows. She danced the polka and Viennese waltzes, turned across the floor by partners in white ties and black tails, until Leopold Winter introduced himself. She could not ignore how they read each other's movements, anticipating each turn, each gesture.

When the music stopped, the lights of a hundred chandeliers above his head seemed to be captured in his hair, and she wanted nothing but to talk with him until the sun rose in the east over their splendid, magnificent city.

Giddy with the elixir of young romance, Maria hardly listened as neighbors spoke of trouble across the border in Germany. Her grandfather, who had come to Austria from Hungary, recalled the magic of young love and patted her hand. "Never mind, *Engelchen*," he told her. "There have been Jews in Austria as long as Austria has been Austria. We built this empire, and she will not forget those who served in the Great War." He waved toward his medals displayed on the wall.

And because Maria wanted to believe him, she did.

Die Wahrheit, the Vienesse-Jewish newspaper, also recommended they remain calm. "Antisemitism has been part of life for European Jews for centuries," it reminded its readers. "And here we remain." Hitler too would pass.

On the other side of the border, Nazis spoke of *Grossdeutsch,* the greater Germany, and they claimed they could unite all German blood in one land. Divisions began to fragment Vienna—first a telephone booth exploded, then a tear gas bomb, next a demonstration. But these were minor events of isolated political extremists, and the more responsible Vienna could surely not forget the two hundred thousand upright and law-abiding Jewish citizens who were doctors, lawyers, and shop owners indispensable to any community.

Mesmerized by Maria's full and rounded sweet face, her quick tongue, and her laugh that sounded like a silver bell, Leopold Winter begged Papa to forget he was a Gentile, promised to love her always, and promised: as soon as he found a job, they would marry. Surely, soon, he said, the rampant unemployment in Vienna, forced artificially high by Germany to hold out the promise of sweeping economic reform—it would have to soon come to an end.

On March 11, 1938, just before the Bauers turned off the radio for the Sabbath, Austrian Chancellor Kurt Schuschnigg announced his capitulation to the Nazi party.

"And so I take leave of the Austrian people," he said, "with a German word of farewell uttered from the depths of my heart: God save Austria!" A Nazi official took over abruptly, proclaiming that Austria was now part of Germany.

With shaking hands, Mama lit the Sabbath candles.

The next morning it seemed all of Vienna had taken to the streets to shout, scream, or celebrate. "Common blood belongs in a common empire!" some yelled. "One people, one land, one leader!" cried others.

Great crowds, with hastily fabricated swastika armbands, threw Nazi salutes. Maria held tight to Papa's arm as they navigated the sea of people, passing Hitler Youth on the street corners, offering lapels to all who donated, noting those who did not.

Four days later, German tanks arrived, crossing the medieval cobblestones with a ghastly metallic clatter. Luftwaffe planes skimmed across the rooftops, and Hitler spoke before two hundred thousand wild and cheering people in the Heldenplatz.

"Heil Hitler!" they screamed, with their arms locked at an odd angle.

Making their way through the streets of Vienna on Monday, Maria tried to steer her mother away from the jeering crowd but stopped when she saw an old Hasidic Jew down on the street, beaten and bloody. As people mocked his confusion, Maria recognized a young woman her own age pretend to help the man up. He reached toward her, expecting help. And then she spread her skirt and urinated on him, as the crowd roared with laughter.

Disgusted, Maria hurried her mother away, but not before the man's bloody, exhausted face had been etched upon her mind in indelible strokes that would never leave.[10]

Another crowd, just a block from home, surrounded their own rabbi, Israel Taglicht, who it seemed had been forced to his knees to scrub the sidewalk. "I am willing to clean God's great earth," Maria heard him say as they hurried past, ashamed she didn't dare try to help him. *What could they do?*

Overnight, they'd been denied their Austrian citizenship,

proclaimed by Germany to be stateless. Grandpapa clutched his medals from the war. "Stateless?"

"Don't go out," Maria told him. "None of you go out."

Drunk with power, people forced their way into Jewish homes, looting cash, jewelry, and fur coats. Papa barred the door, put out the lights, and prayed no one would come with an axe.

In synagogues, fiends tore up Torah scrolls, cut the beards of rabbis with knives, and dragged hundreds of people to the Prater where they beat them, then forced them to eat grass. In the parks, cafes, and streets of Vienna, uniformed *Sturmabteilung*—storm-troopers, or the SA—forced girls to sing, "Perish, Jew," as they had their heads shaved and scalps painted with a swastika.

Signs went up in store windows across Vienna: *"No dogs or Jews."*

Outside the yeshivas in the second district, Hitler Youth waited to hurl objects at students as they left to walk home. The crowds grew daily, circling Jews, forcing them to scrub floors, toilets, and sidewalks in their nice clothes, to sing as they cleaned with a tooth-brush or scrubbed with acid burning their hands. If they fell down from hunger or exhaustion before the jeering crowd, they were beaten.

Where had these people come from? Maria wondered. These people who had lived beside them their whole lives as neighbors, friends, and co-workers—*who had they become?*

Papa came home the following week, hands hanging at his side. His business partner had forced him out. Out of the business they had built together, with no compensation for the years they had worked together. "You are lucky," his partner had told him. "Other owners have been forced to stand outside their own shops holding a sign that read: 'I am a Jewish pig.' Now go home."

Lifelong friends pretended not to know them. Anneliese Lang

and Margot Wimmer had been Maria's friends since grade school. Maria would never have believed it possible, yet they had joined the crowds of people who had seemingly lost their minds. They passed her in the street now with a look of loathing, as if one touch, one word would spread the filth. The Jewish filth. "To preserve the city," Vienna's parks, swimming pools, cinemas, and public benches were now forbidden to Jews.

Tales of hysterical depression and whispers of suicide began to circulate. Five hundred in two months, the rumors went. Wealthy professionals. Whole families who took their lives together with a pistol. A bit of rope. A coal gas oven.[11]

"We need to leave, Ezra," said Mama. "They're taking people and locking them up in Hartheim Castle, near Linz."[12]

"But where can we go?" Papa asked miserably. "We are Viennese."

The SS came for Papa the next day, breaking down the door. They took Grandpapa too. They were going only to the police station for processing, the soldiers promised. They would, of course, be back. Grandpapa pinned his medals to his lapel, head held high as he marched through the door.

"Don't worry, Irma," Papa said, kissing Mama goodbye. "See you tonight."

She threw herself on their bed when he was gone and didn't get up for hours.

◇·· ··· —··◇

It had been weeks since Maria had seen Leopold, with so many dark questions raging at the corners of her mind. All that they had promised each other seemed empty and hollow now. It had been a promise made in a different lifetime. In a different world.

His knock came at the door, after dark. Furtive, muffled. "Maria, it's me," he whispered against the wood, and she opened the door, bracing herself for his words, knowing what he must say and that she alone now could protect her mother from the insanity that had descended on the streets outside.

"You could have sent a note," she chastised, scolding him. "It isn't safe to come here." She crossed her arms over her chest, protecting her heart, waiting for him to spit at her. To mock her like the others.

He tried to pull her to him. "I came as soon as I could."

"Don't," she said, pulling away. "They've taken Papa," she choked out. "Grandpapa too." Spasms ratcheted against her chest. "You shouldn't have come—it isn't safe for you to be here."

"I had to." He tried again to reach after her. "I needed to see you before I left. I'm going to Switzerland."

She reached behind her for a chair, a table—something to hold onto as the last of her world fell to pieces, as it inevitably must now that he would leave her.

"The Nazis have offered me a job," he said. "Made it plain I must not refuse. But I told them I needed medical attention in Switzerland first, with my brother. I will wait for you there."

"Wait for me?"

"Yes. Wait for you, my soon-to-be-bride."

"Leo, don't you see? That's impossible now. We can't—"

"What is impossible?"

"Everything. Us. The Mosers have taken poison—the *whole* family of them. Papa and Grandpapa—gone. I'm Jewish," she stammered. "You're Aryan. We can't—"

Leo Winter dropped his satchel to the floor, grabbed both her elbows, and turned her to face him. "Ilse Maria Bauer, I adore you.

And if you think the entire Nazi army could keep me from your side, you do not understand the depths of my love. But you will before our lives are over. You will."

Great sobs welled up from her chest then, and she sagged into him, amazed to find that in the midst of this spinning world gone mad, he still remained. This man had appeared beneath the dancing chandelier lights of an opera ball; but unlike so much that is magic, he stayed when the sun rose in the east. And somehow, he remained even now as the rest of the world disintegrated back to particles of swirling dust. When she could speak, she said desperately, "Leo, what can we do?"

"Listen carefully. Don't write it down, only remember. You must ride the train to Bregenz. You know it? Make your way west to the shores of Lake Constance."

She nodded, breathless.

"On the first moonless night, a young fisherman, Léon Moille, will meet you at an abandoned boathouse villa near Fußach. He will row you across to Switzerland, where I'll be waiting, and somehow I will survive the two weeks until I can hold you again."

"I can't leave Mama."

"Of course not. You must bring her too."

Switzerland. Yes, she remembered. On the other side of an arbitrary political border, the world continued on as it always had. A world without jeering crowds and power-drunk SS men. Hope glimmered in that beautiful and shining word: *Switzerland.*

<hr />

Two weeks later, the lights from a hired car cut through the Fußach twilight. Irma wore a gray wool suit with a white handkerchief folded neatly in her breast pocket. Maria sat beside her, nervous and still. In the fading light, the great expanse of lake glimmered ahead, the shore outlined with lights from small villages that dotted the alpine landscape rising from its shores.

Lake Constance, or the Bodensee in German.

"You can leave us here," Maria told the driver, gesturing vaguely to a cluster of villas near an orchard on the outskirts of Fußach. "We're visiting friends," she added, knowing he would not believe them. She paid him extra, hoping it would be enough to keep him from alerting authorities to two dark-haired women carrying handbags, bound for the lake near the border.

The driver grunted, pocketed the money, and drove into the night, wheels churning against gravel. The abandoned villa lay ahead, but they cut away toward the barn at the back of the property, navigating overgrown weeds, and pushing the barn door open with a creak. They turned on a torch just long enough to ensure they were alone, then settled down to wait in the fragrant darkness, as the sky grew dark and stars came out.

Near midnight, clouds rolled in, gray and luminous, and a light rain began to fall. Maria and Irma pressed open the barn door, creaking on unoiled hinges, and made their way through the muddy pasture down to the row of boathouses that rose and fell with the rise and fall of waves slapping their timbers. A gusting, southeasterly wind from the Alps churned the water, and heavy mist obscured the opposite shore as they slipped inside.

Sometime later, out in the expanse, Maria could just make out a dark shape, floating flat against the water. A rowboat moved silently, headed in the direction of shore. She took Irma's arm, helped her shuffle noiselessly toward the door. Maria eased the gateway open an inch.

Like a lightning strike, a searchlight pierced the darkness, sweeping across the waves, resting on the darkened shape of a rowboat.

"Halt! Im Auftrag der Polizei!" came the voice from the patrol boat that had risen from the shadows.

Maria froze, gripping her mother's arm.

The patrol boat drew alongside the rowboat. Guards boarded it and bound the pilot, lashing his boat to theirs. Then they motored in the direction of shore, their lights scanning each boathouse as they passed, glazing each window with their glare.[13]

Maria pulled Irma toward her, shaking, as they sank to their knees just below the sill of the window.

They spent the night like that, startling at every sound, straining to hear beyond the moody lake lapping at the moorings. But after the soldiers had left with their prey, there remained only the creak and give of soaked timbers.

At dawn, they struggled out, darted back to the barn, out to the road to Fußach. Back to Bregenz, and a train bound for Vienna. Third class, the only cars still open to Jews. Maria watched the jagged lines of the Swiss Alps recede in the distance. There were whispers people were crossing there, through wild, forested mountain ways, but her mother would never make it, she knew, so she could only watch as they shrank into the distance.

Back in Vienna, they sidled down streets and pressed themselves against walls like shadows, then tumbled back to their apartment, barred the door, and collapsed on the sofa. Maria covered her face with her hands as the world shivered to pieces. *Oh Leo,* she cried, *what do we do now?*

PART 2

"The idea that a poem could make a dent in a
regime or a symphony rally a revolution sounds absurd,
but all tyrannical governments move first against the artists.
When you kill the artist, you kill the protest.
And Hitler knew it."

—IDA COOK

PESACH

AUSTRIA, APRIL 16, 1938

On the eastern edge of Austria, Jews gathered round seder tables, lighting candles to mark the passing from day to night, from the ordinary space to the sacred. In Hebrew or in German, voices across the cities of Pama and Sittee repeated the ageless Passover blessings.

By the light of flickering candles, families and friends broke flat sheeves of matzah bread, setting aside a portion to be the afikomen. "This is the bread of affliction that our fathers ate in the land of Egypt," they recited.

> *Let all who are hungry come and eat;*
> *whoever is in need, let him come.*
> *This year we are here; next year in the land of Israel.*
> *This year we are slaves; next year, we will all be free.*

And they went on, retelling the story of the Israelites in Egypt, affirming that the light of freedom could not be extinguished, that the story, would be repeated through time immemorial.

Even as they reclined, though, they listened for the sound of the jackboots, for Austria was not as it had been some weeks before.

Into the gatherings, the feasts of wonder, came the SA soldiers, rolling into town in trucks, left in the streets, their engines idling.

Screams began to punctuate the Passover gatherings as soldiers loaded up the rabbi, the new mother, the little child, the barber, the goldsmith, the leatherworker.

Forced outside without their belongings, the Jews of Pama and Sittee were pushed into trucks, then transported in darkness to the banks of the Danube. Rowed by boat and left upon the sandy island—floating in the no man's land between Austria and Czecho-Slovakia. Surrounded by rising tides and the dark flash of the river, they were left to think of the matzah they had left behind, and of Moses, raising his hands over the shimmering vastness of the Red Sea.

THE DEMONS IN THE FIELD

FRANKFURT, APRIL 1938

"What is the purpose of your visit?" demanded the German border official.

"Opera," said Ida, trying to sound breezy.

He flipped through their passports. "You were also here last year—twice?"

"We come often to see performances." That sounded reasonable enough, surely; but they both waited, breathless and anxious.

He turned his head to the side, suspicious. "What opera have you come to see?"

Curses. They should have checked.

Ida spat out the first title that came into her mind. "*Rigoletto.*"

The official waved them through, and they both exhaled. Once out of earshot, Louise whispered, "Hopefully he won't check what's on, but we need to be more careful."

The air seemed tenser than when they'd last traveled to the continent. Now that Hitler had taken over Austria, a flood of refugees advanced in his wake, and even Papa admitted that perhaps Neville Chamberlain had been wrong to try to appease the führer.

◇ ⸱⸱ ⸱⸱⸱ — ⸱⸱ ◇

A few hours later, Mitia's husband, Paul, opened the door to their apartment in Frankfurt and hurried them inside. "Thank God you're here," he said as he closed the door behind them. "So many of my neighbors have been taken. They must come for me next, I am thinking."

He was a brilliant man, they knew. A distinguished professor, an expert in his field. They'd been working, desperately, on an appointment with Cambridge that would allow him a legitimate reason to travel; but the university needed documents—official documents that could far too easily be confiscated if sent through the post. "Here they are," he said, pressing the papers into their hands even as they still stood in the hallway. "Sorry," he apologized, "I should let you set down your things. What am I coming to?" He ran a shaky hand through his frazzled hair.

"Please don't bother," Ida assured him. "What a relief it will be for us all to have these safe." She tucked the papers into her bag, in a concealed compartment she'd sewn just for this purpose and would later stitch shut. "We have them now."

"Come in, come in," he said, lifting their bags, carrying them into the parlor. Some of the expensive furnishings they'd remembered had disappeared. Sold or bartered for food, surely. For a little soap and paper.

"Mitia and Else send their love," Louise said. "They are anxious to have you in London." She handed him a letter in Mitia's handwriting, and the man tore it open, devouring it as though it were water and he'd made his way through a desert to find it.

Pressing the letter to the table some minutes later, he said, "Miss Cooks, I know you've done so much, but I must ask you: there are others who have heard you're trying to help us. Could you meet with them and help them understand the system? Perhaps offer them some hope?"

Ida and Louise exchanged glances. "Herr Mayer-Lissman, we still are trying to get out Uncle Carl and Elfriede," said Louise.

"And her husband if he returns from Dachau," Ida answered. "I don't know—"

"Elfriede will not leave without her husband," Paul interrupted. "Silly woman. Uncle Carl says to tell you to work on every other case before his."

"We have exhausted most of our resources," Louise admitted reluctantly.

The man looked deeply disappointed, and he set down a piece of paper they hadn't noticed.

"What is that?" Ida asked.

"A list," he explained, offering it to them. Silently, Ida took the paper and scanned the shaky handwriting:

> *Friedl Orlando*
> *Helmut Rosental*
> *Bela Cukierman*
> *Mirjam Sonneberg*
> *Jakob Taube*
> *Sura Lewin*
> *Abram Zylbersztajn*
> *Perla Galaznik*
> *Frajda Bekerman*

It went on that way. "Who are these people?" Ida asked.

"Friends," he explained, shrugging his shoulders. "Neighbors.

Colleagues. All of them desperate to talk with you, to gain more information. To find any way out."

"But—" said Louise. "I'm afraid we can't promise anything."

Ida couldn't stand his look of sadness. "But since we're here, Louie, I suppose we could talk with them. Just hear their stories?"

Louise looked concerned, but she nodded.

"That would be of help to them," Paul said thankfully.

◆┈━┉━┈◆

The next day brought a telegram from Clemens Krauss saying that he and Viorica would meet them in Frankfurt. "That seems odd," Ida said, reading it out to her sister. "Why would they come all this way?"

"Certainly seems like an odd time for a social visit," Louise agreed. But then the first of a steady stream of visitors tapped gently at the door, and they didn't have time to think more about it. Paul slipped each person inside and led them silently into the music room where the sisters waited to talk with them.

Friedl Orlando, a dear friend of Else's, came in with her dark hair pulled back and knotted. "Guten Tag," she said, lodging herself into the curve of the piano as if it might hold her up. "I am speaking to you today, hoping for proper evaluation of my situation." Her accent was heavy, and it seemed as though she'd memorized this speech, expecting to give it to people with far more authority than they had. Louise and Ida looked at each other, wondering how to explain that this wasn't any sort of official hearing.

"We are all living in one world,"—Friedl continued. She pronounced, "one" as "vun." "We must consider: not all these worlds are the same. I was living in Austria, when my father, he died, and then, I returned to Germany. The authorities, you see, they have

91

taken my passport. I am engaged to be married with a man, he is still being in Italy. We are both journalists."

Ida wanted to stop her, to say there was too little they could do, but she couldn't stand interrupting the girl's story.

Friedl continued, "If you allow me this opportunity, I go to England, and I am working there. I am eating nothing, you see? I am needing nothing. I want to work very hard. I will do anything that is necessary to be alive."

Ida sighed when Friedl had finished and turned to her sister, miserable at witnessing her obvious suffering.

"*Wie alt sind sie?*" Louise asked. Her German was getting better. *How old are you?*

Friedl's face lit up at the sound of her own language, and she began rattling off rapid-fire German.

"*Langsam bitte,*" Louise said, raising her hand. "I'm afraid I do not know very much."

But she knew enough.

"I'm afraid we can't promise anything," Ida repeated as the conversation wound down. She worried the woman was putting far too much hope in them.

"Understand," Friedl assured them, clasping her hands. "Understand."

They had time to exchange a hopeless glance before the next person came in.

Helmut Rosental needed a letter, just a letter, he explained, his hat in hands. He was a chemist who had managed to obtain a post in London, but the German authorities were refusing to return his passport. Ida looked more hopeful. Perhaps this one, they could do. She wrote down the details on a sheet of paper, explaining she would read them a hundred times over until she was sure she knew them all by heart, then put the paper in the fire. Though they cautioned him they could promise nothing, he wouldn't stop shaking their hands.

The day went on like that, working down Paul's list as they listened to stories of desperation and pleading. Louise took careful notes—notes she told Ida she would also memorize and burn. Several people were so nervous they couldn't stop shaking.

A woman named Perla held back tears as she begged them to take her mother's furs to England, holding out a mink and fox coat more luxurious than any they'd ever touched before.

Frajda barely batted an eyelash as she told them in near-perfect English that her son had been taken and imprisoned with no further notice, her only son.

Jakob spoke scarcely any English but still managed to explain that his wife was dead from suicide. "She could not . . . " he said, hands shaking, falling to his side. He shrugged, helpless to explain better. "She could not." When he left the room, Ida and Louise clung to each other, the tears they'd been holding back, tumbling from their eyes. Now, at last, Ida began to feel she understood the shadow's that haunted Mitia's eyes. How had they lived with this? *How could anyone live like this?*

Clearly. Some could not.

Even for those who managed to escape somehow, would they ever sleep again without fear, no matter how far away they went? Could they ever smile or laugh again? Remembering Jakob's shaking hands, Ida thought if they did, it would take miles beyond miles, years beyond years.

They stayed up that night using a seam ripper to remove the German labels from Perla's mother's coats, ripping English labels from their own coats and sewing them into place, using tiny even stitches their mother had taught them when embroidering pillow-cases had seemed like a reasonable use of someone's time. As they worked, every so often one of them would ask a question: "Did you see the way Jakob held his hat?"

"As if it were all he had to hold to in the world?" the other replied, and then they would tear up again at the mounting frustration, knowing that no matter what they did, no matter how hard they tried, they could never help them all.

"What would we have done without your German?" Ida asked, in awe of her sister.

"You would have been fine," Louise assured her. "Did you see the way they trusted you immediately? Loved you too?"

"Oh, Louie, I'm so glad we were here together. I couldn't have stood it alone."

<hr />

Krauss and Viorica arrived the next day, lighting up Mitia's music room. Though Ida and Louise met them gladly, an odd twinge of distrust lay beneath their greetings. In the past year, Krauss had taken over the position of director for the Bavarian State Opera after Hans Knappertsbusch was dismissed for his refusal to join the Nazi Party. Krauss was clearly working closely with the Nazi regime, then, and the safety of everyone they had talked to weighed on their shoulders as they greeted them. They kept conversation light when Paul was present, but later when he excused himself to take care of somethings, Ida picked her words carefully, hoping to determine where their friends' true sympathies lay.

"We've spoken with several of Mitia and Paul's friends while we've been here," Ida began, hesitantly.

"Others who need to escape?" asked Viorica, her voice sympathetic.

"It seems they must." Ida watched their expressions closely. "We thought since you were working closely with the regime, you might tell us how worried we should be. Is the worst perhaps behind them?"

Ida knew Friedl and Perla could not be exaggerating, but did Krauss know that? The details they'd heard could be disastrous in the wrong hands.

A look of intensity fell over Clemens's face—and he swept back his dark shock of hair. "No, no," he insisted. "They are not exaggerating. This is why we traveled to see you. We needed to talk without risk of interception. My position is a precarious one, you see. The Party trusts me, and I must give them no reason to reconsider. This is why it is much better if the help comes from you."

"For Mitia's family?"

He nodded. "And for others. We hope you'll help them. The government has cast out Schoenberg, arrested Erwin Schulhoff, and now that they've taken over Austria, they'll gut the Salzburg Festival too. Bruno Walter was fortunate enough to be in the Netherlands during the Anschluss, but his daughter has been arrested, and Arturo Toscanini has resigned in protest."

"Yes," Ida said, shifting in her seat uncomfortably. "There are many who would say resignation is the most ethical course of action."

Krauss looked discomfited. "Believe me, we have considered it. But ultimately, I believe we can do more good from this side, with full access to those in power here than we could beyond Germany's borders."

"Then it's not just Mitia's family you're hoping to help?" Louise asked.

"Heavens no." Krauss threw up his hands. "We're helping everyone we possibly can."

Viorica nodded intently.

Ida leaned against her sister with relief. "We're so glad to hear it," she admitted. "We couldn't be sure. There are more who need help than we realized." She paused, trying to convey what they'd heard. "Their stories are—we couldn't sleep last night—"

Viorica leaned forward, touching her knee. "We understand. Will you be able to help them, do you think?"

"We're going to try. We have some ideas," Ida said vaguely.

"I'm not sure how many more trips we'll be able to make safely," Louise interjected in a strained voice. "We want to help, but they questioned us in Cologne. Relations with the UK are only getting more tense."

"That, I think, we can help with," Viorica said.

Krauss nodded. "As director of the Bavarian State Opera, I set the schedule. Next time you need to make a trip, just send me the dates, and I will schedule a performance. I'll send you the details and a private invitation you can show at the border. You should come by air to Munich or Berlin, where I'm conducting—as our special guests—then to Frankfurt afterwards, if you need to. That should make things much easier at the borders. The two of you make a formidable team."

"Your *guests*?" said Ida, squirming and feeling they could never be convincing in that role.

"Bring your nicest gowns," Viorica suggested. "You should look the part."

Ida and Louise exchanged looks. The outfits Ida had made for the Salzburg Festival were the only gowns they owned that might be reasonable.

"You must stay at the Adlon in Berlin and the Vier Jahreszeiten in Munich—that's where we stay, and many of the party leaders. You'll attract less attention if you're right under their noses. We have rooms there—you'll be our guests. There are others in the city who would love the chance to talk to you. Do you have opera requests—something you'd like to see?"

"*Requests?*" Ida and Louise repeated, nearly together. This was beginning to sound like a much bigger commitment. Actively work to aid escapees? How many trips would they have to make? Could it put their family in danger?

Through Ida's mind flashed the faces of Jakob and Friedl, Sura and Mirjam. Could they really return home to Morella Road and resume their former lives as if nothing had happened? If they did, Ida knew their faces would haunt her for the rest of her life. She swallowed hard against her fear. "How do you do it?"

"Do what, dear?" Viorica asked.

"How do you pretend like the music even matters anymore?"

The light of understanding lit up her face. "In some ways, it matters less," she said simply. "But in some ways, it matters more than ever."

Ida nodded, sensing there was a greater truth than she could yet grasp, beginning to love this woman who had become like a mentor to her. She tried to smile at Louise through an odd pinch of guilt for having doubted them.

"Can you tell us what the government's plan is?" Louise asked.

"The Party's position," Krauss explained, "is that Jews are incapable of creativity, incapable of artistic utterance from the nature of their being. It's utter nonsense, of course, but they claim that for centuries Jews have been bolshevizing art, using it as a political tool of control. The party has promised to eradicate the Jewish presence from literature, art, and music, to 'rout the demons from the field' in Wagner's words. Holding that music is the pinnacle of artistic expression and therefore the climax of Jewish distastefulness, the party's goal is to purge their influence completely, to 'wash away the traces of his origin.' They've banished all Jewish professors, directors, and composers to prevent the 'bastardisation of the nation.' They've removed all Hebrew and Old Testament references from Handel's *Messiah*. They've re-written Mozart's *Requiem*."

Ida and Louise sat in stunned silence for a moment, shocked at the extent of the rationalization. Louise recovered first, the wheels turning in her mind. "So you mean, if we use your opera performances as a cover to help those they've targeted, we'd be using their Nazi operas to undermine their own goals completely?"

Krauss smiled, nodding at her comprehension. Viorica laid a warm hand upon Ida's arm. "No one would blame you for choosing not to, my dears. We can't promise it won't be dangerous. Hitler is a madman and there's no telling where this will end."

"Well, in truth," Ida said, thoughtfully. "We've never seen a top rate *Tosca*. . . ."

THE SYSTEM

On Monday they took the earliest boat back from Amsterdam under a just lightening sky. The sun burst across the stainless blue bowl above them, as if welcoming them back to sanity. Looking up, Ida asked, "Remember how it was sunny every time we queued to see Rosa? This sky reminds me of those mornings. We used to call it Ponselle Weather."

"Rather shocking for April," Louise agreed.

"*Rosa*," Ida repeated just to hear the word aloud, wondering at the contrast between the new work they were embarking upon when only months ago they'd spent every waking moment waiting for the next performance, mad about the next letter from Lita.

"Even in the midst of all this mess, there's still Rosa," she said.

How odd and heartbreaking to know that the perfection of sound that was Rosa Ponselle coexisted in the world with all that was evil and rising behind them—what a marvel that somehow one did not manage to extinguish the other.

When they arrived in London, Louise headed straight to the office to make apologies for being tardy, while Ida stopped at the bank to deposit Perla's furs for safekeeping. When she walked into the kitchen on Morella Road sometime later, she found Mum making pastry, up to her elbows in flour. Prince Igor wound himself around her legs and meowed at Ida when she entered.

Ida stopped short on the threshold, overwhelmed by the mundanity of the beautiful and ordinary sight. "Oh, Mum!"

Her mother looked up, startled as Ida burst into tears. "What is it?" With her hands covered in bits of pastry, she couldn't move, but she gave a sympathetic nod to draw her daughter close and continued arcing the pair of butter knives across the bottom of the bowl, cutting the butter into the flour, with steady, even slices, as she'd done as long as Ida could remember. The simplicity and familiarity of that rhythm was more comforting than anything, and Ida drew her handkerchief from her pocket, sobbing into it, before taking a deep, steadying breath.

"There," Mum said reassuringly. "It's no good tearing yourself to pieces. Whatever spot of bother this is, I'm sure you're doing the best you can. Now tell me all about it."

Ida crept behind her, circling her mother's waist with her arms, and hugged the whole floury, doughy mess of her.

Mum laughed. "You haven't done that since you were little. Remember how you used to hug me around the knees when I was making your tea?"

Ida laughed through her tears. "Mum, you've no idea. Neither does father. Mitia is right. Right about everything. They need to leave. They *all* need to leave."

"Who does?"

"Ever so many people. All of them, possibly."

"There are thousands of Jews in Germany, Ida."

"Perhaps not for very long."

◇⋯—⋯—⋯◇

In the afternoon, Ida submitted her resignation to the Civil Service. "We're sorry to see you go," her supervisor said, trying to understand why she would suddenly resign after so many years.

"Thank you very much," Ida replied vaguely. She had no desire to explain, and felt only relief, twinged with a pinch of guilt over the loss of the pension. "I have a new job," she told Louise that evening. "Writing serials and scrounging up visas."

"Now then, Ida," Louise said briskly. "Here's what we must do. We've got to screen out those who are in the most desperate situations and decide which of these have the best chances of being rescued. We have to either find guarantees for them, or we'll have to go back and smuggle out their belongings so they have valuables waiting that can be used to convince the British government."

Ida nodded, relaxed at the confidence in her sister's voice. If her sister said a thing, it was as good as done. "Tomorrow we begin."

◇⋯—⋯—⋯◇

Ida wore a trim wool suit and neat hat to visit the British firm that had agreed to hire Helmut Rosental. A secretary ushered her into the director's office. "You've visited with Mr. Rosental in person?" he asked, surprised. "We'd very nearly despaired of being able to hire him."

"Yes, sir, in Frankfurt."

"How are you acquainted with him?" the man asked, clearly intrigued that a total stranger would show up and attempt to work out these details.

"We have mutual friends," Ida said vaguely. "Mr. Randall, I believe Mr. Rosental will make you an excellent employee. What is needed is a letter verifying that you wish to hire him because of his specialty training and necessary qualifications, and a statement that you will provide the necessary emigration documents."

"Thank you very much indeed, Miss Cook," he said, shaking her hand. "We appreciate the information and will send the letter promptly to the German authorities. We do, indeed, wish to hire Mr. Rosental." He paused, then, hesitant. "We also understand that it's likely vital for his personal safety—"

"It is," Ida assured him.

She wished the man a good day and left his office feeling like the sun had begun to come out from behind a dark and ominous cloud.

◇ ·· — ··· — ·· ◇

They'd been home a week when Mum said, "Ida, do you remember Mrs. Baker with the League Club?"

"Quite possibly?" Ida said, trying to place the woman.

"They've decided to sponsor a lecturer to discuss the refugee crisis in Europe," Mum said, "and Mrs. Baker wondered if you might attend, seeing as you've just returned from Germany."

Thinking it might lead to a guarantee, on Wednesday evening, Ida followed Mrs. Baker into the Church of the Ascension at Lavender Hill in Battersea. The speaker was a professor, and the lecture was quite academic. He reviewed the issue of refugee resettlement, touching on historical occasions when immigration to the UK had been done successfully.

Ida stifled a yawn, annoyed that this academic conversation did so little for the desperate people she'd met in Frankfurt. A person seated to her right whispered to their neighbor that it was a complicated situation. "Jews," she said, as the presenter fumbled with some maps, "were Jews first and members of their nation second, and this must be kept in mind."

Ida squirmed in her seat.

Near the end of the presentation, a person in the audience raised her hand to ask the presenter to explain the current guarantor system.

To Ida's great surprise, the professor said, "Actually I'm told there's someone here who has more experience than I do with the current situation. Miss Cook, would you be willing to share a few words about the guarantor system and your recent trip to Germany?"

Ida felt the color rise to her face. She'd never done public speaking except for some brief, awkward encounters in secondary school, but she managed to stammer out "certainly" and rose to her feet. She heard a rather faint and squeaky version of her own voice explain haltingly how the system worked, and how it was even possible for two or three people to band together and assume responsibility for a single case.

It was past teatime, and someone's stomach made an awkward sound. A woman on the front row gazed into space. This isn't working, Ida realized. She cleared her throat, wishing she could channel some of Viorica's stage presence.

"Perhaps if I may provide you an actual instance? My sister and I were in Germany last week. We met a man named Jakob Taube, a carpenter. He's a kind and gentle man—" she broke off, wishing she could convey the sincerity of his face, the way he had held his hat. "He has asked us to save his life, for he is under orders to return to Buchenwald concentration camp, and almost certain death."

Ida's voice grew strange and pinched, but she struggled on. "— unless he can be removed from the country in the next few weeks. I have no guarantee. I have no means of saving him. He must die unless I can find the means—and find them quickly. I'm afraid his wife has already committed suicide from the dreadful stress of the situation. And there are a dozen other stories we heard, just like this one. They're people. Kind people. Just like any of you here in this room," she looked slowly round the group, "who need help desperately. Right away, in fact." She paused. "Thank you."

"Thank you," said the professor thoughtfully and concluded the meeting as Ida returned to her seat. Many eyes remained on her, fully open now. After polite applause and thanks, some people filed out without a backward glance. But others waited to speak with the presenter while others gathered around Ida. An elderly women said, "Would you have time to speak to our church circle, my dear? They would like to hear what you have to say."

Ida agreed, wondering if she would have time to better prepare for public speaking.

Another woman laid her hand on Ida's arm. "I need to talk to my husband, love, but perhaps we can help that sweet man you spoke of."

Another asked, "Do you think you could write up the things you said? We could put some bits in our newsletter and send it out to people."

"*Write?*" asked Ida with palpable relief. "Yes. Certainly. I can write you an article."

The next day, the phone rang. It was the woman who had promised to talk to her husband. "My husband says we better go ahead and offer it," she told her. "I couldn't stop crying all night after hearing your story about that man in need of rescue. What was his name?"

"Jakob," Ida said, tears welling in her eyes.

"Yes, that's it. Jakob. Just tell us what we need to do so that nice man will be all right."

PROMISES

Ida sat before her typewriter in the attic, eager to flee into a fictional world where each event was caused by one that came before, and each mishap was waiting to be teased out and resolved neatly in the end. Try as she might, though, the worries of the real world weighed down her hands, and when she tried to write, echoes of those waiting found their way into her characters' dialogue.

"You will come back, won't you? Promise you will come back," the orphan boy Max demanded on her page, as he threw his arms around Vicki's neck.

"Yes, darling, I promise to come back, and then we'll go away and make a lovely home together," Ida wrote, wishing she could say it to everyone they'd met with in Frankfurt.

"Vicki wanted to take him away with her that first afternoon, but realized there would be certain formalities," Ida typed, burning with the frustration of a bureaucracy that halted the exercise of all that was humane in the world.

"I don't want you to go," Max whispered.

To Vicki, who had known so long the dreariness of being unwanted, his clinging fingers were indescribably dear. He gazed with astonished blue eyes at all the things his little world had never held before. She quite understood his sense of insecurity about all this new happiness. She had experienced something like that herself, and she took unlimited trouble to promise herself that eventually he would develop a natural confidence in everyday happiness.

"You are all mine, aren't you?" He asked anxiously.

"Yes, darling, I'm all yours," Vicki replied.

Ida wrote of Christopher's first journey to Salzburg, luxuriating in the accurate description of that lovely city, where musical airs float from open window casements. This was pre-Nazi Salzburg, reclaimed from an Austria that no longer existed, pulled from the rubbish bin of time and dusted off at the edges by the incantation of clicking keys. The peak of the Untersberg mountains, half hidden in clouds, rose up from her pages.

Finally, she had arrived at the novel's final scene. Chapters of conflict and misunderstanding brought the sweet, cobbled-together family of mismatched humans together at last—an orphan child, a divorced man, and a woman many had written off as a spinster:

"Vicki," asked Christopher, "won't you ever forget anything about me?'

"No."

"But—why?"

"Because I love you. I loved you almost from the first. And I sup-pose I shall still be loving you when they shovel the earth on my coffin."

Christopher understood the depths of her love at long last, and, all miscommunication resolved, drew Max apart. The little boy returned flushed with excitement.

"Mummie!" he said, "Did you know he was my daddy?" He ges-tured toward Christopher.

There were a few seconds of breathless silence. For a moment Vicki could not find her voice, but when she did, it was clear and steady. "I hoped he was, Max, but I wasn't sure until I saw him kiss you just now." Her eyes travelled beyond her child to her husband, in a smile of complete understanding.

"The End," typed Ida, sniffling.

Prince Igor jumped onto her lap, as if to comfort her. She laughed with the sheer and utter relief of setting things right in some small corner of an alternate universe. Drawing the final page from the typewriter, she laid it upon the growing stack. Yes, it needed work, revision, and cleaning up. But the manuscript was complete from beginning to end.

What an odd mishmash of reality writing fiction was, like the kitchen-sink stews Mum made from time to time, cleaning out the root cellar and icebox and dumping everything into a pot, adding spices and other ingredients, stirring it about until the pieces trans-formed into something entirely different from the original elements tossed into the pot.

This was not her story, not really, and Vicki was certainly not Ida. And yet, on some level, she was. "Madame Bovary, *c'est moi*," Ida quoted to the shadowed garret of the attic. Tomorrow she'd dive into the revisions, but for now, she was going to savor the satisfac-tion of having a complete draft, messy though it might be. She felt as though she stood upon a stage after a gritty, exhausting performance, taking a well-deserved bow.

Fingering the title page, Ida returned to the question of a pseudonym and considered also to whom she should dedicate the book. Her sister was an obvious choice, of course. Her parents. But it was Viorica Ursuleac who kept returning to her mind. It was Viorica who had set them down the path of helping refugees. It was her artistry and accomplishments Ida had tried to channel when she'd felt destined to fail. Ida's pen hovered over the title page.

"To V. U." she scrawled.

"By Ida Cook," she wrote, then crossed it out, thinking. Her mother's name, Mary, would make a lovely author name. Her grandmother's last name before marriage had been Burchell. She quite liked the ring of them both together, and using a pen name added a touch of drama to the entire project. "By Mary Burchell," she wrote beneath the title.

BERLIN

A month later, at Croydon Airport, south of London, Ida and Louise boarded a Douglas DC-3 for the first airplane ride of their lives. Clutching each other's hands, they tried to reassure each other as the drafty cabin shook and the engines roared so loudly they had to shout to communicate. They bounced in every direction, lurching on airstreams and exclaiming over the ground receding below. Once they hovered over the Channel, water stretched out like a vast, gray blanket.

Finally, they dipped down over the rolling pastures of Germany. As they bumped to the ground in Berlin, Ida let out a shriek and clutched Louise's arm. The plane rattled down the runway, as the faint smell of vomit rose from the back. Ida exhaled a long sigh of air she'd been holding since London.

"Well, it's not quite like the adverts, is it?" asked Louise.

Ida laughed and straightened her hat. "With the glossy photos of people sitting back and taking tea in the air? No, not at all like that."

"Though I do like how quickly we arrived. Since one of us still has a proper job and never enough leave, this buttons things up nicely." They gathered their hand baggage and stumbled down the ladder with other shaken passengers.

"Also," Ida added, "air people don't talk to boat people typically. It's quite clever to come in one way and leave the other. Personally, I am relieved to skip the airplanes and go home the regular way."

They directed a hired car to take them to an address scrawled in Viorica's handwriting—the house of Krauss' friend on Arndtstrasse. They arrived at a street of elegant apartments adorned with Corinithian columns, and a woman with a dark scarf tied over her thinning hair welcomed them inside in a heavy German accent.

"You may call me Frau Jack," she said, indicating they should hand their bags to the servant and follow her down the hall. Wordlessly, she swept open an interior door, gestured them inside, and shut the door behind them.

It was a large, well-appointed sitting room, part of a guest suite most likely. Near the other end of the room, sat a woman with a bag firmly in her lap. She had a white cap on her head and a rounded chin and wide, eager eyes which gave her a look of curiosity. Ida thought under different circumstances, she would have wanted the woman as a friend. She darted up nervously as they entered, dipping her head in greeting. "Please, don't bother," Ida said.

"Danke schoen," the woman replied. "*Sprichst du Deutsch?*"

"*Ja*," Louise responded. Relieved, the woman unleashed a steady flow of words. Louise nodded along, saying only once, "*Langsam bitte.*"

After a few minutes of conversation, the woman opened her leather flight bag and pulled out a fur stole—rich brown with a slight blue cast and silver-tipped ends. "It's sable," Louise translated. "From Russia originally, she says. And her name is Lieselotte."

The woman withdrew another piece—a mink cape, with tails still attached.

Ida took it from her, gasping at how luxurious and soft it was—the pieces belonged in a museum. Were they really planning to waltz into the hotel wearing these? "You'll attract less attention hiding right under their noses," Krauss had said. Well, they'd look the part.

"This represents the guarantees for three families," Louise translated. "There's jewelry too."

Beneath the furs, the woman fumbled for a small purse of black, ruched silk with a gold clasp. She opened it and withdrew an Edwardian engagement ring—a central pearl surrounded by cushion-cut diamonds set in platinum. The matching necklace featured delicate platinum filigree of metal worked like lace. A pear-shaped diamond lay at the center of the design. There were earrings, too, finished with pierced loops.

"We can't take these, Louise," Ida protested. "We haven't got pierced ears, so we can't wear them. A guard might notice."

Louise regretfully explained the problem in German. Lieselotte accepted the earrings back, but revealed a second ring, a glittering dark amethyst surrounded by a diamond pave.

They wrote down their names and their address in London.

"Danke schoen," Lieselotte said again, nodding furtively. The door swept open and shut behind her. She was gone.

Louise tucked the jewelry into the black silk purse, and Ida settled the mink around her shoulders awkwardly. "Will anyone possibly believe this is mine? What a ridiculous thing, having to trust a perfect stranger with your most valuable possessions," Ida said. "How can she know we won't just take them home and keep them?"

"She doesn't," Louise said somberly. "And there's nothing to stop us from doing it either."

They interviewed a mother named Irmgard who spoke some English and explained that her only son had been imprisoned in a small country town. She was in despair over the possibility of his being transferred "to the east," the obscure direction where Nazis claimed to be resettling the Jews.

"Tell me everything about him," Ida prodded.

"He's an architect," the Irmgard said, shrugging. "A good one."

"Hmm," Ida answered, letting her mind run down several different directions. "What else?"

Irmgard talked on, and they listened, sifting through details and following paths like circuitous corridors.

After several more stories, they left for the hotel, exhausted by the weight of so many new, haunting stories. The hired car crossed a wide and busy boulevard directly across from the Brandenburg Gate. "At least we'll be a stone's throw from the British embassy on Wilhelmstrasse if we have to make a run for it," noted Louise, quietly.

"We can throw ourselves on British soil and beg for mercy," Ida murmured.

The car pulled up beneath a massive, six-story stone building whose elegant roof ornaments were decorated with scores of Nazi flags flying at crisp attention. Sixty-foot Nazi banners streamed from the roof, interspersed with an emblazoned Bear, the icon of Berlin. "Have you seen the list of who has stayed here before?" Ida asked. "The likes of Tsar Nicholas II, Albert Einstein, and every star from Josephine Baker to Louise Brooks. Enrico Caruso as well."

"I very much appreciate that Krauss insisted on paying for the hotel when he insisted we stay here," Louise said.

A porter in a brass-buttoned suit and spotless cap whisked open the car door and helped them out. Ida tried to wear the mink casually, as if it were her own. It was cool for July, but the furs were more ornamental than designed for actual warmth anyway. As they entered the breathtaking lobby, eyes turned upon them, sweeping up and down. Their clothes were not expensive, but the furs and jewelry marked them as elite.

"We're guests of Clemens Krauss," Ida said just loudly enough at reception. She tied not to gawk at the coved ceilings, decorated with ornate paintings and sculptural reliefs, at the rich rugs upon the floor, and the sweeping staircase with glittering people descending.

Ida bent her head to confide to Louise, "I just want to sit down in the lobby and stare at all the clothes. Look at the hats!"

Tiny toy, or doll, hats resembling saucers piled with flowers, fruits, and feathers tipped over the foreheads of several fashionable women, wearing styles straight from Paris. Pencil skirts were nowhere to be seen, Ida noted, and dresses were flared, tiered, and billowed. They milled about and dawdled, fussed over hand baggage, and tried not to gawk. The goal, above all, was to be seen.

"And here they are!" Viorica exclaimed, coming to meet them in a spun rayon dress that flared dramatically. "Looking lovely as always, my dears." Her eyes rested a moment on their furs. "Exquisite, both of you. But I must run. Finishing touches for tonight, you'll understand. Your tickets are waiting at the theater, and you must dine with us after the show." She blew a kiss from her perfect lip-sticked mouth.

As they turned away from reception, Ida felt the eyes of the lobby upon them. She straightened the mink about her shoulders and tried to walk as though she knew where she was going.

◇··—··—··◇

Later that evening, they hurried to the performance, still trying to shake off the weight of the stories they had heard that morning and trying to adjust the furs effortlessly as if they meant nothing at all. The sumptuous grandeur of the Berlin State Opera house made the sisters gasp, and Ida thought out of all the opera houses they'd seen, this was most exquisite. It was a palatial space oriented around a grand stage with four distinct gallery floors, and at the center, hung a magnificent chandelier suspended from an elaborately gilded ceiling. Directly opposite the stage, where musicians tuned their instruments, hung the magnificent Imperial Box adorned with festoons of roses and an elaborate swastika. Once reserved for the emperor of the Weimar Republic, it had now been re-christened, "the führer's box." Sumptuous draperies had been drawn back, and now top party officials and their wives wearing splendid evening gowns and suits decorated with military insignia greeted one another. The front and center seat remained conspicuously vacant.

"What a spectacle!" Louise marveled.

"They're top of the game of pageantry, I'll give them that," Ida murmured, gazing round the blazing edifice in awe. "Looking at this, Germany seems to be the pinnacle of evolution, order, achievement, and artistry. You'd never—"

"Quite," Louise interrupted smoothly, adjusting the sable stole about her shoulders.

At once, the audience rose. In the orchestra pit, the musicians also came to their feet, and turned en masse toward the "führer's box," where a man with a clipped mustache and decorated military medals entered with a steady step, Herr Hermann Göring on his right.

Adolf Hitler looked over the crowded theater, the festooned stage, and raised his arm to an angle out over the crowd. Like a sea beneath the pull of the moon, they moved in response, raising their arms in kind, deferring to his direction. Louise and Ida followed suit, knowing they could hardly do otherwise. "Heil Hitler," rose from a chorus of voices.

"Hell Hitler," Ida chimed in before dropping her hand, adorned with a dazzling amethyst ring. Close enough to hear her altered words, a corner of Louise's mouth twitched ever so slightly. The lights came down then, and the curtain rose. Clemens Krauss picked up his baton, plunging the crowded auditorium into a dream. Viorica Ursuleac had transformed into Tosca, a passionate and fiery soprano who dominated the stage, her voice plunging to depths and heights as she marveled at the beauty of the night and her matchless love. Ida had reviewed the translated score in English, and had brought her copy. "Listen," Tosca sang in Italian to the dazzling crowd:

> to the voices of the night
> as they rise through the starlit,
> shadowed silences:
> from the woods and from the thickets
> and the dry grass, from the depths
> of shattered tombs . . .
> rain down desire, you vaulted stars!

They watched as the villain Scarpia concocted his plot during a Mass, sung in holy Latin. With a crucifix hanging upon a nearby wall, he confessed to the audience:

> *For myself the violent conquest*
> *Has stronger relish than the soft surrender . . .*
> *I pursue the craved thing, sate myself and cast it by,*
> *And seek new bait. God made diverse beauties,*
> *As he made diverse wines, and of these*
> *God-like works I mean to taste my full.*

But Tosca's strength and intelligence carried her, through plotting of her own, as she wrangled out the villain's plan to ravish her body then murder her lover, Cavaradossi, at dawn. Devising a plan to save herself and rescue her lover, Tosca convinced Scarpia she had acquiesced, though he did not see the dagger she carried in her sleeve. When he moved to embrace her, she plunged the blade deep into his heart.

Carrying the bloody knife to her lover's cell, Tosca admitted what she had done, and Cavaradossi marveled at the strength of her gentle, loving hands. He was stunned by the chiaroscuro of the human heart, its capacity for dualities and contradictions beyond what he believed possible.

Tears sprung to Ida's eyes. Louise handed her an extra handkerchief, and she poured out the grief she'd not been able to show in the interviews, her grief at the glories that humanity could raise up a building such as this one, could compose a score of soaring melodies, could be capable of exquisite sound, without acknowledging the chasm of suffering that lay beneath all gilded surfaces, a yawning pit where tortured souls were deprived of their most basic needs. All irony and contradiction hung together, over the stage. Cavaradossi sang:

> *And only you invest this life with splendour.*
> *All joy and all desire, for my being,*
> *Are held in you as heat within flame.*

The opera plummeted on, to its inevitable end. The shot that was supposed to be a blank, tore through Cavaradossi's heart, and he fell to earth. Tosca rushed to his body, realizing that he lay dying. Voices called out, demanding justice for Scarpia's life. With all her desire for life gone, Tosca hurled herself off a castle parapet, and a long stillness stretched out over the audience as they sat with the finality of death.

The lights came on and applause rang out. Ida brushed away tears and struggled to calm her emotions. Without a word, Louise took her sister's hand, and they stayed like that through the bows and applause and glittering chatter around the theater.

A woman seated to their right spoke English in a sea of German, "The soprano had a lovely, airy top register."

"Opulent tone . . . poise and restraint," her friend replied.

Puccini had just vividly demonstrated the greatest evil and cruelty to humankind lay not in what you do to a person directly, but in separating them from those they love most. *She could not,* said the voice of Jakob in Ida's mind, his hands falling to his side, as he spoke of his wife. *She could not.*

Ida squeezed Louise's hand once more.

Opera patrons in resplendent gowns waited for the führer's departure before the rest found their way to hired cars that would whisk them through the streets of Berlin, clean and shining under cover of night. Joining the milieu, Ida and Louise made their way to Krauss and Viorica's rooms at the Adlon for a late supper. With wait staff on hand, conversation remained light and airy, focused on the gossip of the musical world: which singers had been stepping out with whom, and Strauss's new composition and musical fetes. They avoided the trappings of anything remotely tied to politics, including the increasing numbers of singers and composers on exodus from Germany, either by force or protest.

Stars danced outside the hotel window by the time they had finished eating, and the gas streetlights' illuminated halos hung in the heavy night air. When the last waiter departed, Krauss sank into the recesses of a wing chair before the fire. Eager to speak freely, Ida pushed exhaustion aside and collapsed against Louise on the settee. Viorica sat beside her husband.

"Now then," said Louise, "what news since we last spoke with you in private?"

"Only top Party officials know for sure," said Viorica, "though we have our guesses."

"It's an odd feeling to sense the weight of societal shifting," Krauss said, sipping a brandy. "The ground beneath us is disintegrating, and historians may be writing about this time for generations to come. In the musical world, Goebbels and Göring are fighting tooth and nail over Nazi artistic control. Göring proclaimed himself overseer of artistic policies, but Goebbels claims that as propaganda minister, he should have that right.

"As we spoke of last time, they're attempting to develop a repertoire that matches the aesthetics and ideology of National Socialism. They want 'pure' German content, drawn from national fairy tales, and legends—anything that deals with the glorification of the fatherland, or the politics of race. They've targeted the new jazz out of America because it's linked with Africans, but the music is so popular, Goebbels can't keep the people away from the swing bands, so they pretend it's German. They recently broadcast Duke Ellington's 'Caravan,' repressing its origin. They rewrote Handel's *Judas Maccabaeus* with Judas rebirthed as a powerful military dictator."

"It's as if they're trying to erase reality," Ida said, incredulously.

"It's exactly that," Viorica said, nodding.

"And the exodus of the artists continues. They've forced out Hans Heinz Stuckenschmidt for writing a positive review of Berg's *Lulu*. Schoenberg is condemned for obliterating the Germanic element of the triad, the holy trinity of musical theory; and his twelve-tone composition represents the complete destruction of the natural order, according to the regime.

"How far will they go in their quest for purification? That's anyone's guess, but you've heard the stories from the lips of those who are living it. I imagine you could tell, as much as anyone right now, the lengths to which they're willing to go in pursuit of their exalted utopia. Hitler has stated that war would mean the extermination of the Jewish race in Europe. Some say he's using hyperbole, but empty words have an alarming way of morphing into action."

Could masses of Germans truly be convinced that Mitia, Friedl, Jakob, and Perla would degenerate society? The idea was incredible and yet, to some degree or another, this warped perception had infiltrated German air, twisting the concept of humanity.

"There's a man we've been trying to get out," Louise said. "But we've lost track of him. Have you heard anything about Abram Zylbersztajn?"

"I believe he's been taken to Buchenwald," said Viorica.

Ida's heart sank. One more person beyond their grasp—beyond help.

"And Mirjam Sonneberg and her family? What of them?"

"We thought you'd heard," Viorica said, sadly, as the sisters shook their heads.

"I'm afraid they turned on their coal gas oven."

"Oh no," Ida said, miserable. "No, no."

Suicide. The bodies were mounting—not in those clean swept, elegant parade streets, but at the edges, in the alleyways, in the forgotten attics and overlooked apartments.

"We'll keep doing everything we possibly can," Louise assured them.

"That still remains all that any of us can do," said Krauss quietly.

◇┄┄─┄┄◇

Their mother was waiting at the door to embrace them. "Thank heavens, you're home. We were worried sick about you both."

"I must get to the office!" Louise said, dropping her bag with Ida by the front door.

"Several letters arrived by post for you." Mum held out half a dozen envelopes for them.

"What's this?" Louise asked wonderingly. The envelopes had been addressed to Miss Ida and Louise Cook sent by way of the British Refugee Headquarters with postmarks from Germany. She recognized none of the names.

"No idea," said Mum. "I thought they were correspondence about your cases."

Ida tore the first one open:

"Dear Madams, we have heard you are helping people find passage to London. Please. We must leave as soon as possible."

The others continued in similar variations of the theme.

We must leave.

We have no other option.

Please. Please. Please.

Overwhelmed by her own ineptitude, Ida sat down on the step, resting her head on her hands, offering the pages to her mother. "What shall we do?" she asked with tormented eyes.

Mum scanned through the lines. "Whatever you can do," she said practically. "No more. No less."

Ida hugged her mother fiercely as she tried to dry her tears, then she nodded and carried their bags upstairs. She went straight to her typewriter to type out a pompous official letter stating that a very important man in the city of London was giving a guarantee for Irmgard's son because he was exceedingly interested in the extraordinary methods employed by architects in a particular town. Using all her fiction-writing skills, Ida explained that the architect would be asked questions in the British House of Commons, and a good deal of public interest was likely to be taken in the case. In order to authenticate these statements, she wrote, the letter was being transformed into a legal document.

Later that morning, Ida carried the letter to her father's local solicitor in London and persuaded the astonished officiant to put a seal to the document and witness her signature, with a note that he was a solicitor of the Supreme Court of Adjudicature in London. With absolutely no idea if the ridiculous nonsense would fly, she sent it all off to Germany.

◇···——···—··◇

That evening, Louise handed Ida two quid.

"What's this, then?"

"A couple of my friends at the office have scrimped on bus fare so they can contribute."

"Bless them," Ida said. "People want to help when they begin to understand."

"Your father and I have decided to make a guarantee too," said Mum across the table.

"Are you sure?" Ida exclaimed, knowing they'd only barely qualify for it.

"Can't have our daughters spending all their time helping without us. Find out what we qualify for." With war pressing down the corridor and money as tight as it was, Ida and Louise understood the depth of their parents' sacrifice.

The others at the table were still eating when Ida excused herself to return to the attic. She scribbled revision notes onto the pages of her novel, furiously crossing out, scratching in, moving, changing, shifting, revising—revising as though her life depended on it. As if many lives depended on it.

ALICE GERSTEL

Alice Gerstel's millinery shop in the busy thoroughfare of Hausvogteiplatz was a world unto itself. Behind the glass door that opened with a tinkling bell, reigned a world of elegance and style, the essence of *Berliner Chic*. All of it spilled out of Alice's fingertips, which had been trained to hold a needle by age five and had been pinning laces and velvets into creations for her doll collection by age six. Opening a shop in the bustling Hausvogteiplatz square, home to all of Berlin's premiere fashion salons, had been a dream for nearly as long, and when she married her husband, Oskar, he'd said, "We will make this true."

Together, they did. Oskar ordered the carefully lettered gold sign above the door and kept the books, totaling long columns and ordering supplies—the ostrich feathers and glass bits from Murano, the finest laces from Brussels. The taffetas and dimity, felt wool and rabbit fur. He derived the pleasure a good man does at seeing his wife do the work she had been placed upon the planet to do.

One small corner of the shoppe held men's hats—fedoras, bowlers, and chapeau—and another corner displayed notions for trim. Handmade buttons, peacock feathers, and iridescent seed pearls were arranged in cut-glass containers interspersed with bottles of perfume: Joy by Jean Patou and Je Reviens by House of Worth. Elizabeth Arden's Blue Grass. Cut glass shelves reflected the light, turning the display into a jewelry box of color and refraction. The rest of the shoppe was taken up by fantastical women's hats too beautiful for belief and Alice's work space—an artist's studio.

In the midst of a global depression, people needed mischief, and they sought escape in the form of whimsical hats. People stopped in front of the glass storefront to look longingly at Alice's window displays. The brave opened the door and set the bell tinkling, breathing in the rich elegance of the shop, inhaling it like the aroma of an exquisite meal. The illusion of the space left you wondering why all the earth couldn't be just as lovely and well-ordered as Alice's hat shoppe.

As she worked, she perched each new, custom-made *konfektion* upon a hat stand left for customers to view. A cloche hat perched upon a mannequin, hugging the silhouette like an embrace; a boudoir cap awaited top stitching; a "mad cap" with a striped grosgrain band stood beside pillboxes, halos, and tams mimicking popular dress lines. When Alice turned each creation just so, the little piece seemed less a hat and more a story that made you want to sit down and listen for the rest of the night.

Berlin elegants like Annelies Ribbentrop and Magda Goebbels

swept regularly into Alice's shop in a controlled explosion of mink furs and gold-studded gloves. Frau Ribbentrop often wore a swastika pin made of diamonds. They admired her bonnets, berets, and toques; and one day Frau Ribbentrop asked slyly, "You're only *half* Jewish, aren't you, dear?"

The artist looked up from blackbirds she had fastened onto the brim of a halo hat and nodded blankly, trying to remember for all the world how this woman had become so important.

"You know," Frau Goebbels said, lowering her voice to a smooth simper. "If you would divorce your husband, I could see to it that you kept your shop."

Alice blinked, thinking of Oskar in the backroom right now, sorting through shipments and labeling them carefully. She tried to keep her voice soft and charming. "Thank you very much, Frau Goebbels, but I suppose if it comes to that, I think it is better I keep my husband and lose my shop."

"Hmm," Frau Goebbels replied, perching an inkwell hat upon her head and admiring the effect in the looking glass.

The following day, Frau Ribbentrop's manicurist set the bell tinkling.

"May I help you?" Alice asked, looking up from a hat she was fashioning for Germany's former crown princess.

The manicurist's voice was sickly sweet. "Frau Ribbentrop asked me to tell you that she likes your hats very much and wants to go on having them. But in the future, she will not come to the shop herself. Instead, you will deliver the hats to me."

Alice looked round the magnificence of her chic hat shoppe, resting perhaps too securely in the present rather than the more precarious future arriving in Germany each day. Her voice remained as charming as the perfume bottles, but just as faceted. "Please tell

Frau Ribbentrop that I may be a Jew, but I don't yet do business by my back door."

"I see," the manicurist replied. The tinkling of the little bell spun round the edges of the elegant shop.

That conversation spelled the end of Alice's hat shoppe. Some months later, when the inventory had been seized and given to an Aryan owner, Alice and Oskar attempted to escape to Holland. At the border, officials informed Alice that her papers were incomplete, and she was turned back. Oskar at first refused to leave, but she insisted. She would be fine, she told him firmly.

He reached back over the barrier, promising they would find each other again. Then, when he was completely out of sight, Alice collapsed at the loss of him and the realization too late that the jewelry she'd planned to bring across the border to fund their future was still with her, in her bag, trapped on the wrong side of a frontier. Nearly unconscious, Alice rode a cold, shuddering train back to Berlin, where she marooned herself with friends, spiraling into a depression so severe her Aryan cousins who took her in watched her carefully. They agreed among themselves never to leave her alone, particularly near a knife or the gas stove.

THE EVIAN CONFERENCE ON JEWISH REFUGEES

FRANCE, JULY 1938

Along the south shore of Lake Geneva, representatives of thirty-two civilized nations gathered to discuss the refugee crisis. For nine days, the delegates savored the purity and healing properties of mineral waters purified by their descent down the French Alps.

They dined on lake fish and local cheeses and the most exquisite wines—Jacquère, Altesse, Roussanne. They sipped from their goblets as thousands of desperate people fled Germany, Austria, and Czecho-Slovakia, and the peaks of the alps rose above the waters of Lake Geneva like a benediction.

With their hair neatly combed, their dark suits tailored and ties firmly knotted, the world diplomats consulted papers splayed before them and discussed what should be done. Trying not be distracted by the thought of the lakeside promenade outside, they debated various strategies, encouraging each other to take action to relieve the suffering of the refugees. After more than a week of discussions and presentations, representatives from each country rose to deliver a statement to the assembly.

Canada had much sympathy for the impossible situation in which the refugees found themselves, but could do no more than it was already doing—which was a great deal, they reminded everyone.

France, who felt they'd been quite generous to host the conference in the first place, said they'd reached, the "extreme point of saturation."

"The United Kingdom is not a country of immigration," Lord Winterton reminded the assembly crisply. "The idea of settling Jews in Palestine is wholly untenable. The question of Palestine stands upon a footing of its own and cannot be usefully taken into account at the present stage."

America, who had called for the conference in the first place, but who was represented not by the secretary of state, but by industrialist Myron C. Taylor, offered: "Our country's contribution is to make the German and Austrian immigration quota, which up to this point remained unfilled, fully available." The savvy businessman tried to pretend he had done more than shifting numbers around in a sleight of hand, like a magician.

The Australian delegate gave voice to the thoughts of many: "As we have no real racial problem, we are not desirous of importing one by encouraging any scheme of large-scale foreign migration." However, he assured the group, "I do hope that the conference will find a solution of this tragic world problem."

Only the Dominican Republic was willing to admit one hundred thousand refugees. Mainly out of guilt, but also in exchange for money from everyone else. And, thus, the conference concluded with one final clink of the wine glasses.

When the negligible outcomes of the conference were published, the German papers noted that while foreign governments criticized their policies, none wanted to open their own doors to those being targeted. Hitler crowed at the rejection of the Jews. "I can only hope and expect that the other world," he said, "which has such deep sympathy for these 'criminals' will at least be generous enough to convert this sympathy into practical aid. We, on our part, are ready to put them at the disposal of these countries, for all I care, even on luxury ships."[14]

NO GUARANTEES

Louise dropped the paper onto the breakfast table. "So. After nine days of talks, there's a piddly shift in US numbers and an offer from the Dominican Republic to take some if everyone else will pay. It's astounding, the apathy."

"People don't understand what the people are fleeing from," Ida replied. "Though you'd hope diplomats would have access to better information. I did, however, hear this morning that the sham papers

I had father's solicitor sign worked, and Irmgard's son is on his way to London.

"And Helmut?"

"Received the employer's papers and he's also on his way," Ida said giddily.

"Well done, you!" Louise said, her eyes shining.

That evening, they spoke once again to a small church circle, pleading for sponsors. "I'm afraid it's a great deal worse than we can possibly convey," Ida explained. "Many of our cases are in desperate circumstances. Their livelihoods have been taken away, their assets seized, and they're left with no way to support themselves or feed their families. They're starving. And being daily removed to work camps."

"Can you explain how to help?" a sweet woman in a pink hat asked, and there were nods all around the circle.

"Yes, of course," said Louise. "The British system requires that a citizen agree to give a guarantee, covering the person's expenses while in the country until they are able to emigrate permanently. Right now, we have many people waiting: all ages, genders, and situations, with a broad range of circumstances. Most need a guarantee and a place to stay for three years' time. If a person can't offer a guarantee but still wants to help, the financial donations will be used to help those who are able to host."

After the presentation, women circled around the sisters. "I'd no idea it was as bad as all that," said the woman in the pink hat.

"We'd no idea before we started ourselves."

"I'm afraid I'm not in a position to guarantee anyone," said a young woman who worked as a secretary. "But I'd like to donate my bus fare weekly. I can walk until things get better."

"Thank you very much," said Louise. "That would help a great deal."

Two retired schoolteachers exchanged glances. The elder said: "If you can find us a woman near our age or a little younger who would be comfortable in our modest home, we're happy to host and offer the guarantee."

"I am certain I can!" Ida gushed, overwhelmed by the generosity. These people were not wealthy. They had little themselves, and times were uncertain with the chaos in Europe threatening to spill across the Channel. Yet they were willing to sacrifice for strangers they'd never met.

As requested, Ida had written an article called "Will Somebody Save Me?" In the piece, she briefly explained the system and said they desperately needed to find an elderly man three years' hospitality and a guarantee, and a young man six months of the same.

The piece was printed in several church newspapers and circulated around the UK.

The week following, a telegram came from Scotland offering to guarantee the elderly man and keep him for three years. The next day a postcard arrived from Yorkshire offering to do the same for the young man.

Another win came in the days that followed. With tears in her eyes, Ida told her family, "Paul is now safe."

"How incredible," said Mother "What kindhearted people there are in unexpected places. Well done, the both of you."

⬥ ⸱⸱ — ⸱⸱⸱ — ⬥

By September, London looked like it was already at war, with sandbags stacked to protect historic buildings and kilometers of trenches dug through all the parks in the city. Their father laughed at the fuss being made. "It will come to nothing. Hitler's threats are empty." As if in fulfillment of his words, within a few weeks the empty trenches began filling with rain.

◇·· — ···— ··◇

Friedl Orlando arrived from Frankfurt, and Ida soon found herself spending hours at the Dolphin Square flat, becoming fast friends with the skilled journalist who had landed work in the growing news fury despite her still-developing use of English. One night, as Ida joined Friedl for dinner at the flat, Mitia and Else rushed about, arranging spare things they had purchased, pure joy shining in their eyes. Paul would be there soon. The flat would be crowded, but no one complained.

Friedl took a small helping of food and placed it on her plate.

"Take more!" Ida encouraged.

"It's too expensive," Friedl said, laughing. "I only want to eat a little." Friedl had kept every word she'd promised in Mitia's music room. She was a hard worker and utterly refused to allow the Cooks to buy anything for her beyond the most basic needs.

Ida scooped more turnips onto Friedl's plate. "You're wasting away. We've plenty, and you're our dear friend now. If you don't manage better, your clothes won't fit you!"

Friedl clucked her tongue but picked up her fork and made short work of the food.

"We go now to meet Paul," Mitia said, pausing at the table, looking as though she'd swallowed a star.

"Shall I come with you?" Ida began to rise to her feet.

"No, thank you, we can manage," said Else, and Ida knew indeed they could. In the months they'd spent in London, the women had become adept at managing public transit and were now quite comfortable navigating the city's many institutions as well. They kept up a steady flow of correspondence with cousins, aunts, uncles, nieces, and nephews—all attempting to escape Germany no matter the destination, and Mitia worked tirelessly to reunite their loved ones on the other side of the Atlantic. Ida had no doubt that they would manage the feat as efficiently as they'd learned their way around London.

Ida sat back down at the table.

"He will be anxious to thank you," Mitia said, brushing off her protests.

The door shut behind them, and Ida turned back to Friedl. "I am so happy for them."

Her friend's expression turned wistful. "Yes, happy, but also, I worry about the others."

"Of course," said Ida. "And your fiancé, have you heard from him?"

Friedl nodded. "Ruggero is an Italian, a journalist like me. Not Jewish, though. He hopes to find a job in London so we can be together."

"That's so romantic," Ida said, pressing Friedl's free hand. Friedl's voice chattered on, and they giggled together like schoolgirls.

Though it was late when Ida returned home, she climbed the stairs to the attic where she'd begun a new story. Shutting the door and placing a pillow at the edge to muffle the sound, she typed away, long into the night.

"A JOLLY GOOD FELLOW"

Prime Minister Neville Chamberlain's luxurious car navigated the treacherous roadways through the Bavarian Alps to the Berghof, where servants ushered him into the great hall. There, he could lean against the expansive, red marble fireplace and listen to the Harz Roller canaries in cages, singing their pleasant, melodious songs, assured the air was free and clean. Miles above him, workers scaled the cliffs, working feverishly to finish the Kehlsteinhaus before Hitler's birthday.

The führer entered, and the men shook hands warmly, sitting down together, chatting lightly about the beautiful mountain view with the help of an interpreter. *He was such a reasonable man,* Chamberlain thought. *Surely, they'd be able to reach an agreement.*

Hitler appeared to be enjoying himself greatly. "From my youth," he told the prime minister earnestly, "I felt with all my being, that Germans belong as one. There are places, of course, where it's impossible to bring them into the Reich, but other places, it's possible. I'm concerned, you understand, with the three million Germans who are in Czecho-Slovakia. Those Germans want to come into the Reich, and I'm determined to have them."

Chamberlain gripped the side of his chair, anticipating each word from the translator's mouth. A bit too eagerly, he held up his hand. "Hold on, Sir. You say you will be satisfied with the three million Germans in the Sudetenland? This and nothing more? Because many people think you wish to dismember Czecho-Slovakia."

He had to wait then, while his words were translated into German, then Hitler responded, and the translator at last reported: "I want the three million." Hitler had emphasized each word with a hand tap upon the table. "I want racial unity, nothing more. I've been very misunderstood. My patience is growing thin, you understand? By now, I am willing to risk a world war rather than have the problem drag on, but the solution is quite simple. Very practical."

"But I have nothing to say against the separation of the Sudeten

Germans, provided the practical difficulties could be overcome," Chamberlain sputtered.[15]

The führer smiled. Here, at last, was someone who could be reasonable.

◇·· —···—··◇

"Come to Munich," Hitler invited Chamberlain weeks later. The British House of Commons cheered the announcement of another trip. Hearing that Chamberlain was on his way to Munich, President Roosevelt cabled: "Good man!" across the Atlantic.

Flattered by Chamberlain's attention, Hitler had increased his demands. He now wanted the Sudetenland occupied by the German army and the Czechs evacuated by the end of the month. Rejecting the proposal, France and Czecho-Slovakia began mobilizing for war as the world held its breath.

Dread blanketed London like a debilitating fog, and older people exchanged glances in the street that still held the losses of the Great War. As Chamberlain negotiated, his wife knelt down before the great altar at Westminster Abbey to pray for peace.

Days later, the British prime minister stepped onto the tarmac at London's Heston Aerodrome and waved aloft a flimsy paper flapping in the breeze. A wildly cheering crowd welcomed him with glee as Chamberlain read the nonaggression pact signed by Hitler. "This confirms," he said proudly, "the desire of our two peoples never to go to war with one another again."

Cheers drowned him out. Photo journalists snapped pictures, and the BBC broadcast it all. "We have achieved peace with honour," Chamberlain claimed. "I believe it is peace for our time."

◇· —···—··◇

On Morella Road, the whole family had gathered around the radio to hear his words. "Peace for our time," Louise repeated thoughtfully. Ida began crying, holding onto her mother.

"You, see? You, see?" Father insisted. "Haven't I told you Mr. Chamberlain would come through?"

◆·· — ··· — ··◆

Thousands lined the route Chamberlain's car would follow to travel to Buckingham Palace and report to King George. They flooded the plaza in front of the palace, cheering him on. The king and queen themselves stepped onto the balcony, inviting the prime minister to come forward for well-deserved applause. The crowds outside Number 10 Downing Street sang, "For He's a Jolly Good Fellow," and Chamberlain addressed them all from the second-story window: "I recommend you go home and sleep quietly in your beds tonight."

So, Ida and all of London slept as German tanks moved into the Sudetenland under the cover of night. Thousands of refugees hastily threw together their possessions, fleeing ahead of the army, moving in soft waves through the darkness.

◆·· — ··· — ··◆

"He's a hero," father declared the next morning over breakfast.

Brits would send forty thousand letters of congratulation to Chamberlain over the coming days.

"Is he, though?" Louise countered, the thrill already abating. "Italy, France, and Britain bought peace with Germany by carving up Czecho-Slovakia without Czech permission. They were told they could either fight Germany alone or agree to be carved up. I fear all the miserable events in Vienna will soon be happening in Prague."

Winston Churchill, it seemed, agreed with Louise, for he had given a statement for the morning papers: "I assure you this will only increase Hitler's confidence, not to mention his power and supplies. Mr. Chamberlain was given the choice between war and dishonour. He chose dishonour, and he will also have war."

THEO

Theo wore his brown wool cap pulled low, so his sharp eyes could observe the world undetected. When the Nazis told him he could no longer go to school because he was Jewish, he shot back with an impish grin, shrugged, and spent his days playing skat and finger wrestling in the streets of Frankfurt instead, despite his parents' chiding.

SS soldiers knocked on the door of Theo's house in October and ordered his family to pack small suitcases for resettlement in the East. "But my boys were all born in Frankfurt," his mother protested.

The SS guards did not care. "Get ready. You leave in five minutes," they told her.

Gelle scrambled to shove clothing and bits of food into satchels. "Where are Anya's socks?" she asked in a voice more strained than any her children had heard before. "Moses, find your gloves. It's cold."

"What about Papa?" Theo asked his mother.

"Schneller!" commanded the waiting guard.

"NUR JUDEN"

Near the end of October, Ida and Louise risked another trip to Frankfurt. This would be the last one, they reassured each other—the last one until things were safer. They followed Mitia's instructions to an unobtrusive home, where they conducted more interviews in whispers. More jewelry traded hands.

Their first stop was at Julek Zunz's home. They'd been corresponding with Julek for more than a month and had arranged safe shelter for him in Scotland, but when he opened the door to meet with them, it was his wife who greeted them first. Flustered by the surprise, Ida stammered: "I'm so very sorry, but there has been some misunderstanding. We didn't realize you had a wife, Mr. Zunz." Louise translated her words into German, as surprise and consternation passed over the couple's faces.

"Today is our wedding anniversary," Herta Zunz explained. She shifted in her seat, covering her husband's hand with her own, the two wrinkled and frail lovers, still holding firmly to each other. "Forty years ago, we promised never to part, but perhaps the time has come."

"I won't leave you," Julek Zunz said.

Ida looked to Louise in dismay as she finished translating the interaction. "We will certainly do our best to help you both, now that we understand the situation," Louise said, adding Herta's name to their ever-lengthening list. The heaviness of one more—always one more—weighed down both of their shoulders.

Herta looked at them steadfastly. "All I ask is that you save my husband. I shall be all right."

◇ ·· — ··· — ·· ◇

Louise and Ida arrived at their hotel hours later, exhausted by both travel and the grueling, familiar weight of the interviews. Around them, the ebb and flow of Frankfurt continued. A neatly dressed mother and her children peered eagerly into shop windows, admiring tailored coats on display. In the center of the street, a policeman in shiny brass buttons and white gloves directed the smooth flow of motor cars, with an occasional horse-pulled cart navigating the fray. Men in fedoras bicycled their way to the office, and a streetcar crossed the thoroughfares, traveling on electrified wires. *Adrienne Lecouvreur* was playing at the theatre across the street, and patrons patiently queued up to pay twenty reichspfennigs to see the play about an actress's ill-fated love affair with a Polish prince. The city was all charm and order.

A porter stepped forward and reached to take their bags, but Ida turned, hearing a sudden commotion across the square. Threading their way through the normal traffic of shoppers, workers, and holidayers, wound a long line of people: men in ties and overcoats with briefcases in hand, women in wool suits hefting small parcels, children skipping along, though a few of the more cautious little ones apprehensively darted looks at their parents, who kept their eyes straight ahead. The men and women tried to step forward with confidence, for they were Germans, born in Poland, but Germans for decades now. Many spoke no Polish at all.

Young boys in caps followed girls in thick stockings, their hair swept neatly to one side. Elderly women in shawls hobbled along, and one woman was using a plaid blanket as a cape, propping a basket on her shoulder. A rabbi shuffled forward with his long white beard and cane, carrying holy books in one arm, accompanied by yeshiva boys with side curls. A mother hushed an infant in arms, as her toddler in small shoes ran to catch up, holding up his hands to be carried.

They had done nothing wrong, they reassured each other. Many had fought for Germany in the Great War. *Follow the rules*, they agreed. *Let them see how orderly and reasonable we are.* Policemen watched over the scene, their guns slung casually across their backs.

From across the square, Ida and Louise watched the people coming, still coming, winding their way in a seemingly endless line through the town. People around them glanced at the travelers. Some laughed. Some looked away. All let them go past. "What is happening over there?" Ida asked, and Louise translated the question into German.

The porter shrugged. *"Nur Juden."*

"Only Jews," Louise repeated quietly.

A boy in a cap pulled low caught Ida's eye. Keeping step with the others, he hefted the largest bag for Mutti. He would follow her, she would follow the soldiers, and the soldiers were following orders.

"But where are they going?" Ida asked, and Louise posited the question.

"Richtung Osten," he replied. *Going east.*

"What is east?" Ida implored. "Poland? Ukraine?"

The porter shrugged once more. Going east. No one knew where. Only east.[16]

Hefting their bags, the porter led the way into the lobby, where he set their baggage on a brass polished luggage rack that whisked the items away. They reappeared in a neat stack on the dresser in their room sometime later. Each item had been turned with precision and arranged just so.

DIE BIBLIOTHEK DER ISRAELITISCHEN KULTUSGEMEINDE

On the other side of the Reich, a man wearing a long, leather trench coat and black, hobnailed jackboots knocked on the door belonging to the cantor of the largest synagogue in Vienna. The cantor's wife, Amalie, answered the door as her children scurried into corners at the sight of the imposing officer. He was Adolf Eichmann, he said smoothly, and was kindly requesting the key to the library at the Israelitische Kultusgemeinde Wien—the Jewish Community of Vienna—the world-famous library that held more than two hundred thousand volumes representing four hundred years of Jewish life. A twelve-volume edition of the Talmud sat among twenty-eight incunabula dating from 1476, rare Hasidic writings, kabbalah, and manuscripts of the Jewish renaissance.

Reluctantly, Frau Moses delayed, wishing her husband would come, then leaving at last to fetch the key.

Eichmann said hello to the only child who had not retreated, resting one muscled hand upon the boy's blonde head, considering the lad and how he might pass for an Aryan child in a different family. The child recoiled at his touch.[17]

Some minutes later, Amalie listened to the sound of Eichmann's jackboots retreating down the hall, keys grasped firmly in hand. A few hours later, he returned. "I've taken what I want," he informed her. "I'm sending trucks to collect the rest."

Without a response, she took the key from his outstretched hand and began to close the door.

"And fraulein," he added, inserting his boot in the closing door. "Tell your husband to be sure there is nothing missing, eh? It would be a shame for Leopold Moses to be taken also along with the books."

"Da," she said, locking the door tight.

That night, the cantor and his wife put their children to bed and spent the rest of the darkened hours hiding volumes in crates in the basement of the Leopoldstädter Temple. A few friends who could be trusted worked alongside them. In blackened rooms, they wrapped and interred ancient volumes in subterranean passageways of the synagogue complex. Under a cloudy night sky, they wrapped priceless books with lengths of cloth, then buried them in tombs in the Jewish Central Cemetery.[18]

ZBĄSZYŃ

Theo and his family were taken in trucks to the train station, where most of their carefully packed possessions were taken away. They were shooed into train cars, and the heavy rail doors clanged shut on steel tracks. For long, hot hours, they traveled in the cramped, hot cars without food or water. Without any idea of where they were headed. Small children cried until they realized the crying made no difference.

When the trains came to a stop, the doors ground open on their long steel tracks, and the people who were still alive were herded into trucks that rattled their way toward a fence. The Polish border.

As the truck gateways were opened, the German police began shouting, herding the occupants out of the trucks and toward the fence. "*Lauf*! *Lauf*!" they screamed, barely restraining their dogs, lashing out at slow legs with sticks and whips.

"Run, Mama," Theo said, tugging on her hand, trying to pull his sister too. Guns fired into the air. With a heavy thud, some toppled lifeless into ditches.

With their hands raised, Polish officials rushed to the fence. "Stop!" they yelled.

But the German soldiers would not stop, and there were too many being herded forward. Thousands pushed toward the border, swarming over and around the fence.

Theo didn't care where they were going, as long as it was away from German guns and dogs and thrashing sticks. As long as it was away from the trains and trucks.

Overwhelmed Polish officials cursed at the German guards but threw up their hands and allowed the people entry. What else could they do? On the other side of the fences, in the small town of Zbąszyń, were abandoned horse stables, an empty army barracks, and the remains of a large flour mill. Desperate for somewhere to rest, people claimed spaces in these buildings, setting down anything they had left.

"Look, Mutti," said Theo, pointing out the enclosure. "A horse stable can hold us all." It was damp inside, smelling faintly of mouldy hay and cow dung, but far better than the crowded train car they'd left behind. Thinking of her home in Frankfurt, of her husband across the border, Gelle burst into tears at the sight of the stable, but Theo hugged her tight. "It's all right," he assured her, "we're going to be all right."

"Mutti!" shouted his sister. "People have food!"

In the square of the town, the Central Jewish Rescue Committee had set up tables to hand out fermented soup and sourdough rye. The refugees rushed to beg for their first meal in more than a day. Some twelve thousand people tried to carve out living space among the abandoned shelters of Zbąszyń.[19]

◇ ·· — ··· — ·· ◇

On the other side of the square, Berta Grynszpan had been forced out and herded just like Theo's family, and she wrote a frantic postcard to her brother Herschel in Paris. "People in the streets were shouting: *Juden raus! Raus nach Palastina!*" she wrote. *Out with the Jews! Off to Palestine!*

"They marched us three kilometers, then forced us over the border into Poland with their guns and dogs. We said: 'Run, dad, otherwise you'll die.' But we've found shelter now, in a horse stable in a place called Zbąszyń. We have a little food. Some Polish Jews are trying to help. Those who tried to escape back to Germany were shot. I have no idea what will happen, my dear brother. But under no circumstances should you try to come home."

A POUND A WEEK

Ida and Louise returned to London and wrote promptly to the Scottish couple to ask if they might possibly extend the guarantee to Mrs. Zunz, as well. The wife replied, saying they would come to London to discuss it.

The Scottish couple wore simple clothing and carried bags worn with use. Ida worried they might change their mind, but the woman said, "Of course we shall give the guarantee for the wife too, but I'm afraid we can only afford the maintenance of one. We wanted to meet you, to make sure everything was above board, you see."

Ida nodded.

"We wouldn't dream of having them separated. What would you advise us to do?"

Her husband interjected, "If there's a possibility of finding someone who could pay a pound a week for the wife's keep, the matter is settled."

Ida's heart swelled at the generosity of these strangers, so willing to trust her, to help people they had never seen. "I will be very glad to contribute that myself," she said, with a breath of relief, though she knew her own finances were tight. But that sweet old woman—perhaps she would be all right.

78 RUE DE LILLE

In Paris, seventeen-year-old Herschel Grynszpan read the post-card from his sister and thought of his kind, hard-working father, whose careful hands had spent years tailoring clothes in his own shop. Recently his customers had begun to dwindle before an emp-tying register, though all knew his work to be the best in the city. His mother had buried three of her six children in her adopted country. As Herschel read the postcard, his chest filled with shock, which turned to rage.

How dare they. How dare they load law-abiding citizens onto a train like cattle? How dare they take his parents, who should be retiring in their own home in Hannover, and force them to live like animals in a refugee camp on the border of Poland?

Anger and injustice welled up inside with a mounting pressure that could not be contained. In a hazy delirium, he walked to the Rue du Faubourg Saint Martin, where he bought a 6.35 mm re-volver and a box of twenty-five bullets. Carefully, he boarded the metro to Solferino Station and stormed through the street, heading to the only place he could think of to find someone to blame: the German embassy at 78 Rue de Lille.

Herschel's feet exuded white hot fury with each step, and he avoided the German bastards ahead of him in their Nazi uniforms, the swastikas on their arms that had spelled the end of hope for his family.

The guard at the entrance approached, alerted by the accusatory look on the boy's face, but Herschel's voice remained calm as he asked to speak with the topmost senior diplomat. The thin veil of control reassured the guard, who indicated he could enter.

He was a German citizen, he explained to the receptionist, with an important document to show the most senior diplomat available, preferably His Excellency, the ambassador. The ambassador had just stepped out, the secretary explained, had just walked by Herschel, in fact, as he departed for his daily morning walk.

Instead, the secretary led him to the office of Ernst vom Rath, third secretary of the German embassy in Paris, who rose to introduce himself. "I'd like to see this important document," vom Rath said, holding out his hand.

"You're a filthy Boche!" Herschel screamed. Dropping the veneer of control, he let loose his rage for his parents, his sister, and all those shivering in the camp of Zbąszyń. "In the name of twelve thousand persecuted Jews, here is your document!"

Vom Rath drew back, but not in time, and Herschel drew his gun, with rage running through his arm and down the trigger. Rage carried the bullets across the polished marble floor and into vom Rath's chest, his spleen, his stomach, his pancreas. The diplomat staggered and fell, as guards wrestled the boy to the ground to restore the shattered order.

When Herschel was restrained, they searched him, drawing from his pocket a postcard addressed to his father. "With God's help," he had written:

> My dear parents, I could not do otherwise, may God forgive me, the heart bleeds when I hear of your tragedy and that of the 12,000 Jews. I must protest so that the whole world hears my protest, and that I will do. Forgive me. Herschel[20]

The world heard him.

Enraged, Hitler sent his two best doctors to Paris to save vom Rath. For two days, his life hung in the balance. At noon, Hitler promoted the unconscious man to the rank of Legal Consul, First

Class. The act could not save him any more than the doctors could. He died at 5:30 pm.

BROKEN GLASS

That night, the Reich threw back its head and howled long and low.

In Munich, where celebrations were underway for the anniversary of the Beer Hall Putsch, the mood turned sober. Joseph Goebbels spoke, announcing vom Rath's passing and promising all listening that the Jews would "feel the anger of the people."

Radios carried his speech across German lands. Nazi soldiers changed into civilian clothes to lead "spontaneous" demonstrations of the country's outrage. Hitler Youth and stormtroopers picked up clubs and sledgehammers—anything useful for smashing. The sound of splintering glass echoed through the night. They began with storefronts and moved onto homes, shattering windows into oblivion. The shards of glass reflected the glare of buildings going up in flames, devouring the rooftops of a thousand synagogues, consuming the work of centuries.

Torah scrolls, painstakingly written by scribes with quill and ink, were tossed into the blaze, scattering the ash of 304,805 Hebrew letters on hand-sewn parchment. Dark smoke rose in billowing embers into the night sky, where the bitter cold shards scattered across the pavement like fallen stars.

Fire fighters stood by and watched the great structures burn, interfering only if the conflagration threatened nearby buildings. A woman in Frankfurt was dragged down the street by her hair. Rabbis were hauled into the street to be shot or beaten. They were left to be buried in the rubble of the collapsing buildings.

Confused children picked up rocks and threw them through the brightly colored stained-glass windows, for what child has not secretly wanted to break glass until it crunches under the feet like shards of jagged ice? Charmed by the tinkling sound of little chimes, mothers held up babies to watch the fun, while others wept, watching from behind closed curtains.

In the light of a rancid dawn, thirty thousand men were rounded up, taken to police stations and shoved into trains bound for Dachau, Sachsenhausen, and Buchenwald. When he learned of the destruction, Former Kaiser Wilhelm II remarked, "For the first time, I am ashamed to be German."

FINALLY

The mood at breakfast in 24 Morella Road the next morning was somber as Louise splayed the *London Times* across the table, and the family looked at images of the carnage. Ghostly, charred synagogue skeletons pierced with shafts of smoky light rose from the ground, littered with charred remains. Timbers in the hull of the great Aachen synagogue lay fallen like scattered matchsticks. One could trace the elegant dome of the synagogue in Frankfurt as it was consumed by a black cloud, devilish flames licking round the dome before a crowd of onlookers.

"No foreign propagandist bent upon blackening Germany before the world could outdo the tale of burnings and beatings, of blackguardly assaults on defenseless and innocent people, which disgraced that country yesterday," Louise read from the front page.

"You can't go back again," said Mum. "It's far too dangerous now."

Their father agreed.

The phone rang. Ida answered it and returned.

"Who was it?" Louise wanted to know.

"A stranger," Ida said, amazed. "Someone who wants to help."

❖ ⸺ ❖

In the days and weeks following the synagogue attacks, it seemed the world had finally begun to listen. Ida no longer had to beg or explain when people asked why help was needed. In response to the riots, Hitler levied a fine on the Jews for "provoking" the destruction of their own property, and hundreds of thousands of people stampeded to leave Germany. Suddenly, friends, relatives, and strangers all over England wanted to help refugees. Signs went up petitioning the government to increase Jewish immigration into England and Palestine, encouraging voters to write their local MP. There was talk of creating a makeshift camp in northern England, so more refugees would be able to enter.

Aid organizations asked for government permission to rescue children, who could make no demands on the labor market of a fragile economy. "Here is a chance of taking the young generation of a great people," Home Secretary Samuel Hoare told the House of Commons, "a chance of mitigating to some extent the terrible sufferings of their parents and their friends." The British Parliament announced that if aid organizations covered transportation costs and provided fifty pounds per child, children could come to Britain to stay just until the refugee crisis was over—they called the project the Kindertransport. Surely, they told themselves, these children needn't be in England for long.

The first Kindertransport left Germany with each child identified by a label hung round their neck. Some clutched toys, or perhaps a violin—all vestiges of a different life. Two hundred children from

Hamburg and Berlin caught the night boat from Holland.[21] Most had parents, though some also came from an orphanage that had been damaged in the riots people had begun calling *Kristallnacht. The night of broken glass.*

DOMESTIC PERMITS

A week later, as the wet, London fall turned toward the coldest and wettest days of winter, the phone's shrill tones ripped through the silence of the flat.

"Ida Cook?" a woman's voice said from the telephone.

"Yes."

"I am calling from an Austrian aid organization in Vienna. I have a woman and her daughter here, and they were given your name somehow. They were scheduled to come to England next week on domestic permits, you see. The daughter's papers have come through, but the mother has been refused by the consulate at the last moment due to rheumatism in her knee."

Ida could imagine the women's growing desperation as their options dwindled daily. "How may I help?"

"I am wondering if you know one of the British consuls in Germany well enough to ask him to reverse the decision of another? I'm afraid I see no other way for them."

"I know the consul in Frankfurt quite well," Ida said, "but I hardly think one consul has the power to reverse the decision of another, even if inclined to do it."

"I see," said the woman. A pause ensued. "In truth, Miss Cook, I've spoken with these women personally and they're quite distressed. Their father and grandfather have been taken. The family business has been seized. They've been removed from their home and are staying with a friend temporarily. Soon they will be entirely out of food and money or removed to a camp. I would love to find help for them, to have someone who knows the consul personally inquire on their behalf. I understand you come regularly to Germany to work on cases like this. Do you think you might be here within the next few weeks?"

"I would like very much to help," Ida said, shifting uncomfortably, "but my sister and I feel it's far too dangerous to travel to Germany just at the moment, you understand."

"I do," the woman said.

But perhaps, Ida thought. *Perhaps* they could travel to Frankfurt. They'd heard nothing from Frau Basch for weeks, and they could check on Uncle Carl as well. Did they dare?

"Perhaps . . ." she heard herself say aloud to the aid worker. "Perhaps we could meet them there, to speak to the consul? I'm afraid I really have no other ideas."

The woman grasped at the idea as if it were her only hope. "We could assist them with the cost of their journey to Frankfurt. The Kristallnacht pogroms were particularly brutal in Austria, Miss Cook. Vienna is a terribly dangerous place for them at just the moment. But of course, no hotel in Frankfurt will permit them."

"Of course. Give me a day to see if I might sort this out," Ida promised and rang off, a sinking feeling at the base of her stomach.

◈ ·· — ··· — ·· ◈

"Travel to *Frankfurt*? Now?" Louise said. "Oh, Ida. Things are *dreadful* in Germany. And I've no more annual leave for the year. You'd have to go alone." Louise's face said the idea was simply out of the question.

"But it is the only chance for this mother and daughter," Ida said miserably. "They're trapped in Vienna."

"As so many, many others are trapped. We can't possibly help them all."

"True," said Ida, knowing she was right. "But—we might be able to help these two. And we could try to tie up the last loose ends for bringing out Frau Basch. We've heard nothing from her. And Uncle Carl."

Mother exchanged worried glances with father. "If you feel you must go, then you must," Mum said with a deep breath. "But we shall be very thankful to see you back again."

The inhabitants of the flat in Dolphin Square weren't any more enthusiastic than her family had been. "You can't possibly be thinking of going, can you?" asked Mitia. "Without Louise?"

Ida felt sick at her words. How could she possibly manage without her sister? "I'm terrified," she admitted, but I can't bear to think of this mother and daughter trapped in Vienna. If I go, I will be able to see Elfreide and Uncle Carl too, maybe be able to get them out this time."

Else rose. "Well, if you're determined to do it, you must borrow my thick winter coat. You've no idea how cold Frankfurt can be in December."

When Ida explained she needed somewhere for the women to stay, Friedl interrupted. "Oh, they must stay with Mother. She's on the outskirts of town, which keeps her safer than many."

Friedl's mother. Another woman who needed a guarantee but kept insisting others needed help first. "That's perfect," Ida said. "Thank you."

"You're very brave," Mitia said, expressing the thoughts of all in the room as she laced her arm around Paul's shoulder. "God go with you, dear Ida."

Ida rang back the woman in Vienna. "I am coming," she told her. "I will meet them in Frankfurt. Please send them to meet me at this address. What are their names?"

"Bauer. Irma and Maria Bauer."

MOTHER AND DAUGHTER

The train pummeled its way through snowy mountain passes, and Ida rested her hand on the windowsill to watch the white powdered wonderland slip past, each tree spire turned by the alchemy of snow into a flocked castle spire. The tension in the air was palpable, and SS guards watched over the carriages with sharp attention. Ida gripped her British passport emblazoned with the royal coat of arms.

"What is the purpose of your trip to Germany?" the border guard asked.

"I'm going to the opera," she managed, trying her best to sound unfettered by fear. "I am a personal friend of Clemens Krauss and Viorica Ursuleac."

He waved her through.

In spite of the tension, Ida thought she'd never seen Frankfurt so lovely, as she pulled Else's coat tighter against the cold. On Römerberg square, a fir tree hung with baubles reached toward the sky, and a thousand fairy lights reflected off wavy glass windowpanes in the old town. From the ancient Christmas market rose the scent of baked apples, chestnuts, gingerbread, and mulled apple wine.

Occasional downy flakes drifted down on a night wind, and tower horns hung from the balconies were decorated with swastikas, wreaths, and velvet bows. A life-sized nativity graced the center of the square. Ida stopped to admire a window display of marzipan cookies decorated with dried plums and nuts. How easy it was to forget the menorahs that once shone from many of the same windows.

She stayed that night on the outskirts of town with Friedl's mother, who was safe only because of her neighbors who had been willing to protect her. The next morning, two women knocked hesitantly on the door, and she hurried them inside where they removed the shawls from their heads. Maria Bauer had a full round face and dark hair that fell in soft waves. Her mother, Irma, was an older version of her daughter, with the same lithe step when she walked, as if she were setting out to explore the world. Irma's face was thin, though, with a haunted expression reminiscent of Mitia's before she came to London.

"Danke schoen," Irma said to Ida several times.

Maria spoke more English than her mother. "We are most grateful, Miss Cook."

Not wanting to see them disappointed, Ida held up her hands. "I'm very much afraid that I cannot guarantee our success. I have no idea what to expect from the consul, but we'll do our best. I usually have my sister to translate," she gushed, "and she couldn't come this time." Ida struggled against an overwhelming feeling of inadequacy.

"Yes, yes, we understand," said Maria.

Irma pointed to her daughter. "Maria," she insisted, struggling after the English. "She go, not me."

"You know I won't go without you," Maria insisted.

"We'll do our best to keep you together," Ida assured them both, understanding Irma's love for her daughter.

Ida, Maria, and Irma left early for the British consulate, just as the morning light bloomed over the frozen city. The building was already packed with desperate people, dusty bags splayed at their feet. Pale and anxious, they checked and rechecked their papers. An edge of despair circled the long, marble corridors.

After an hour, they'd managed to get near the door. When Vice-Consul Dowden appeared momentarily, Ida showed him her British passport. "Mr. Dowden, might I speak with you for five minutes? I have come from England to do it."

He glanced down at Ida, then looked around the room at the dozens of waiting people. "I'm very sorry, but do you realize that some of these people have been waiting since seven this morning to speak to me? I'm afraid you must take your turn."

"No, *I* am sorry. Of course, you are right," Ida said, realizing nowhere in the whole of their horrible country did those people have any rights left, except in that room.

His face softened. "Did you come on refugee work, my dear?"

"Yes, sir."

"And you know Mr. Smallbones?"

"I do."

"Then perhaps you could visit him after hours? Our official hours belong to these people, you see, but he's working day and night at the moment."

"Oh yes," Ida said, with great relief. That would be very helpful."

He scrawled an address on a slip of paper. She tucked it away like a hidden treasure and walked back along the long and endless lines of men, women, and children, bent over and weary with the forever waiting.

◇ — ⋯ — ◇

Robert Smallbones' home lay behind heavy walls covered in bare ivy vines and heaps of snow. "We've come to see Mr. Smallbones

151

about an immigration case," Ida explained to the servant. "The vice-consul sent us, and I have met Mr. Smallbones before on several occasions."

The servant led them into a lovely foyer with knotted rugs and a chandelier, and a teenaged girl came down the stairs to greet them. "I'm Irene," she said, tucking a strand of smooth, dark hair behind one ear. "The consul's daughter. Very pleased to meet you." Ida drank in the sound of her gorgeous British accent, like a taste of her mother's rum cake far from home. "Can you tell me about your case? I'm afraid Daddy has been working night and day since the November pogroms. Sometimes it saves him a few minutes if I can hear about the issue first."

Impressed at all they were doing, Ida explained the situation to her, and when the door to her father's office swung open, Irene ducked inside. She returned a few moments later. "You can go in. I've explained things."

"Would you like to come too?" Ida asked her charges, but both Maria and Irma shook their heads.

"You're the British citizen."

A balding man with a fringe of white hair and round spectacles gestured her into the office. Stacks of papers surrounded him, and his red-rimmed eyes spoke of many late nights. "Hello, Miss Cook. Irene explained your case. I'm very sorry, for I know you've come a long way, but you must understand it's quite outside my province to reverse the decision of another consul."

Ida felt the floor drop out beneath her. "They're waiting out-side in the hallway, Sir. They've come all the way from Vienna and they've no other hope." She wrung her hands. "I can't go outside and tell them there's no chance for them."

The consul blanched and leaned forward to rest his head upon his hands, rubbing his closed eyes. "It may surprise you to learn there are many in Vienna who have no chance at just this moment."

"I do see that," Ida said, realizing that this man more than anyone else could understand the overwhelming frustration she felt when letters piled up with fervent pleas she would never be able to answer.

"This is most difficult, I'm afraid, when a decision has already been made." Mr. Smallbones tapped his pen, deep in thought, while Ida waited breathless. "Perhaps . . . perhaps I could write to the chief consul in Berlin, telling him I have a case from Vienna where the visa was refused on health grounds, but I'm now satisfied the woman's health is restored. I could ask if it would be in order for me to grant the visa without referring the case back to Vienna."

"That seems like an excellent idea," Ida said, with a flood of relief. "How long might it take?"

"I've no idea," he replied. "I can send the post at once, and consuls typically answer each other quickly, but beyond that, I simply cannot say as I've never made such a request before."

"I see," Ida said, rising. "Well, there is no more we can do, then. I do appreciate your efforts."

"As I appreciate yours, Miss Cook. I sincerely wish there were more I could do."[22]

Irma and Maria waited with such looks of hope that when Ida left his office, she could scarcely face them. "He has written to the chief consul in Berlin," she promised. "I'm afraid we must wait now, but we can return in a few days to see about a response."

The women attempted to take the news bravely, but as they travelled back toward Friedl's mother's house, tears slipped down Irma's face, then Maria's, until Ida too felt her eyes brimming.

"Oh please, let's not cry," she begged. "If we start, we won't be able to stop."

Maria drew her mother close, wiping her tears away. "I'm sorry. Papa and Grandpapa." She shrugged. "Our home is gone. My fiancé, Leo, escaped to Switzerland. We tried to get over the lake. We've tried to get out ever so many times. We're losing hope."

Irma said something to her daughter in German. Maria nodded. "Mama reminds me we must have faith."

"Indeed," said Ida, watching sleet descend upon the frozen world outside.

OFFENBACH

The car swept up the circular drive toward the Baschs' elegant villa where thick, knotted vines had grown over the walls, attempting to overtake the stones. Ida climbed out beneath the stone porte cochere she hadn't seen since the first time she'd visited there with Mitia and Else. She thought numbly of their conversation that day, when she'd wondered if they hadn't been overreacting. How foolish and naïve she had been.

She knocked on the door again and once more, letting the silence fade away. "Frau Basch?" she called. "It's me. Ida Cook. Did you receive my note?"

The door cracked open, and Frau Basch herself peered round the heavy frame. Her hair was disheveled, and she had aged more than the eighteen months that had passed since they'd last been together. "Oh, Ida Cook, it's you," she said, falling back with relief.

Surprised not to see a servant, Ida began to step inside, then stopped in horror. The lovely grand entrance hall lay in fresh ruin— a cacophony of shattered glass and splintered wood. "Frau Basch!" she exclaimed. "What happened? Are you all right?"

"For now? Yes," Elfriede answered, though her hand shook

as she took Ida's outstretched arm. She called out something in German, and from the other end of the hallway came the sound of furniture being scraped aside and footsteps coming near them.

The man who appeared had obviously once been quite handsome, that was clear from the finely chiseled face, strong nose, and wide jaw. But now his shoulders stooped from hard labor and his face was gaunt.

"Oh!" Ida exclaimed. "Herr Basch! You've been released! We hadn't heard!"

"Only two days' past," said Elfriede. "And now here is our dear Miss Cook, who helped Mitia and Else and Paul get to London."

"A pleasure to meet you," said the still stately gentleman, inclining his head as though he were in a drawing room rather than his recently destroyed entry.

"Herr Basch, your wife simply refused to leave without you," Ida said. "But now that you are reunited, we must get you both to London right away. We have the jewelry you gave us before in a bank deposit box waiting for you."

"How can we ever thank you, my dear?" Elfriede said.

"Please don't," Ida said. "What happened to your beautiful home? What senseless destruction."

A hammer had been thrown at the Venetian mirror, and fragments of perfect glowing glass remained about the edges. The curio cabinets from the upper landing had been thrown down the staircase, sent smashing against the marble floors below.

"Would you like to see upstairs?" Elfriede asked. "You of all people will understand what it means."

Ida followed them up to the music room, avoiding the glass shards strewn on the stairs. She stopped short at the entrance to the magnificent room. That gorgeous grand piano with wooden inlay of palisander, lemon, and boxwood lay gutted, the keys torn from the keyboard, the strings hammered and stretched to breaking. Ida felt she was looking at a shattered carcass. "Oh, how could they?" she said, distraught.

Herr Basch led her to the remains of a Dutch painting hanging in tatters. "That is—*was*—a Frans Hals. Any museum in Europe would have been proud to add it to their collection. If the Nazis had stolen it from us, I could understand. But you see what they have done?" The frame bore marks of heavy blows from a hammer, and the canvas now hung in shreds.

Ida turned away with tears in her eyes. "Why would they do such things? What heedless waste."

"Then again," Herr Basch said, patting her arm. "These are only smashed pianos and paintings. They are doing far worse to people."

Ida nodded, believing him fully. "How can you possibly stay here like this? Have you food to eat?"

"Our neighbors have been very kind, fortunately for us. We can manage a few more weeks," said Elfriede.

"They gave me a few weeks to get out of the country before they will come back for us," Herr Basch admitted quietly.

Ida handed them nearly every banknote she had in her purse. "Keep this. We will get you out. Now that we know you are both together, we will find a way."

SHADOWS OF THE CITY

As dusk fell across the city the next evening, Ida made her way across town to a house undergoing extensive repairs. The heavy scaffolding lent the structure an uninhabited appearance, probably the only reason Uncle Carl had been spared so long. Ida went to the back of the house and knocked on the door leading to the basement.

It swung open. "Come in, quickly," he whispered, and she slipped inside.

Uncle Carl was Mitia's last relative in Frankfurt, and though he'd refused to allow them to work on his case at first, now that he was willing, it had become impossible to get him out. Somehow, he had been overlooked during Kristallnacht, but his removal seemed like only a matter of time.

The small apartment was lit dimly by a carefully shaded lamp turned down so low it illuminated little beyond his carefully combed, thinning white hair. The old man checked the heavily draped windows to ensure no light escaped.

"Uncle Carl!" Ida said, embracing him impulsively once they were safely back inside. It had been well over a year since she'd met the man at the Baschs' estate, and though she'd met him only once, he seemed like a family member after hearing so many stories from Mitia and Else. "How good to see the final Mayer-Lismann in Frankfurt!"

He chuckled at her unexpected gesture, fondly patting her back.

"That hug is straight from Mitia and Else," Ida assured him.

"You must think me rude for wearing my hat indoors," said Uncle Carl, attempting to remove it along with his gloves. "As you can see, it's quite chilly in here, but then, I don't usually have company."

"Oh, please don't," Ida stopped him. "Don't make a fuss over me. I'm not company. You must think of me as family now. Please leave your hat on."

He insisted on making her tea. She watched the shrunken pads of his fingers move methodically from the simple sink to the chipped enamel kettle. They sat down together at the chilly table with the lamp between them, the only source of light. The skin of his cheeks hung slack on either side of his face, but his dark eyes shaped like Mitia's burned with the same intelligence and humor that Ida had come to know well.

"How *are* things in Frankfurt, dear Uncle Carl?"

"They're fine, my dear, if you're not a Jew." He chuckled. "Less food and fuel, more rules and restrictions. Daily news of friends who have gotten out, been rounded up, or ended their lives. Let's not talk of Frankfurt," he said in a gravelly voice. "Tell me of my sister and my niece. Tell me of London. I want now, above all, to remember a world beyond this one." The man had travelled much during his career as a soldier turned businessman and had seen London many times in better days.

"London is all a-fizzle," said Ida. "There's endless talk of war, and everyone has an opinion as to whether it will happen or not, but they're all preparing, just in case. They've given gas masks to the lot of us, and children think it's quite clever to wear them in the streets. Mitia, Paul, and Else are navigating it all and hoping to leave for America, though not without you."

"America," Uncle Carl repeated. "Our family has been German for over two centuries. And now we're scattered across so many continents. My little sister is brave. She is lucky to have her daughter and husband with her. Few have been so fortunate. I am grateful my wife isn't here to see what's become of the country she loved."

Ida covered his hand with her own. They sat in silence, feeling the weight of the ghosts who had passed through and on, of the near-ghosts who still remained in the shadowed corners of Frankfurt, behind thick drawn curtains, in the corners of uninhabited buildings, in darkened alleyways and emptied attics.

Hours passed on, and still they talked, spinning time from the future, holding the inevitable at bay. The past year she'd stayed in hotels and opera halls far grander than any she'd seen in her life, yet holding his hand and speaking of how things used to be, Ida realized there was nowhere she would rather be in all of Germany than here in this scaffolded apartment, listening to this dear old man's stories and wondering if she would be able to save him from a concentration camp in time.

GOODBYES

Maria, Irma, and Ida returned to see Mr. Smallbones as soon as it seemed reasonable. Irene shook her head as she opened the door. "Sorry, I'm afraid there's still no word from Berlin."

They rang the following day, and the next two as well. "I promise to ring as soon as I've word," Irene told her.

As they sat in Friedl's mother's kitchen holding cups of hot, watery tea, Irma told Maria, "You must go without me. There's no other choice."

"I cannot leave you, Mama."

"I'm afraid I agree with your mother this time," Ida confessed. "Your own visa will expire soon and then you could both be stuck. As difficult as I know it will be, I think it's best if Maria and I travel back together and work to find another way to bring Irma."

Maria clung to her mother, hugging her fiercely. "We will get you out, Mama. We will do it. No matter what. We won't be separated after all we've been through."

"No worry," said Irma, drying her daughter's tears. She switched into German, and Ida for the hundredth time felt the absence of her sister to help her navigate this work that had always been theirs together. Turning back to Ida, Irma said to them both: "I am being all right. We be together in London, God willing."

◆ —··—··—◆

As the train wrapped through the frigid, snow-clad landscape, Maria sat quietly, watching icy forests slip past outside. They passed the checkpoint at the border, where an official checked and re-checked their documents before waving them through. Both women breathed a sigh of relief, and Maria began talking more.

"Your fiancé is in Switzerland?" Ida asked.

She nodded. "When we last saw each other in Vienna, we wondered how we would possibly bear being separated from each other for a few weeks until I joined him there. But our attempt to cross the border failed, and now . . . it's been nine months." Her voice faded to silence.

Ida patted her arm reassuringly. "In London you should be able to work out a reunion."

A TOUCH OF ROMANCE

Maria and Friedl seemed destined to become inseparable when Ida introduced them at the flat. "I will show you all around London," Friedl promised. "You'll need to get used to suspicion because of your German accent." She laughed, but there was a hard edge to her laughter. "I want to explain to these Brits that not every German speaker supports Hitler. People forget that the German Jews are *not* on his side."

"I'm sorry this flat is becoming so cramped!" Ida said, wondering how they would manage.

"It won't be forever," said Mitia, plying Ida for every detail about her dear brother.

Carl. The Baschs. Brave, sweet Irma. Their safety weighed upon Ida's shoulders, their faces haunting moments when she could do nothing at all. Though she tried to enjoy the company of these wonderful people safe in the walls of her flat, those missing were there at the edges, dancing in the corners of her mind.

Ida began looking for new guarantees the next day. She'd long exhausted the resources of herself, her family, and every personal friend she had. She'd worked through all offers from strangers, church circles, and those who had responded to her articles. She'd begged, borrowed, and stopped short only of stealing. Where in London could she find someone else?

In the afternoon, Maria stopped by 24 Morella Road to say that she'd had a telegram from Leo in Switzerland. The Nazi army was trying to force him back into service, which he had refused on moral grounds. To escape, he offered to take the first available visa, and now he was heading to Brazil.

"Brazil!" said Ida. "How exotic and romantic! Will you join him there?"

"I'd never considered a foreign wedding, but I suppose it will be romantic," said Maria. "We always said we'd go to the ends of the earth for each other." The corner of her mouth turned up in a wistful grin. "And I suppose now we really shall."

❖ —— ┄ —— ❖

A week after they returned to London, a telegram arrived from Mr. Smallbones saying Irma's visa request as a domestic had been permanently denied. Panic mounted on Maria's face when Ida told her.

"Don't worry," Ida reassured, trying to sound more confident than she felt. "I'll start over again with a visa for an elderly person not permitted to work. I just have to find someone willing to make the guarantee."

"Do you know someone?" Maria said hopefully.

Ida sighed. Her parents, her brothers, her cousins, all her close friends, every colleague, and so many church groups—she'd begged them so many times. She and Louise had provided guarantees to the maximum allowed of their income. The thought of all the money she'd promised to pay back made her feel ill. "Not yet," she admitted, remembering the way Maria had clung to her mother, thinking of how she would feel with her mum trapped in Germany, while her beloved Leo traveled on a storm-tossed ship to Brazil.

People could lose everything, she realized—their houses, their wealth, every possession, even their culture, and their community. But without the people they loved best, life was scarcely worth living.

"I will try to manage it, Maria. Truly," she promised. Families stranded like flotsam strewn across the Channel, tossed and pulled by currents, in the midst of a howling storm.

◇··——··◇

A week after Christmas, Ida headed toward Oxford Street to have lunch with a friend, coat pulled tight against the bitter, gusting rain. Despair settled in her heart as the drizzle rained down upon London. She had no guarantee. Not for Carl. Not for Irma. Not for her dear Baschs.

Raw numbness clawed at her stomach, an empty helplessness that followed her into sleep, wearing ragged the edges of her dreams until she awoke, screaming, after SS soldiers hauled off Louise in front of her or threw the weight of an iron hammer through the paneled edges of her parents' parlor mirror. Her bed became a pale, white island adrift upon a cold dark sea as her mind scrambled through every subterranean passageway looking for a way to save them all. *What if she failed?* Louise handled the stress rather better on the whole than Ida did. Her job distracted her and was more demanding than ever; while Ida spent more and more time trying to puzzle out escape routes.

Refugee groups in London were working frantically now, helping to coordinate Kindertransports; everyone it seemed had become aware of the refugee crisis all at once, and now everyone was more sympathetic than ever, but so many were now committed to the extent of their financial resources as they eyed an uncertain future warily, with the carrion of war turning circles overheard.

<hr />

"Minority groups have no national perspective," a man was saying to another on the street. "Their religion and culture tell them they are an independent entity—so let them be!"

Ida shrugged their words aside and crossed the street to the restaurant. She shook the water from her hat, shook out her brolly, slick with winter slush, and greeted her friend with a kiss on each cheek as she tried to leave all the gloom and conflict behind in the streets. They lunched, catching up on the gossip of the office where they had both worked together. Thelma recounted the latest unreasonable demands of Ida's former office supervisor, and they giggled over an unexpected romance that had sprung up. Ida shared the news of her book, which had managed to win an award from the Romance Association, and she confessed sales had been better than she'd hoped.

"Turns out during strange and tense times, romance sales climb upward," she said, repeating Miss Taft's explanation.

"We all have plenty to escape from, just now," said Thelma. "Speaking of escapes, I've heard you're still making refugee trips into Germany." Shock raised her eyebrows in admiration touched with envy. "What a time to be going to the continent! Tell me all about it."

Two women were lunching at the table next to theirs, their proximity too close not to have overheard. One of them, with upswept curls, glanced over in Ida's direction.

"It's every bit as terrifying as you could imagine," Ida confessed, the gaiety falling from her voice. A chill blew through the restaurant as someone opened the outside door. "Perhaps worse. People are in the most desperate of circumstances—without the most basic necessities. Without any hope of things improving unless they can leave right away. I've exhausted my resources for guarantees, and the resources of everyone I know well enough to ask, plus many I don't know at all. But there are still so many waiting, and we receive more requests every day from people who have already lost so much."

They struggled their way through a few awkward bites, both feeling along the edges of the worry that underlay every conversation now, every casual plan for the future—would England go to war with Germany? And if so, when? And when they did, what would happen to all those trapped on the other side?

The woman with the upswept curls at the next table over cleared her throat. "I'm terribly sorry to interrupt. It's horribly rude of me to listen to your conversation, but I couldn't help but overhear you, and I feel I *must* do something. You're helping the European refugees, are you not?"

Ida nodded, mutely.

"Is there something I could do?"

Stunned, Ida felt dazzled by a strange and sudden shaft of hope. "If you haven't yet made a promise of a guarantee for one of those trying to leave Europe, you can do a great deal."

"My sister-in-law and I were speaking of it just last week. We should very much like to help, though we haven't the first idea of how to go about it."

"If you are looking to help a refugee," said Ida with a hard glee, "I have everyone from five to seventy-five, and you may have your pick from my photographs, though I have an elderly woman whose daughter is here with me in London who would be more grateful than you can possibly imagine knowing her mother is safe."

"Consider it done," the woman said. "I can't imagine my own mum trapped in Germany at this moment."

Ida tried to hold back tears at the unexpected mercy of strangers as the woman wrote down her contact details on a card. Sometime later, she stepped into the darkened street, where newly illuminated streetlamps cut a glow through the gathering gloom. Ida had to hold her feet back from running, as she rushed to the flat to tell Maria, tears of relief stinging the corners of her eyes, joining the rain in its downward descent.

ANNIHILATION

THE REICHSTAG, JANUARY 1939

Beneath a massive, glowing bronze eagle, Hitler delivered a stirring speech to a wildly appreciative audience. "The peoples of the earth will soon realize," he proclaimed into the knobby microphone, "that Germany under National Socialism does not desire the enmity of other peoples." The men assembled around him in trim ties and polished military uniforms nodded appreciatively. He desired only peace, the führer maintained, and sought only Germany's war-lost colonies, which he hoped to acquire without force.

As the text of the speech was broadcast, the world collectively exhaled.

◇·· —— ··—— ··◇

"You, see?" Father asked over breakfast the next morning. "What did I tell you? Hitler doesn't war any more than we do. 'The greatest libelous claim ever levied against a great and peace-loving Volk,' Hitler calls it. No, the man won't be foolish enough to start another war. Chamberlain was right to appease him. Look here." He pointed to a line in the paper he'd been reading. "Hitler says, 'If Europe today is plagued by strenuous tensions, then this is due primarily to agitation in an unaccountable and irresponsible press.'"

Ida and Louise exchanged glances and continued eating their soft-boiled eggs and marmalade toast. When their father left the table, Louise lifted the discarded paper, reading Hitler's words aloud: "'It is truly a shaming display when we see today the entire democratic world filled with tears of pity at the plight of the poor, tortured Jewish people, while remaining hardhearted and obstinate in view of what is therefore its obvious duty: to help.'"

"Well, he does have a point there," Ida conceded. "It's difficult to maintain a position of outrage when the other countries also refuse to do anything." She scanned down the column, reading back to her sister: "He says, 'Should international Jewish financiers succeed in plunging the nations once more into a world war, then the result will not be the Bolshevization of the earth and thus the victory of Jewry, but the annihilation of the Jewish race in Europe!'" Ida shuddered and pointed to the word her father had so easily dismissed: *Annihilation.*

Louise nodded. "He's spelled it right out for them, though people tend to overlook that part."[23]

Ida stood up and swept the crumbs from the table. "Have a good day at the office, my love," she said, then climbed the staircase to the attic, where the sound of furious typewriter keys soon rained down from above.

HORSE STABLES

Though many of the refugees in Zbąszyń had spent the winter in horse stables, they had been busy. By December, they had established a hospital, an emigration office, a post office, and a small library; they set up occupational training workshops, began holding choir concerts and Talmud school, and voted to use Yiddish in camp to bridge the various dialects. Polish courses were popular, and two hundred students squeezed themselves into a classroom set up at the old flour mill.

Rumors flew through the camp. Some said they would be permitted to stay in Zbąszyń, for who could ignore all that the refugees had done with only a handful of abandoned buildings? Others worried Hitler would not be content until he had taken over Poland as well. The sooner they traveled onward, some said, the better. Many in the camp bid their children goodbye, sending them off on British Kindertransports, promising they would soon follow.

THEO MARKUS VINEBERG

In January, Ida ripped open yet another envelope. *Zbąszyń, Poland,* the postmark said. Letters had become commonplace, but she still dreaded opening each one, knowing it would lead to

167

another desperate search for a guarantee she probably couldn't fulfill. *Zbąszyń*. She had heard of the place. It was a town-turned-refugee-camp on the Polish border.

"Dearest Madams," she read:

> *I, Jewish of both Polish and German nations. My father were taken away since six months. I have 16 years of age and for now I am with my mother, my sister, my brother. I look not so much for help as for hope. I have migration quota for United States of America, but it will not be ripe for three years. It is hard to keep alive without encouragement. Your sustaining is appreciated. I try to get this letter out.*
>
> *—Theo Markus Vineberg*

There was a photo enclosed, a snapshot taken at school probably. The boy, who couldn't have been more than fourteen when the photo had been taken, gazed up at her with an impish grin and sharp eyes. He wore a crisp school uniform, and a cap rested lightly on his head. How clever, playful, carefree he had once been. The sweetness of the photograph tore at her, as she imagined this boy spending the winter in a horse stall near the border.

Theo Markus Vineberg. Whose father had been taken—somewhere. The photograph was a relic of another life now, offered to a stranger in hopes that she might help. Ida sat down on the Chesterfield, resting her head in her hands. *Zbąszyń*. The name would play through her dreams.

◇ ·· ─ ··· ─ ·· ◇

As she stood to address a church group the following day, Ida remembered the sweet letter and decided to scrap her prepared speech and spent the time begging for help for Theo instead.

When she sat down, Louise squeezed her hand, and the pastor rose to his feet: "Miss Cook, you are a persuasive speaker. As a congregation, we have been considering the adoption of a refugee child. Theo is somewhat older than what we had in mind, but you've convinced us. We will all share the cost."

The church members present held up their hands to signify their assent, and relief flooded Ida's heart. She could send back to Theo the hope he so desperately wanted.

Afterwards, members came forward to ask more questions and thank her. One woman, a dry unimaginative type, said, "Is it true that you write romance novels under a pseudonym?"

Ida blushed, wondering how that had been spread around. "Yes, she does," Louise interjected protectively. "Her first book won an award too."

"Well," the woman replied. "Of course, I don't read books like that."

"No, and I suppose you can't write them either, can you?" Louise snapped.

Ida laughed, surprised to see her sister defensive. "It's okay," she said, trying to pacify them both. "Romance novels aren't everyone's cup of tea, but they are mine. Thank you ever so much again for your support of the refugees, madam."

◆ ·· ··· —— ·◆

The next morning, Ida rushed to send Theo the paperwork with detailed instructions about how to fill it out. In a fortnight, she received back the completed paperwork with one of the most joyous letters she'd ever received. She scurried the papers off to the immigration office at Bloomsbury House, where Francis, a clerk in charge of processing forms, was by now more than familiar with her name.[24] Encouraged by Ida's frantic tone, Francis hurried through the application forms as quickly as she could scribble.

But, then, she paused midway down the page.

"Oh, dear," she said, raising her pen. "How terrible. We just had an order today saying we cannot accept anyone with a US quota higher than 16,000. This boy's quota is 16,522."

Ida gaped at her. "My dear, I am *not* going to write this boy and tell him that. I *can't*. We must think of something."

Francis, who didn't look like she enjoyed being hurried or prodded, looked up at Ida helplessly and her eyes began to fill.

Ida tried to keep her voice calm, though her fingers gripped the counter. "Please, dear, let's do remember that we aren't the ones in a concentration camp. Can you please look in your rule book and find us a way out?"

Francis looked down, fiddling with the edges of the paper, while Ida did her best not to scream. A few minutes later she straightened her glasses.

"Miss Cook! I think I know what we can do. If you take these papers home with you, I'll write a letter, dated a few days ago, asking for these 'missing papers.' That should start this case file several days before the new rule."

"That's simply brilliant, love," Ida replied.

IN THE GARDEN

NEW YORK CITY, FEBRUARY 20, 1939

Twenty thousand people streamed into Madison Square Garden, past protestors and mounted police, beneath a marquis advertising a "Pro-America Rally." Inside, the crowd faced a thirty-foot-tall portrait of George Washington, surrounded on both sides by American flags—and swastikas. Long files of clean-cut boys in ties marched in, followed by a row of wholesome girls wearing modest dark skirts. They were graduates of youth training camps—summer camps, many called them—sponsored by German loyalists.

Fritz Kuhn, leader of the German American Bund, took the stage and promised to be "the Hitler of America."

"Ladies and Gentlemen," he said, "American Patriots, I am sure I don't come before you tonight as a complete stranger. You have all heard of me through the Jewish controlled press as a creature with horns. With cloven hooves and a forked tail." He laughed, and the crowd applauded. "We, with American ideals, demand that our government shall be returned to the American people who founded it. . . . If you ask what we are fighting for . . . First, a socially just, white, Gentile-ruled United States. Second: Gentile-controlled labor unions, free from Jewish Moscow-directed domination."

Cheers rose up at his words, and people in the crowd raised their right hands, palms out in salute.

"The spirit which opened the West and built our country is the spirit of the militant white man," Kuhn proposed. "It's always been American to protect the Aryan character of this nation."

Overwhelmed by such rhetoric, twenty-six-year-old Isadore Greenbaum, a plumber from Brooklyn, rushed onto the platform and pulled on the cords connected to Kuhn's microphone to halt the stream of grotesque language coming from his mouth. "Down with Hitler!" he screamed before guards pounced on the man, pinning him, beating him, and swarming over him. Greenbaum's pants were ripped off and he was beaten, then forcibly ejected.

Kuhn continued his speech.

Outside the Garden, policemen attempted to keep order in the streets. While anti-Nazi protestors toted signs that said, "Drive the Nazis out of New York," one protestor set up a loudspeaker near the entrance and told the crowd: "Be American. Stay at home."[25]

QUOTAS

In the early months of 1939, a proposal sponsored by a Quaker relief organization, and written by Senators Robert Wagner of New York and Edith Rogers of Massachusetts, came before the floor of the United States Senate. The bill would permit twenty thousand Jewish refugee children under the age of fourteen to enter the United States without being counted against the immigration quota. When the children reached eighteen years of age, they would either be counted against the German immigration quota or forced to return to Europe. First Lady Eleanor Roosevelt allowed reporters to quote her on pending legislation for the first time in her husband's administration.

"England, France, and the Scandinavian countries," she said elegantly, "are taking their share of these children, and I think we should too."

Opposition groups claimed the Wagner-Rogers Bill would increase unemployment and deprive American children of aid. Joint hearings began in April, but despite public adoration for Mrs. Roosevelt, only 26 percent of Americans supported the idea. Recognizing the lack of public support, many in Congress said the child refugee issue was "too hot to handle." By summer, Senator Wagner quietly withdrew the bill without a vote, and the immigration quota remained as it was—one small trickle against a rising flood on the other side of the ocean.

ANTI-SOCIAL ELEMENTS

From one terra cotta roofed town to the next, the Roma of Moravia traveled in their finely carved, horse-drawn wagons, forming caravans reaching in intricate silhouettes against the horizon. Shy children peeked out at town dwellers from behind lace curtains.

They set their *vardo* in wide circles on the edges of towns, and soon bricklayers, tinkers, blacksmiths, and roadmenders offered their services. By night, the flames of firelight played near the forest, along with the sound of hand clapping and the clicking of wooden spoons keeping time with the violin, guitar, and accordion. Smoke from the wagon stove pipes smelled of stuffed peppers and rabbit stew. The light of the carriage lamps winked into the darkness like fireflies.

"Anti-social elements," the German government labeled the Roma and Sinta. "Career criminals."

Many across Europe agreed and did nothing to stop the creation of new "Gypsy camps"—Lety, south of Prague, and Hodonin, along the Morava River.[26]

Forced from the swaying of the wagon caravans, they were brought to the camps, placed behind wire fences with guards on every side.

Though their ancestors had wandered for centuries, they were now forced to return to the same desolate ground each evening and there they awoke each dawn.

A NOBLE REPETITEUR

In late February, Mitia knocked on the door at 24 Morella Road. Ida swung it open.

"Do you recognize the names Georg and Gerda Maliniak?" Mitia said, and Ida smiled at her abrupt greeting.

"Come in, come in, Mitia." She settled her on the Chesterfield. "I'm not sure . . ."

"He's a brilliant Polish musician," Mitia explained. "Residing in Vienna. Krauss calls him 'Jerzy.' In truth, I thought they were already gone. They're dear friends and colleagues of Clemens and Viorica. They were inseparable in Vienna."

Ida tapped the arm of the sofa. "Wait, is he the one Krauss refers to as his 'noble repetiteur?'"

"The very same. Krauss says he's finest operatic coach in Europe."

"How has Krauss overlooked them until now?"

"I've no idea, but he has written that it's likely hopeless to try to save the poor man, but he wants us to try and help his wife and their daughter, Krysia."

Ida sighed, feeling the growing sense of futility.

◇·· — ···— ··◇

The next day, a telegram arrived from Krauss himself. "Get Alice out!" was all it said.

"Alice?" Ida asked Louise blankly. "Who is Alice?"

"He's being cryptic," said Louise, "but she must be rather famous if he thinks we'll be able to sort it with the first name alone."

They carried the cipher to Dolphin Square to enlist help decoding it, but everyone in the flat met their questions with the same blank looks.

"A famous Alice," Friedl said, thinking. "Perhaps an actress, like Marlene?"

"A ballet dancer, like Jeanmarie?" Mitia offered.

"What if it's a fashion designer of some sort," Louise wondered. "Someone like Chanel?"

"A designer. Yes, that has to be it!" Friedl interjected. "Alice Gerstel is the best-known milliner in Berlin. She made hats for Frau Ribbentrop and Frau Goebbels before they confiscated her shoppe."

She bent over the telegram to make sure they'd missed no clues. "But I don't think she's Jewish, though her husband is. I should have thought she was safe."

"Well, we've only fifty others waiting for help," Louise said. "What does Krauss want us to do?"

"Perhaps he wants us to go to Europe?" Ida said. "We could meet the Maliniaks in Vienna and then go onto Berlin. We could see Krauss in person so we don't have to talk in riddles and meet with Alice. I wish we could see Theo, but Poland is too far."

"It's a dreadful time to go to Germany," Friedl gushed. "Don't go, my dears."

"Do you think it could it be a trap?" Mitia said sharply. An uneasy silence fell over the flat.

"Of course, it could be," Ida said breezily. "But there's only one way to know for sure. And going with Louise will be far better than going without her."

"I suppose," said Louise, "If we meet Krauss in Europe, we will have to see one of his operas."

They looked at each other. The idea sounded all at once trivial, dangerous—and alluring.

◇·····——···◇

Irma arrived a week before their departure. She rushed to hug Maria with a bone-deep hug, clinging to her with such longing, Ida felt embarrassed for viewing the intimate moment.

"Now 'ze only thing remaining is to get ourselves to Brazil," Maria said, laughing through tears. "Oh, Ida, we cannot ever thank you."

"Don't," Ida protested. "Don't thank me. Welcome to England, Frau Bauer. Your arrival has made your daughter so happy."

The old woman's eyes shone with a vibrant joy Ida wanted to bottle up and take with her to face the journey ahead. For all her flippant remarks, she was deeply worried.

VIENNA

Hundreds of Nazi banners draped Vienna's magnificent edifices. The streets hosted dramatic military spectacles, flag pageantry, and parades of youth glowing with the vitality of the fatherland. The pogroms of Kristallnacht had been more dramatic and violent than the slow creeping erosion of Jewish liberties that had taken over Germany. Here, the swastika had fallen like a hammer, and battle scars remained about the city in the form of gutted storefronts sprayed with crude graffiti and in the hulking remains of synagogues that had been destroyed on Kristallnacht. SS soldiers roamed the city in military cars, their guns a constant reminder of government power.

Still, with little effort, it would be easy enough to forget why they were there. If one stayed only in the wealthy part of the city, one found smartly dressed patrons tasting ice cream on terraces overlooking the domes and spires of the city. Expensive automobiles stopped in front of the opera house, which was now adorned with Nazi banners. Elegantly dressed people of means lingered over glasses of wine in cafes. The League of German Girls organized a spring parade, marching proudly before a crowd of onlookers waving small swastika flags. The crowd saluted and cheered for the girls, a symbol of German heritage and pride, the greatest country on earth. With such youth, how bright was their future?

Near the edges of the city, the picture began to crumble. In the old Jewish quarter, Café Rembrandt lay empty, with stars of David painted in crude strokes on the windows. Crowds gathered round Jews kneeling on the streets and scrubbing the sidewalks, as storm-troopers shoved men forward, marching them down the street.

Throngs of people queued outside each embassy, every passport office, and the Central Office for Jewish Emigration. They checked their paperwork to make sure the right boxes had been filled, inching forward in line, attempting to leave this City of Dreams behind forever. They wished to leave the Liechtenstein Palace, the Museum of Fine Arts crowned with its octagonal dome. They wished to leave the glittering golden canvases of Gustav Klimt, the lilting Danube, and the grand fetes (four hundred balls a year!).

And incredibly, they wished to leave it for an unknown future—nearly anywhere. People whose families had been in Vienna for generations told officials they would go to the United States, Great Britain, or Palestine if they could, but would also gladly accept China or Australia. Argentina might work. Chile or Bolivia would be fine. Or any place else on earth, really.

With hundreds of others, Ida and Louise queued up outside the IKG, the Israelitische Kultusgemeinde Wien, or Jewish Community of Vienna.[27] The primary IKG building rose near the banks of the lower Danube, five stories of graceful arches decorated with friezes of angels and curling feathered scrolls. "Miss Cooks?" asked a man walking toward them, hat in hand, accompanied by a woman and a little girl.

"Mr. Maliniak?" Ida replied.

"Yes," he said, and they all broke out in smiles of relief. Georg and his wife, Gerda, both wore an air of intelligence and artistry as easily as they wore their worn but once stylish clothing. Their daughter had her mother's curls, swept back in a large bow.

"Mitia sends her regards from London," said Louise.

"Please return them," Gerda said. "We're so relieved you're here."

"I'm afraid we've done nothing yet," Ida said, eyeing the long queue. A man stood in front of them, hat in hand, next to a woman so old and bent with age, it seemed unlikely she'd be able to stand for long. Toddling children looked up at their parents with a mixture of trust and confusion. Every adult clutched papers—their only weapon against the endless line that had wound out the door and down the street by sunrise.

At the Central Office for Jewish Emigration, a person needed to present their quota number, an affidavit, and a passport. They musn't forget entry and transit visas, exit papers, and boat tickets. Certificates of work permits were required as well as a tax clearance certification with the longest name Ida had ever seen— *Steuerunbedenklichkeitsbescheinigung*. Valid for only one year. If the other pieces didn't come before the clearance expired, a person must start over again and pay all the government fees for a second time.

Gold Hebrew letters had been painted over the doors, and Louise tried to puzzle them out. "Something about thanksgiving, I think? Mitia's been teaching me a little Hebrew, but I can't get much further on it."

Georg scanned the epitaph. "It's a line from Psalm 100," he explained. "'Enter into his gates with Thanksgiving and into his courts with praise.' City Temple is the only synagogue left standing after Kristallnacht. One remains out of ninety-four in the city, and this only because the façade facing the street doesn't look like a synagogue."

When they finally stepped inside the building, Ida sucked in her breath. Every corner of the building—every stair, every hallway, every alcove—was crammed with people, papers in hand, waiting.

"Oh!" she said. "We've not even begun!" Though it was chilly outside, the building was hot with the warmth of so many breathing bodies.

Krysia needed a toilet, and Gerda took her hand. Watching them walk away, Georg turned back to the sisters. "Miss Cooks," he said in a changed voice of urgency, "they've denied my request to go to Poland. I'm afraid it's clear the party has decided I won't live through this. All I ask is that you save them." He nodded after his family. "My wife is Aryan. Why should she die because of me?"

"Mr. Maliniak," Ida said calmly, "I'm sure you are sincere, but I'm quite sure they wouldn't want to lose you. Let's not give up hope just yet."

"But you understand me, should it come to that?" he asked intensely.

They both nodded.

By afternoon, they had made their way inside, through the foyer, up the stairs, and part way down a long, endless hallway. Exhausted, Krysia sagged against her mother. Georg picked the girl up and let her head rest upon his shoulder. When her eyes had drifted closed, Ida said, "We may be able to get your daughter on a Kindertransport, if you're willing to let her."

"Yes, that's best. As soon as possible," Georg said, fingering a stray curl of his daughter's hair. Gerda nodded tearfully.

A short, wiry man wearing enormous horn-rimmed glasses

approached them. "Are you by any chance the Miss Cooks?" His voice echoed off the marble floors.

"Yes?" Louise and Ida said with surprise.

"Pardon me." He turned his hat in his hands. "I heard the English accents and hoped it was you."

"I'm terribly sorry, but have we met?" asked Louise trying to place him.

"No, ma'am, but I have a friend in Frankfurt."

"Frankfurt?" Ida repeated, stunned. The city was more than a day's journey away.

"She wrote to me you were coming to Vienna and that you have been trying to help some of us get out." The man cleared his throat. "I've been round to every hotel in Vienna asking for you. Then I thought you might have come here."

Ida and Louise exchanged looks of amazement. "You've been looking for *us*?"

He nodded and introduced himself as Jacques Heliczer.

Louise started. "I believe I've heard of you. Aren't you a sculptor?"

"I am, ma'am. I'm afraid I've been told that the order for my arrest will come at any time. Most of my family is already in the concentration camps. I was jailed for three weeks for making critical remarks about the Nazis, but they released me, and my friends helped hide me, then sent me to you."

"Heavens," said Ida with a sinking sensation. "We can try our best to help, but this is our very first morning in Vienna. I'm afraid we have no contacts at all here, Mr. Heliczer." She introduced him to the Maliniaks, her mind racing through his terrible predicament. After a moment, Ida took a deep breath. "Though we have no contacts to offer, what we do have just now is time to talk," and she gestured to the endless line.

Louise nodded at her sister. "We've learned that often the best way to find a solution is to explore the story for all potential leads. While we're waiting, can you tell us about your career? Perhaps we might find something there for a lead."

Jacques began recounting his training, his work, as Ida and Louise both nodded, encouraging him with little questions and murmurs of assent. He went over his prize won at the World's Fair in Paris in 1937, and his first-place prize at an exhibition in Prague, which was what Louise had read about in the London papers.

"How fascinating. And what subject did you sculpt for the Prague exhibition, Mr. Heliczer?" Ida wanted to know.

"A bas-relief of Tomas Masaryk."

"Isn't he the president of Czecho-Slovakia?" Louise inquired.

"Yes, ma'am. You're very knowledgeable."

Ida looked between the man and her sister. "She's quite the memory," Ida said admiringly. "And did he sit for you, when you did this piece? Did the president meet with you?"

The man nodded.

"Could he be of help to you?"

"I'm afraid he's dead, ma'am."

"And what about his family?"

The man looked thoughtful. "There is a son who I've met, Jan Masaryk is his name. But do you think . . . ?"

"Yes," said Ida. "I do. Why shouldn't he help the artist who sculpted his father?"

Louise nodded in agreement.

"Heavens. Hold on. Tell you what, let's try to ring him. Mr. and Mrs. Maliniak, will you hold our place in queue?"

Fortunately, the queue to use the telephone was a great deal shorter than the one to see a clerk. Ida asked the operator to place a call to Jan Masaryk and had him on the phone a few minutes later. She turned on all her full Ida charm. "Yes, hello, Mr. Masaryk, how are you? Yes, the sculptor who did the lovely work of your father— I'm sure you must remember? A remarkable likeness, oh you still have it in your collection? Yes, it won quite a prize." She nodded, smiling into the phone. "Well, I'm afraid it's quite a dreadful situation. He's in Vienna and his whole family has already been taken, you see? We were hoping you might know of a way—" She nodded, listening. "Very good. Yes, indeed. I will tell him. Thank you very much indeed, Mr. Masaryk. It's ever so much appreciated."

Ida rang off and turned back to Louise and Jacques Heliczer. "Mr. Masaryk says that the work you created of his father is a treasure in their family, sir. It would be their honor to provide you with a visa. You should get your papers in order now and expect the Czech visa to be cabled over to this bureau shortly. You should be able to leave at once."

The dear man's mouth dropped open in amazement. "How did you possibly?" His hands began to shake. "You've no idea . . . God bless you both."

"Oh don't, Mr. Heliczer," Ida replied, taking the man's shaking hand. "You can see it took hardly any of our time at all. It was nothing. It's just that we've more practice than most navigating this wretched system just at this moment. It's you who has done this, with your marvelous sculptural work. Won't you come and look us up if you make it to London?"

His eyes swam, and he pressed Ida's hand. "Of course, of course. God bless you."

They shuffled back to the Maliniaks, who had managed to move a little further down the hall. Mr. Heliczer bid them goodbye, and the couple looked at them both as though they were angels, then after the man a bit enviously. "Did you really get him a visa just now?" Gerda asked wonderingly.

"I'm afraid things almost never sort themselves out that quickly," Ida assured them, feeling amazed by the miraculous events and wishing she could work such a miracle for everyone in the queue. "He just got terribly lucky."

By late afternoon, they had finally approached the front of the queue. Louise explained the situation in German, and they both signed the paperwork verifying they had British guarantors lined up for Georg, and a domestic job waiting for Gerda. They inquired about a Kindertransport for Krysia, and explained a family friend would care for her until her parents arrived.

"We can reserve a spot five days from now in Berlin if you can get her there," the agent told them as Louise translated.

"We can take her there ourselves, if her parents agree," said Ida.

Conflict raged on Gerda's face, but Georg showed no indecision. "Yes. Get her out. As soon as possible."

"*Sehr gut*," the clerk replied, stamping and signing over the paperwork.

Louise translated for him: "Here you are then. If the guarantor is approved by the British government, they will notify you and cable the visas."

He slid the paperwork across the transom to Louise, and it was finished. She gathered up the pages and handed them to the Maliniaks, the papers flimsy in the stagnant air.

They stumbled into the hallway, exhausted, hungry, and far from relieved. "The guarantee still needs approval," cautioned Ida.

"In truth, it's not ideal. The couple is not wealthy, but it's all we have."

"And it's far more than we had yesterday," said Gerda. "Thank you."

◇·—···—·◇

Krysia arrived at the Vienna train station the next morning in a navy trimmed coat and travel bonnet, holding tightly to her mother's hand. Gerda spoke to the girl in German. "You must go with our friends now," Louise understood. "Be very good and we will be together soon in London." She pressed the child to her with fierceness that belied the certainty of her words.

Georg too clasped his daughter. "Be sure to do everything they ask of you, my dear."

The seven-year-old straightened her hat and lifted her satchel bravely. She did not cry, only pressed her lips together tightly until the edges grew white.

"*Wir lieben dich*!" Gerda called to her.

"*Du auch*," Krysia turned to call back.

Ida and Louise held her hand, small and pale, as they boarded the train. Ida looked back over the girl's dark curls in time to see Gerda collapse against her husband, giving way to the tears she'd held back in front of her daughter.

KRYSIA

Berlin thrummed with a pensive, building fever. For the first time, their English accents captured attention, and not the positive kind. The hotel manager was polite, but not cordial, and more than once they felt the weight of hostile stares thrown after them on the street. Mindful of their accents, they stopped speaking outside entirely when it could be avoided.

On the first night away from her parents, Krysia had cried herself to sleep and woke the next morning with rings circling her eyes. But she wiped away the tears and scarfed down her breakfast so quickly they worried she would be ill. "You may certainly eat as much as you like," Ida told her. "But perhaps not all at once."

The girl nodded.

They delivered her to an austere institutional building that sheltered children waiting for the Kindertransport. Inside the well-scrubbed walls, parents clutched their children, handing them over like precious pieces of glass wrapped carefully for a long journey. Some of the little ones cried, but a few looked gleeful, as though they were leaving for a holiday adventure. Others, sensing the gravity of the situation, stood solemnly, bidding their families tearful goodbyes.

Krysia looked about her with large eyes that seemed to absorb each detail, carefully lining them up in a row in her mind. Louise signed the necessary German paperwork, as Ida knelt before the girl, her hair bow tugged slightly to one side. "These kind people will take you to England," Ida explained, "and there will be many other children you can play with."

The girl nodded solemnly. "And my parents, they will be there too."

"In time, yes," Ida told her, hoping that she spoke truth to the child. Krysia let Ida hug her, then lifted her small linen satchel and followed a nurse through the door. As Ida and Louise left the building, a boy of ten refused to leave. "No, Papa!" he shouted in German. "I won't go!" As his father turned away, the boy ran after him, begging the man not to leave. The father shouted then, embracing him hard, as tears streaked jagged pathways down both of their faces.

Ida and Louise turned away, overwhelmed by so much heartbreak, tracking the labyrinthine streets of Mitte, attempting to push away such indescribable sorrow.

ALICE

Alice Gerstel had powder-white hair, hyacinth blue eyes, and soft powdered skin. Though she was as old as their mother, she carried herself with a grace that marked her as one of the prettiest women Ida and Louise had ever seen. Somehow, she managed to wear even her threadbare bias-cut dress with the elegance of a popular cinema star. She locked the door and sat down before them, with the calm composure that comes long after someone has ceased trying. Tears laced the side of her powdered cheeks.

"Oh, please don't cry," said Ida. "Clemens Krauss asked us specially to help you. We'll do our very best to help you get to London. Can you tell us a bit about what happened?"

Alice dabbed at her cheeks with a lace-trimmed handkerchief and told them of her millinery shoppe, of the visits from Frau Goebbels, the trip to the border with her husband, the jewels, and the long cold train home.

"Do you still have your jewelry?" Louise asked.

Alice nodded. "But I don't have my husband."

"Have you heard from him?"

"Not in some time."

"We're so sorry," Ida said. "Will you trust us with the jewelry? We will try to use it for a guarantee in England. They're getting harder and harder to find, but money helps offset the risks."

Alice pulled a box from her purse and opened it to reveal an Edwardian era engagement ring with a matching négligé pendant of platinum filigree. Despite all the magnificent jewelry they'd been wearing of late, both sisters gasped at the glimmering flicker of metal woven as expertly as lace.

"Do we dare take that?" Ida asked Louise in a hushed voice, but one look at Alice's pained expression told them that they must.

When they had finished the interview and the jewelry exchanged hands, Alice led them back into the rest of the flat, which belonged to a distant cousin who had been willing to risk sheltering her. Two women were seated in the living room, talking together, and they glanced up when they entered. One of the women seemed to have a bad cold, but Ida soon realized she had actually been crying.

"This is Elsbeth. I'm afraid she's just lost her husband in a camp," Alice explained.

Elsbeth showed them her husband's photograph. A kind and ordinary looking middle-aged man looked up at them from the paper. "He was such a good man and never harmed anyone," she said, as though he could have possibly deserved his fate.

Her friend leaned forward and rested a hand upon her arm. "Don't grieve so, Elsbeth." Anger flashed across her face. "They'll be punished, the people who've done these things. Their turn is coming."

Elsbeth raised pained eyes to her friend and said in tones of lead: "But still, you can't un-kill people."

"ALL WOMEN ARE LIKE THAT"

In a magnificent edifice commissioned by King Frederick II of Prussia, beneath a glittering chandelier, Ida and Louise did their best to appreciate Mozart's opera buffa, *Così fan tutte,* under the direction of Krauss' inspired baton. The Berlin State Opera house was resplendent, the crowd dazzling, the orchestra crisp and polished. The clarinets shone, and the lilting singing accompanied by timpani, seemed nearly divine.

The show began with Don Alfonso claiming there was no such thing as a faithful woman and wagering two officers he could prove their fiancées unfaithful if they attempted to seduce the other's lover in disguise. True to his prediction, the women did indeed capitulate, and all agreed, quite hysterically, that *"Così fan tutte"*: *all women are like that.* To Ida and Louise, the frothy show seemed like one more charade belying the decay, like a gaudy carnival tune turned to a manic pitch to hide the grinding of blackened gears.

When they finally had Krauss and Viorica alone, they dismissed the servants and begged for information.

"The Party has decided to kill Georg Maliniak, it is true," Krauss confirmed. "You did the right thing in bringing his daughter. If you're able to save his wife, you'll be working a miracle."

The fire log turned with a brandish of embers in the grate as the sisters digested the new information. "How can you keep on staging operas for these people?" she said with disgust. "I'm starting to loathe them all."

The fire in the grate burned low, turning the wood swiftly to ashes. Krauss looked more exhausted than they'd ever seen him. "It's the work itself, of course, that pushes us forward, but also the knowledge that this is the best way we have to undermine them."

"As we're too old to join the army directly," Viorica said with a shallow laugh.

"If war comes—" began Louise.

"*When* war comes—" Krauss corrected. "I'm afraid at this point, there's little doubt, though many outside of party circles have accepted it. Incredibly, the average German still believes Hitler's professed desire for peace."

"*When* war comes," Louise corrected herself, "all emigration will be halted immediately."

"Yes," Krauss agreed. "It is like a great clock winding down, though no one knows when exactly it will finally stop."

"Be very careful that you're not trapped here when it happens, my dears." Worry puckered Viorica's brow. "Thank you for coming, for Alice, for the Maliniaks, but just be very careful. And remember that the more they perceive you as being wealthy, the safer you will be."

Trapped. It was true. They all knew it; the sisters felt the possibility hanging before them each time they set foot in Germany. The weight of it followed them down the cobblestone streets of Berlin, present like a piece of worn hand luggage you can't be rid of.

"Last time we were here," Louise began, "we spoke with a man who knew you. His name was Markus Horovitz. Do you remember? We have guarantees worked out for him, but he hasn't returned our post."

Viorica shifted uncomfortably. "Oh, my dears, I hate to tell you this." She fumbled after words as her hands moved to the necklace around her throat. "I'm afraid he and his family turned on the gas. As so many others have done. It's so horrible, but they simply lost all hope."

The weight of her words settled over the room, and into a pit at the base of Ida's stomach. They hadn't done it in time. The visas they'd arranged. The papers. All useless now. That lovely man believed it was better to end his life in a gas oven than continue gambling with his wretched chances, waiting to be hauled off to a camp. She stretched one hand across her stomach, warding off a sinking nausea.

"Every day, every minute war is delayed means more people to be gotten out," Louise said quietly. "In a sense, the music distracts them, prolongs the inevitable."

The fire sputtered on, slowly dying, the unknown pressing upon the city like a great clock unwinding. Each passing second spelled out the name of another soul who might pass now to the great beyond, of another soul who might live.

SECRET WEAPON

As they boarded a train bound for Holland, Ida and Louise pulled the mink coats around their shoulders and attempted to wear Alice's jewels casually. Two jackbooted SS men fell in step behind them, and they hazarded a worried glance at each other as they entered the railway car. The men followed them into the compartment, eyeing them up and down.

With a shaking hand, Ida fished a book she had been reading from her hand luggage and opened it tensely. Scanning down the page, she nudged her sister and pointed to a word on the page. "Calm," it said. Louise followed suit, drawing out her own book and skimming through pages before resting her finger on the phrase: "In trouble."

Ida licked a finger, turned a page, and pointed to: "Breathe." The train jolted forward, carrying them through the grimy outskirts of the city.

"Deeply," Louise marked back. Suddenly, she began to giggle.

Good grief. Was she becoming hysterical? Ida wondered. Her sister never giggled.

Acting as if she were on holiday, Louise opened her purse and drew out a package of chocolates, unwrapped them, and offered one to her sister. Loudly she said, "What an opera! Krauss was magnificent as usual. Let's come back in a few weeks and hear *Tosca*!" She held the box out cheerfully toward the men who were still watching them closely.

Shocked to be directly addressed, the guards each took a piece, nodding their thanks, jostling their weapons as they bit into the chocolates. It's utterly impossible to look threatening while eating chocolates, Ida thought, blinking. What a brilliant, brilliant sister she had.

"What a diverting book this is," she said, scanning ahead, for she'd read this one before. Her nail skimmed the word "secret," then "weapon" a few pages later.

Louise giggled again and bit into a decadent German truffle.

When the train came to a halt, the men rose stiffly to their feet and said something to each other in German before exiting the car. "Did you catch what they said?" Ida asked when they were gone.

"I did," answered Louise smugly. "They were laughing about crazy English ladies who spend all their money on chocolate and German opera."

Ida giggled. "I guess we better eat the rest of these chocolates."

<hr />

The customs inspector at the border ogled the glittering lustre of Ida's négligé pendant. "That is a very beautiful necklace you are wearing, Fraulein," he said, looking as though he might be gathering his nerve to make an arrest.

Ida tried to calm her quavering heart and fought the urge to flee. She willed herself to stand up straighter and remember Viorica's advice. "And why not?" She forced her voice not to squeak. "Do I look as though I were accustomed to imitations, Herr Inspector?"

"Certainly not," he said, taken aback. "I only meant to ask whether you bought it in Germany."

"My grandmother's necklace?" Ida replied contemptuously. "Scarcely."

Louise looked just as offended. "You seem to be implying there is something wrong with my sister's appearance. Does your superior know that you feel free to insult single lady travelers?"

"*Nein, nein*, no offence, frauleins."

They swept through, heads held high. When they stepped onto English soil a few hours later, they could have both knelt down and kissed it.

MORNING INVASION

MARCH 15, 1939

They'd been home a week when Hitler ripped up the Munich Agreement and drove his tanks into the rest of Czecho-Slovakia. The country no longer existed, he declared, and henceforth Slovakia would be a German independent state under the "protection" of Nazi Germany. Tens of thousands of Jews who had fled from Germany were now trapped in Bohemia, Moravia, and Prague, including their sculptor friend from Vienna. Prime Minister Neville Chamberlain was shattered.

Father's hands shook so hard he could barely take his morning tea. "You were right," he said, miserably. "You girls were right."

"Don't bother with it, father," Louise said kindly. "We wish we hadn't been."

One week later, five thousand paintings, drawings, and

sculptures burned on an enormous pyre in Berlin, while twenty thousand protestors marched through the streets of New York City to "Stop Hitler." Like England, America had finally begun to wake up.

Attempting to save face, Chamberlain announced the UK and France would absolutely guarantee Poland's sovereignty, but he had said the same of Czecho-Slovakia too, and of Austria before that. And no one, including Hitler, believed him anymore.

OVER TEA

Ida scrambled to find a guarantee for Alice Gerstel, but no one wanted to sponsor a German hatmaker, even if her husband was Jewish, so Ida did what she always did when she was desperate: begged her friends. Sometimes she wondered if anyone would still be willing to talk to her by the time this whole mess was over.

After apologetically turning her down, one school friend rang back a few days later. "Could you come to tea this afternoon? I have a friend coming, and I *think* she might be good for a guarantee. She's awfully nice and has an understanding husband."

"Brilliant. Of course. You know I'll ask anyone," Ida replied.

Her friend laughed. "Yes, Ida. I *do* know."

Over tea Ida gave her pitch, a speech her family had begun referring to as "Ida's little piece."

When she finished, the kindly older woman stirred her tea, spoon tinkling against the side of the china. "I'm sure my husband would agree to guarantee this woman if, as you say, she has jewelry here to support herself."

A great weight lifted from Ida's chest. Alice, then, perhaps was safe.

SPEAKERS' CORNER

But the following day, an official letter arrived stating the domestic permit requested for Georg and Gerda Maliniak had been denied—stamped in red-inked finality. The post brought a scrawled, frantic letter from Vienna in Gerda's handwriting, saying Georg was expected to be arrested at any moment.

The familiar weight returned, descending with a crushing burden. Ragged panic pulled at the edges of Ida's vision, pulling her back to Vienna, to the Maliniaks' whispered conversations, the dimming of lights, the scratching after food, Gerda slumped against her husband as her daughter was taken by strangers. And Krysia. An orphan in London.

When the emptiness of the house became unbearable, Ida pinned on a hat and rushed into the street, without the faintest idea of where to go. She wandered the streets of London, calling unexpectedly on one friend after another.

"No, I'm so sorry."

"I'm afraid we couldn't possibly."

"We've already done everything we can, love. I don't know anyone who isn't already helping. Terribly sorry."

They closed their doors with an odd mixture of guilt and pity, and Ida felt terrible for asking at all—they were already helping, one way or the other. A bracing breeze gusted through the streets, carrying hints of spring rain, as tulips pushed their way up through the wide lawns of Hyde Park.

Nearly incoherent, Ida did the only thing left to do. She made her way to Speakers' Corner and set up a cheap wooden crate abandoned by some other fellow—a religious preacher calling London to repentance perhaps, or some bloke ranting against government waste. Here is where the people of London came when they needed a platform.

Ida stepped up to the crate, found her balance, and tried to clear her throat.

"Good people!" she called. "Hitler is overrunning Europe, threatening Jews, Roma, the handicapped, and homosexuals with imminent arrest. I myself just returned from Germany and Austria. I have seen the desperation of these people. They are just like you and me."

A few people strolling through the park stopped in their path, listening curiously to this middle-aged woman in a soggy straw hat and disheveled wool suit. She was not the typical corner speaker selling hair tonic.

"I have seen women grieving husbands who died in the camps," Ida continued. "I've seen old men who have committed no crime forced to hide in their homes, unable to purchase food. I have seen mothers give up their children. I've seen wealthy homes ransacked and destroyed, their owners forced to trade priceless artwork for a sack of potatoes. I've seen hardworking shopkeepers humiliated in the streets."

A little crowd had gathered around her now, listening to her words—words far more personal than those in the papers. They'd plenty of concerns at home, but this respectable woman getting quite damp with moisture was harder to dismiss. She was obviously just an average, ordinary Londoner. And so, some paused. Some listened.

"All these people need to survive is the ability to come to England for a time, until they can settle permanently," Ida explained. "They need guarantees from Londoners, assurance of employment, and adopted families to care for the children. Many of them have more than adequate means to support themselves, but the government requires assurance that a citizen is willing to support them. Most likely, this will never become necessary. I have now, a husband and wife," she explained. "The husband is a Polish Jew, and his loving wife is also accused because she refuses to divorce him. He was a solo repetiteur at the Vienna State Opera. Their young daughter is already here, hosted by a British family. He is threatened with imminent arrest in Vienna. I beg you, I implore you, is there anyone listening who would be willing to help?"

The crowd looked at each other. "Guarantee a perfect stranger?" one man said. "I can't guarantee my own children's expenses, ma'am, that's a fact."

A few people tittered. A man at the back in a scruffy suit pushed forward. "I myself just escaped from Germany," he said. "I promise you, every word this woman says is true. They're trying to kill us."

"I wish I could help, love," one woman said, "but it's hard enough to feed my own brood right now." Others nodded, shoved their fists into their pockets, lowered their hats, pressed on into the park, toward their homes, back to wherever they'd been heading before the woman in her soggy suit caught their attention.

Devastated and damp, Ida stepped down from the crate, as the mist turned to drizzle. Only the man in the scruffy suit remained. "Once you've seen it, you can't forget about it, can you?" he asked sympathetically.

"No," Ida replied, with a defeated shrug. "I can't."

"Did you know? The Talmud says he who saves a life, saves the world entire," the man told her, helping her put back the crate. "Or *she* who saves, in this case."

"And she who loses a life? What about her?" Ida's voice hung heavy with exhaustion.

"The world is being lost many times over at the moment," the man said thoughtfully. "But none of that is your own fault." The drizzle became rain, and the lampposts came on. "Good night, ma'am. Thank you for what you're doing."

"Good night," Ida said, taking his offered hand. As she made her way home, the dark clouds parted and she could see the stars spread like cold jewels across the night sky. It was dark when she arrived home, blustering up the steps all wet and wrung out.

"And where have you been?" Louise asked, opening the door.

The story and tears tumbled out.

Mother hung up her wet hat and coat, and father handed her a cup of warm tea.

"There's simply nothing else to be done," Ida said. "I've failed them. There are no other options. Their daughter is here in London, and Gerda and Jerzy will both be taken to a camp. It's too awful for words." She set the tea on her lap, wrapping her frigid fingers around the warm porcelain.

Her brother Bill sat across from her. He was busy with a wife and young child of his own, with never enough money to make things comfortable. They were already paying Ida and Louise a pound a week to help with their cases. He was a man who seldom wasted words when silence could do just as well, but he spoke now.

"I haven't got a bank account," he said, "but you can take my Post Office Savings Bank book if you like, and a statement that I'm a permanent civil servant. You can see if they will accept me as a guarantor for the two of them."

It was the flimsiest of offerings, and Ida and Louise both knew it was unlikely to fly, but for the first time all day, Ida felt a mild fluttering of hope. "Perhaps if I get one of the big-name officials to take responsibility for the irregularity. Oh, Bill, it's incredible of you to offer. Thank you. Tomorrow, first thing, I will try."

PERSISTENCE

Ida managed to sleep a few hours on the whisper of flimsy hope, though she awoke long before the room began to lighten. She rang Mitia as early as she dared to see if she had any ideas.

"Hmm . . ." Mitia said, pondering. "Perhaps I can make an introduction to someone who can get us before Sir Benjamin Drage."

"The head of the Guarantee Department at Bloomsbury House? Oh, Mitia, someone like Sir Benjamin is exactly who we need!"

Thanks to Mitia's connection, Ida found herself ushered into Sir Benjamin's quarters that afternoon. She began to speak, then stopped, realizing the man was quite deaf. She needed to start over again, speaking into something that looked like a small radio set.

He gave each detail his utmost attention, and when she had finished, sent his assistant to fetch the right file, which he promptly started filling out. The horrified assistant watched, protesting, "But I'm afraid you really can't do that, Sir Benjamin!"

The form was signed, dated, stamped, sealed. "You can't do that, either!" the assistant insisted.

"But I've done it," replied Sir Benjamin. "Now," he said, turning back to Ida, "That's four weeks saved in your case. It has to go to the Home Office, where it will normally take four weeks more. I can't do any more for you. But if you have any sort of government string to pull, I'd suggest pulling it now."

Ida did a quick bit of thinking. "I do have a friend in Downing Street come to think of it."

More accurately, her father had a man she'd met exactly once. "May I ring him from your office?"

"Of course," said Sir Benjamin, gesturing towards his royal Victoria telephone.

Her father's acquaintance answered, and Ida explained the case once more. "Miss Cook, I'm afraid I can't do anything for you officially, you understand, but could you see about telling me the name of the official who would normally deal with this case?"

Ida asked Sir Benjamin, and he supplied it.

"Very well. I'll ring him up and ask him to see you personally. After that, I'm afraid there's really no more I can do."

Sir Benjamin bundled Ida into a taxi and insisted on paying the fare. After a short street brawl through the traffic of London, she was introduced to an official from the Home Office who was very courteous but could clearly see no reason why the case should be specially hurried. "But their little daughter is already here," Ida explained, "and the parents are threatened any moment with arrest. They're rounding up the last of the Polish Jews in Vienna, you see."

The official, a Mr. Hutchinson, looked thoughtful. "You had better telegraph that White Form 227A is about to be authenticated." He nodded. "That should stop the Gestapo." The man had greased back hair, wild bushy eyebrows that straggled about his face, and no imagination.

Ida stared at him helplessly. "Sir, do you really suppose anything will save him but a telegram that British visas are on the way? I don't imagine the Gestapo cares a fig about white forms."

"Madam," he said, falling back against his chair, "to be frank, I am exhausted. I have worked a very long week, and my wife is waiting for me at home. There's only so much I can do."

Clear now of her most persuasive tactic, Ida settled herself quite firmly into a chair opposite. "I do apologize for your long week, sir. I am also fatigued, but I am not, most thankfully, threatened with imminent arrest. I am not currently just at this moment trapped in a concentration camp."

Mr. Hutchinson raised an eyebrow, measuring the likelihood that she might remain indefinitely in his office. He began sorting through documents. After a several minutes of reviewing the papers, he said, "Ah! Miss Cook, I have discovered the source of the problem. As you say, you applied for the wife to come as a domestic, and at that time, a file was opened on the Maliniaks' behalf, but unfortunately, that file was lost." He shut the folder with a small sigh. "And of course, it's quite impossible to take action without the file." He began to stand apologetically.

Ida stayed firmly seated and raised an eyebrow of her own. "So. We must open another file, then?"

He looked horrified at the suggestion. "We couldn't possibly."

"And what might be the good of finding the file after my friends are dead?" Ida asked carefully.

"Madam," he said, adjusting his spectacles. "I understand the case is urgent. I can have the night guard conduct a search for the file. Once we've found it, I can promise I will take immediate action, but that is all I can do."

"Very well," Ida said, gathering her purse, clear that the usefulness of the office chair had spent itself. "I'll telegraph my friends that their British visas are on the way."

Mr. Hutchinson looked up as sharply as if she had suggested treason. "But suppose we don't find the file?"

"Your guard has got all night, hasn't he?"

"Well, it should be all right," he conceded. Ida staggered out and sent the cable, returning home to another evening of compassionate glances from her family.

The next morning, a telegram boy came roaring up to the door. Ida ripped the message from Vienna open. "Georg not home. Helpless. *Gerda*."

Oh, God. *He'd been arrested.* Ida fell down upon the stoop. She was too late. She pulled herself together and snatched up the phone to ring the Home Office.

"I'm afraid we haven't found the file yet," Mr. Hutchinson's secretary said briskly.

"Well, they've got the husband," Ida said, trying to keep her voice steady. "What are you going to do before they get the wife?"

"Gordon Bennet!" cursed the secretary. "Please hold." A few moments later she returned to the line. "Mr. Hutchinson said we will manage to telegraph the visas somehow."

"Thank you," said Ida, hanging up the phone feeling as though she'd walked a dozen miles since her morning cup of tea.

STREET GHOSTS

Gerda Maliniak walked her husband to the Munich police station, clasping his arm tightly. When they were a hundred yards from the building, he turned at the corner stoop and kissed her goodbye. She watched him walk inside, watched them take him. Brushing tears from her eyes, she retraced her weary steps, eyes darting up and down the street, for Vienna's streets weren't safe anymore. Not for her.

She was two blocks away from her apartment, when her neighbor approached. "Good day, Frau Becker—" Gerda began wearily, but the elderly woman lay a finger against her lips.

Taking her arm, she gently turned Gerda back the same direction she'd just traveled, and whispered, "Come, my dear."

They turned down one street and then another, and part way down the following block, Frau Becker confided in a low voice, "The Gestapo is waiting for you, just outside your apartment."

Gerda stiffened. The dear woman. "And you risked coming to tell me?"

An SS soldier passed them on the street.

"Thank you for helping me to market," Frau Becker said brightly. They wandered on, thoughts shooting through Gerda's frazzled mind like the rapid shots she heard fired at night, when the city was supposed to be asleep.

At the end of the next block, Frau Becker passed her the small satchel she carried over one arm. "Thank you, my dear. You can just leave me here to pick my veggies. Have a lovely day." The clever woman waved as blithely as if they'd been out for a pleasant stroll.

Gerda rushed on, trying for all the world to appear as calm as Frau Becker. After three more blocks, she darted into an alley, and dared a glimpse inside the bag. A bottle of water. Some bread and cheese wrapped in cloth. The humble contents of her neighbor's pantry. At the end of a dark corridor, she slumped into an alcove, letting tears come. She couldn't dare stay in one place for long. If the Gestapo didn't find her, a street gang might. She wandered, changing position every hour or so as darkness fell, seeking out the very alleyways she would have usually avoided. By the time the sky began to lighten, Gerda felt she'd lived a year. Her pumps pinched impossibly, and she bit off a corner of the loaf, wondering how long she could make it last.

Making her way to the British consulate, Gerda smoothed back her hair and tried to straighten her rumpled dress, hoping for news from Ida and Louise Cook across the Channel. Nothing. She remained all day, agents casting her pitiful glances. At last, when it came time to lock the doors, they told her she must depart.

She nodded, knowing it wasn't their fault. Somehow, this wretched situation was no one's particular fault. Gerda struggled out into the street where reasonable German women hurried their children home for supper, and her mind turned to Krysia, her dear, dark curls pressed against a pillow in an English woman's bed. Dashing away tears, she struggled toward a public park, forbidden to vagrants and Jews. She stayed as long as she dared, then sought out a shadowy corner of the Jewish cemetery, where she might be mistaken for a shadow. With her back pressed against a stone wall, Gerda hoped against hope that no one would stumble into her, for the streets of Vienna were full of exiled ghosts at the moment.

Her food and water gone, she pressed her empty stomach to still it and tried to ignore the noises of the night. Near dawn, a light rain descended, mingling with morning dew, and she took shelter under the branches of a spreading tree. How much longer could she survive like this? She wondered numbly if she should turn herself in to the police.

As light reached over the city, Gerda tried to wipe stains from the side of her skirt. In one last wild attempt, she presented herself at the Polish consulate. "My husband is Polish," she explained. "He's been arrested, but we still have family there."

The woman on the other side of the counter looked sympathetic, though Gerda was only one in an endless line. "If you're Polish by marriage, I may be able to send you there. Is that what you wish?"

Doubt clawed at Gerda's mind. The hunger gnawed so she couldn't think clearly. If she left Austria, would she ever find Georg again? "Yes," she said, thinking of the Gestapo waiting at home. "I have no other choice."

"Where is your family in Poland?"

"Warsaw."

The woman filled out forms, stamped, signed, and handed them over. "I can put you on a train to Warsaw tomorrow, but without the proper Austrian exit papers and your passport, I cannot guarantee they will let you through. The situation changes hour by hour. Do you want to try?"

"Yes, I understand," Gerda said. "Thank you."

"Coffee?" asked a woman from a local relief group. Gerda snatched it up, gulping it feverishly. The woman handed her biscuits, which she also made short work of. Done with her business, she haunted the hallways until they locked the doors for the night. By the light of a slivered moon, she made her way back to the cemetery, holding back waves of panic at every strange noise.

When light broke over the city for the third time, she struggled upright. By now it was impossible to hide her desperation—the dirty, rumpled clothing, unwashed hair, and hands that shook from hunger revealed more than words. As she made her way to the train station, she looked back over her shoulder, expecting to hear the footfall of the Gestapo's slick back boots and a shouted "Halt!"

The train puffed into the station, and she climbed aboard, so weak she had to haul herself up the stairs with her arms. She settled into a seat, slouching toward the furthest window from the platform, wishing she could melt into the space between the seats. One moment passed, and then another. Guards swept through the cabin, checking tickets. They moved on, as Gerda tried to remember how to breathe.

At last, the train pulled out of the station. Chugged its way across Austria, the scenery falling away in smears and spatters of green. An hour into the journey, a conductor approached her, and his brown eyes and salt and pepper hair reminded her of her grandfather. Disoriented with hunger and exhaustion, she held out a paper that was not her ticket, then hurriedly replaced it with the right one.

"Are we far from the border?" she asked.

"Just a few hours yet, Ma'am," he replied, looking around her for husband or friend. "Are you all right there?"

She hesitated.

"Where is your luggage?"

She shook her head, refusing to answer.

Understanding her hesitation, he pulled out his own Polish passport, opening it. "See, madam, I am also Polish. Will you trust me now? I will help if I can."

In a lowered voice, she admitted: "They've arrested my husband. I had to flee without my passport. I'm not sure they will let me cross. The Polish embassy gave me papers, but I cannot answer their inquiries." Faced with his kindly, steady gaze, she began to cry.

The man's eyes swept across the empty carriage. "If you give me your papers, I will see what I can do." He fumbled in his pocket and produced an orange.

"*Dzięki*," she said, using one of the few Polish words she knew and reaching for the orange like it were fruit from the Garden of Eden. She handed over the papers from the embassy. He secured them in his pocket and moved on. Suddenly a conviction that he might betray her seized her throat. *How could she have been so stupid? Idiot. She would never see her husband or her daughter again.*

Pushing down the terror, Gerda devoured the orange. With a little food in her empty stomach, she began to nod off, lulled by the rocking of the train. She fought the exhaustion as long as she could, lest she be awakened by SS guards, but the sleep deprivation was too much, and she succumbed at last, her head lolling in time with the train's movements.

Hours later, she startled awake, jolted upright, and chastised herself for sleeping. Outside the window, the sky grew light, and she anxiously waited for a sign to explain her whereabouts. The words *Mszana* and *Świerklany* on large signs slid by her view. Poland. Then, incredibly, he had not betrayed her.

Beside her, she realized, he had left her papers, stamped and processed. Somehow, he had managed to get her through. Relief flooded her body and tears crowded her eyes. She looked around to find the man and thank him, but like an angel, he was nowhere to be found.

Perhaps. Perhaps, she might dare hope to see her daughter again. Perhaps, her husband. The Polish countryside slid by outside the window, lovely and peaceful, and Gerda thought it looked like the dawning of the first day of the world, before wickedness had come.

◇·· — ··· — ·◇

With the last of her strength, Gerda knocked on the door in a neighborhood of Warsaw.

It creaked open tentatively, revealing an elderly woman with crepe paper skin. Her eyes grew wide when she saw her daughter-in-law. Beckoning her inside, Zofia Maliniak checked the passage, shut and locked the door, then pressed the disheveled Gerda to her chest. *"Mój boże,"* she said, touching her head, her chest, crossing each shoulder. "My prayers, are answered. How did you do 'zees? Where is Jerzy?"

Zofia spoke little German, and Gerda less Polish, but they clung to each other, speaking with embraces that needed no translation.

"Slowly, slowly," Zofia said, as Gerda ate. "You see?"

Gerda nodded, forcing herself to hold back so she didn't throw it up. Food was too precious to waste. Even here in Poland, with Hitler's army massed against the border, threatening to invade.

In Austria, Gerda had worried most about her husband's safety. Zofia, Georg's siblings, they had seemed far away from any immediate danger. But now, seeing Zofia's sweet face, Gerda worried also for this kind woman who had accepted her into the family even though it meant her son would not be married beneath a canopy. Remembering all that had been done to Austria's Jews and knowing what lay ahead for them if the Germans rolled into town as they had done in Vienna, Gerda fought back waves of nausea that had nothing to do with starvation.

BON VOYAGE

As the UK began conscripting soldiers for what seemed like inevitable conflict, Father still voiced his opinion that Hitler would never fight, but his words were meeker since the Czecho-Slovakia had been carved up. Frequently now, his voice wavered as he spoke.

The Mayer-Lismanns left London in spring to sail to New York. Ida and Louise went to the docks, where they hugged Mitia, Paul, and Else goodbye fiercely. "When all this is over, we will come to America," Ida promised.

"We'll be waiting for you," Mitia said.

"Goodbye," said Else simply. "We owe you our lives."

Her plain pronouncement caught in Ida's throat. They waved until their friends were no more than specks aboard the mighty steamer pulling out of port, bound for another side of the world, a place far away from madness.

Thanks to the Tea Guarantee, as Ida called it, they got Alice out. She arrived, disheveled, hungry, and as elegant as ever, and Ida settled her into the flat with Friedl, while she worked to extricate her husband from Holland.[28]

Friedl's Italian fiancé, Ruggero, also arrived. Since he was still employed by the Italian government, he couldn't marry a Jewish girl, but they spent nearly every free, waking moment together. Looking at their glowing faces, it was easy for Ida to forget about anything as mundane as war.

ADRIFT

In May, the German refugee ship *St. Louis* left Hamburg with landing passes for Cuba and quota numbers permitting entry to the United States three years hence. After crossing the ocean, the ship docked in Cuba, but Cuba made extortionate demands for money no one wanted to pay, so the passengers were denied the right to disembark.

Hoping for mercy, the ship sailed slowly along the eastern coast of the United States, as various refugee organizations tried to persuade the government to allow the immigrants to disembark. But President Roosevelt ordered the Coast Guard to prevent any passengers from landing, even if they were desperate enough to jump from the ship into the sea.

Having failed in his mission, the captain could do nothing but regretfully turn the ship back across the ocean, docking weeks later in Antwerp, Belgium. Though the refugees had traveled all the way to the new world and back, a handful of European countries were left to divide the passengers, and they were settled in neighborhoods across the Netherlands, Belgium, Britain, and France, hoping that there, they might be safe.[29]

In late June, a Romanian-Jewish refugee ship bound for Palestine ran aground and burned near Rhodes, Italy. It began to feel at times as though the whole world had run aground, that all humanity had burst spontaneously into flames.

GOOD COMPANY

In early summer, Georg Maliniak appeared quite suddenly at his mother's home in Warsaw. Gerda opened the door and found him there—scruffy and scraped, but very much alive. She reached for him frantically, touching his face, his neck, his shoulders to reassure herself he was truly her husband.

Somehow, they had released him, he said. Clemens Krauss had pulled some strings perhaps. "Prison wasn't too bad," Georg told his wife dryly. "I imagine I was surrounded by all the best company in Vienna just at the moment."

They telegrammed Ida and Louise, who cabled over visas, though they could still do nothing for Zofia.

Georg wept as he told his mother goodbye, pressing her slight frame against his shoulder, trying not to wonder if he would ever see her again. "*Do widzenia, Mamo*," he said, as they parted. "We won't give up until you join us in London."

"*Tak, tak*," she replied. "*Będzie ze mną dobrze.*" *I will be all right.*

◇··—··—··◇

Ida and Louise went to the docks in London to meet Georg and Gerda, holding Krysia's hands between them. The Maliniaks rushed down the dock, swept up their daughter, and held her tight against their chests, and Ida wiped tears away, watching the one small corner of the world that was put right again.

A WHITE ROSE

Theo's paperwork seemed likely to be approved for immigration, but now there was no transportation left to take him to Britain. Every vessel, train, and bus out of Poland was irrefutably booked. Ida agonized over the case, knowing that if they didn't get him out quickly, his visa would expire and they would have to start over again.

◇⸱⸱—⸱⸱⸱—◇

One afternoon, a woman with a neat hat and dress called at 24 Morella Road. She had read one of Ida's articles in a church paper, she explained, and she was hoping Ida might be able to help.

"What is the issue?" Ida asked, hoping it didn't involve adding another name to their endlessly growing list.

"My dear friend Lulu Cossmann went to finishing school with me," the woman explained. "That was fifty years ago, but, when you came and talked about the dreadful situation in Europe, I thought I better write to her to find out if she were all right. Lulu sent back a letter saying that she and her brother, Paul, needed a guarantee, so my husband and I offered one for each of them. We've bothered with forms and references, and the necessary permit for the British visa was sent to Berlin. But when Lulu applied to have hers transferred to Frankfurt, they said no such visa had been received. A great deal of correspondence has passed between us, but we haven't been able to sort it. I thought that since you go regularly to the continent, perhaps you could check in with the head office in Berlin and make enquiries for my friend?"[30]

Ida looked apologetic. "My sister and I *were* going regularly to the continent some months back, but it's becoming more and more dangerous, I'm afraid." Krauss had sent numerous coded warnings that they should be careful, particularly to make sure they didn't aid anyone with Communist or anti-Nazi sentiments lest they end up in a camp themselves or be shot on the spot next time they entered the country. However, this case was tempting only because the guarantee was already assured.

"Let me think about it," Ida offered. "If we can do it, we will."

"Would certainly love to see Strauss' *Arabella* in two weeks' time," Ida cabled to Krauss, just to test his response.

"Arabella," he telegrammed back. "24, 25, 26. Take Walter Stiefel too. Needs another."

Needs another guarantee, he must mean. And where would they find that? It was an invitation, though. Did they dare accept? Ida rang the Home Office, seeking reassurance, but the secretary seemed shocked she'd even consider it. "You're thinking of going to Germany right now? Oh, Miss Cook, you must know that if war breaks out while you're there, you may find yourself interned in a German camp until this is well and over."

"Thank you," Ida said, swallowing. Hoping Krauss wouldn't have invited them if it were hopeless, Ida and Louise flew into Berlin. At each security checkpoint, their documents were closely scrutinized. They were Brits, true enemies of Germany now, and the cold, suspicious glances didn't let them forget it.

The air in Berlin was tense, and SS guards with guns kept watch over a precarious new order. Swastikas proudly hung from every building, but in some alleyways, anti-Nazi pamphlets fluttered in the gutters. Near the university, they found a Nazi poster painted over with graffiti. *"Freedom! Down with Hitler!"* someone had written in scrawling ink. The corner of the poster had been decorated with a white rose.[31]

"Who could have dared to do that?" Ida asked, astonished.

"Someone very brave," Louise replied.

News waited for them at the hotel that Theo's British visa had, indeed, been granted, but every escape route was jammed. They needed to send money for his fare, but doing so from Germany was impossible. Ida sent him a vague, brief cable hoping he would understand that they would send it as soon as they were back in London.

At the central emigration office in Berlin, Louise translated for Ida as they tried to sort out the situation with Lulu. After several dead ends, Louise managed to understand that the English friend had promised her guarantee in the name of Lulu, but Miss Cossmann had filled out the forms using her proper name, Louisa. They spent the morning straightening out the muddle. By afternoon, they sent a reassuring message back to London. Next, they met with her brother, Professor Paul Cossmann, and found him a brilliant and shrewd man who had been unable to be employed at the university since the Nazis had forbade it. He'd been jailed once for open opposition to the regime, and they were worried about the difficulties of helping him.

Krauss had also asked them to get out Walter Stiefel, the son of an older couple they had rescued a few months previously. He had a young daughter who had gotten out on a Kindertransport, but he needed a guarantee for himself and his wife. From their hotel room, they rang the number Krauss had provided.

The man's voice sounded tense. "No, no," he said to an invitation to meet at a private apartment. "Somewhere else."

"Where?" Louise asked. She explained to Ida: "He's asking us to meet him at a railway station—the Anhalter Bahnhof. He says we'll recognize him because he will be carrying an English newspaper under his left arm."

Ida raised her eyebrows. "Does that seem suspicious to you?" when her sister hung up the phone.

"Everything seems suspicious to me at this point," Louise replied.

The next day, they waited nervously, scanning the crowds at the Anhalter Bahnhof. A man with a briefcase walked by holding a Swedish newspaper, gesturing them to follow him. "Do you think—?" Ida asked.

"We can't compromise in the slightest," Louise whispered crisply. "One wrong step, and we're never leaving this country." She took Ida's arm, and they brushed off the man, hurrying off in the opposite direction. They returned to the hotel Adlon, stopping in the lobby to make sure people saw them gazing admiringly at a top Nazi official as he passed.

Their phone in their room was ringing when they opened the door. "I'm going to get into a taxi and drive around Pariser Platz," Walter's voice said. "If you stand on the corner, I'll pick you up."

Back down to the street they went, fighting down a desire to take the first flight back to London. A cab turned the corner and stopped right in front of them. The door opened and a man wearing a dark hat, pulled low over his face, leaned away from the darkened windows of the cab. "This is the last thing Mum would ever advise us to do," Louise said.

"But she isn't here," Ida shot back. "Quickly then." She darted inside the cab and pulled her sister in with her, slamming the door.

The cab sped off down the street. Walter looked up from the front seat, and Ida recognized him as the man who had carried the Swedish paper at the station. "It's you!"

"Yes," he replied dryly. "Clever of you not to bend, but unfortunately English papers were banned in Germany just this morning."

"Ah," said Louise.

"You were right to be worried," Walter Stiefel explained. "Things are very tense here right now, and you must not be seen with me. It's of the utmost importance. My wife and I appreciate your help more than you can understand, but we don't want to put you at risk."

They wanted to ask why being seen with him would put them at risk but thought of the anti-Nazi literature lying in the gutters of Berlin and decided not to ask questions.

"I'm hoping you can possibly find a guarantee for me and my wife? It would have to happen quickly. There's not much time left." Surreptitiously, he slipped an envelope into their bag. It was full of money, Ida realized with a start. Probably he needed it out of the country. She nodded to show she understood. They did their best to answer his questions, to assure him they would do all they could. "There's not much time left," he had said, and there was that word again—*time*—like a great clock winding down. No one wanted to think about what would happen if they ran out of time.

That night, in a sumptuous Berlin theater, they tried to enjoy Richard Strauss' *Arabella*, staged for their very own benefit. There wasn't enough velvet and crystal in the entire German empire, Ida thought, that could distract anymore from the quickly cracking façade.

IN HOSPITAL

That next morning they took the train to Frankfurt, and, following Krauss' instructions, traveled to the Jewish Community hospital in Gagernstrasse. As a doctor led them through the ward, they realized that every patient there had been released from a concentration camp and they were stunned to see how emaciated the people were. Only two surgeons remained to look after the very large ward, and one had a septic thumb and could not operate.

Heads turned in their direction and staff greeted them warmly, as though they knew who they were. A Doctor Hirsch led them to an alcove holding two beds, where a woman with thinning hair stood waiting for them with three scrawny little boys who seemed unnaturally well behaved for small children.

Dr. Hirsch introduced Corine and Silvio Ahrens. The man in the bed had lost a leg to frostbite and looked beyond ill, but he opened his eyes, and you could see the intelligence and strength within. "Hello," said Ida, wishing she could hug this sweet, suffering family. "You're not feeling so well just at the moment, I'm afraid."

Mr. Ahrens shook his head. "I was in Dachau," he said simply. He gestured to his friend beside him. "And he was in Buchenwald."

Silvio nodded slightly. "It was even worse in Buchenwald," he acknowledged graciously. "Thank you for coming, Miss Cooks. We've been told you may be able to help our children." He seemed moved beyond tears at the thought. It was clear that both he and his wife believed he was dying.

"Silvio was taken in the November roundups last year," Mrs. Ahrens explained. "I've done my best to support my children by cleaning homes for the few people brave enough to employ me. But now—" her voice broke off. "I can't part with my little girl. She is too young. But my boys you can take, for they are absolutely starving."

She nodded at the three sweet boys waiting patiently by their father's side. "I'm afraid we can't take them just yet," Louise cautioned.

"It's rather unlikely we'd find a place for your boys all together,"

Ida said, thinking quickly, "but perhaps we could get them placed in the same village, perhaps near the Northumberland village of our old childhood home? Then they would be eligible for a Kindertransport."

They spoke with Mr. Ahrens quietly but didn't want to tire him out. "Please rest now, Mr. Ahrens," Louise said. "We'll do our best to help your children." The man's face relaxed at her words, and he sank back into his bed, exhausted with the effort of speaking.

"Stay here for a minute," Corine instructed her boys. She led the sisters away from her children's small ears.

Louise said tactfully, "When your husband is better," though her tone implied—*when he is dead*—"we can try to get you a domestic permit some place where you can bring your daughter too. Then we will work to reunite you all."

Corine shrugged, choking back tears. "He's lost a foot from frostbite. He was nearly dead from carrying weights beyond human capacity."

"It's unbelievable," Ida said sincerely. "No one should have to go through such a thing. We're so sorry. We'll do our best to help your children. In the meantime, please use this to buy them some food." She handed Corine most of the money in her purse.

"Thank you," Corine said, hugging them impulsively. "It will help ever so much."

They turned away, stumbled toward the door, sickened by what they'd seen. Just before they reached the corridor, the young doctor returned, beckoning to them. "I'm awfully sorry. Could I bother you for one more minute of your time?" Surprised, they followed him into a small office. "I know you are helping people here," he explained, "and I was hoping I could ask your advice about something?"

"Our advice?" Ida said, bewildered.

"Yes. You see, I've been given a chance to escape. All my papers are in order to go to America, but it means leaving these patients behind. I have no idea if the regime will replace me or just leave these people to—to suffer." He raised agonized eyes, and they saw the depths of his dilemma. "Have I the right to take this chance, or should I stay?"

Ida looked at Louise in horrified silence. "I'm terribly sorry," Ida said, at last. "We couldn't possibly undertake to decide such a thing for anyone."

Louise nodded.

"I will tell you, faced with such a choice, I would seek refuge in prayer," Ida said, touching his arm compassionately.

"Thank you," he said solemnly. "I appreciate your counsel. It's brave of you to come to Germany right now and try to help."

"There are so many who need it."

He nodded. "After seeing the work you are doing, I think I will try to stay."

"It's very brave of you," Ida said, patting his arm again. "Very brave and kind."

They left the building, trying to shake off the weight, holding onto each other as if there was little else to hold onto. "How much money did you give Mrs. Ahrens?" Louise asked.

"Almost all of it."

"Will we have enough left to get home?"

"We'll have enough. Oh, Louise—" Ida began, tears falling down her cheeks.

"Don't. Please don't," Louise begged. "If you start, I won't be able to stop."

As they stepped into the late July sunshine, Ida felt an urgent, swift, and driving hatred for those responsible for so much suffering. The overwhelming personal desire to retaliate scared her in its intensity, and she knew unequivocally, that were it in her power, she would gladly draw blood, would even take their lives. The feeling, an entirely new one, overwhelmed and terrified her. She lapsed into silence and leaned on her sister as they made their way down the street.

TICK TOCK

The moment they were safely back in London, Ida scrambled to cable visas and entry permits to Lulu. She frantically tried to find a sponsor to take Walter Stiefel and his wife and pleaded for more sponsors for Corine Ahrens and her children. She went over routes again and again, determined to get Theo out of Poland, knowing that every hour that passed made success less likely.

"I'm afraid every airline, train, and bus is overbooked out of Poland," yet another refugee office explained to her for the hundredth time.

"Are you quite sure there's nothing?" Ida asked, wanting to scream. "He's just a boy. He's been living in a horse stable in Zbąszyń for nearly a year now."

"I'm very sorry, Miss Cook. Thousands of people are trying to get out of Poland right now. There's nothing at all." She heard the maddening shuffling of papers through the line as he verified it. "Well . . ." he stopped, and hope tore against the edges of despair. "There is one packet steamer leaving Gdynia on the twenty-fifth."

"There is?" Ida demanded.

"Yes, a Kindertransport, but it is, of course, restricted to children twelve and under, with only a very few exceptions made for older children."

"I must find a way to get him on it," Ida said and rang off. She rang the owner of the shipping line next, patiently explaining the situation and begging him to help. "I can pay extra for his fare if it would make a difference."

"I'm very sorry, Miss, but I can do nothing. Kindertransport is run by the government now. Any vacancies for older children are filled on a first-come-first-serve basis. He can come to the dock on the day of departure if he likes, but beyond that, I cannot make any promise."

The sound of a delivery man outside sent Ida scrambling to the door to receive a telegram from Lulu's guarantor: "Documents received," she had written. "Brother taken." Ida wanted to crumple. That sweet man. The swift sound of stormtroopers in long black boots knocked on the door of her mind. Knocking, beating. The image of the professor's anguished face lodged itself into her memory, refusing to disappear.

She withdrew money to pay for Theo's passage, ignoring her empty bank account and the credit that had been extended against her future book projects too. Every penny of her earnings had been promised away. *Could she ever write enough books to pay it all back?* She shoved the niggling thought away, just one more worry lodging itself in the base of her stomach. She couldn't think about it now. Bugger the bank loans. All that mattered was Theo. And Lulu. And Corine. And ever so many others.

Frantically, she cabled Theo the borrowed money with instructions to get himself to Gdynia on the twenty-fifth. Ida threw a briskly whispered prayer toward the heavens, sure that there were many requests in line before her. There was no guarantee of his place on the transport, she explained in the cable. But there were no other options either.

HAPPY BIRTHDAY

On Ida's thirty-fifth birthday, London received word that the Soviets and Germans had signed a nonaggression pact, adding even more strength of force to Germany's seemingly unstoppable ascent. The Cook family struggled their way through a sugar-rationed cake and half-hearted singing, trying to tease a smile from Ida, who had found few reasons to smile as of late.

Trying to cheer her, Father said, "Maybe there won't be a war, Ida, owing to a cataclysmic collapse in Germany." His family rolled their eyes, but he continued. "Hear me out. Maybe this pact is just a wild clutch at a swirling away straw by a drowning führer. It seems reasonable enough."

"Perhaps so, Father," Ida said, patting his arm absentmindedly and trying to eat a bit of cake that tasted like sand in her mouth. At midnight, just as they were going to bed, the phone began ringing urgently.

"Who is that at this hour?" Mum asked.

"Must be for you, Ides," said Louise. "It wouldn't be for anyone else.

"Call from Germany for you," the operator told her when she picked up.

"Thank you," said Ida.

In the hurry to connect her, there was a muddle and the line was not properly isolated. From every side of the telephone ether, there came a rush of voices speaking a jumble of different languages—like a great, approaching flood of sound. It was as if Ida alone were listening in to a mad and terrified Europe pleading for help. Standing in the silence of the hall, she seemed to wait on a distant island, witnessing the cries of those about to be engulfed in an imminent tidal wave. Helplessness overwhelmed her, sweeping her into the outer currents of the swell, unable to do anything more than listen to the sound of all that was coming.

At last, the line clicked into place. Ida tried to cast off the weight of need as the voice of Frau Jack in Berlin insisted urgently: "Ida, I have one more. A young man and his wife. Is it possible? They're going to be taken any moment."

"Yes, yes," Ida choked out, knowing it had to be impossible. "Of course, yes. Give me the details." Even as she wrote them down, she felt a great sinking beneath her.

"Thank you, then," Frau Jack said, hesitantly. "Goodbye." Her voice broke off into silence.

"Goodbye," Ida answered, feeling a dreadful finality to the word. She placed down the receiver but could not free her ears from the sound of thousands of desperate voices still echoing across the line in Europe, calling out for rescue.

The line clicked shut.

WARSZAWA

On the twenty-fifth of August, one final packet ship loaded with Jewish children slipped through the Kiel Canal and sailed in silence past a menacing German cruiser with its red and black Nazi flag flapping in a brisk breeze.

Ida received word the *Warszawa* had sailed. Desperately hoping Theo had made it aboard, she called at the refugee office for the passenger list, which she dragged back to the street, where Louise waited.

They read it aloud to each other, scanning down the long list of two hundred names: Bernard Kessler, Erich Reich, Karen Gershon, Hella Pick, Alfred Dubs, Karol Reisz, Heinz Danziger, Eva Rosner, Simon Markel, Herbert Haberberg, Edward Pachtman, Josef Kamiel.

Ida dropped the sheet to her side, disappointed. "He's not on board," she said, bracing herself to lose yet another. *Theo*. Why him? That boy's quick eyes looking up from beneath a jaunty cap had haunted her heart since she'd first seen his picture months ago.

"We can still go meet the ship," Louise said. "There's the slightest chance that he came aboard late and isn't listed here."

"I love you," Ida replied.

Five days later, the *Warszawa* steamed up the Thames estuary, passing beneath the raised Tower of London bridge. It docked at Cotton's Wharf at the Port of London, with a sea of children's faces at the railing, watching a new country come into view, small bags and satchels perched on their thin shoulders.

From the dock, Ida and Louise watched sailors ready the planks for the small passengers. Adults from the refugee office waited at the bottom, beckoning them down. Ida held the passport photo of Theo Markus Vineberg as the children descended: little chubby toddlers clinging to an older one's fingers. One carried a violin, shyly. The faces were alternately apprehensive, eager, excited, terrified, and sobbing. All of them gazed about in wonder, few understanding the language spoken by the adult strangers they'd followed. Ida dropped the photo to her side as the line began to thin. Only a final few children remained now, and she prepared herself for the loss of him.

An older boy crossed the dock with a big, lanky stride, reminding her of an American cowboy. He had blond curly hair and gray eyes and wasn't carrying so much as a knotted handkerchief. But he was smiling, and she had seen that smile before.

"Theo!" she called, waving fiercely. "Theo! It's me! Ida Cook!"

He grinned as he came closer, hurrying towards them, surprising them both by leaning in impulsively and hugging them around the waist. Ida and Louise laughed aloud, sharp jagged fearful laughs, and hugged him back.

"Theo! You weren't on the passenger list, but here you are!"

In Polish-laden English, he responded, "Some problems wis my papers. I was only allowed to go at ze last possible moment. Just as they remove the—how you call it?"

"Gangway?"

"Yes," he nodded, gesturing emphatically. "I was ze very last."

Ida and Louise exchanged looks of horror above his blond and curled head. The last passenger on the last civilian ship out of Poland. Some God in heaven wanted this boy alive, one way or another, this miracle boy. "And you've brought nothing with you!" Ida exclaimed.

The lad shrugged, still smiling. "I had nothing left to bring."[32]

WIELUŃ

Two days later, German soldiers pretending to be Polish staged a planned attack on a German radio station. In "retaliation," German tanks rolled into western Poland, launching simultaneous incursions from the western, southern, and northern borders—the troops all converging steadily on the capitol of Warsaw.

A "Defensive War" (*Verteidigungskrieg*), Hitler called it. Because, as he explained, Poland had provoked first and "Germans in Poland are persecuted with a bloody terror and are driven from their homes. Poles no longer are willing to respect the German frontier." Luftwaffe bombers screamed overhead, descending on the quiet, medieval castle town of Wieluń. The town had neither military significance nor defenses, but war planes sent forty-six tonnes of bombs swirling through the pre-dawn sky, dropping like brightly colored candies upon a Red Cross hospital, a nineteenth century synagogue, and a fourteenth century Augustinian cloister.

Civilians woke to a strange roar they'd never heard before, watched cracks spreading across ceilings and glass shattering in their panes. The marketplace filled with rubble as fierce flames enveloped the square. People ran in all directions, some without clothing, crying out for help, stumbling over dead bodies. When the plumes of smoke began to dissipate, the planes circled back to strafe civilians fleeing the wreckage.

After leaving most of the town's center destroyed, German pilots landed their new Ju 87B bombers, proud of their newly tested technologies. Any Jews who had survived the assault were set to work clearing the rubble.

In all occupied territories, Germany issued ration cards to all remaining Roma and Jews, restricting them to a starvation diet of two hundred calories per day, so the flood of refugees continued, flowing outward and away from Germany in streams that washed ashore in England, China, Australia, Syria, South Africa, Bolivia, Argentina, and Palestine.

SEPTEMBER THIRD

A thin drizzle fell on London and wisps of fog laced across the tops of her tallest buildings as Neville Chamberlain reluctantly mobilized the British army. Small children boarded trains, as London sank into the darkness of the first blackout and the country waited, and still waited, for a formal declaration of war.

The prime minister's ultimatum that Hitler leave Poland expired, unanswered, at 11 am.

The family gathered around the wireless to listen to the clipped voice of Neville Chamberlain speaking from number 10 Downing Street:

> You can imagine what a bitter blow it is to me that all my long struggle to win peace has failed. Yet I cannot believe that there is anything more, or anything different that I could have done and that would have been more successful. . . .
>
> And now that we have resolved to finish it, I know that you will all play your part with calmness and courage. . . . It is of vital importance that you should carry on with your jobs. . . . Now may God bless you all and may He defend the right. For it is evil things that we shall be fighting against—brute force, bad faith, injustice, oppression, and persecution. And against them I am certain the right will prevail.

This was it, then. The war everyone had anticipated, feared, cautioned each other about.

Ida, Louise, Mum, and Father looked at each other, nearly expecting that everything should appear changed somehow. It seemed that at any moment, bombs would descend, obliterating them all. But all was silent, except for the slow and steady ticking of the clock upon the wall.

At 11:27 am, the air raid sirens began to wail.

They fled to their garden shelter, sodden and damp, and huddled there until the all clear sounded. A neighbor peered over the fence as they straggled out of the corrugated contraption. "False alarm, that was. Set off by a French plane."

"Can't they invent a different signal to say so?" Ida said crossly, brushing dirt from her skirt. "How do they expect anyone to take alarms seriously?"

"I expect when we hear bombs exploding around us, it will be easy enough to take them seriously," said Father. To the neighbor, he called, "Has France joined us yet?"

"Not yet," the man replied. "Anytime. Hitler will have a hard go of it, getting through the French."

"Let's hope so," said Louise. "Since we're sitting right on the other side of them."

More false alarms followed in days ahead. Boxes of gas masks showed up on every doorstep, along with fliers on preparing for air raids. The tops of mailboxes were painted with special paint that changed colors in the presence of gas. Street signs were removed to confuse Nazis who might attempt to navigate the streets of London.

In the first move toward combat, Royal Air Force Whitley bombers sent millions of leaflets raining down like snow flurries over the city of Kiel. *A Message to the German People from the British People*, each leaflet announced in crisp type.

> *German Men and Women:*
>
> *The Government of the Reich have with cold deliberation forced war upon Great Britain. They have done so knowing that it must involve mankind in a calamity worse than that of 1914. . . .*
>
> *It is not us, but you they have deceived. For years their iron censorship has imprisoned your minds in, as it were, a concentration camp.*

From the east, an exhausted Poland mockingly pointed out that the Germans had arrived with incendiary bombs, while Great Britain fearlessly retaliated with some millions of leaflets.

CONFETTI

On Morella Road, the phone lay silent.

Their work was done.

Letters kept arriving, though, dropping through the mail slot and littering the entryway like confetti. Some were addressed simply "To Ida and Louise" and had been sent on from London's Jewish Refugee Headquarters. Mother carried the letters to Ida's room and tucked them under her door. Ida lay in bed alone after Louise departed for work, with the curtains closed and more of the missives scattered about her.

Adrift upon an endless sea of gray, she floated, listlessly staring at an unfinished novel in the typewriter, pressing her eyes to her palms, trying to think of a reason she should get out of bed. She lay still, trying to tear the haunting images from her mind, trying to extract them, wishing she could perform surgery on the gray mass of her brain.[33]

My departure is of the upmost urgency because I have no way to live here anymore, I have no income. Also, spiritually, I cannot manage living here anymore my soul simply cannot bear to be so degraded.[34]

I am a doctor of philosophy and have been a math teacher for 32 years. On no account should I become a burden to you or anyone else. Will you then, be kind enough as to help me get an affidavit? Hoping that I am so lucky to find in you a rescuer, I remain, thanking you beforehand.[35]

Especially since I am a widow and have no possibility of taking care of my children here in Poland. . . . My daughters are sensible,

227

*intelligent, healthy and independent girls. Surely it must be pos-
sible for you to rescue my children from this state of misery. I beg
you to help me quickly, for the winding up of the camp is gradually
beginning.*[36]

Their words swirled through Ida's head, came out onto the pages, and haunted her twisted nightmares, where she tried and failed. Over and over, she failed. All those they had tried to help on their final trip. Lulu's brother, Professor Cossman. All those people in hospital in Berlin. Corine Ahrens begging them to take her boys. All gone. All trapped in the rising floodwaters that had burst their wall at last.

"I beg you to help me," played on repeat through Ida's mind, like a tangled opera chorus chanted by a sickening voice from the shadows. From her window mainly, fighting ironic resentment, Ida watched London burst into a flurry of activity. *Too late*—the city awoke and began moving in response to the mess on the other side of the Channel. For three days, the main routes out of London become one-way streets as people fled, fearing imminent attacks on the capital. Children were shepherded aboard outgoing evacuation trains, while troops arrived, massed and awaiting orders.

Planes and troop carriers droned in an endless procession through the air overhead, streaming toward an unknown destination, moving in what seemed like an endless formation taking over the sky.

WARSZAWA

Two thousand German tanks and a thousand fighter planes descended on the Polish capital of Warsaw, encircling it, laying siege to the city. Plumes of great incendiary bombs descended on infantry barracks, on water supplies, on hospitals and marketplaces. On grade schools and on the Warsaw Royal Castle. In response, the Royal Air Force's Wellington bombers finally turned to dropping lead instead of leaflets, raining fire on German warships navigating the North Sea's Jade Bight. Leading with air attacks and artillery shelling, the Soviet Union invaded Poland from the east.

The weight of the German army hammered again and again against a beleaguered Warsaw, which for eight days stood the test of siege, hunger, and air bombardment.

Still in control of their air waves, Polish radio operators broadcast defiance and courage, then proudly played the African American jazz music so hated by the Nazis. During the second week of siege, a German radio operator located the same wavelength as a Polish station, and broke over the airways calling out for instant surrender. "*Warschau, gib nach*!" he screamed. *Warsaw, surrender*!

After several long moments of static, the Polish announcer regained control of his airwaves once more. In response, he crowed into his microphone: "*Warszawa będzie walczyć do końca!*" Don't believe the Germans! Warsaw will fight to the end.[37]

Then with a sultry *wa da do* from Ivie Anderson, the announcer turned up the sweet strains of the Duke Ellington band's "It Don't Mean a Thing," sending it streaming across the airwaves, both a solace and a battle cry.

PART 3

"There is never a complete answer to anything
that stems from man's inhumanity to man."

–IDA COOK

FALLING

Louise cast a worried glance in Ida's direction as she got ready for work. "Isn't your manuscript due next week?"

"Right," Ida said, waving her away. Half-heartedly, she sat up and pulled on clothes, then noticed a spot on her dress and absent-mindedly rubbed at it. She picked up a book to read, but her eyes kept straying to the windowsill—to the brickwork outside lined with gray mortar that reminded her of the brickwork lacing up Uncle Carl's flat in Frankfurt.

Uncle Carl. *Where was he?* Still crouched behind closed curtains? Scraping the last of his food from the cupboards while Luftwaffe planes screamed overhead? Or in a camp trapped by men holding a gun against his aging skin? The papers said leaflets had rained down over Germany, flimsy papers drifting like snow over the buzzing city, where people rushed with the purpose of wartime, while ghosts haunted abandoned buildings, pressing themselves into shadowed corners. Leaflets couldn't stop bullets.

And if they found him? Her imagination hurtled forward, impossible to stop—the sweet old man, stripped and shaved. A rocking train. A length of concertina wire.

The book dropped to her lap, and Ida buried her face in her hands.

Eating was difficult. She forced herself to bite methodically. Chew. Then swallow. There was no joy in it. Just duty. Just something else that needed to be finished and gotten through. Another hour of another day with the phone brooding in the background, stiff and silent. The sound of another letter dropping through the slot, landing cross the mat with a muffled, final clap.

WARSCHAU

Within weeks, the city of Warsaw lay in ruins. Two hundred thousand Polish citizens lay dead in the streets amidst the rubble. There was no water left with which to fight the fires, and children sat down upon piles of broken cobblestones and wept. Overwhelmed by the losses, General Juliusz Rómmel signed a cease fire agreement and surrendered the city to the German army.

Once bombs stopped falling, the Jews who were still alive in the merchant districts of Muranów, Powązki, and Stara Praga were forced to help clear the rubble from the streets. Zofia Maliniak worked among them, her frail bones straining to lift the weight.

Months later, when the autumn weather snapped and turned cold, the Warsaw Jews would be compelled to stack bricks and begin to set them into mortar. Together they would work, forming the rough and rambling outline of a slowly rising wall.

POSSIBLE

"I wouldn't be a bit surprised to learn that Hitler is insane and Göring has taken over," father said to the family gathered round for tea. "Mark my words: this won't last long."

"God, grant you're right," said Louise, picking up the paper he had dropped. Off the coast of southwest Ireland, Germany had sunk the HMS *Courageous*, one of Britain's seven aircraft carriers. A

German U-boat struck the port side with two torpedoes, and seventeen minutes later, the ship had sunk, dragging five hundred British soldiers into the frigid sea. It would be days before the full casualty lists were compiled.

War, war, *war*. It was all anyone spoke of. The radio kept up a constant stream of noise as papers flew off shelves. "My daughters are sensible, intelligent, healthy and independent girls," Ida's head informed her as she tried to eat her pudding. She tried to wave the voice away and listen vaguely to father and Louise sizing up the navies of Britain, France, and Germany.

"France will hold," her father was insisting. "The Maginot Line is unbreachable. Mark my words, France will be the undoing of Hitler, a strong and faithful ally through the long months ahead."

Months. If not years. Ida swirled her spoon through the custard, observing the swirls left in its wake. "Surely it must be possible for you to rescue my children from this state of misery," the voice intruded. *Surely.*

Surely, it must be possible . . .

And yet, I could not.

Ida pushed her chair back from the table, leaving her pudding nearly untouched.

"There's talk of a butter and sugar ration soon," father remarked, gesturing. "I fancy you won't leave custard behind then."

"Would you like mine?" Ida pushed it toward him and drifted toward the stairs. "I need to write." She mounted the stairs as Mum looked after her with a puckered brow.

Upstairs, Ida shuffled through sheets of paper, trying to concentrate. The scene needed reworking. She had read the same lines over ten times. "There was only one world," she had written, had written

235

weeks ago, a line she still heard in her mind spoken in Friedl's voice in Mitia's music room in Frankfurt.

> *There was only one world, and love, however deep, was only a part of it. "Thy people will be my people," only held good in the Old Testament, where an all-seeing Providence was forever leaning out of heaven to put things right—*

Ida's eyes drifted back toward the window. Where *was* the all-seeing Providence? If ever there had been a time for Him to lean out of heaven, this seemed like a good moment for it. Could even God Himself put all that was broken in Europe right again?

On no account should I become a burden. To you or anyone else. Surely. It must be possible.

Surely.

Ida reached for the bottle of sleeping tablets she'd hidden under her mattress. Shoving more than the regular dosage into her mouth, she drew the curtains and buried herself under blankets, wishing she could remain there indefinitely, tumbled in oblivion until their words and faces washed free from her mind. She didn't hear Louise come in.

◇ ·· — ··· — ·· ◇

It was late the next morning when Louise drew back the curtains, letting light stream into the room. Ida kept the pillow firmly over her head and groaned her disapproval. "You've got guests," Louise announced, opening the door to their room.

Ida squinted dazedly at her sister and then, across the room to the threshold, where Friedl and Maria had just entered.

"Well, there's a thing!" Ida struggled to sit up.

"Hullo!" Friedl said, giggling like she were going to a party.

"Come for breakfast, girls?" Ida's groggy hands went to her hair, trying to tidy her halo of frizz. "I've only just woken. I'm sure my hair's a fright."

"Louise told us the news," said Maria.

"That one hasn't heard about it yet," Louise said, pointing to her sister. "She's been sleeping the day away."

"Heard what?" Ida sat up and leaned against the headboard. "I must say, this isn't at all the way I expected this morning to run. Why aren't you at work, Louie?"

Friedl laughed, sitting down beside her on the bed. "Poor *liebling*."

"I'm afraid there's good news and bad news," said Louise. "Which would you like first?"

Ida turned from sister to friends. "I can't bear any more bad news just at the moment. Let's have the good, then. Out with it."

"The good news," said Louise, "is that I have the day off, and we're all skiving off to the cinema together."

"But—" Ida started.

"I told you she'd be a bit dodgy," Louise countered. "Your novel can wait. It's been waiting a great deal of late anyway, we've noticed. And we may as well get the bad news over with, for there's nothing for it. In preparation for the imminent conflict, my office has been packed off to a remote and undisclosed corner of Wales for safekeeping, so I'm going to have to leave you in the care of these girls until I can get back again."

Ida sank back in surprise. "Leaving? To *Wales*? Oh, Louie. We all know I couldn't manage a fortnight without you."

"I'm sorry to be the one to tell you, dear," Louise said, handing her a printed cotton dress. "But we're at war, Ides. This is the moment when dear old Chamberlain needs to call upon our world-famous stiff upper lips."

Ida felt as though she were sinking beneath the cold and engulfing waves of the Atlantic. "But, Louise," she said seriously. "We've never been apart. Not in our entire lives. Not more than a week or two, and we were miserable the whole time." The corners of her eyes began to sting. "Or *I* was at any rate." An avalanche of depression flooded her soul.

"Girls, tell her—" She looked to Friedl and Maria for sympathy, her still groggy mind beginning to process at last to whom she was speaking.

Friedl, looking down at the bedspread, tracing Mum's small stitches with her fingertip, had left behind mother, sister, aunts, uncles, cousins, friends, neighbors—everyone, *everyone*. And they weren't in a remote corner of Wales, either. They were trapped in Hitler's Germany, barricaded behind concertina wire. And Maria—her father, her grandfather had been taken right before her eyes, disappeared. Her own love was en route to Brazil, and she with no way to join him. Ida's eyes narrowed and she saw her sister's cleverness.

"Well then, get out, the lot of you. Let me get dressed, if this is how it's going to be."

"Don't be a prude," Friedl said, laughing as she reached to unbutton the back of Ida's nightgown. "We've seen knickers before."

"Far nicer ones, I'd wager," added Louise.

"Not mine, you haven't," Ida replied, but she let herself be helped out of the nightgown and into a dress like a child, let them fuss over her hair and makeup in the looking glass, patting each curl into place, clucking over her like they couldn't bear to leave her one minute. She blessed them for not leaving her alone, surrounding her like sisters—pulling her out of bed, then downstairs to tuck away a cup of tea, and out the door and into the streets of London, where Ida found the city transformed in the time she'd hidden herself away—transformed into a city at war.

Holding onto her gas mask box and identity card, Ida followed the girls through a park that had been dug up into trenches. Sandbags had been stacked ten feet high to protect historic buildings, some even covered telephone booths. London's streets thrummed at a fevered pitch. Closer to the city center, men and women waved to friends as if it all were a gay party. A group burst spontaneously into "It's a Long Way to Tipperary," a ditty which had been remembered and found as good for war in 1939 as it had been twenty-five years ago in 1914. Air raid shelters and blackout curtains now covered the city. Wartime mobile canteens doled out tea to anyone walking by.

"Are the cinemas even open?" Ida asked.

"Only just," Louise explained. "They were shut down for weeks, but then nothing happened, so they realized they couldn't lock down the city forever, waiting for Hitler's invasion. But they're rationing petrol, so we have to walk."

"What if we get caught outdoors in a gas attack?"

"We pop these on," said Louise, holding up the fastened box holding her gas mask, "and dart into a tube station. London has decided it will have business as usual."

As they neared a train station, they met a group of children in wool overcoats toting satchels and gas mask boxes over their shoulders, identity cards hung round their necks. Bobbies in domed caps hurried the children through the throngs of crowds. In the station, soldiers in uniform hoisted duffels, grinning like they were going to a party, while a brass band played brightly. Nearly everyone carried a newspaper.

Advertisements had been plastered up on the streets, reminding Brits: "Register today as a Life Donor!" And: "YOUR courage, your cheerfulness, your resolution WILL BRING US VICTORY." Barrage balloons three times the size of a cricket pitch floated over London from cables fixed to winches on lorries. Ida ogled the massive contraptions.

"They keep dive bombers from hitting their targets," Louise explained.

"And they use a massive hoover to inflate them," Maria added, laughing.

Judging by the line outside the cinema, they weren't the only ones in need of an outing. Inside, the newsreels flashed images of Nazi tanks rolling through Poland, cutting back to British lads being outfitted for battle. Then the Metro-Goldwyn-Mayer titles rolled up the screen, and Hollywood's Greta Garbo played the title role, Ninotchka, a Russian girl sent to Paris to reclaim confiscated jewelry who accidentally discovers capitalism isn't as bad as she's been led to believe.

Afterwards they relaxed over coffee at a nearby café and Friedl said of the film, "'Zis is the same, how I felt coming from Germany to London." Maria nodded in agreement. "Finding the whole world was different from that I had supposed."

"The costumes. The jewels. Paris. Melvyn Douglas." Ida sighed. "It was all so romantic. The jewelry we brought back from Europe is just as grand as the stuff she was smuggling. Louise, doesn't Alice remind you of an older Greta Garbo?"

"Mm-hmm," Louise agreed.

"What do you suppose they're doing in Paris right now?" Ida asked dreamily.

"It's midnight," Louise quoted from the film. "One half of Paris is making love to the other half."

The girls laughed around the table in response to the clever line. They dawdled over their coffees, sipping as they basked in the beauty of the autumn evening. The sound of the jitterbug and couples moving across the dance floors streamed unhampered from a blacked-out dance hall.

The sound of "Swingin' the Jinx Away" flushed the street, as Ida looked up at her sister and remembered with a start: she was leaving. "Really, Louise, *whatever* shall we do without you?"

"For one thing, you must commit to getting out of bed."

Ida stirred her coffee pointedly.

"Do we need to come and get you up in ze morning, dear?" Friedl asked.

Ida glanced round the table and looked down, staring into her cup as if seeking answers there. "I can't stop thinking about them," she admitted at last. "The ones we left behind. The ones we couldn't help."

"Ah," said Maria.

They exchanged looks over the top of her downturned head. "You did everything that was possible, yah?" Friedl asked her gently. "We've seen you, all of us. Working to help another one, always another one."

Maria put a warm hand over Ida's. "There is nothing more you can do. Not right at this moment."

The fact that they of all people were comforting her made Ida feel a deep sense of guilt and shame. She should be able to go on. If *they* could, she should be able to. She took a deep breath and tried to banish the images from her mind.

"How is that boy from Poland?" Friedl asked, prodding.

"Theo?" Ida smiled. "He's fine. He's staying with such a kind family now. He wants to go to school."

"And Krysia, the little girl?"

"With her parents, in the countryside."

"And 'zis other man? From Berlin, you told me, who has come with his wife?"

"Walter Stiefel? He and his wife are safe," said Ida, dimpling again. "Reunited with their daughter and staying with our friends in the north of England, near Alnwick, where Louise and I went to school. And do you know? He told me the most remarkable story once he got here. Louise and I noticed how very strange he acted in Berlin." Louise nodded her agreement. "Well, it turned out he was working for the anti-Nazi underground the whole time, doing very dangerous work, and they were tracking him. If we'd been found helping him—" her voice broke off. "Well, we might not—"

Louise, Maria, and Friedl exchanged horrified glances over her downturned head.

"Oh, Ida, you see?" asked Maria, pausing for her words to sink in. "You, see? Think about *them*, Ida. Think about *us*—where would I be? And Mama? And Friedl" she gestured across the table, "—about 'ze ones you helped. I know some of the ones who come without their families, they are like you. They can do nothing now." She shrugged. "Of course, there are many days where I feel so heavy I don't want to go on." Her eyes grew round with emotion. "But I do not think my family, my friends would be wanting this, wanting me to be even so sad, not able to leave from my rooms. My papa, even though he may be gone from this world, I feel that he is wanting me to live."

Ida felt her vision blur at her friend's brave words. She squeezed her hand. "Sometimes it seems like if I forget about those we left—they will be gone forever, abandoned." She dropped her face to her hands.

Maria nodded, rubbing her shoulder. "I understand. Believe me, I do. There may be others you can help, after all of this is over. But we need to be trusting them to God, for just this moment."

Maria's imperfect English made the phrase so much more memorable. *Trusting them to God.* Ida caught onto the phrase, repeated it. Tried her very best to believe it. Dear Maria, on the train fleeing for her life, repeating her mother's expression of faith, surviving, to encourage her here in London once again, when Hitler might easily still catch up with her.

Louise and Friedl exchanged glances, remaining silent, for not even Louise had been able to get this far.

"They will not be gone forever," Maria said, "but you need to be letting them be in peace now, yah?" Maria's deep brown eyes assured her, and Ida felt the truth of her words wash over her heart. "You have done so much already, Ida. So much for us all."

BLITZKRIEG

Autumn stretched into winter, and still the German land invasion did not come. Life almost returned to normal in London, and people began calling it the "Phoney War," though sugar, butter, and bacon rations were real enough.

In the flush of a spring thaw, German panzer tanks rolled into adjacent countries, spreading their reach further, a plague spreading north. On April 9, 1940, Denmark surrendered six hours after invasion. Without waiting for a formal declaration of war, the Luftwaffe began bombing Belgium, Luxembourg, and the Netherlands, dropping high explosive bombs on each capital city that capitulated, falling before the enemy like leaves dropping in autumn. Finally, Germany turned towards France, with the full hypocrisy of Hitler's claims for peace now utterly revealed. Not only did he have territorial desires for all of Europe, but he had been building an army capable of grasping it with a blitzkrieg—a lightning war.

The British military whisked an exiled Norwegian government to safety as an overwhelmed Neville Chamberlain took to the radio: "Early this morning Hitler added another to the horrible crimes already committed by this man by a sudden attack on Holland, Belgium, and Luxembourg. . . . It was clear, that at this critical moment in the war . . . the essential unity could be secured under another prime minister though not under myself."

Shock hung over the breakfast table as he continued:

> As this is my last message to you from number 10 Downing Street, there is one more thing I should like to say to you. . . . The hour has come when we are to be put to the test as the innocent people of Holland and Belgium and France are being tested already. And you and I must rally behind our new leader, and with our united strength, and with unshakeable courage, fight and work until this wild beast that has sprung out of his lair upon us, be finally disarmed and overthrown.

The sound of the national anthem carried across the airwaves, dissolving into an awkward silence. "Dear, old Chamberlain," said father thoughtfully. "I did so want him to come through."

"Perhaps he has," said Ida, feeling keenly the absence of her sister.

Father nodded. "We're in God's hands now."

"God's and Churchill's," Ida added quietly.

VIVE LA FRANCE

The world held its breath as German troops approached France, bracing themselves for battles to come. "The Maginot Line will hold," everyone assured each other, referring to the 280 miles of fortresses, underground bunkers, minefields, and gun batteries that helped Parisians sleep better at night. Fifty-five million tonnes of steel embedded deep into the earth had been designed to withstand months of artillery fire and poison gas attacks.

Instead, in May, new superior Nazi tanks simply bypassed the Maginot Line through the Ardennes and along the Somme valley, rolling through Belgian territory deemed impassible, flanking the armies and moving on toward Paris. French prime minister Paul Reynaud telephoned newly appointed prime minister Winston Churchill. We have been defeated," he said. "We are beaten; we have lost the battle.

Shaken and attempting to offer comfort, Churchill reminded Reynaud of all the times the Germans had broken through Allied lines in the First World War only to be stopped. Reynaud remained inconsolable. Churchill flew to Paris the next day, where he found the French government burning its archives and preparing to evacuate the capital. In a meeting with top French commanders, Churchill asked, "Where is the strategic reserve?" referring to the reserve that had saved Paris in the First World War.

General Maurice Gustave Gamelin replied: *"Aucune." There is none.*

When a shocked Churchill asked if they could launch a counterattack, Gamelin simply replied, "inferiority of numbers, inferiority of equipment, inferiority of methods."

All of Britain reeled at the news.

DUNKIRK

By the end of May, German armies had cut off the Allies, pushing the British, Belgian, and French forces west, back toward the coast. Soldiers massed on the beaches and harbors of Dunkirk, in the north of France, with their backs against the sea. An impassioned Winston Churchill rose and addressed the House of Commons: "The whole root and core and brain of the British Army has been stranded at Dunkirk and is about to perish or be captured," he informed them. "Every available vessel must be brought to help."

Churchill's emergency call went out across the southern coast of England. One cruiser and eight destroyers headed across the Channel, while naval officers combed boatyards for small private craft that could bring soldiers from the beaches to the larger ships. Removing men from Dunkirk's beaches via cruiser and destroyers was a tedious and slow process. Soldiers lined up along the east and west moles—great walls of toppled cement pilings that reached into the sea. Men in khaki, carrying any supplies they had left, flowed out along the stone and concrete breakwaters, waiting to be loaded into incoming ships.

The Luftwaffe gleefully scried overhead, bombing Dunkirk's town and docks, knocking out the water supply, lighting fires up and down the coast. The Royal Air Force fought dog fights for control of the skies, far from beaches where soldiers waited on, imagining themselves abandoned. To reach the ships more quickly, soldiers at De Panne and Bray-Dunes constructed improvised jetties by driving rows of abandoned vehicles onto the beach at low tide, anchoring them with sandbags and connecting them with wooden walkways.

German troops surrounded thirty-five thousand Allied soldiers in nearby Lille. When the army ran out of food, they surrendered. King George declared a national day of prayer and the Archbishop of Canterbury England led prayers for the soldiers in dire peril in France.

The call was passed from vessel to vessel. Private cruisers, passenger ferries, hospital ships, destroyers, gunboats, all turned into the Channel, heading into the churning sea, wary eyes on the sky. Minesweepers and trawlers, torpedo boats and Dutch schuyts joined the fray, followed by yachts, tugboats, and car ferries, pleasure craft, and motor lifeboats with civilian crews. Streaming across the Channel, into the range of the army that had swept mercilessly across Europe, they came as a rising tide.

Luftwaffe planes screamed overhead, strafing the beaches and managing to sink a few transports, though low hanging clouds kept them from doing more damage. Waiting men scrambled onto the ships, teeming on the decks and packed into galleys. Once full, the pilots headed back across the choppy sea, hulls sunk low in the water. Dog fights screamed overhead, exploding around them.

At the far shore, the White Cliffs of Dover met them like a benediction. From hell to heaven, the men said they had travelled, as they fell with relief onto British soil.[38] Nearly three hundred forty thousand troops were rescued. And all of Europe knew that the war had come perilously close to ending just as quickly as it had begun.

◇ · · ── · · · ── · · ◇

On June 14, the German army arrived in Paris. Shock swept through London. The photographs of the Nazi flag spinning out over the Eiffel Tower were unthinkable. The French republican motto from 1790: "Freedom, equality, brotherhood" became the German, "Work, family, fatherland" instead. General Philippe

Pétain signed the armistice at the Forest of Compiègne in the same railway carriage and chairs that had been used for Germany's 1918 surrender at the end of World War I. This time Hitler sat in the victor's chair, his revenge complete.

It was finished. In Paris, a baker placed a framed photograph of Pétain in his shop window. "Sold," the image was labelled with a flourished sash. Holland surrendered, then Belgium and Norway. The unthinkable had happened. And now England would have to fight on alone.

COLD SUMMER

1940

Sandbags mounted on London streets and air raid sirens sounded regularly, but weary of alarms that never materialized, a trickle of the refugees who had fled to the countryside made their way back to the city. Despite the inconvenience of blackouts and the eerie presence of soldiers in the streets, London returned to shaky normality.

Ida began writing again, a mad and furious type of writing with little joy. She punched keys with desperation, the panic of money breathing down the back of her neck as she continued paying promised guarantees, having leveraged more than half her income to the support of those they'd been able to help. But anything seemed better than the gray and hazy sea through which she had passed.

Their youngest brother, Jim, had enlisted the day after Dunkirk. Two days before his ship date, he married his girlfriend, Ena. To everyone's delight, Louise came home from Wales and she and Ida helped their mother scrape together enough butter and sugar rations to make a wedding cake. Their brother Bill was also in uniform, his wife Lydia beside him, wearing the uneasy air of all that lay ahead, the uncertainty just as intoxicating as the rationed champagne.

The day after the wedding, the family listened to the BBC radio, broadcasting Churchill's latest speech into homes across the commonwealth His powerful voice pronounced:

> I have, myself, full confidence that . . . we shall prove ourselves once again able to defend our Island home, to ride out the storm of war, and to outlive the menace of tyranny, if necessary for years, if necessary alone. At any rate, that is what we are going to try to do. . . .
>
> Even though large tracts of Europe and many old and famous States have fallen or may fall into the grip of the Gestapo and all the odious apparatus of Nazi rule, we shall not flag or fail. We shall go on to the end, we shall fight in France, we shall fight on the seas and oceans, we shall fight with growing confidence and growing strength in the air, we shall defend our Island, whatever the cost may be, we shall fight on the beaches, we shall fight on the landing grounds, we shall fight in the fields and in the streets, we shall fight in the hills; we shall never surrender, and if, . . . this Island or a large part of it were subjugated and starving, then our Empire beyond the seas . . . would carry on the struggle, until, in God's good time, the New World, with all its power and might, steps forth to the rescue and the liberation of the old.[39]

Thunderous applause met his words, both in the House of Commons, and in the kitchen of 24 Morella Road. "Dear Churchill," Louise said, wiping tears from her eyes. "He has quite a way with words, doesn't he?"

Ida, who was crying as much from the joy of having her sister there as from the prime minister's speech, wrapped her arms around her sister and wouldn't let go.

Father lay an arm across mother's shoulders thoughtfully. "We shall never surrender," he repeated. "Just so."

The following day, Ida and Louise were catching up with Friedl and Maria at Dolphin Square when a call came from home. Ida was surprised to hear her mother say, "Can you please come home and help me reason with your father?"

In confusion, Ida reported the unheard-of request to Louise, and they hurried home to find Mum looking out of sorts and Dad marching up and down the garden path.

"What's this about?" Ida asked.

"Your dad has gone and signed up to be a stretcher bearer!" Mum said. "I think his mind is slipping. He's seventy-five!"

"Churchill needs us all!" he announced, puffing out his chest. "I'm just as hale and spry as a lot of younger ones, and I'm not going to let our boys do all the fighting."

"Mark my words," his wife replied, "if you try to carry the wounded, you're more likely to be *on* the stretcher than at one end of it!"

"I don't care what any of you think," father insisted. "Churchill said we must all do our part, and this is what I think is right."

"Well, I guess that's the most that any of us can say, Father," said Louise, taking her mother's arm reassuringly. "Maybe you can find another position where you don't have to carry so much weight? But of course, if you feel that way about it, I don't suppose there's anything else to be said."

He said nothing, but the next day he returned from the city wearing an air raid warden's uniform.

"It's better than a stretcher bearer," Mum said, running a shaking hand over his lapel. With both of their brothers now in uniform, and their father now arrayed as an air raid warden, the war became more real with each passing hour. Mum tried to smooth back his hair and hide the fear that had settled behind her eyes.

FIREWORKS

Throughout June and July, Soviet forces occupied the Baltic states. Lithuania surrendered. Then Latvia and Estonia fell. The sole remaining enemy of the Axis powers now lay across the English Channel. A tense summer dissolved into an exquisite August of clear skies. The city converted public gardens, parks, golf clubs, and tennis courts into stodgy rows of vegetables. Dig for Victory! the signs reminded everyone. Father installed an Anderson shelter made from corrugated steel in their own backyard and covered it over with vegetable starts.

From Normandy, Göring could now train his binoculars in the direction of the English coast with only the oily slick of a channel between them. Luftwaffe bombers could be over London in less than an hour. On the last week of August, the bombing of airfields and factories began—lighting the horizon with sudden, distant flares and glow.

In early September, Louise escaped from Wales for a long weekend visit home. Ida screamed when she opened the door and saw her sister on the other side, grasping her into a tight hug. Friedl and Maria joined them for the evening, and the fears of war retreated as they drank mulled wine, ate Mum's lemon drizzle cake, and listened to Rosa Ponselle and Ezio Pinza records on the gramophone.

"This was the first song Leo and I danced to," Maria said

wistfully as they listened to a quadrille by Johan Strauss. "At the Grand Ball in Vienna."

"What another lifetime that sounds like," Ida said, hugging her.

They had settled in for a long evening of records and conversation, when the sirens came from the east, a long low wail carrying across the city.

Father, who had been out in the garden, came inside. "There may be some fireworks tonight."

Ida went to the windows overlooking the back garden, Louise and the others close behind. On the eastern horizon, a midge-like cloud of fighters rose to the attack. A thud followed by a dull explosion played on repeat, as high explosive bombs showered down over the city. "Those don't look like warehouses," Louise remarked.

"Should we go out to the shelter?" asked Maria.

"I don't think we'll all fit in there," Ida said, gesturing to the metal structure. "And it will take too long to get to a tube station. We're probably better just waiting it out." There had been small skirmishes before, small dog fights hurtling across the sky. But this was a different, playing out on a much larger scale. As darkness fell, slow-moving clouds began massing in the eastern part of the sky. Darkness fell over the city, and a curious red reflection hovered over the city like an aura.

"Why, those aren't clouds at all," said Louise with realization. "It's billowing smoke, rising from a fire."

"The docks are ablaze, I'd guess, from the position of it," said Father.

The red glow and billowing black clouds looked like something out of a film; only this wasn't a Hollywood set, Ida reminded herself. Their cat, Prince Igor, who had no such difficulties keeping that fact straight, set up a plaintive yowl as he tried to climb inside a bottom kitchen cupboard for shelter. "Oh, look at Iggie with the right idea." Ida laughed.

In the distance, a dog began to bark, and others took up the chorus. Sparks and red plumes spiraled through the night as, in the distance, red clouds continued mounting. "Looks like there's nothing for it but for you two to stay the night," Ida told Friedl and Maria. "You can't go home in this. Louise and I will bring our pillows to the living room, and we'll make an evening of it."

Long after midnight, they lay together on the living room carpet, listening to the sounds of explosions overhead, some of them close enough to shake the house. The hurtling of a bomb screamed through space and exploded in the garden of the flat opposite their own. At 24 Morella Road, windows blew in with the tinkling sound of disintegrating glass falling into shards. The scream of the siren was followed by a Spitfire chasing after a Luftwaffe plane. "Is everyone okay?" Ida asked, shaken. Heads nodded all around, as they huddled close, waiting for the endless night to be over.

Louise went over to the gramophone and set Rosa's sumptuous, unhurried voice playing through the darkened house. Somehow the music made the sound of the bombs retreat into the distance, less important and faded.

The all clear finally sounded at 6 am. They sipped down cups of tea and tried to remind themselves it was actually morning. "We'd best start back," Maria said.

"We better walk you part way," Louise insisted, taking her overcoat.

"Be careful," warned Mum.

In the chilly gray dawn, neighbors swept up the mess—calling "you all right?" to them as they passed on the street. Ida followed after her sister, as they walked over slate roof tiles and shining bits of crystal scattered over the pavement. Beyond Morella Road, they stepped onto the streets of London, looking around curiously as if they'd never been there before. As they came through Battersea, dawn rose behind the silhouette of a skeleton, a collapsed and crumbling building hit by a bomb with a single wall standing through the dawn and smoke. They wondered who had been inside, no one wanting to point out that it could easily have been the flat on Morella Road.

The bombers returned that night. And the next and the next.

THE BLITZ

Official government policy forbade the use of tube stations as shelters, but after two weeks of nightly bombings, the public no longer cared what was forbidden, and thousands descended into the caverns with their bedding, flasks of hot tea, cards, and magazines. Below the streets of London, they waited warm and dry, with the sounds of air raids playing in the distance.

Within a few weeks, more than a hundred thousand people were regularly sleeping in the Underground, and the government reversed its policy. They weren't entirely safe, though. Ten days into this blitz on London, Marble Arch Station took a direct hit, crushing twenty people.

London was not Germany's only target. Coventry, Nottingham, Glasgow, Birmingham, and Southampton were also pummeled with incendiaries. Plymouth, Exeter, Sunderland, Bristol, Bath, and Cardiff were hounded by the Luftwaffe fighter bombers. Every decent-sized town in the United Kingdom was soon equipped with air raid sirens that began with a low mechanical whirring building to a shrill, constant cry, rising and falling.

On the walls of boarded-up shop windows, scrawled in paint and chalk were the words that marked the attitude of London: *Business As Usual.*

⋄⸱⸱—⸱⸱⸱——⸱⸱⋄

Within weeks, thousands of London civilians were dead. Thousands more were homeless. They had been killed by high explosive bombs sheering their way through rock walls, turning century-old buildings to rubble. They died from incendiaries that sparked great fire storms of super-heated winds fanning massive walls of flames. Historic churches near St. Paul's Cathedral lay in piles of ruin, and even Westminster Abbey and Buckingham Palace showed signs of damage.

In October, Ida sat down to tea with her parents when the air raid siren sounded. Only a few moments later, an explosion shook the house that sent them all scurrying under the table. When the all clear sounded hours later, Ida went to investigate and found the hulking remains of the nearest railway station. "I think it's time for Mother to leave London," Father said when she returned with her report. "While she still can."

"Why should I leave if you aren't?" Mother protested.

"Papa is a warden, and I can't leave my friends in the flat," said Ida. "But there's no reason for you to stay." She rang up Bill, who had been moved to Devonshire, where he awaited his next assignment.

He arrived in London the next day to fetch his mother back to Devon to wait out the war with friends.

The house seemed empty with only Ida, her father, and poor Iggie for company, but Ida was glad to have her father nearby. For all his ridiculous political predictions, in a real pinch, he unflaggingly remained cool and level-headed. In many ways, there was no one she'd have rather had with her, other than Louise. His work as an air raid warden was serious now, and he returned each morning with tales of devastation from London's East End, which was undoubtably taking the worst of the pounding.

A few days after her mother left, Ida was alone in the house, writing, when the siren sounded. She hurried downstairs, heading for the garden shelter, when a scream overhead told her the planes were coming too fast to make the shelter, so she bolted under the kitchen table instead with Iggie clawing at her legs.

A tearing sound ripped through the air before something hit the ground like a giant mallet. All the front windows blew in and the back windows out, showering glass around her in a rectangle, protected only by the table she knelt under. When the shaking came to a halt, a lovely, weak, thankful feeling washed over her, and she hugged the wretched cat tighter. *Only windows.* They were only windows. The bomb had not fallen on her, though it must have been a direct hit for someone, and not too far away either.

"It's not safe for you here at nights," Father said when he returned home in the morning.

"I won't leave you and Iggie," Ida said, "or the girls at the flat either. But perhaps I ought to volunteer for one of the East End night shelters you keep telling me about. It's better than staying here waiting for one of the incendiaries to pick out our flat."

BERMONDSEY

The Women's Voluntary Service was more than happy to have her as a volunteer, so a few nights later, Ida made her way to a large shelter in Bermondsey between Tower Bridge and the Elephant and

Castle, arriving just as the sirens sounded and the guns started up. A heavy curtain covered the entryway, and Ida realized it was there because sudden shifts in pressure would have blown a door right off its hinges.

Making her way down the dark and damp concrete steps, the smell of cement, disinfectant, coffee, people, piss, and sawdust rose to greet her, along with sweet phrases of Cockney English— her Mum's English still, when she was relaxed with an old friend. Brother shifted to "bruvver," "water" became "wa'er", and she heard "a bit dodgy," "telling porkies," and "fanks."

Ida gazed around in wonder at the little neighborhood they'd created on the underside of the streets—scores of people exchanged greetings and shared supper, while others made up beds, some on hastily constructed frames, and several directly on the cement floor. She adjusted her new Night Watcher pin, feeling both at a loss for what to do, but also like she'd come home. A section set off with heavy sheeting seemed promising, and she rattled one corner in place of a knock. "Hullo? May I come in?"

"'Course you can, duck," came a motherly voice. Ida parted the curtain and found a plump woman in a jumper sorting supplies into crates and parcels. "You're the new night watch? But of course you are. I'm Afton. Afton Foskett."

"Hello, I'm Ida," she said smiling.

"I reckons as 'ow you can find your own way 'bout the shelter. But let's take a looksee, come wiv me, lovey." She led Ida around the space where families were bedding down for the night. "We're mos' of us factory workers during the day, come here at night."

"'Les we've already had our flats buggered off in a raid," a man pulling on old faded slippers interjected.

"True," agreed Afton. To Ida she explained, "You and me, we

gives out hot drinks, aspirin, the odd bandages with a heap of free advice to alls who wants it." She led Ida toward a coffee pot in one corner, where a small group was gathered.

A woman was talking, but she stopped as Ida approached. "Evening," the woman said to them both. "Whole 'ouse came down around our ears, two nights back."

"How dreadful. I'm terribly sorry," Ida said.

"Nevermind. We'll build Bermondsey again after the war, better than it's ever been. See if we don't."

Ida smiled. Above, brazen hordes of Germans might be pounding the island into what they fondly supposed was submission, but here below, this woman knew that eventually the nasty men would stop, and when they did, they'd carry on and rebuild Bermondsey.

"If you're new heres," said a man with a cup of his own, "you dinna see the Queen."

"The Queen?" Ida asked, wondering if he were teasing her.

"Oh, yes!" he nodded smugly, quite serious, and others nodded too. "She visits us a few days back. To build morale. Afton done tole Her Majesty that Nellie there had lost her home, and Nellie says back to the Queen she says, 'It donna matter as long as we beat him." He paused to let that sink in. "She says that to the Queen!"

"And what did Her Majesty say?" Ida asked, properly impressed.

Nellie beamed. "Why, didn't she pats me shoulder and says, 'That's the right spirit!" She absently rubbed the place the Queen had patted as if it might have been a dream.

An elderly grandmother joined in the conversation near her bed. "I helped me sister sweep up remains of our father's old home today. But I says to her: 'Well, Em, we must always remember we'd be much worse off under Hitler.'"

Her little grandson danced by, doing a clever parody of Hitler in a German accent. "I tell you 'zis! We Germans want only peace!" There were smiles and chuckles around the circle.

"Five minutes before lights out!" Afton called out across the cavernous stone structure. "You lot too," she said to the small group near the coffee pot. Then to everyone: "Prayers if you're so inclined." The Hitler mime scampered off to his grand-mum, as parents hushed babies and settled toddlers. The murmur of hundreds of voices began to repeat in the cavernous gloom:

"Our Father which art in heaven, Hallowed be thy name. Thy kingdom come, Thy will be done in earth, as it is in heaven."

The distant sound of bombs began crashing overhead. Children lisped the words in the darkened shelter:

"Forgive us our debts, as we forgive our debtors. And lead us not into temptation, but deliver us from evil: For thine is the kingdom, and the power, and the glory, for ever. Amen."

The lines seemed more poignant than ever before, and Ida remembered her father praying with her before bed.

People settled in, drawing together in clusters, pulling blankets over their bodies, saying good night. A few fussy children cried as their parents tried to hush them toward sleep in this strange new bedroom. A mother sang a lullaby, her voice haunting and simple, echoed on by the walls of concrete: "Lavender's blue, dilly, dilly, lavender's green . . . "

Listening from the curtain of the sick bay, Ida blinked tears away, as hundreds of people turned to their concrete and bedraggled mattresses, a community set on sleep though war raged overhead. Here, beneath the streets of London lay unconscious courage, unselfishness, and blazing confidence no bombing could dim. It seemed to Ida that here, in a cave collapsing into darkness, beat the unconquered heart of Britain.

"Off with you too," Afton said, so Ida lay down in her clothes and tried to ignore the sounds of distant air raids. Eventually, she nodded into an uneasy slumber, but far too soon, Afton gently shook her awake. "Two o'clock. Your turn to watch, duck." Ida drew back the blankets and pulled them back across wooden slats, tugged on her shoes, and yawned her way toward the dim lamp with a chair beyond a partition set out for the night watcher. She tried for a while to read *Mab's Fashions* and crochet a blanket, but then she set down her work and looked around.

From the darkened, cavernous space came the occasional sound of a person mumbling in their sleep, a sleepy giggle, or a snore ranging from basso profundo to coloratura soprano. In gradual crescendos, they continued on, trusting the structures above to hold back the deep and monstrous rising battle. At 5 am, the all clear sounded, and Afton showed Ida how to wake the first shift of workers who needed to depart: an elderly baker, a big kindly fellow who worked at the docks, an energetic grandmother who cleaned offices in the city. Her little grandson who had done the clever Hitler impression the night before grumbled at being wakened, but Ida slipped him a sweet to tease a smile from his face. At 6 am, they lit the lights. People still weary from sleep tried to stretch the stiffness from their bodies as they folded blankets, stowed bundles, and sipped tea from enamel mugs.

Ida made her way home from the East End in a heavy drizzle, noting fresh piles of rubble, with children's toys shattered among the debris. She met her father arriving at Morella Road, and he told her about his night as a fire warden, spying fires around the city. They shared breakfast and Ida mounted the stairs to the attic and seated herself before her typewriter, though exhausted.

She began typing, methodically at first, but then, more

smoothly. As they'd not done for more than a year, the words flowed, inspired and moved by the wonderful people in London below with their will to survive. An elderly baker and an energetic grandmother with a wry little grandson found their way onto her pages, filling her with hope and purpose, refreshing her far more than the missed sleep could have done.

"ROLL OUT THE BARREL"

The next evening, Ida eagerly returned to the Bermondsey shelter and found crates to open, filled with intricate patchwork quilts from the Catskill Mountains. "These are from America?" she asked a teenage girl who helped her unpack them.

"You wouldn't believe how good the Americans have been to us, miss. Bales and bales of stuff, not a rubbishy thing among it. I don't know what we'd have done this last month without the Americans."

Ida thought of Rosa, Lita, and Mitia, of sewing parties in Maine, Connecticut, Boston, and Philadelphia. Beneath the patchwork quilts, slept people who the makers would never see or know, but whose association with America would forever be connected with deft stitches across pieced cotton and snug warmth. She thought of her longing to go there, to hear Rosa sing again, but heard only the constant reverberation of war playing out above.

◇ ·· — ··· — ·· ◇

Over the next month, Bermondsey began to feel like a community. There were grumblings, of course, domestic spats that were impossible not to hear, and wry observations about the reaction from the government if it were the West End being bombed relentlessly every night rather than the less affluent East. The domestics arguments ended naturally enough, though, when the frequency of bomb hits caused the earth to shift strangely beneath them. The sound of death prowling overhead made life seem too precious to fritter away on petty disputes.

The group organized lectures, discussion groups, and a dress-making class. A Bible study was followed by a film show and dart matches. It was the concerts Ida loved more than all else. Impromptu singalongs happened in the middle of particularly nasty air raids when they sang to drown out the sound of screaming notes. Somehow it made the terrors recede to manageable levels when they defiantly bawled: "Daisy, daisy, give me your answer do," in competition with German bombers. They repurposed old songs from the Great War and found that "Roll it out, roll it out, roll out the barrel!" sounded grand accompanied with a gunfire obbligato.

After lights out, there were always a few adults who remained talking quietly on into the night about the war, the latest casualties, the latest homes destroyed. One long night as the place shuddered under assault from above, a woman with her hair tied up in ribbons confided to the circle, "Whenever I feel I can't go on, I think of Mr. Churchill and the weight he carries. And then I feel better. We've only got to hold on."

"But for how long? That's the question." Mrs. Coffee-shop said, and heads nodded in agreement. "I'd feel best abouts it if my hus-bind would come down."

"Why won't he?" Ida asked.

"He would, only he won't leave the dog, he gets frightened, and we can't bring him."

Moments later, an old hop-picker began recounting watch-ing the Battle of Britain from Kent fields: "Falling out of the sky, they was—just falling out of the sky. And often enough, our boys coming down by parachute as their own planes caught on fire. They'd pick themselves up almost before you could ask 'em if they was all right, and off they'd go crying, 'Give me another machine and let me get at 'em again.'" He looked round the circle, shaking his head. "Ah, what boys." Smiles and head shakes spread round the circle. For how could they not be safe with such boys battling for the skies above?

Another old woman had lost both her sons at Dunkirk within three minutes of each other. "One shot through the mouth," she explained. "And his brother, hearing him cry out, goes back for him, and is killed beside him. They was such good boys. Both of them gone." She sniffed and swiped at her eyes. "But there, perhaps it's best that way. They were that fond of each other. My Bill wouldn't have wanted to come home without my Harry." Ida rubbed the woman's shoulder, feeling her own eyes prick for her catastrophic loss. "The sergeant came and told me hisself," the woman continued. "'We know what you're feeling,' he says. 'We been a long time together and we wasn't pals, we was brothers. We couldn't stay to bury them, but we did the best we could, leavin' them side by side, with their hands touching.'" Another swipe, and a look round the circle at a ring of sympathetic faces. "But there," she said, managing a deep breath, "we must all make sacrifices these days."

Ida thought it seemed those in the shelter were making more sacrifices than most. Over the next few weeks and months, she heard stories of families wiped out, of shelters that collapsed under a direct hit. After attending a couple of mass funerals held for residents of whole streets, it began to seem illogical that anyone would still be left alive. They reassured each other with platitudes: "I heard our shelter is particularly safe," one would say, nodding.

"If you can hear it, that's the way you know you'll be fine," another replied.

But catching each other's eyes above the heads of the children, they exchanged glances that said it was, all of it, utter nonsense. No one was safe. Not here, not anywhere in London. No one was fine, and they would not be fine for some time to come—months, years, decades? Until sometime after this madness stopped, this reality as harsh and constant as the smell of sulfur and gritty particulate suspended in the air.

Sometimes the raids started up during moments of relative quiet, and there was nothing to do but listen to the sounds of bombers diving to attack. There would come a screaming note, melancholy as a banshee wail, then a nerve-rasping warning, as people pretended it wasn't happening, their sentences tailing off into futile banalities. For one moment of fatal certainty, Ida would brace herself, knowing this was their bomb, their shelter, their death—just before a fearful thud came a blessed distance away and flooded her with guilt at the realization it meant death to someone else. The relief washed in waves before it happened all over again.

When she left in the mornings to walk home, there was a tinkling of broken glass underfoot, and the unnatural crunch of roof slates as she passed buildings that had been solid last night and now held ragged holes through which she could see the pale light of morning.

"WE'LL MEET AGAIN"

Ida arrived one evening to find the shelter buzzing with excitement. Four men were hauling a piano down into the depths, laughing as they brought it along, children scurrying out of their way. Vera Lynn was a popular singer who regularly performed in London's West End, and now she was going from shelter to shelter, aiding the war efforts by toughening morale.

Vera arrived wearing a pressed gingham skirt, her hair curled and jaunty. Perching herself on a stool as the accompanist ran his hands up the keyboard, she pulled them all into her song. Vera sang. They sang together. And the accompanist played on, plunking out songs Ida distantly remembered from childhood. "Pack up your troubles," turned to "There's a long, long trail," which became "Keep the home fires burning." The same words had once been sung by khaki columns of soldiers marching through Belgium and France in 1914, and now the children of those men, sang the words anew.

"While there's a Lucifer to light your fag, smile boys, that's the style," the audience bellowed.

Vera asked the group to choose a song, and they called out for her most popular. "We'll meet again," she began to croon. "Don't know where, don't know when, but I know we'll meet again some sunny day."

Children dandled on the laps of people who took a stubborn delight in not only surviving an air raid, but in lustily bellowing their way through it. Watching their faces reminded Ida of the first time she'd heard Rosa sing.

This was romance as a distraction from war hammered out on a battered old piano. On all the faces shone the human capacity for art to lift others entirely out of this world and into another. There among the East Londoners, singing as loud as she could, Ida very nearly forgot her longing for Mum and Louise, the gnawing fears that stalked her waking hours and her ever-dwindling bank account.

INCENDIARIES

In mid-November, the incendiary bombs came. Their cast iron noses were designed to pierce through roof tiles and spew flaming thermite sure to catch curtains and carpets on fire. Government instructive films showed a young woman pouring buckets of water on a bomb that had fallen into her living room. Signs went up around the city: "If you find a bomb soon after it has fallen, you can put it in a bucket of water. If no water is available, smother it with a quantity of sand."

The city of Coventry was leveled by ten thousand incendiaries with such destruction that people began using the name of the city as a verb—meaning to achieve complete destruction: "to Coventrate."

BRISTOL BLENHEIM

Ida received news that Peter Bailey had been shot down in North Africa when his Bristol Blenheim—with its all-metal, stressed-skin construction, powered-gun turret, and variable-pitch propellers—could not hold up under the fire of a Messerschmitt Bf 109. Its liquid-cooled, inverted V-12 aero engine carried an MG 17 machine gun that dropped 7.9 caliber of encapsulated lead through its belt at a rate of 1200 rpm.

Though it had been years since she'd thought of him romantically, for weeks and months after she'd received the news, Ida dreamt of his plane, hit, freewheeling through the sky, plunging into the sand of the Libyan desert in a gorgeous explosion.

There was nothing left of him to send home to his mother. Ida sensed great sands shifting within her, barren, dry and rainless.

WILDERNESS

"Seems it'll be a lively night," Afton observed dryly when she came to wake Ida for her watch, though Ida had long given up the idea of sleep for the night.

Ida pulled herself out of bed and drank some coffee. The sirens had gone off hours before, and now, when bombing would typically begin letting up, the frequency only seemed to be escalating. The pummeling came again and again, shaking the very bowels of the earth. Ida struggled to read a newspaper, realizing her eyes had passed over the same line several times before she set it down. The bombs were so intense, so close, that the tarpaulin over the doorway was lifted almost to the ceiling again and again by the force of the blasts. The sound of muffled sobbing came from a darkened corner of the shelter.

Finally, near 4 am, a momentary lull fell upon the city, and Ida hesitantly ascended the steps. A fire warden near the top beckoned her closer. "May I take a look?" she asked.

He nodded. "Go ahead, I think the worst is finally over."

Pulling back the edge of the tarpaulin, Ida sucked in her breath at the sight of the smoldering remains of London bathed in a warm, eerie glow. The light cast upon the remaining stone skyline didn't come from the moon obscured by smoke and haze or from an early dawn's sun—the city was lit by *firelight* on a colossal scale. London lay before them, smoking and twisted, transformed by war into an unrecognizable landscape of Mars. Ida drew back to the darkness, beating a soft retreat from the doomsday apocalypse above.

Shortly after dawn, the fire wardens announced to the entire shelter that it was safe to leave, if such places as home and work still existed. "Do you know if 23 Ettrick Street is still standing?" a man asked the warden.

"Unlikely, sir," came the kindly reply. "That entire neighborhood was badly hit last night."

The man's wife began to cry. "That's our home, gone too, then. And just before Christmas."

The man hugged her fiercely. "Never mind, then. Here we are, love. Here we are."

When Ida finally stepped outside the shelter, she felt as if she'd been plucked up in the night and set down in a totally unfamiliar part of town. The skyline had shifted dramatically. Picking her way homeward through the rubble, the acrid smell of burning stung her lungs. The last of the book publishing centres had been hit, the warden said, and as Ida walked homeward, bits of charred paper swirled down through the sky.

She turned up Morella Road and breathed a sigh of relief to find the row of familiar houses still standing. Louise and mother were due home in a few days' time. Ida went out into the back garden as still the ash fell, as silent as snow—fragments of a million exploded books sifting down upon the city.

One charred sheet, still nearly complete, bent in the breeze above, floating into the garden. In wonder, Ida reached for it, scanning the lines. It was a page from some ancient Bible. From Jeremiah, she read: "I will make thee a wilderness, and cities which are not inhabited. And I will prepare destroyers against thee, everyone with his weapons." She barely had time to skim the phrases before the sheet disintegrated into fragments in her hand.

The shrill ring of a telephone called her into the house.

Friedl's frantic voice waited on the other side of the line.

"It's Maria and Irma," Ida could barely make out. "Caught in the raid." Friedl choked. "At hospital."[40]

"Which one?" Ida cried.

"St. Thomas's."

"I'll come right away."

Ignoring her rumpled clothes and intense exhaustion, Ida ran down the front steps, frantically considering the fastest way to Westminster. The thought of waiting for a jolting bus seemed impossible, so she rushed down the pavement, shoes clapping, relieved by the movement, willing her body to forget she hadn't slept the night before.

Such a scene of devastation surrounded the blocks around the hospital it seemed surprising anyone had survived. Ida scurried up the steps of the brick building with its white, tile-clad arches, rushed inside, and gave her name to the attendant.

Friedl was waiting, tears streaking her red cheeks. They had to wait, then, holding each other until the nurse said they could enter Maria's room. They found her lying in bed, bandaged from head to foot, moving with repeated and frantic agitation. Her arm was suspended from above, her face almost completely obscured.

Ida and Friedl approached, softly calling her name, but Maria's confused eyes registered no recognition. Friedl collapsed into tears.

"Speak to her," a nurse hovering nearby encouraged. "See if you can hold her attention and persuade her to rest. We haven't been able to manage it."

"Maria, dear," Ida said, through her tears. "It's me, Ida. And Friedl is here with me too. Can you hear us?"

"We're right here, love," Friedl added.

There was a moan in response. A nonsensical muttering.

Ida wracked her brain, wondering how to get through. "Maria,"

Ida tried again, "try to go to sleep and dream of dancing with Leo to Strauss' quadrille—you remember?" She began humming the tune. "Bah bah ba, bah bah ba, bah—"

Maria stopped moving her bandaged head, and a muffled sound emerged from the wrappings.

Ida repeated the tune. There was a long pause, then Maria's balled-up fists relaxed a bit against the coverlet. Ida gently let her hand rest upon the two exposed fingers. She continued, still humming.

"Thank you," said the nurse. "You've done the trick." After a long moment, they edged back toward the door, trying to stop the flow of tears.

Irma Bauer lay a few doors away, in similar condition, though one eye was useable through the bandages. She opened that eye wearily as they approached, and she seemed to recognize them for a moment.

"Dear Irma," Ida said. "It's me, Ida. And Friedl is here to see you too. I'm sure they told you, your daughter is only a few doors away."

"Maria, yes," said Irma, nodding imperceptibly. She muttered something. "And Ezra? Where is Ezra?"

Friedl's grip tightened on Ida's hand. She was calling out for her husband. "Still in Germany, I'm afraid, love," Ida wanted to choke on the words as she said them. How terribly unfair that after everything, they had now been caught in a London bombing. If only they'd been able to get to away to Brazil before the bombs had begun.

"Leo," Irma mumbled. "Leo will worry about my Maria."

"We'll telegram him," Friedl promised.

"It's best if she rests now," the nurse told them, and they nodded.

"We'll be back to see you tomorrow, dear."

Friedl and Ida leaned into each other as they passed through the hallway and back into the street, dashing away tears. "See you tomorrow?" Friedl asked when they'd reached the street.

Ida nodded.

"And the day after?"

"And the day after that. And as many days at it takes us to bring them home."

FROM THE ASH

Ida climbed through rubble strewn streets just beginning to be swept up the next morning, trying not to think about the fact that Louise and her mother had decided not to come home for Christmas given the level of destruction in the city. What a cold and lonely Christmas it would be this year.

She met Friedl at the entrance, and they made their way inside, stopping short in front of the waiting attendant, who met them as they walked through the door. "I'm dreadfully sorry," the woman said, her face fully of sympathy and agitation. "We were just about to telephone." She kept her voice calm and steady, as if she had done this many times before.

"What happened?" Ida managed, reaching for Friedl's hand.

"I'm afraid Irma Bauer's injuries were too severe," the woman explained. "She has passed on, just moments before you arrived."

She couldn't be gone, that sweet old woman they'd just spoken with the day before. She'd seemed out of danger. Ida cried out, "Does Maria know?"

The attendant shook her head. "She's not been conscious enough to tell her. Do you know any next of kin we should notify?"

Ida shook her head. "Not outside of labor camps in Germany."

271

The woman's face creased in genuine sympathy. "I'm so sorry," she said.

They made their way to Maria and found her much the same: bandaged from head to toe, her eyes still covered. This time, she didn't respond to anything they said. Ida hummed the tune again but received no response.

"She seemed calmer after you left yesterday," the nurse told them. "Even if she doesn't respond, it helps to hear your voices."

"Considering everything," Ida said. "It's much better for her to sleep."

They made arrangements for a simple burial for Irma, wondering if Maria would know her mother was gone by the time she was laid to rest. Friedl and Ida said goodbye again outside the hospital, hugging each other close before the sheer frailty of life.

Turning away, Ida wandered home through streets of devastation and debris, as a soggy, sodden rain descended over London's freshly bombed streets. Freed for the first time from her thoughts, Ida truly began to take in the destruction of the city. Piles of plaster, shredded timbers and bricks, whole walls. These had all been flung onto the streets and had to be navigated around. Row houses with their ends sheared off met buses that had been flung upside down by a giant's hand as easily as a child knocks down a stack of blocks. She made her way past smouldering ruins, still smoking, as people in overcoats pushed prams past the mess or tried to navigate it by way of bicycle. Skeletons of twisted steel support beams raked the sky. Whole streets had been reduced to rubble, the concrete thrown about like sheaves of paper.

Passing close by a shattered home, Ida noticed photographs and broken ornaments among the ruin. Bits of furniture, books, papers, clothes—all rain soaked and horribly familiar. An engraving of Earl

Kitchener greeting someone that once had hung on a sitting room wall, now lay exposed to rain and snow.

She felt an oddly uncomfortable sense of voyeurism, looking over the personal items.

From the uninhabited shell of a demolished building, came the sound of a voice speaking. Ida stopped on the ruined street, in the gray chill of the December afternoon for one frantic moment, wondering if someone needed help. The voice was coming from the basement of the deserted house and Ida called out, panicked.

The voice continued and, finally, she realized it didn't come from a survivor, but a *radio*—still operating from the ruins of the bombed-out building, broadcasting a voice that had become entwined with the struggle faced by the nation and the world. Winston Churchill's Christmas address was winding to a close: "Let the children have their night of fun and laughter," he said from the ruins. "Let the gifts of Father Christmas delight their play." His voice was tinny and faint from the depths of the fallout, but unmistakable. She stopped, short, to listen to his message:

> Let us grown-ups share to the full in their unstinted pleasures before we turn again to the stern task and the formidable years that lie before us, resolved that, by our sacrifice and daring, these same children shall not be robbed of their inheritance or denied their right to live in a free and decent world.[41]

Though the gray drizzle soaked her wool coat as she stood on the deserted, smoking street, Ida stood still, choking back tears.

"And so, in God's mercy," Churchill said, "a happy Christmas to you all." A reed band with horns and basses started up then, a modulating brass fanfare of rising arpeggios. The sweeping strains of Britain's national anthem rose from the smoking wreckage. Ida began humming the verse that had always been her favorite and had never seemed more relevant:

> *God bless our native land!*
> *May Heav'n's protecting hand*
> *Still guard our shore:*
> *May peace her power extend,*
> *Foe be transformed to friend,*
> *And Britain's rights depend*
> *On war no more.*[42]

The sound of the battered, faint music filled her with emotion and her eyes spilled over at last. It would still be a cheerless Christmas. Her mother and Louise and brothers were far from home. Dear Maria still lay in hospital, dear Irma had passed on, and so many others were trapped in Germany. She barely had a penny to her name, and the street stretched before her, a bombed and smoking ruin.

But somewhere beneath the rubble, from the very ashes of devastation, the heart of Britain rose, and would beat on. Where there seemed to be only ruin and destruction, life and hope waited to rise. Ida wiped away tears, straightened her shoulders, readjusted her bag, and continued down the debris strewn pavement.

LA VESTALE

Weeks later, Ida walked the same route in reverse, noticing the clean-up crews' attempts to remove the rubble, though full repairs would take years. She and Friedl had visited Maria every day, though she remained unresponsive. Today, as Ida hurried toward the building, she tried to push aside the weight of bills and notices pressing upon her. *Eight pounds.* She owed eight pounds, and she didn't want to bother family over it either. She'd been racking her brain trying to figure it out. Two pounds support promised to Alice Gerstel in West Yorkshire, three pounds for Theo's hosts, ten pounds for the flat. She'd borrowed hundreds of pounds for the refugee work—everything that had been allowed. And then she'd promised half her income for maintenance for refugees who were unable to support themselves. There was simply nothing left.

As she hurried up the wide hospital steps, she pushed the gnawing worry from her mind. She must concentrate on Maria, who had bigger things to worry about. Ida forced a smile for the nurses and made her way to Maria's room. She stopped at the open door, shocked to see Maria with one eye uncovered and—open. "Oh! You're awake!" Ida rushed to her. "Dear, I can't tell you how happy I am to see you looking at me!"

The edges of Maria's mouth moved faintly.

"Can you hear me?"

She blinked. "Hello . . . Ida." Her voice sounded dusty from long lack of use, but the words were unmistakable.

A nurse hovered nearby. "She just woke up," she explained. "Not more than an hour ago." She gestured for Ida to remain calm. "Maria, Ida and Friedl have been to see you every day since the accident."

Maria looked up at her friend with quiet appreciation. "Thank you," she said, squeezing Ida's hand. She struggled to say more. ". . . where's Mother?"

Ida raised agonized eyes to the nurse. Should they tell her? What if the shock were too much? The nurse, understanding, nodded. Ida knelt down and took both her friend's hands in her own.

"Darling, I'm so terribly sorry, but your sweet mother didn't make it. She died quite peacefully from her injuries, right here at the hospital. I saw her before she passed, and her last words were about you."

Shock covered Maria's face, but she said nothing, processing.

"You buried her?"

"We had to, I'm afraid. We had a local rabbi help, but we were waiting for you for the memorial service. We'll do it however you like."

Tears clouded Maria's eye, and she grasped Ida's hand more tightly. "Thank you. My only family is in Brazil now . . . and maybe Germany."

"And right here in London," Ida said. "Me, Louise, and Friedl—we're right here."

"Yes," Maria replied softly. "Here too."

"When you're feeling better and a bit stronger, we'll have the memorial service, just as she would want it."

Maria rasped. "In a synagogue?"

"Of course. The best synagogue in London."

Maria nodded slightly. "I didn't want to leave her behind," she said, tearing up again.

"And you didn't," Ida answered. "She died free."

"I have so few items left. So little left." Maria lapsed into silence, tears silently descending the contours of her bandaged face as she clung to Ida's hand. After several minutes, she said, "Ida, there's something else, worrying me. It's silly."

"What is it, dear one?"

"The nurse put my things there." She gestured. "Some of the money you gave us is in my purse, but I don't need it here. I don't want to lose it. Could you take care of it for me?"

Ida laughed a bit hysterically. "I will gladly help keep it safe. May I please borrow eight pounds of it? I'm in an awful jam."

"Borrow the lot if you like," Maria replied. "I shan't need it for some time, I wouldn't think."

"Thank you so much, dear."

Ida walked home thinking about friends who become as good as family and a God who provides when all seemed lost.

◇ · · — · · · — · · ◇

Maria would never have full use of one eye again, and her right arm would bear the scars forever. After another month, the doctors transferred her to a hospital further away for reconstructive surgery, and Ida had to ring her up every few days instead of visiting.

One day when Friedl and Ida were in the parlor at 24 Morella Road, listening to records, they rang Maria. "Wait a moment," Ida told her. "We think you would like to hear this."

Friedl placed Rosa Ponselle's *La Vestale* on the gramophone. The supreme beauty of the sound filled the flat, poured out into the war-dusted street, and carried through the receiver all the way across town to Maria's hospital room.

"It's so beautiful," Maria said when they had finished. "There is still sublime beauty in the world. Thank you for reminding me."

V FOR VICTORY

The rains of winter passed into spring, as flowers struggled to come up in the smoky haze of war-torn London. Winston Churchill began raising two fingers in the shape of a V to signify "Victory!" Soon, Londoners flashed the two-fingered slogan everywhere, and Vs were painted in bright slashes on street corners and in tube

277

stations. Much more dangerously, they also appeared throughout occupied France.

Someone cleverly pointed out that the letter V in Morse code was three dots and a dash: da-da-da-DAH, just like the opening notes of Beethoven's fifth symphony. Soon these notes were played on the timpani for station identification on all BBC broadcasts to Europe. "The symbol of the unconquerable will of the people," Churchill called the rallying cry.

WAR TIME WEDDING

Friedl married her Italian soldier, at long last, in the middle of an air raid. They scrounged up flowers, a little bit of flour and butter to make the semblance of a cake, and drew lines of eyeliner up the back of their legs to pass for stockings. Maria sat beside Ida, her arm bandaged, and though there were no ringing church bells since they were saved for a land invasion, Ida thought the joyous celebration still seemed like an open defiance against Hitler. Despite his air assaults, a Jewish girl and her lover could still exchange vows surrounded by friends and family. She helped throw blossoms and rice like a benediction before the couple dashed off for a few days' honeymoon in Southampton.

FISSURES

In the shelters of London, life continued with lectures, concerts, and quibbling over space and belongings. The air raids ranged from brief to endless affairs, when they had no idea if they would live to see the morning. One April night, Afton woke Ida for her shift. "It's a bit blitzy up there tonight," she warned.

Ida rose and tried to settle in the chair. Desperate thudding came from above. Scudding shells landed quite close, rumbling through her feet like a tremor through the foundations of the earth. A nearby building sheared apart, and more than one person screamed involuntarily. A fire guard who came down hourly to report on the situation above snapped at Ida to shut off her light.

"How goes it, sir?" she asked, as she extinguished her lantern.

"It's a bad night for casualties, be glad you're down here," he replied.

She shuddered at the ripping sounds of mortar and shattering masonry from above. *I shall never see Mother again, nor Louise,* Ida thought, trying to shake off the conviction she wouldn't live to morning. *I shall never hear Rosa sing again.*

A woman reaching for the coffee pot next to Ida's shoulder overheard the fire guard's remark. "You can buy fresh homes, but you can't bring back dead people," she observed.

Just then, a wild shriek from a descending bomber thundered through the shelter, followed by the whizzing descent of a bomb. Ida braced herself for the final thud, which seemed to hit right over their heads. Time held suspended, then came the new and terrifying sound of masonry crashing overhead for endless, horrible moments. Shrieks, gasps, and screams came from the darkened corners of the shelter, as children cried and called out for their parents.

Ida darted beneath her chair, wondering if the roof would hold. Massive groans and shifting came from the darkness as falling plaster pelted her arms and dust choked her throat. More screams from the darkness.

"A wall has collapsed!" someone cried. From the darkness, came sounds of agony. Torches flashed on, lighting the space in disjointed patches. A wall had collapsed, tumbled inward, blocking off a doorway and trapping people beneath the rubble on the other side of a new gaping hole. Fire wardens rushed from above, scurrying toward the collapsed portion. A boy of nineteen who sometimes played the piano accordion scampered into the opening, torch in hand, looking for survivors.

Flashes of light. Groans of pain. The boy re-emerged, carrying a woman bleeding from her head and covered with masonry dust. From the shelter side of the opening, people reached for the woman, carrying her down the rubble pile and over to Ida and Afton, who lay her on a cot and began bandaging her wounds.

There were others. A man whose hand had been sliced by a falling beam, a little girl whose foot had been crushed and would need to go to hospital. Her mother had been the first carried out. They were, all of them, covered from head to toe in layers of thick dust. Afton and Ida wiped their faces, bandaged their wounds, and made coffee while assuring them they were still alive, and that the ceiling, for now, held. They did not say, of course, that this meant it would go on holding.

When all the injured had been helped out, the piano accordion player joined Ida's little circle, taking the coffee cup she offered with shaking hands. "You were the first in," Ida told him. "Very brave of you."

"First thing, I sees a woman quite dead," he admitted quietly. "Me stomach came up and hit the roof of me mouth. I'll never be nearer to heaven than I was tonight. I almost heard them harps playing."

Ida nodded shakily. When the dawn rose at last, she gathered her things and prepared to face the streets. "Be careful out there," the warden warned her as she left. "Last night they dropped eight hundred tonnes of bombs on us. Westminster Abbey is damaged and the House of Commons has been destroyed. A third of London streets are now impassable."[43]

Ida struggled home through an unfamiliar landscape, making her way through a smoking London filled with fresh jagged piles of rubble. As she turned up Park Lane, a riot of purple, white, and golden crocuses confronted her, somehow, incredibly, unmarred by all the trenches and bombs. The sun rose into a sky of patched blue beyond the billowing pyres of bombed carcasses. Relief washed over Ida, mingled with a strange and manic joy that she could have been killed but had lived instead. Still here to see this incongruous and raucous spring rained down on with ashes.

LOUISE

By summer it became clear that Hitler's bombing routines over London had dwindled to a minor tantrum. To everyone's surprise, Stalin's most of all, Hitler tore up his non-aggression treaty with Russia and diverted his forces away from England. Britain heaved a sigh of relief. Mother came home. Ida hugged her close, breathing in the familiar smell of her, feeling the sweet release of tears. But when Louise arrived, Ida held her sister close and couldn't stop laughing. "There's *always* Rosa," Ida said, holding her close.

"Except there isn't anymore," Louise said practically, hugging her back just as fiercely. "Rosa's gotten married and gone and retired from the stage. Lita is retired too."

"We'll never hear either of them sing again," Ida said sadly, tracing her sister's cheek, feeling as though she were a whole person again for the first time in more than a year. "Nothing has worked out like I thought it would."

"We can't go back to that past," Louise said, still hugging. "Only forward."

"Oh, Louise," said Ida. "I feel like the worst of the war, for me, is over. Rosa or no Rosa, I can't tell you how awfully glad I am to have you home."

AMERICA CALLS

DECEMBER 7, 1941

At 7:02 am, young soldiers George Elliott and Joseph Lockard on Kahuku Point were monitoring the radar on the north coast of Oahu when they picked up the signal of dozens of approaching planes. Private Elliott looked over, concerned, but Private Lockard only shrugged. "It's probably nothing. We're going to miss breakfast."

Elliott called the Information Center at Fort Shafter in Honolulu just to be safe. "Don't worry about it," Lieutenant Kermit Tyler told him. "We're expecting a dozen planes from San Francisco."

"It looks bigger than that," said Elliott, recalling the shape of the blip.

"It's nothing," came the reply.

At 8 am, 79 Japanese fighter jets descended from the skies, followed by 40 torpedo planes, 103 level bombers, 131 dive bombers, and 35 submarines. An 1,800-pound bomb smashed through the deck of the USS *Arizona*, which exploded and sank with more than one thousand men trapped inside. Torpedoes pierced the hull of the USS *Oklahoma*. With four hundred sailors aboard, the *Oklahoma* rolled onto her side and slipped under the water. Within two hours, the Japanese fleet had killed more than two thousand Americans and decimated a fleet of airplanes left out on a runway. Ships and destroyers lay shattered about Pearl Harbor, turned to flotsam floating beneath the glinting rays of the Hawaiian sun.

Franklin D. Roosevelt called the Pearl Harbor attack a date which would "live in infamy."

"No matter how long it may take us to overcome this premeditated invasion," he promised, "the American people in their righteous might will win through to absolute victory. . . . [we] will make it very certain that this form of treachery shall never again endanger us."

When the United States declared war on Japan, and Hitler declared war on the United States just days later, Britain breathed a long sigh of relief. At last. At long last they were no longer standing alone.

A month later, the first American forces landed on British soil. For the first time, Hitler began to seem vulnerable.

NORMANDY

JUNE 6, 1944

Carried on a rising tide and guided by the light of a full moon, battleships, cruisers, and destroyers crossed the gray, tumultuous Channel in the early hours before dawn. The warships neared the coastline and deposited more than a hundred thousand Allied soldiers across five beaches in occupied Normandy. Released at the high-tide mark, soldiers met with hidden landmines, tangles of barbed wire, and metal tripods. But most of the soldiers navigated the obstacles, and pressed on, ever inland. Within a week, the five beaches had been combined, and the Allies held territory in France once more.

Perhaps. Perhaps, then, the end was in sight. London raised its battered head, proud that many buildings turned to rubble had already been rebuilt, with a firm look to a time that must exist beyond this one.

The Allied spy network began warning the Brits to expect a reprisal from Adolf Hitler. Vague rumors of secret vengeance weapons intended for London made their way along the channels, and people walking streets that had only just been swept clean cast their eyes skyward and wondered how much more the city could take.

RETALIATION

In the predawn hours of June 13, 1944, the staccato throb of a V-1 rocket engine shattered the city's early morning silence. Seconds of terror followed, then the warhead exploded. The air raid sirens began blaring, announcing the first bombs released on London since the Blitz. Searchlights crossed purposefully under the low, cloudy sky. A warning wail announced approaching enemy planes, followed by the sound of antiaircraft fire. London listened ominously to the clatter of the Bofors rather than the heavy boom of antiaircraft that tackled high flying bombers. Wherever they were, people stopped to listen.[44]

These new, unmanned flying bombs—the V-1—fired from Nazi-occupied French coasts approached at incredible speed, a short trail of brilliant flame tracking their path across the sky. With their bullet-pointed noses, the bombs dove diagonally toward the earth as the reverberating throb of an engine sputtering out led to seconds of silence, followed by ear-shattering explosions. Every antiaircraft gun in southeast London blazed hopelessly away at the "buzz bombs"—or "doodlebugs," as some called them—falling on barracks, depots, arsenals, and dockyards. There came the shudder of buildings, the crash of falling glass, the sharp chink of shrapnel falling on roofs and roadways, and the clanging of civilian fire engine bells—a cacophonous symphony played on repeat as night dragged on toward dawn.

DOODLEBUGS

Ida was more scared of the flying bombs than she'd been of the incendiaries because victory was in sight and the thought of being killed now seemed unbearable. In rare moments, they'd each begun cautiously thinking of a future beyond the war, and they couldn't bear the idea that it might still be snatched away. One night, Mum and Dad made it to the Anderson shelter out back at the first sound of the air raid sirens, but Ida and Louise were still rushing down the stairs at the sound of the first explosion. They darted under the dining room table, side by side, trying to coax Igor to join them.

Doodlebugs whirred overhead, their deep-throated whirring descending in pitch, growing louder with the pulsejet engines. The all clear siren was followed almost immediately by another warning. Hours after the attack commenced, the antiaircraft guns gradually fell silent as each battery used up its supply or became too hot to fire.

Bombs came in groups of five, each one closer than the one before. Still crouching under the table, they held their breath until the fifth one, listening as it passed over. If the engine stopped, they knew it was about to crash and explode. From under the table, Ida sent up an unholy silent prayer that it would land on someone else's home.

There was a pop of explosion, like the backfiring of a car followed by a loud and rattling noise. Sick of hiding, of bombs and air raids, Ida held onto her sister. "If we live to see the end of this war," she shouted above the din, "you and I are still going back to America!" The pulsejet engines grew louder like an overwrought hoover. "We'll do ourselves well over everything!"

Louise clutched her knees. "Will we?"

"Yes! We'll go to California and see Lita and maybe, somehow, find Rosa, even if only to stand in front of her and look at her!" Ida insisted fiercely. The ack-ack of antiaircraft drowned out Ida's words, and Igor yowled.

Louise grabbed him firmly and pulled him under the table with them. "How soon after the end of the war do you think we can go?"

"The first minute they open travel again."

Defiantly, Ida rushed out from under the table and put Rosa's record on the gramophone, set the needle down, and sent her glorious voice ringing through the flat.

"You better write some more books," Louise advised.

They both jumped at a flash of explosion, of ornamental masonry shooting skywards, accompanied by a boom of explosion. The ground shook beneath their knees, but for one moment, none of it mattered. With her sister's arms around her and Rosa's voice in her ears, the sounds of war retreated and Ida could picture America, the Metropolitan opera, and Rosa. Beautiful Rosa, singing. It was so real, it felt nearly like she could smell the flowers of her bouquet.

Hitler couldn't hold out forever. It was only a matter of time.

BLOOD FOR TRUCKS

Sixty-two railway trucks filled with Jewish children left Hungary bound for an unknown destination in Polish Galicia. Even as the tide of the war turned against them, the German army continued removing Jews from Hungary, where the largest Jewish population left in Europe remained. The Pope, the king of Sweden, and President Roosevelt clambered for the Hungarian regent to intervene. In response, Adolf Eichmann proposed to hand over one million Hungarian Jews to the Allies in exchange for ten thousand trucks, plus tea, coffee, and military equipment. The British media marveled at a nation that would propose exchanging Jews for Lorries and vowed to keep fighting on.

THE CAMPS

That summer, two inmates escaped from Auschwitz to Slovakia. Leaders of the Jewish community compiled testimonies and a report detailing the systematic murdering of Jews, including the use of gas chambers and the incineration of thousands of bodies. The report was so gruesome, many refused to believe it. In July, Soviet troops liberated the first concentration camp at Majdanek, freeing five hundred prisoners and occupying Lublin. What they saw behind the camp's barbed wire, confirmed the testimonies of the men who had escaped Auschwitz. Forced labor camps had been transformed into centers for mass annihilation where children were killed in front of their mothers and prisoners were forced to engage in deadly sports. Typhus epidemics ran rampant through the camps, while soldiers machine gunned people into trenches, forcing them to kneel down on warm corpses and wait to be shot. Dance music blasted from loudspeakers was used to drown out the sound of machine guns and murder.

EVACUATION

In August, Charles de Gaulle went to Paris and received the document signed by the German commander agreeing to give up the garrison. Parisianers ran from their houses, flooding the streets to meet the triumphant troops and welcome de Gaulle home as a hero. "Paris has been liberated," the BBC announced.

From the ports in Holland and Calais, though, the bomb attacks on London continued. V-2 buzz bombs replaced the V-1s, travelling faster than the speed of sound, so the projectile appeared out of nowhere, the explosions heard only *after* they landed, leaving sixty-foot craters in their wake.

Walking through the streets of London each morning, Louise found fresh mounds of rubble and gaping chasms.

When she arrived home one evening after navigating around several wreckages, she told Ida, "Did you see they bombed Clapham Commons? I think we really must send the parents away."

"Right," said Ida. "Where can we send them?"

"Remember your old school chum Saanvi Patel in Northumberland? She might have space, mightn't she?"

"It's worth a try."

Ida sent off a telegraph and received a prompt reply from Saanvi the next day: "We've seen the photographs. Have them come to us now."

Their parents protested only feebly. "And what about the two of you?" Mum asked. "You're not any safer than we are."

"Hitler cannot hold out much longer," Ida said, reassuringly. "We can't leave our work, or Maria either. We'll be all right, Mum. We'll all sleep better knowing you are safe."

Their father found someone to cover his night shifts as air warden, and Ida and Louise bundled them off to the train station the next morning, feeling the oddness of reversed parenting roles. They both breathed a sigh of relief as the train pulled away from the platform. Louise headed to her office, while Ida headed for the publishing house. She was still out when the sirens started up again, and she headed to a public shelter to wait for the all clear.

Hours later, as dusk began falling, Ida headed home alone. As she neared Morella Road, she met scenes of more and more devastation. *It must have been close this time*, she thought, hurrying her pace. Turning onto the street, she traced the familiar roof lines, but where the rowhouses had once continued complete, there remained now a massive pile of rubble and a crater, eight rowhouses missing from view.

Panicked, Ida hurried onward, counting the homes of neighbors, turning the final corner to find a splendid disaster of bricks and slate all over the street.

Ida began to run. *What about Louise,* she thought, icy with panic. *Had she been home?* Scarcely daring to look, Ida strained to see through the dimming light and haze of rubble-filled air. Someone stood outside the house, on their front doorstep. "Mrs. Beer!" Ida cried. Her mum's best friend. And someone else standing beside her.

They turned at the sound of her voice. By her side stood Louise looking mildly annoyed. "Louise!" Ida cried hysterically, closing the space between them and grabbing her tight. "Oh, Louise, I didn't know. I wasn't sure."

"I'm fine, Ida," Louise said, hugging her back. "I was worried about you too. We've been bombed, as you can see. But never mind the house. Igor is missing."

Ida laughed at her sister's utterly practical announcement. "Oh, poor Iggie! Do you suppose he's buried in there? It's too dreadful to think of it."

"And here's our dear Mrs. Beer, come to make sure there were no looters."

"There's me ducks," Mrs. Beer clucked affectionately. The front door of the house hung open into the plaster-strewn hall. The front room looked fairly intact, though lacking windows for the third time now. Where there had once been a proper back to the house, now stood gaping walls, torn away like paper in more than one place.

"And to think we only just sent off Mum and Dad!" Ida said, marveling. "They could have been here!"

"That's Providence, that," Mrs. Beer said thankfully. They climbed the steps and entered the plaster-strewn hall. Everything was covered in a thick layer of dust, photos had fallen off the wall, and Mother's vases had knocked over and shattered. In the kitchen, a gaping hole now opened onto the back garden. "You look for Igor and fetch anything salvageable from upstairs," Mrs. Beer said. "I'll grab me husband so he can re-hang the doors and board up the windows before it gets completely dark. I'll bring a torch as well." She didn't wait for a response before she darted off down the street.

"What a gem she is," Ida said as she retreated. They pushed inside, moving things aside, past doors that had been blown apart, navigating the stove tipped sideways and piles of splintered furniture. "Mother's table," Ida said mournfully.

Louise picked up a broom and began to sweep the hall.

Ida laughed at the utter futility of her sister's action. "You've quite a job for yourself there."

"We can at least have one room clean," said Louise.

"Do you suppose it's safe to go upstairs and fetch our things?"

"I imagine so, so long as you don't run out a hole in the back wall."

Ida gingerly climbed the stairs. "Igor!" she called, trying to stay hopeful. She fetched a basket, dusted it off, and threw some clothes inside, trying not to look at the mass of rubble in the room across the hallway. She tossed in shoes and dresses, pajamas, a brush, and makeup, all covered in debris, but useable. *Where could they go?* She thought of the Bermondsey shelter couple hugging each other. "We're right here," they'd said. Well, she and Louise were still right here though so many others weren't. Nothing else mattered.

From below came the sound of Mr. and Mrs. Beer screwing wood panels over missing windows and gaping holes to make the home secure.

"Igor!" Ida called again. In the last fading light, Ida climbed over rubble into the back garden, sorting through the piles of things that had been blown out of the house. Their bedroom had been left intact, but her attic writing room was in shambles. Thank heavens she had delivered her most recent manuscript to Miss Taft just a few weeks before.

Between the piles of rubble lay books and pieces of books, fragments of stories blown into bits. The edges of a photograph protruded from the debris, and she tugged it out. Clemens Krauss and Viorica Ursuleac smiled up at her from the Salzburg Festival, a younger Louise and Ida by their sides, glowing in their homemade opera gowns. How careless and frivolous it all seemed now. What a lifetime it had been since they had met them at the station in Salzburg and been asked to take care of Mitia. The music matters less and also more, she remembered Viorica saying. *Where were they now, Clemens and Viorica?* It had been years since they'd had any word.

Ida lifted the photo and dusted off the fragments of masonry, placing it in her basket as a reminder of the world they were fighting to return to—a world where two sisters could listen to sublime music played freely beneath the Austrian Alps. She looked over the rest of the mess. Who had known so much of a house was made up of wall and ceiling materials? There were only a few recognizable objects mixed into the mess—here her mother's cutting board, there her father's pipe—tossed in the melee of plaster. "Igor!" Ida called again, less hopefully now, terrified she might come across a patch of unmoving fur.

By the time Ida and Louise had cleaned and moved anything salvageable from the bombed part of house to the front, the Beers had boarded off the shattered part, rehung the front door, and hammered wood over the broken windows.

They expanded their search, calling Igor's name down the street and realizing that eight houses near them had been demolished completely, some with people inside. It would be entirely dark soon. "Oh, Igor!" Ida called, feeling both gutted and guilty, knowing their neighbors had lost much more than a cat, but mourning his soft fur and gentle purring.

Louise shoved aside a splintered cabinet and a strangled sound came from inside, followed by an indignant meow.

"Igor?" Ida cried, and out he came—plastered in dust, walking stiffly, and looking as though he held them both personally responsible. "Louise! We've found him!"

Louise let out a small cry of joy, and they both sat down upon the stairs amid the ruins and congratulated themselves on being alive, petting their poor confused darling.

Ida unceremoniously loaded him into a second basket.

"There now," said Mrs. Beer. "All's well then. Are you coming over with us?"

"I think we'll go to the flat at Dolphin Square," Ida said.

Louise nodded. "But how can we ever thank you?"

"We're only that glad to help, and beyond relieved your parents weren't here."

They said goodbye and carried two baskets away from the ruined house. Louise stopped to look back. "You do realize," she said, "that we are now the refugees? If this continues much longer, there will be no buildings left standing in England."

Ida laced her arm through her sister's. "We're refugees in name only because we're still together. That's more than the other inhabitants of Dolphin Square."

"You're a keeper," Louise said simply, patting Ida's arm. Igor meowed from his basket, and they made their way up the rubble-strewn street, joining the thousands of Londoners left homeless by Hitler's revenge.

LIBERATION

In September 1944, the Canadian First Army swept up the French coast and freed Boulogne—the last stronghold of Hitler's "Atlantic Wall." As part of the Allies' "Clearing the Channel Ports" campaign, the Canadian army also retook the port of Calais, with its launching site for V-1 and V-2 bombs. The flying bomb attacks came to an abrupt end, and the skies over London began to clear.

A few months later, Soviet troops captured Warsaw and liberated Auschwitz, and a Polish-born American jurist invented a new word to describe the atrocities discovered with each new unveiling: *genocide*.

As the Allied armies advanced across the continent, they discovered stolen art and wealth hidden in German salt mines. They liberated the Buchenwald and Belsen camps, and the German forces in the Ruhr surrendered. The Soviet army reached Berlin as the Allies captured Venice and liberated Dachau.

The world waited to see what end would befall the man behind so much madness, but in a bunker beneath his headquarters in Berlin, Adolf Hitler married his mistress one day, then swallowed cyanide capsules with her and their dogs the next, shooting himself in the head in one final act of violence. In announcing his death, the *Daily Express* refused to show a picture of the world's most hated face. The Associated Press's Berlin correspondent, Louis Lochner, wrote: "I still find it difficult to believe that Hitler is really dead . . . I cannot escape the feeling that he is some place where nobody expects him to be."

CELEBRATION

In May, seventy thousand German troops laid down their arms in the surrender Hitler had said never would come.[45] His successor signed Germany's unconditional surrender in a ceremony with General Dwight D. Eisenhower, and the BBC interrupted their scheduled programming to announce that though the battles in Japan struggled on, the war in Europe had indeed ended, and Victory in Europe (VE) Day would be a national holiday.

In the flat at Dolphin Square, Ida, Louise, and Maria hung flags and bunting, hugging each other in disbelief. Out in the streets, people lit bonfires, dancing with their neighbors. Against the darkening night sky, lights shone out from each rooftop and unfettered window of the city—blazing light—pure, glorious, and glowing for the first time in more than five years. Parades and street parties were hastily thrown together, while St. Paul's Cathedral offered ten consecutive services of gratitude for peace. The pealing of the city's church bells, full throated and resonant, rang out all over the city like a million weddings performed all at once, shattering the long silence of scarred belltowers, many barely still standing.

By the light of the next morning, most of London seemed to drift into the streets and parks, milling around the palace, waiting for the royal family. Churchill addressed the House of Commons then went to Buckingham Palace where thousands stood outside the battle-scarred palace with blackout curtains and bricked-up windows still in place. The King appeared, wearing his naval uniform, the Queen stood beside him, and Princess Elizabeth emerged wearing a uniform for the women's branch. Lines of unknown people linked arms and walked the streets, swept along on a tide of happiness and relief.

To Ida and Louise, it seemed they must all live happily ever after. It felt as if the whole city had stumbled out into the sunlight again, blinking at each other after a long, nightmarish sleep.

Rumor that Churchill would speak next from the balcony of the Ministry of Health sent the crowd shifting in the direction of Whitehall. It was unusually hot for May, and people fanned themselves with newspapers and handkerchiefs. "We want Winnie!" someone began to shout, and others took up the call. "We want Winnie!"

"Why don't 'e come out?" Ida heard a cheeky man demand.

"E's 'aving a drink!" a woman called back to applause and laughter.

Finally, Churchill and labour minister Ernest Bevin appeared on the balcony of the Ministry of Health building with thousands of rejoicing Londoners waving from below. Churchill wore his famous boiler suit with black hat, an iconic cigar placed in his mouth. He walked onto the balcony holding up two fingers in the V sign. The crowd roared. When they quieted enough to hear him, he shouted: "This is your victory!"

The crowd called back: "No. It's yours!"

"[This is the] victory of the cause of freedom in every land," Churchill pronounced when they had quieted enough to hear him.

> In all our long history, we have never seen a greater day than this. . . . The lights went out and the bombs came down. But every man, woman and child in the country had no thought of quitting the struggle.

He held up his hands proudly. "London can take it."

There were cheers of agreement before he continued:

> I say that in the long years to come not only the people of this island but of the world, wherever the bird of freedom chirps in human hearts, will look back to what we've done and they will say "Do not despair, do not yield to violence and tyranny, march straightforward and die, if need be, un-conquered."

More cheers rose in response. Then, as if filled with so much emotion that it could only spill over into song, someone in the crowd began singing spontaneously, "Land of hope and glory." Other voices joined in, the impromptu chorus rising to a great crescendo:

> *Land of hope and glory, Mother of the Free,*
> *How shall we extol thee, who are born of thee?*
> *Wider still and wider shall thy bounds be set;*
> *God, who made thee mighty, make thee mightier yet,*
> *God, how made thee mighty, make thee mightier yet.*

The crowd sang with the full strength of their voices, as Churchill conducted from his balcony, jubilantly beating out time and bellowing along. From somewhere in the crowd, drums started up.

Their beloved Winnie had tears in his eyes when they had finished. "God bless you all," he said as he bid them goodnight.

⋄ ·· — ··· — ·· ⋄

That night, London's street parties could not be contained. Lights blazing, bonfires sprang up at street corners lit by people who grabbed anything that could burn. Kids roasted potatoes in the blaze. Neighbors stopped by with cakes, tarts, biscuits, tea, and lemonade. Pianos were dragged into the street for singing "Roll Out the Barrel," and people burned effigies of Hitler. People sang, music spilling out of homes and into the streets. In Soho, all the dances of central Europe were performed as people stood round clapping time.

Arms linked with Louise and Maria, Ida laughed and pointed to a boy carrying a sign: "I have no further territorial claims in Europe," it said, with "Europe" crossed out and "Hell" scribbled in. Little children who weren't old enough to remember the city properly lit up, watched on with wonder, the dancing flames reflected in their wide eyes. A few little ones asked why they weren't sleeping in the shelter anymore.

Flood lights outlined every stone on the National Gallery. Big Ben wore a grin on its great, illumined face. The Tower of London and the Dome of St. Paul's were lit by the ATS unit's powerful searchlights, setting St. Paul's golden cross ablaze. Two bright searchlights behind the cathedral projected a triumphant V against the night sky.

Even as they laughed and danced, Ida thought it was a cathartic, ragged laughter, for none of them could shake the thought that the same dancing lights had only days ago been searchlights seeking out aircraft during raids. The smell of bonfires was an uncanny reminder of London burning as she had huddled in the Bermondsey shelter. Pin wheels, roman candles, and bangers echoed the thousands of bombs that had fallen. The lights along the embankment strung like a necklace of pearls along the river, recalling the jewels they had brought out of Germany and of so many others they'd been forced to leave behind.

CORRESPONDENCE

Weeks later, Mum and Dad returned home, and they all moved back into the repaired flat on Morella Road. Their brothers Bill and Jim were both discharged safely and would soon return to their families. Filled with joy and hope for the future, Ida announced to Louise: "I'm writing to Rosa."

"Have you an address?"

"No. I am addressing it to Rosa Ponselle, Baltimore, USA."

Louise scoffed. "The American postal office will have harsh words for you. What are you saying?"

"I've told her what she's meant to us during all these years, and that we hope to come to the States when the war is over on both sides of the Atlantic. If we get near Baltimore, we would perhaps pluck up courage and ask if we might see her."

Louise snorted. "Well, if there's one thing I've learned by now, it's not to dismiss a letter of yours. Stranger things have happened."

Weeks later, Ida ripped open the reply, feeling as if she tore away all the years that had separated them. Rosa wrote as though they had parted yesterday:

*No words can describe how happy and touched I am to be remem-
bered thus in London, where I spent some of the happiest days of my
whole career. We are moving on to a brighter future now and at least
we are both alive and able to make contact, which means so much. If
you and your sister come to the States, we absolutely insist you stay
with us so we can see and hear each other and know we are real once
more. Please remember me to all the Covent Garden admirers.*

Ida raised eyes filled with wonder to her sister.

"Well, there's a thing," said Louise, smiling at her impractical,
magical sister.

"There *is* always Rosa." Ida sniffed as she impulsively embraced
Louise. "Oh, Louie. We said it during all those dreadful years, just
to survive them. But it was true."

Louise hugged Ida back, her own eyes misty.

Ida straightened. "Lou, do you suppose we could have a gramophone party? To celebrate the anniversary of Rosa's London debut
so many years ago?"

Louise laughed. "You do understand people are swimming in
Trafalgar Square fountain to celebrate the war's end? A gramophone
party wouldn't be the strangest celebration. Of course, we should!
Why not?"

Feeling ten years younger, Ida rang Maria at Dolphin Square:
"And who do you think wrote to me today?" she asked, trying to
keep her voice calm.

PARTY LINE

Ida invited everyone she could think of: family, friends from the
Bermondsey shelter, opera friends, refugee friends and those who

had sponsored them, and neighbors—anyone who could be mustered into a party.

"And what do you plan feed all these people?" Mum asked when she saw Ida's list. "There's still food rations on, if you haven't forgotten."

Ida wrote to her school friend from Northumberland who had taken in Dad and Mother during the flying bombs, imploring her to rustle up a chicken or fish.

"I'll do better than that!" Saanvi wrote back. "I'll bring you a Coquet salmon personally. I will catch the first train down in the morning!"

Few of the people knew each other, but they got on like a house on fire. They played opera records, reminisced about the war, and ate the food. Everyone was cheerful and lovely, though there were lines upon their faces and gray hairs that hadn't been there before. Beneath the revelry ran an undeniable undercurrent of sympathy and tenderness from the collective shared suffering that had touched them all the past few years.

Promptly at eight o'clock, the phone rang, and dead silence fell upon the room. None of them had ever spoken on a telephone call across the Atlantic before. The whole project seemed like an unnerving attempt to bridge both time and distance. Ida picked up the receiver and the operator checked over the details of names and time, and then said: "Go ahead."

Rosa's beautiful Italian American voice came through the line: "Hello, Ida! Is that really you?"

In the sound of Rosa's voice lay all the shades of their youth. It still captured all the times they had sat in the gallery at Covent Garden. Of the days Ida had followed her through London, not daring to ask if they might snap her. Of the day she had appeared at their home for the party, singing in front of their marble fireplace.

"Hello, Ida! Is that you?" Rosa said again.

Magic. It was like raising the dead.

Ida forgot to call her Madame Ponselle and called her Rosa, as they always had among themselves. Rosa laughed and asked how many there were. "Thirty of us," Ida explained, "and all as silent as they were when we waited for your Casta Diva in Covent Garden years ago."

"Would you like me to sing for you now?" Rosa asked, almost hesitantly.

"Will you?" Ida gasped.

"Call them around and hold up the receiver. I'll see if I can get it over to you all." People gathered closer then, kneeling or standing as close as possible as Ida held up the receiver.

A moment's silence followed. Then, in miniature, but in a clear, matchless, tremendous voice, Rosa's "Pace, pace, mio Dio" from *La Forza del Destino* crossed the years and the ocean. Her pianissimo grew to fortissimo and back to the golden thread of her unrivaled pianissimo once more.

Ida would have recognized the voice anywhere as Ponselle singing—had she been at the North Pole or on the banks of the Styx. Ponselle's listeners nearly went crazy. She sang for the remaining minutes while they passed the receiver around so that each person got to hear a few notes at full volume.

"My suffering has lasted for so many years, as profound as on the first day," Louise translated the lines quietly after the call. "Peace, peace, my God, peace!"

BRAZIL

A few short days after the party, Ida and Louise hugged Maria goodbye as she boarded the steamer that would take her at last to meet her fiancé, Leo, in Brazil. "When we parted, we didn't know how we would stand to be apart for three weeks," she told them as she held Ida's hand absently. "Now we've been engaged for eight years. I still remember how I felt, though, and all I want is his arms around me again."

"Goodbye, dear Maria," Ida said, and Louise hugged her too. She boarded the ship, and Ida and Louise remained below, still waving, feeling the weight of the empty ones, the lost ones, the ones who could not sail back to their loved ones anymore. They felt the presence of those others, still hovering out over the sea.

KRAUSS AND VIORICA

When Japan finally surrendered, the Nuremberg war crimes trials began, and humanity tried to grapple with all that had been lost. Ida and Louise heard that Clemens Krauss had been subpoenaed to stand before a de-Nazification committee, and they wondered if he would contact them to testify that he had been undermining the Nazis even as he outwardly complied. It had been years since they'd last heard from either him or Viorica. Where had they spent the war years? Munich, Vienna, or Salzburg? The once enchanting musical cities had since filled up with ghosts.

◇·· — ··· — ··◇

In time, they heard that Krauss had been released. When the Vienna Opera Company came to perform in Covent Garden, he sent a tremulous telegram—one that assumed nothing and gave them plenty of room to make excuses to not see them, for their countries had gone to war. There were many who said Krauss' career had benefitted far too much from working with Nazis.

Ida replied they would meet them at Victoria Station, so a few weeks later, Ida and Louise made their way through a cacophony of crying porters and whistling engines. The Vienna opera personnel tumbled out of the trains and into the station, and the sisters scanned the faces of musicians, singers, set designers looking for, and finding at last, Krauss' distinctive, sharply cut nose and his black curtain of hair now nearly white. Viorica looked older too, refined with a look of suffering that hadn't been there five years previous.

"Hello!" Ida cried, and Viorica hesitated, for who knew how friends on opposite sides felt toward each other when so much blood had been spilt? But Ida threw herself into her friend's arms and hugged her until the opera singer laughed.

"London wouldn't be London without you!" Viorica said, returning the hug. "We were so worried about you."

"Did you receive any of our letters?" Louise asked.

"None at all," said Krauss, recovering from the shock of their welcome. "We weren't sure if you were alive and had made it out of Germany until we had a recent postcard from Mitia. And then we weren't sure . . . well, who can know?" How deep and ominous their silence must have seemed.

Louise took his arm, the way she often did with their own father, and Ida led Viorica. "We're so very glad to have you here and safe in London."

They navigated around the city, ignoring the suspicious looks of passersby at the sounds of German accents. They walked them through the Dolphin Square flat, empty for the first time since Maria's departure; and Viorica admitted their own flat in Munich had been hit by a phosphorous bomb that destroyed everything. They'd fled to Vienna where they had both found employment.

Ida began to say something sympathetic, but Krauss dismissed it with a gesture of his hand. "Why complain? We are alive, when so many are dead. We are the lucky ones. Let's admit it." They sat down at the table, speaking of those they'd helped escape, and Ida understood for the first time how clearly Krauss and Viorica had co-operated on occasions when they hadn't even realized it. Their work had not ceased when war broke out, either, and they had continued helping with escapes, though it became riskier and riskier.

"We heard you were called to Nuremberg," Ida said, tentatively.

"Yes," said Krauss, pain passing over his features. I'm thankful Wallerstein returned to testify on my behalf at the de-Nazification proceedings."

"But you were working to help so many people escape. They must have seen that, surely?" Louise asked.

"Of course, but now everyone is claiming they were never true Nazis and are using any excuse to escape punishment," Krauss said. "I understand why they needed to be careful. On the outside, as you know, we were quite complicit with the regime."

"Though people do say hurtful, careless things," Viorica added thoughtfully.

"Of course, they do," said Ida.

"Figuring out who is who is a difficult task," said Krauss graciously. "I don't envy them that. The lines were very blurred."

"Tell them what they asked you," Viorica prompted.

Krauss smiled wryly. "At one point in the trial, they demanded,

'Have you ever visited Hitler at Berchtesgaden?' 'Certainly,' I told them. 'When did you go last?' they asked."

"When had you?" asked Louise.

"I said, 'I cannot recall the exact date, but it should not be difficult to check. It was exactly one week after Mr. Chamberlain visited him there.'" Krauss chuckled at the memory and passed his hand across his face, though the lines settled back into sorrow and he looked as if he wished to erase the memory entirely.

Louise and Ida exchanged a quiet glance. So much suffering and pain below the surface. So much darkness, and so many lives that would never be put right.

◇ ·· — ··· — ·· ◇

They had dinner together at a quiet Soho restaurant. The three Maliniaks joined Krauss and Viorica—all moved to meet again after so many years. As the waitress set down a carafe of water, she whispered to Ida, "Is that Clemens Krauss?"

"It is. Are you a fan?"

"Am I? Do you think I could ask him for an autograph?"

"Certainly, you could. And you should ask her too, for she's Viorica Ursuleac."

"Of course!"

"Krauss," Ida said, "You have an admirer."

Flushing and laughing, the girl explained, "I come from Vienna and have heard Mr. Krauss conduct many times." Ida realized she was part of a thousand grains of sand in Europe, stirred by the tide of history and set down upon new shores.

Krauss gave the autograph, and Ida impulsively added, "Go and fetch yourself something to drink with us. We're together for the first time in many years and are drinking a toast to reunion and peace."

The girl returned with a wine glass, and the entire party stood to clink glasses. They drank to the fact that they had survived the hurricane that swept over Europe and lived to smile at each other in a London restaurant, and they drank in remembrance of the many more who had not.

When they saw Krauss and Viorica off at the station a week later, Ida told them: "I hope you will look upon the Dolphin Square flat as another home. Come and go whenever you like."

Louise held out a key for them.

Viorica teared up at the unexpected gift: a home, to replace one that had been lost, in a land that had been filled with enemies. "Thank you," she said, hugging Ida close. "I hope you know, my dear, that you have an astounding talent for love."

AMERICA

JANUARY 1947

Three months later, Ida and Louise stepped down from their first trans-Atlantic flight, their steps a little wobbly after thirteen long hours in the air. *New York City*. How they had dreamed of being there—the mad bustle, the museums, the architecture—the chaos of life happening at full tilt. A cab whisked them through the city across the bridge to Manhattan and set them down in front of their hotel.

Inside the lobby, sitting on a bench waiting for them, just as she had once waited for them in a train station in Frankfurt, sat Else Mayer-Lismann. They fell upon each other, laughing and crying over the reunion. Walter Stiefel and his wife and daughter arrived, and the scene repeated itself. They had first known these friends in the shadow of great danger and tragedy, had waved them away from the shores of Europe as refugees; now they were there to welcome them as citizens of a country that had always enthralled them.

Together, they went up to their hotel room. Ida fumbled to turn the key in the lock and opened the door. She stood back in stunned amazement. The room looked like a film star's: every corner had been filled with flowers, telegrams, candy, cakes, cards, and phone call slips. In shock, Ida and Louise looked around the room before Ida spontaneously burst into tears.

Else wrapped her arms around her. "Don't cry, dear. The time for crying is past, and now we can enjoy being happy and safe."

She was right, of course, and Ida wiped away her tears and reached for candy which had always had the power to raise her spirits in every phase of existence. "Louise always told me you shouldn't expect a reward just for doing what's right," she said, trying to control her voice. "And yet, look at all of this."

Every few minutes, the phone rang. Mitia, along with half of her extended family, were waiting to greet them. Maria and Leo had sent a gift from Brazil. Friedl's mother, who had left Frankfurt two weeks before war and had escaped via the Soviet Union and China, planned to come say hello. Friedl's uncle, who they had seen when he had been released from a concentration camp in 1938 wanted some time with them. His wife and family wanted to personally thank them. Everyone, it seemed, had parents, children, uncles, cousins, who could not pass up the opportunity to meet the women who had helped their loved ones escape their darkest moments.

Overflowing with gratitude that evening, Ida and Louise went to watch Ezio Pinza sing *Boris Godunov* at the Metropolitan. The last time they'd seen him perform, it had been *The Marriage of*

Figaro in Salzburg, with war still over horizon. While their refugee work had once taken them away from opera, it now returned them full circle, and the two streams of their lives merged back into one.

They hadn't told Ezio they were coming, so his face blanched when they knocked on his dressing room door after the performance. "Good lord!" he said. "Where did you two spring from?"

"We just arrived from England this morning," Ida said breezily, "and thought we'd come hear the best basso in the world sing tonight."

He laughed and hugged them both, and they exchanged the news of so many years in between. Ida and Louise shrugged off the weight of exhaustion and jetlag, basking in his presence.

Lita, who had retired from singing at the Met but was still thrilled to see them after so many years, drove them to her country home for tea, and they tried to pretend like it was the most natural thing in all the world.[46]

After ten days in New York, they took a train to Baltimore under a beautiful sunny sky. "It's Ponselle weather," Louise remarked.

"How fitting," Ida replied. "Louie, do you remember promising ourselves this trip as we crouched beneath the dining room table with doodlebugs buzzing overhead?"

"I could never forget that moment," Louise replied. "It was the first time I started thinking we might survive."

⋄ · · — · · · — · · ⋄

Rosa's husband, Carle, picked them up at the train station and drove them out to Villa Pace through the Maryland countryside with its quintessential amber waves of grain.

"Rosa is a little scared of seeing you," Carle confessed halfway through the journey.

"What?" Ida exclaimed, laughing. "How on earth could she possibly be scared of seeing *us*?"

"You knew her in her greatest days of fame and glamour, you see, and she is afraid you may be disappointed to find her changed."

Ida waved off the ridiculous confession. "If she remembers us at all, it's as gallery girls, and here we've returned as nearly middle-aged women. What about our scared feelings?"

Carle laughed. "Time changes us all."

They arrived at the stunning villa before Rosa did, and a maid showed them to a room that looked exactly like the set in the last act of *La Traviata*. When Ida sat down at the dressing table mirror, she felt she really ought to start singing the "Addio." The turn of the car outside told them Rosa was home. Without waiting on formality, Ida ran down the stairs from their room and flung open Rosa's own front door for her.

She stood there on the threshold, their Rosa, looking as they had always remembered and had always hoped to see again. Wide and dark were her eyes, like a Verdi heroine, with that indescribable air of drama about her. "Rosa!" Ida cried, Louise just a few steps behind. "Darling Rosa!" And she threw her arms around the star, embracing her.

Ida would later remember those days spent at Villa Pace as among the most transcendent of her entire life—an exquisite aria in the performance of it all. For hours, Rosa sang to them, entertained them with operatic stories, and answered endless questions about the details of her career. She showed them the glorious stage costumes she had worn and allowed them to take their pick of photographs, recreating each moment they had lost to the war.

They found her dark, matchless voice absolutely unimpaired by time. She retained in real life, the fascinating, melodramatic personality that had first enchanted them across the footlights. When Rosa entered a room, it was still impossible to look anywhere else. They spent hours listening to her records. As Rosa sang, her whole appearance changed, the very shape of her face seemed to alter and become young. Her eyes grew wide. She tipped her head back, hearkening across the years. For a few wondrous minutes, she was reincarnated as Norma, Viletta, or Gioconda.

One morning as they listened to a Caruso record, Rosa said: "His voice was not in any sense directional, you understand? The sound did not come from his mouth; it came from his head. It was all around you, and somehow at the back of your neck as well."

They strolled their way through a Chaliapin record, and Rosa remarked: "Listen—for that pianissimo! I always used to listen for that when I sang with him—and tried to copy it."

"You started with perfection as the norm and became slightly irritated with anything that deviated from it," Louise remarked.

"It's so *simple*, really!"

Ida laughed. "Simple for you, Rosa. Not for anyone else. But why don't you sing in public anymore? You must know your voice is still absolutely perfect."

Rosa sat back, stretching into the couch. "For nineteen years, I was a slave to my art," she explained, "but I am not prepared to do that anymore. Nor am I prepared to be anything less than perfect." She shrugged. "So that is all."

Rosa and Carle wanted to hear of their refugee work, speaking of "their work" the way they spoke of hers, which astonished Ida and Louise. The phone calls, notes, and flowers had followed them to Villa Pace. "My dears, the past few years have enlightened us all," Rosa told them. "It is easy to think there are sharp lines dividing the good people and bad people, but most humans have dark passions inside waiting to be stirred up. It's easier than we think to become convinced that decency is for the weak, that democracy is naïve, that kindness and respect for others are ridiculous. The whole world has been reminded these past few years that the things we care about have to be nurtured and defended because even seemingly good people have the potential to do hideous things. That's the evil you were fighting, all those times you risked your own safety and helped others out of Europe. How did you live with so much fear and danger?"

Ida found herself echoing Rosa's words right back to her. "It was so simple, really. The opportunity presented itself. How could we do anything other than what we did?"

"We had our family too," added Louise. "And each other." Ida nodded.

"You underestimate yourselves," Rosa responded. "Many people did nothing. Most people, probably. It's clear there are so many who are so grateful." The golden afternoon sunset streamed in through her windows, making it more difficult to recapture the fear that had been so real. "And how many did you save, altogether my dears?"

"Twenty-nine families altogether," Ida said, sadly. "Twenty-nine complete cases is all we can take credit for."

"Twenty-nine," Rosa repeated in hushed admiration. "How very many people."

Ida shook her head, thinking of all those others. So many, many others. Of letters dropping in the hallway of 24 Morella Road one by one, letters she still kept tucked away, under her bed. Of the voices in her head that would never be silenced entirely, no matter how many years might pass. "No, no, it was only twenty-nine, Rosa, darling. Don't you see? Only twenty-nine families out of all those millions suffering. How very few."

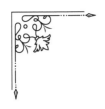

AFTERWORD

It is easy to trace the eventual outcomes for some of the historical people in this account, but others' fates remain unknown.

Dr. Israel Taglicht, former chief rabbi of Vienna was later confined in a concentration camp and escaped to Britain in 1939. Ezio Pinza was arrested in March 1942 and unjustly detained on Ellis Island along with hundreds of other Italian Americans suspected of supporting the Axis. Pinza suffered periods of severe depression for years afterwards. His daughter Claudia later became a renowned opera singer, and the two occasionally sang together in San Francisco.

A less well-known aspect of the war involves the increased risk of suicide among Holocaust survivors. Though Georg and Gerda Maliniak did, indeed, escape to London with their daughter Krysia, like many others who continued suffering from the trauma of their wartime experiences, Georg died by suicide in 1949.

Though Lulu Cossmann was able to escape with help from the Cook sisters, she was unable to help her brother, Professor Paul Cossmann escape, and he died in Theresienstadt camp. The famous milliner Alice did successfully escape with help from the Cooks, but her husband Oskar, who fled to Holland, lost his life when the Nazis took over the Netherlands.

After Clemens Krauss' name was cleared of association with the Nazis in 1947, thanks, in part, to the work he did with the Cooks, he was allowed to resume conducting. He conducted until his death in 1954 while on tour with the Vienna Philharmonic. He is buried in Austria, alongside Viorica Ursuleac, who passed away in 1985 at age ninety-one.

Corine Ahrens, her husband, and their children miraculously survived the war, as the Cooks learned years later. Walter Stiefel and his family also survived. Ilse Maria Bauer and her mother Irma (who in reality survived the war) finally joined Maria's beloved Leo in Brazil after nearly eight years of separation. The couple married and had a child.

The sculptor Jacques Heliczer escaped and emigrated to New York, where he later established an art studio.

Else Mayer-Lismann became a renowned musicologist, lecturing on opera for many institutions. Uncle Carl survived and spent many years after the war living in England, and, in Ida's words, "remained a joy and support to everyone who knew him." Thanks in large part to Mitia and Else's tenacity, nearly all the rest of the Mayer-Lissman family made it safely to America. Ida and Louise stayed in contact with many of those they'd helped for the rest of their lives.

After the war, Ida and Louise continued their refugee work by volunteering with an organization called Lifeline, an Adoption Committee for Aid to Displaced Persons. They helped non-German refugees in Bavaria, particularly Poles who had been brought to the country as slaves during the war but didn't want to return to Poland under the control of the Russians. As part of their work, they also helped Hungarians, Ukrainians, and Czechs who had escaped from the Baltic states and didn't want to return to communism. Ida and Louise fundraised to provide food and medical treatment for the refugees, and they visited the organization's refugee camp on several occasions. During one visit, they met an elderly Hungarian man who had lost his whole family and his culture besides. "What could you say?" Ida wrote of the experience. "I put my arms around him and kissed him."

Louise worked in the civil service until she retired. Ida published 112 romance novels with Mills & Boon under the pseudonym Mary Burchell. She became the president of the Romantic Novelists Association in 1966 and said at that meeting: "Romance is the quality which gives an air of probability to our dearest wishes . . . people often say life isn't like that, but life is often exactly like that. Illusions and dreams often do come true."

After Ida died of cancer in 1986, Louise moved into the London flat which they had bought for the refugees prior to the war. The exact number of people they helped is unknown because the twenty-nine cases mentioned by Ida often referred to entire families; the total number they attempted to help is certainly in the hundreds. They were honored by Yad Vashem as Righteous Among the Nations in 1964 and named British Heroes of the Holocaust by the British government in 2010. In 2017, on Holocaust Remembrance Day, a group erected a plaque in their honor in Sunderland at the site of their childhood home.

AUTHOR'S NOTE

I was raised on stories of World War II, and I was also raised on the absence of stories. My grandfather served in the Tenth Mountain Division, a specialized force of American troops trained to navigate mountainous terrain, who successfully fought on skis in the Italian alps, turning the tide of the war in that region. Like so many veterans of the war, he rarely spoke of his own experiences. What I remember most is the gentle strength of his hands, his remarkable skill at anything related to wilderness survival, and the way he built an American flagpole out of a knotty pine tree on his alpine cabin property. Daily he would fold the flag, taking great care as he raised or lowered it, sometimes with misty eyes. When he died at age sixty-five, he received a full military salute, and one of his war buddies spoke at the funeral, retelling wartime experiences with my grandfather that even his own wife (my grandmother) had never heard before.

I was a grown adult before I realized he had been a hero and longed, too late, to ask him to tell me the stories. Thankfully, he had written my grandmother faithfully during those long years of conflict, and it's those letters that are the best surviving portrait of his experiences. My other grandfather, Harold Monson, spent the early years of the war recommissioning destroyer ships in the Philadelphia harbor, preparing them for use by the British navy. My grandmothers also supported war efforts on US soil, and my father's mother worked inspecting 50 caliber machine gun ammunition at a Remington Arms factory. Even into old age she could still explain the difference between various size ammo gauges.

The war impacted the generation that survived it in a way my own generation is only beginning to be able to appreciate during the last few years of upheaval. Louise and Ida's story is one of many from the era that have been overlooked and forgotten until quite recently, and it's been an honor to revisit and retell it. Their legacy—a dedication to love in the face of violence, art in the face of destruction, and goodness when faced with sheer evil—is a remarkable inspiration.

Like the adept spies they were, Ida and Louise did not use full names for many of the people they helped, protecting their identities in the aftermath of war when many could still be at risk. Many of the names they did include sound so similar as to be confusing when read in a novel. For these reasons, I have changed many of the names. When I needed to flesh out a particular character's experience, I drew upon similar situations people experienced during the war but avoided lifting entire names or stories from real Holocaust victims or survivors. The endnotes, in many cases, can help retrace original sources. For the purpose of creating a more cohesive narrative, I have compressed the timeline and, in some cases, combined characters (Ida had a remarkable gift for keeping track of hundreds of people). I tried to remain true to the essence and lived reality of Ida, Louise, and the many people they assisted.

Attempting to write anything about the second world war is an overwhelming effort, and I'd like to thank all those who helped with the researching and writing of this book, including those who read early drafts: Andrew Behnke, Allison Moulton, Brian King, Lisa Ard, Jennifer Gennari, and Afton Nelson. Thanks to the team at

Shadow Mountain who brought it to life, especially Heidi Gordon, Janna DeVore, and Heather Ward. The European Union graciously granted me permission to travel to Germany, Austria, and London and Sunderland, UK, during the covid-19 pandemic to conduct research, which enhanced the book in a myriad of ways and added a depth it would not have achieved otherwise. My sincerest gratitude is extended to those who operate and maintain the many museums and archives I visited, preserving the past so we can continue to learn from it in the present. In particular, I want to thank the staff at the Museum of Military History in Vienna, the guides of the Third Reich Walking Tour in Munich, operators of The Imperial War Museum and the Churchill War Rooms in London, the musicians of Salzburg, Dr. Peter Black, senior historian at the US Holocaust Memorial Museum, and the gifted guides at the Dachau Concentration Camp Memorial Site in Germany.

In an incredible stroke of serendipity worthy of Ida, I was able to attend an opera at the Staatsoper in Vienna, just as the sisters once did, as I happened to visit in a rare small window of performances still possible amidst the 2020 pandemic closures. The modern owners of the sisters' homes in both Sunderland and on Morella Road in London graciously allowed me to visit their homes and provided me with invaluable information regarding the history and architectural development. Many sincere thanks to Erin Thompson and Martin Bedding for their assistance.

In both homes today, in the corners of the ceilings, hang small plaster ornamentations depicting winged angels. I like to think these are the benevolent reminders of past angelic inhabitants who, as Rosa says in this narrative, had such a remarkable gift for love.

Above all, I extend remembrance and honor to more than eleven million Jews, homosexuals, political opponents, Roma and Sinti,

Jehovah's Witnesses, houseless, and people with disabilities murdered by the Nazi regime, the seventy million military personnel
and civilians who were killed during the war, and the countless millions of survivors whose lives were upended by it. May their legacies
inspire us to work tirelessly for peace.

DISCUSSION QUESTIONS

1. Which scene stuck with you the most, and why?

2. There is a lot of era-specific music mentioned in these pages, from opera to jazz. Were you familiar with the music mentioned? Did you listen to any of it as you read?

3. How did the Nazi regime use music as a tool of war? How did the Cook sisters use music as a tool of healing?

4. Did your opinion of the book change as you read it? How did it impact you? Are there lingering questions you're still thinking about?

5. Who was your favorite character? Did you relate more to Ida or Louise? They are very different people, but how would you describe their relationship? How were their unique strengths both important to their success?

6. Which physical places in the book would you most like to visit?

7. World War II has been written about a great deal. Was there any aspect of the war's suffering you hadn't been aware of?

8. Which events do you find to be most relevant to struggles today?

9. If you could illustrate this book, which scenes would you

illustrate? If you could cast the movie, who would play Ida and Louise?

10. What questions would you have for the author?

11. How does the book title relate to the contents? If you could give it a new title, what would it be?

RECOMMENDED READING LIST

Alexander, Eileen. *Love in the Blitz: The Long-Lost Letters of a Brilliant Young Woman to Her Beloved on the Front.* New York: Harper, 2020.

Cook, Ida. *The Bravest Voices: A Memoir of Two Sisters' Heroism During the Nazi Era.* Toronto: Park Row Books, 2021.

Doerr, Anthony. *All the Light We Cannot See.* New York: Scribner, 2014.

Eder, Mari. *The Girls Who Stepped Out of Line: Untold Stories of the Women Who Changed the Course of World War II.* Naperville, IL: Sourcebooks, 2021.

Larson, Erik. *The Splendid and the Vile: A Saga of Churchill, Family, and Defiance During the Blitz.* New York: Crown, 2020.

Levi, Erik. *Music in the Third Reich.* New York: St. Martin's Press, 1994.

Offenberger, Ilana Fritz. *The Jews of Nazi Vienna, 1938–1945: Rescue and Destruction.* Cham, CH: Palgrave Macmillan, 2017.

Shirer, William L. *The Rise and Fall of the Third Reich: A History of Nazi Germany.* New York: Simon and Schuster, 1960.

Waller, Maureen. *London 1945: Life in the Debris of War.* New York: St. Martin's Griffin, 2005.

Ziegler, Philip. *London at War, 1939–1945.* New York: Knopf, 1995.

NOTES

Pg 4: This account of Germany's hyperinflation is based on an account in *Paper Money* by Adam Smith (New York: Summit Books, 1981), 57–62.

Pg 5: See Harold J. Gordon, Jr., *Hitler and the Beer Hall Putsch* (Princeton, NJ: Princeton University Press, 1972).

Pg 6: The decision of whether or not to leave after the Nazis came to power was impacted by many factors. Women were more inclined to leave than men, but less likely to actually do so. For a full discussion of the factors, see Marion A. Kaplan, "Jewish Women in Nazi Germany: Daily Life, Daily Struggles, 1933–1939," *Feminist Studies* 16, no. 3 (1990), 579–606.

Pg 8: For the purposes of the narrative, the timing has been altered here. Amelita Galli-Curci's tour of Great Britain happened as described but in 1924.

Pg 19: This abbreviated excerpt is a translation of Aldof Hitler's speech on peace given May 21, 1935. Full analysis of the speech, as well as a complete translation, can be found in William L. Shirer's *The Rise and Fall of the Third Reich* (New York: Simon and Schuster, 1960).

Pg 24: On March 7, 1936, Hitler began remilitarizing the Rhineland, despite articles in the Treaty of Versailles that placed all territory west of the Rhine and within 50 kilometers to the east of it under Allied control. He received no pushback from the United States or British governments, as both were eager to avoid war in the region. Many in Europe felt that Germany had been unfairly hampered with reparations after WWI and supported the reclaiming of their previously lost territory.

Pg 29: For the purposes of this story, the timing has been changed here.

Ida and Louise first heard Rosa Ponselle perform in 1929, and the details of that performance match those described here. Ponselle performed again in London in 1930 and 1931 but never returned to the country. Her only other performance in Europe was in Florence, Italy, in 1933. Ida and Louise's great love of Rosa and her music, as described here, is true to Ida's own descriptions in her memoir. See Ida Cook, *The Bravest Voices: A Memoir of Two Sisters' Heroism During the Nazi Era* (Toronto: Park Row Books, 2021).

Pg 49: In 1936, at the outbreak of the Spanish Civil War, both the United Kingdom and France worked to persuade Germany from intervening in the conflict. The hope was that non-intervention would prevent escalation to full-scale war throughout the continent. Although Hitler claimed to agree with this stance, the German air force was already secretly supplying Spanish Nationalists with transport aircraft even as non-intervention talks began. Ultimately, Hitler used the three-year Spanish civil war as a sort of training ground for his army—a rehearsal, so to speak. The Nazis gained experience in ground combat and air technology by aiding General Francisco Franco's rise to power against the legitimate Republican Spanish government.

In the 1937 Battle of Málaga, thousands of Republican refugees—men, women, and children—fled Málaga along the coastal road but were bombarded by tanks on the ground and fire from both the air and sea. Between three thousand and five thousand civilians were killed. See Paul Preston, *The Spanish Holocaust: Inquisition and Extermination in Twentieth-Century Spain* (London: HarperPress, 2012).

Pg 52: For the purposes of this story, the beginnings of Ida Cook's writing career have been altered. In reality, Ida quit her job as a typist in 1931 to begin writing full time for Miss Florence Taft at *Mabs Fashions*. The job paid four and half pounds per week compared to the three pounds a week she'd been earning as a typist. In 1932, Ida began writing standalone fiction articles for the magazine, thus supplementing her base salary from *Mabs*. Ida began writing serialized fiction for the magazine in 1935, and her first serial novel was published in 1936. By the start of World War II, in September 1939, Ida had written eleven novels under the penname Mary Burchell.

Pg 78: Although there aren't any recorded accounts of Maria and Irma Bauer's experiences in Vienna during the Anschluss, the details I've presented here are true to the events of the period and are drawn from firsthand accounts of survivors' testimonies. The story of the unnamed orthodox man being urinated on comes from an oral testimony of Harry Gruenberg, recorded by Dr. Lisa Gruenberg and shared in Ilana Fritz Offenberg's *The Jews of Nazi Vienna, 1938–1945: Rescue and Destruction* (Cham, CH: Palgrave Macmillan, 2017), 34–35.

Pg 80: The notion of suicide by gas stove comes from an era when stoves didn't burn natural gas but coal gas. Sometimes called "illuminating gas," the gas, produced from heated coal, contained large amounts of carbon monoxide. Though it was highly efficient for burning and cooking, with a 10 percent rate of carbon monoxide, it was very dangerous as well and could induce asphyxiation in minutes of exposure. One psychologist called coal gas ovens "the execution chamber in everyone's kitchen." Both Ida's memoir and published accounts of the Anschluss reference use of the method among those who lost hope of escape. After WWII, advancements in technologies made it cheaper and easier to switch over to natural gas, which led to a significant drop in suicide rates overall.

Pg 80: From 1940 to 1944, the Nazis turned Hartheim Castle into a euthanasia center. It is estimated that thirty thousand people—most with mental or physical disabilities—were killed at Hartheim.

Pg 84: Human smuggling was a profitable—and dangerous—venture along the Swiss border, especially after Hitler annexed Austria in 1938. Smugglers risked capture from both Nazi patrols and Swiss border guards, neither group being afraid to kill on sight. Smugglers who were captured in Switzerland could expect to spend months in prison. Smugglers captured in Germany were simply shot. While some smugglers were altruistic, others commanded exorbitant prices to help refugees across the border and were known to abandon their charges or steal from them.

The young fisherman named in this scene—Léon Moille—did, in fact, die during a rescue attempt, but under different circumstances than described here. In 1942, he was rowing across Lake Geneva at night with several refugees in his boat. When he docked on the Swiss side of the lake, a border guard sprang from the bushes. As Moille attempted to flee, the guard shot and killed him. See Valérie Boillat, *Switzerland and Refugees in the Nazi Era* (Bern, CH: Independent Commission of Experts, 1999), 116.https://www. swissbankclaims.com/Documents/DOC_15_Bergier_Refugee.pdf

Pg 125: See United States Holocaust Museum. "Evian Conference." Holocaust Encyclopedia. https://encyclopedia.ushmm.org/content/ en/article/the-evian-conference. Accessed January 19, 2022.

Pg 131: Sudeten Germans were ethnic Germans living within the borders of what was then Czecho-Slovakia. They occupied much of the western portion of the country. The region was given the name Sudentenland in the early twentieth century and became crucial to Hitler's plan for a united, and "undefiled," German populace. The conversation presented here is based on minutes from the meeting between Hitler and Prime Minister Chamberlain, which reveal how Hitler was able to both charm and bully Chamberlain to get his way. (See The National Archives. "Chamberlain and Hitler, 1938: What Was Chamberlain Trying to Do?" https://cdn.nation-alarchives.gov.uk/documents/education/chamberlain.pdf. Accessed January 19, 2022.)

Pg 136: In October 1938, tens of thousands of native Polish Jews living in Germany were forcibly deported, stripped of nearly everything they owned, and marched to trains that would then take them to the Polish border. Many of the deportees considered themselves German, having been there for decades, even fighting for Germany in the Great War. Nearly all of the younger deportees had been born in Germany. Earlier that year, fearing an influx of immigrants, the Polish government had issued a decree invalidating all Polish passports whose holders had lived outside of the country more than five years. This left thousands of Polish Jews stranded in a no-man's-land of small towns just over the Polish border, unable to enter Poland or return to Germany.

Pg 137: Mention here, of Adolf Eichmann paying particular attention to this young boy, is in reference to the reprehensible Nazi practice of kidnapping children in occupied zones who appeared Aryan. They would then place the children with German families. In some cases, children did not know for years that they had been kidnapped from Jewish families and rehomed. Two hundred thousand Polish children were kidnapped, and only a small percentage of those children were ever returned. (See Agnieszka Was-Turecka, et al. *Als wäre ich allein auf der Welt* [*As If I Were Alone in the World*]. Freiburg: Herder Verlag, 2020).

Pg 138: The library of the Jewish Community of Vienna, the Israelitische Kultusgemeinde Wien (IKG), was immense, full of priceless volumes and records. Sometime after the Anschluss in March 1938, Adolf Eichmann traveled to Vienna and ordered that everything belonging to the IKG, including the contents of its library, be catalogued, confiscated, and shipped to Berlin. That undertaking was still in process when the Kristallnacht pogroms occurred months later. Though the violence was clearly orchestrated by the Nazis, the timing in response to vom Rath's death was not; and, therefore, the Nazis were prevented from finishing their precise catalogue of the library's holdings, which allowed time for members of the Jewish congregation to save a number of works by hiding them in Vienna's Central Cemetery. (See Richard Hacken. "The Jewish Community Library in Vienna: From Dispersion and Destruction to Partial Restoration." *Faculty Publications*, 2002. 1335. https://scholarsarchive.byu.edu/facpub/1335. Accessed January 20, 2022.)

My account draws from the firsthand remembrance of Ruth Zimbler, born in Vienna in 1928, whose family lived right next door to the synagogue. She was playing with a friend when Adolf Eichmann knocked on the door and demanded the key to the library. Her description of the event was recorded by the Museum of Jewish Heritage—a Living Memorial to the Holocaust, and is viewable on their website: https://mjhnyc.org/blog/stories-survive-remembering-kristallnacht-with-ruth-zimbler/

Pg 139: Portions of this section are based on the firsthand account of Manfred Lindenbaum, who—like Theo—was exiled to Zbąszyń in the fall of 1938. (See United States Holocaust Memorial Museum. "Oral history interview with Manfred Lindenbaum." The Jeff and Toby Herr Oral History Archive. https://collections.ushmm.org/search/catalog/irn42219?_ga=2.95948766.310408956.1612293637-1928184732.1612039245. Accessed January 19, 2022.)

Pg 142: For a thorough account of Herschel Grynszpan's actions and the events that followed throughout German-controlled lands, see Rita Thalmann and Emmanuel Feinermann, *Crystal Night: 9–10 November 1938* (New York: Holocaust Library, 1974).

Pg 146: There is contradictory information about the first Kindertransport. Many sources incorrectly state that children on the first transport were primarily drawn from an orphanage in Berlin that had burned down, but there's little evidence to corroborate that. The Kindertransport Association claims that half the children came from Berlin and half from Hamburg; the majority were not orphans. (See Judith Tydor Baumel-Schwartz. *Never Look Back: The Jewish Refugee Children in Great Britain, 1938–1945*. West Lafayette, IN: Purdue University Press, 2012.)

Pg 153: British diplomat Robert Smallbones worked tirelessly to expedite visas for Jews from Germany who were awaiting entry to the United States through Great Britain. Forty-eight thousand people were saved under what came to be called The Smallbones Plan; and at the time war broke out in 1939, fifty thousand additional cases were in progress.

Pg 167: Hitler's January 30, 1939, speech from the German Reichstag is often referred to as a prophecy, for he later did, indeed, attempt "the annihilation of the Jewish race." Excerpts from the speech can be found in the archives of Yad Vashem, the World Holocaust Remembrance Center, in Israel. (See "Extract from the Speech by Adolf Hitler, January 30, 1939." https://www.yadvashem.org/docs/extract-from-hitler-speech.html. Accessed February 7, 2022.)

Pg 170: Bloomsbury House was the name of the building—formerly the Palace Hotel—on Bloomsbury Street in London where numerous refugee relief groups kept their offices. It became a sort of headquarters for refugee work. Among the groups working there were the German Jewish Aid Committee, Friends Germany Emergency Committee, the Movement for the Care of Children from Germany, and the International Student Service.

Pg 172: Fritz Kuhn was eventually accused of embezzling $14,000 from the Bund, incarcerated during the war, stripped of his citizenship afterwards, and deported to Germany. For an in-depth look at the rally, see Marshall Curry's documentary film, *A Night at the Garden.* 2019. https://anightatthegarden.com. Accessed January 19, 2022.

Pg 173: On August 2, 1944, the "gypsy camp" section of Auschwitz-Birkenau was closed. It is estimated that four thousand Sinti and Roma were murdered with gas, then burned in the crematoria. August 2 is now Roma and Sinti Holocaust Remembrance Day.

Pg 177: *Israelitische Kultusgemeinde Wien,* when translated exactly, means Israelite Community of Vienna, and that is how it was known from 1853 until the Anschluss in March 1938. It reopened in May 1938 as the Jewish Community of Vienna but retained the IKG acronym.

Pg 208: Alice never saw her husband again. Although he made it over the Dutch border, as described here, he was taken by the Nazis when Germany invaded the Netherlands in 1940.

Pg 209: Of the 937 passengers who were forced to sail back to Europe on the *St. Louis,* 532 became trapped in German-controlled areas. Just under half that number (254) were subsequently killed in the Holocaust.

Pg 211: Lulu Cossmann (b. 1864; d. 1957) was a German school teacher from Frankfurt. Her father, Bernhard Cossmann, had been a celebrated cellist and was colleagues with Tchaikovsky at the Moscow Conservatory. Her brother, Paul Cossmann, was a professor, writer, and editor who participated in the anti-Nazi movement in the years leading up to the war.

Pg 212: Although Ida is depicted seeing a white rose here, the real White

Rose society did not spring up until 1942. The group was led by five students and one professor from Munich University. The group—and others like it throughout the war—distributed pamphlets, wrote anti-Nazi literature, and carried out a graffiti campaign on the walls of the university. In February 1943, three White Rose members—Hans and Sophie Scholl and Christoph Probst—were caught and arrested. A few days later, all three were executed. Hans's last words just before the guillotine fell were, "Long live freedom!" (See "Sophie Scholl and the White Rose." The National World War II Museum, New Orleans. https://www.nationalww-2museum.org/war/articles/sophie-scholl-and-white-rose. Accessed January 22, 2022.)

Pg 223: Theo's story here is retold as Ida Cook told it in her memoirs. Ida, however, never gave the boy a name. She simply and affectionately called him, "our Polish boy."

For the purposes of this story, I have given Ida's Polish boy the name Theo Markus Vineberg and modeled his family after the real Theo Markus Verderber.

Theo Markus Verderber was a real person who did escape Zbąszyń via the Kindertransport program. He was not, however, aided by the Cook sisters, nor did he arrive on the last Kindertransport from Poland.

The real Theo and his family were exiled to Zbąszyń in October 1938. Theo arrived in England on a Kindertransport in February 1929. His mother, sister, and younger brother were killed in 1942 in Limanow, Poland. His older brother escaped and emigrated to Israel.

Pg 227: Ida Cook kept a file of all of the letters she received; however, they were destroyed years after her death in a fire. The excerpts on these pages are from real letters sent to refugee aid organizations or private guarantors requesting help.

Pg 227: From thirty-nine-year-old Paul Berger to the IKG in Vienna. (See Offenberger. *The Jews of Nazi Vienna*, 143.)

Pg 227: From Dr. Flora Hochsinger to a Mrs. Postman in Waltham, Massachusetts. Mrs. Postman worked tirelessly—even writing to

First Lady Eleanor Roosevelt for help—to get an affidavit for Dr. Hochsinger. She was ultimately unsuccessful, and Dr. Hochsinger was deported to the Maly Trostinec death camp in Minsk in 1942. (See Offenberger, *The Jews of Nazi Vienna*, 137–38.)

Pg 228: From Paula Krenzler, a refugee from Gladbeck who had been deported to Zbąszyń, and wrote in May 1939 to Elsley Zeitlyn, a British attorney involved in the Kindertransport program. (See Jennifer Craig-Norton. "Contesting Memory: New Perspectives on the Kindertransport." University of Southampton, Faculty of Humanities, PhD Thesis, 2014).

Pg 229: *Daily Express*, September 19, 1939.

Pg 247: In 2014, ninety-six-year-old Dunkirk survivor Harry Garrett told reporters about his experience, saying: "From hell to heaven was how the feeling was, you felt like a miracle had happened." (See https://www.kentonline.co.uk/dover/news/war-veteran-speaks-of-white-cliffs-18329/. Accessed January 22, 2022.)

Pg 249: This speech, sometimes referred to as "The Finest Hour," is often considered Winston Churchill's most famous. A complete transcript can be found at the International Churchill Society (See "We Shall Fight on the Beaches." https://winstonchurchill.org/resources/speeches/1940-the-finest-hour/we-shall-fight-on-the-beaches/. Accessed February 7, 2022.)

Pg 269: Neither of the Bauers—mother or daughter—were actually injured during the London Blitz. The events described here *did* happen, but to Nesta Guthrie and her mother. Nesta and Jane Guthrie were sisters who met Louise and Ida in the queue at Covent Garden back in their early opera-going days. Nesta and her mother were caught in the attack described here. In an effort to tighten the narrative, I did not include Nesta or Jane in the story. Mrs. Bauer, in fact, survived the war with her daughter Maria and grew to old age.

Pg 273: Winston Churchill gave this speech from the White House on Christmas Eve 1941, just weeks after the Japanese attacked Pearl Harbor and the United States entered the war. For the purposes of this story, the speech has been moved back a year. Ida did, indeed, hear the national anthem coming from an old radio amidst the rubble as she walked home from the hospital after visiting her friend. The speech she listened to that Christmas Day, however, was from the King (see Ida Cook, *The Bravest Voices*, 220). A full transcript of Churchill's speech is available from the International Churchill Society. (See "Christmas Message 1941." https://winston-churchill.org/resources/speeches/1941-1945-war-leader/christmas-message-1941/. Accessed February 7, 2022).

Pg 274: The national anthem verse that Ida sings as she walks home from the hospital was written by William Hickson as part of the Official Peace Version of the anthem, first published in 1925.

Pg 281: The air raid described here, where the building next to the shelter in Bermondsey took a direct hit, occurred in mid-April 1941. A month later, during the late night and early morning hours of May 10–11, Londoners experienced the most intense raids of the eight-month-long Blitz. Eleven thousand houses were destroyed, and nearly fifteen hundred lives lost in that period alone. The British Library, Westminster Abbey, Waterloo Station, and the House of Commons received significant damage. It marked the end of the Blitz, as Hitler turned his focus to the Soviet Union.

Pg 284: The description here is modeled after eyewitness accounts compiled by the BBC. (See, for example, "The First V1 Falls on London." WW2 People's War: An Archive of World War Two Memories. https://www.bbc.co.uk/history/ww2peopleswar/stories/78/a1302878.shtml. Accessed January 22, 2022.)

Pg 289: This number does not include the 1.3 million German soldiers who surrendered between D-Day and March 31, 1945, or the 1.5 million who surrendered in the month of April 1945.

Pg 308: In reality, it was Elisabeth Rethberg, who isn't described in this book but was a famous German soprano and dear friend of the Cooks, who drove them to her country home for tea. Amelita Galli-Curci had retired from the Met at this point, but she welcomed the sisters enthusiastically to her home in California, where the sisters went after New York.

ABOUT THE AUTHOR

MARIANNE MONSON received her MFA in Creative Writing from Vermont College of Fine Arts and primarily writes on topics related to women's history. She has taught English and Creative Writing at the community college and university levels and is the author of eleven books for children and adults. She is the founder of The Writer's Guild, a literary nonprofit, and writes from a 100-year-old house in Astoria, Oregon.